William Shakespeare, William George Clark,
William Aldis Wright

The Works of William Shakespeare

Volume 3

SALZWASSER
VERLAG

William Shakespeare, William George Clark, William Aldis Wright

The Works of William Shakespeare

Volume 3

Reprint of the original, first published in 1863.

1st Edition 2022 | ISBN: 978-3-37500-445-3

Verlag (Publisher): Salzwasser Verlag GmbH, Zeilweg 44, 60439 Frankfurt, Deutschland
Vertretungsberechtigt (Authorized to represent): E. Roepke, Zeilweg 44, 60439 Frankfurt, Deutschland
Druck (Print): Books on Demand GmbH, In de Tarpen 42, 22848 Norderstedt, Deutschland

THE WORKS

OF

WILLIAM SHAKESPEARE.

THE WORKS

OF

WILLIAM SHAKESPEARE

EDITED BY

WILLIAM GEORGE CLARK, M.A.

AND WILLIAM ALDIS WRIGHT, M.A.

VOLUME III.

1863.

CONTENTS.

PREFACE.

THE four plays printed in this volume appeared for the first time in the Folio of 1623, and in the same order in which they are here given.

Of *The Taming of the Shrew* alone is there any Quarto edition. The title-page of this, as it appears in Capell's copy, is as follows:

A wittie | and pleasant | Comedie | Called | *The Taming of the Shrew.* | As it was acted by his Maiesties | *Seruants at the* Blacke Friers | *and the* Globe. | Written by Will. Shakespeare. | LONDON, | Printed by W. S. for *John Smethwicke*, and are to be | sold at his Shop in Saint *Dunstones* Church- | yard vnder the Diall: | 1631. |

From a minute comparison of this Quarto edition with the First Folio, extending to points which are necessarily left unrecorded in our notes, we have come to the conclusion that the Quarto was printed from the Folio. It is necessary to mention this, because Mr Collier, in the second edition of his Shakespeare, maintains that the Quarto was printed long before 1623, perhaps as early as 1607 or 1609; that its publication "had been in some way 'stayed' by the intervention of the author, on behalf of himself and the company to which he belonged; and that, having in consequence been laid aside for a number of years, some copies of it, remaining in the hands of Smithwicke the stationer, were issued in 1631, as if it had been then first published." Mr Collier also conjectures that the title-page was 'struck off long subsequent to the printing of the body of the comedy to which it is attached.' That this could not have been the case appears from an examination of Capell's copy, the only one known to us which has the title-page perfect. In this the title forms part of the first quire, and has not been inserted. The paper on which it is printed is the same as that used for the rest of the play, the wire-marks corresponding throughout. The passages from the Quarto and Folio which Mr Collier quotes in support of his theory seem to us to make strongly against it.

We have not reprinted the old play called *The Taming of a Shrew*, on which Shakespeare founded his comedy, because it is manifestly by another hand. It is referred to in the notes as (Q).

The 'Long MS.,' to which we have referred, is a copy of the Second Folio in the Library of Pembroke College, Cambridge, which was formerly in the possession of Dr Roger Long, Master of the College from 1733 to 1770. It contains marginal emendations, some from Theobald and Warburton, marked 'T.' and 'W.' respectively; some to which the initial 'L.' is affixed, and some without any initial letter at all. Such of these as could not be traced to any earlier source we have quoted as 'Long conj. MS.' or 'Long MS.' For permission to use this volume we are indebted to the kindness of the Rev. C. H. Parez.

Mr Keightley has, with great liberality, sent for our use the MS. of his forthcoming work 'The Shakespeare Expositor.' We beg to return him our best thanks.

To the number of those whom we have to thank for kind assistance we add with pleasure the names of the Rev. G. B. Bubier, the Rev. N. M. Ferrers, and Dr Meredith of Quebec.

W. G. C.
W. A. W.

ADDENDA AND CORRIGENDA.

The Taming of the Shrew.

II. 1. 108. *To*] *Unto* S. Walker conj.

IV. 1. 36, 37. *and...thou wilt*] *is...will thaw* Badham conj. In note on line 37 dele *will thaw* Anon. conj.

IV. 5. 22. Add to note, *so it shall be, so* Mitford conj.

IV. 5. 77. *Have to*] *Have at* Jervis conj.

All's Well that Ends Well.

I. 1. 97. In the note, for *Williams* read *Badham*.

II. 1. 170. *maiden's*] *maid's* S. Walker conj.

III. 2. 108. Add to note, *move the still-reeking* Jervis conj.

IV. 2. 38. Add to note, *make ropes...snare* or *wake hopes...scare* Bubier conj.

IV. 3. 94. Add to note, *he has* Steevens.

IV. 3. 96. For *he has* read *has*, and in the note read *has*] *ha's* Ff. *he has* Steevens.

The Winter's Tale.

I. 2. 147, 148. Add to note, Her. *How my lord?* Pol. *What...brother?*

II. 1. 40. Add to note, *drink deep* Long MS. Mr Staunton's conjecture should be *drink aeep o' t.*

THE TAMING OF THE SHREW.

DRAMATIS PERSONÆ[1].

A Lord. CHRISTOPHER SLY, a tinker. Hostess, Page, Players, Huntsmen, and Servants.	Persons in the Induction.

BAPTISTA, a rich gentleman of Padua.

VINCENTIO, an old gentleman of Pisa.

LUCENTIO, son to Vincentio, in love with Bianca.

PETRUCHIO[2], a gentleman of Verona, a suitor to Katharina.

GREMIO, HORTENSIO,	suitors to Bianca.
TRANIO, BIONDELLO,	servants to Lucentio.
GRUMIO[3], CURTIS[4],	servants to Petruchio.

A Pedant.

KATHARINA, the shrew, BIANCA,	daughters to Baptista.

Widow.

Tailor, Haberdasher, and Servants attending on Baptista and Petruchio.

SCENE: *Padua, and Petruchio's country house.*

[1] DRAMATIS PERSONÆ] First given by Rowe.

[2] PETRUCHIO] PETRUCIO Knight. PETRUCCIO Ritson conj.

[3] GRUMIO] GRUNNIO S. Walker conj.

[4] CURTIS] Capell.

THE TAMING OF THE SHREW.

INDUCTION.

SCENE I. *Before an alehouse on a heath.*

Enter HOSTESS *and* SLY.

Sly. I'll pheeze you, in faith.

Host. A pair of stocks, you rogue!

Sly. Y'are a baggage: the Slys are no rogues; look in the chronicles; we came in with Richard Conqueror. Therefore paucas pallabris; let the world slide: sessa!

Host. You will not pay for the glasses you have burst?

Sly. No, not a denier. Go by, Jeronimy: go to thy cold bed, and warm thee.

Host. I know my remedy; I must go fetch the third-borough. [*Exit.*

Sly. Third, or fourth, or fifth borough, I'll answer him by law: I'll not budge an inch, boy: let him come, and kindly. [*Falls asleep.*

INDUCTION.] Pope. om. Ff Q. See note (I).

SCENE I. Before...] Theobald. A Hedge Ale-house. Capell.

Enter...] Enter Begger and Hostes, Christophero Sly. Ff Q.

1. *pheeze*] *fese* (Q).

2. *stocks*] F_3 F_4. *stockes* F_1 Q. *stokes* F_2.

4. *came in*] *came* Rowe (ed. 1).

5. *paucas*] *paucus* F_4.

7. *Go by, Jeronimy*] *goe by Ieronimie* Q. *go by S. Ieronimie* Ff (*Ieronimy* F_2. *Jeronimy* F_3F_4). *go by, Jeronimo* Theobald. *'go by,' says Jeronimy* Steevens (Capell conj.). *go—by S. Jeronimy* Knight. See note (II).

9. *thirdborough*] Theobald. *headborough* Ff Q.

10. [Exit.] Rowe. om. Ff Q.

13. [Falls asleep.] Ff Q. Falls from off his bench, and sleeps. Capell. Lies down on the ground, and falls asleep. Malone.

Horns winded. Enter a Lord *from hunting, with his train.*

Lord. Huntsman, I charge thee, tender well my hounds:
Brach Merriman, the poor cur is emboss'd;
And couple Clowder with the deep-mouth'd brach.
Saw'st thou not, boy, how Silver made it good
At the hedge-corner, in the coldest fault?
I would not lose the dog for twenty pound.

First Hun. Why, Belman is as good as he, my lord;
He cried upon it at the merest loss
And twice to-day pick'd out the dullest scent:
Trust me, I take him for the better dog.

Lord. Thou art a fool: if Echo were as fleet,
I would esteem him worth a dozen such.
But sup them well and look unto them all:
To-morrow I intend to hunt again.

First Hun. I will, my lord.

Lord. What's here? one dead, or drunk? See, doth he breathe?

Sec. Hun. He breathes, my lord. Were he not warm'd with ale,
This were a bed but cold to sleep so soundly.

Lord. O monstrous beast! how like a swine he lies!
Grim death, how foul and loathsome is thine image!
Sirs, I will practise on this drunken man.
What think you, if he were convey'd to bed,
Wrapp'd in sweet clothes, rings put upon his fingers,
A most delicious banquet by his bed,
And brave attendants near him when he wakes,
Would not the beggar then forget himself?

First Hun. Believe me, lord, I think he cannot choose.

14. SCENE II. Pope.
Horns winded.] Winde hornes. Ff Q.

15. *Brach*] *Leech* Hanmer. *Bathe* Johnson conj. *Breathe* Mitford conj. *Brace* Becket conj. *Trash* Singer.
Brach......emboss'd;] (*Brach Merriman, the poor cur, is emboss'd,*) Grant White. *Brach, Merriman, the ...emboss'd* Johnson. (*Back Merriman!—the...emboss'd*) Anon. conj.

23. *better*] om. Q.

30, 31. Printed as prose in Ff Q, as verse first by Rowe (ed. 2).

37. *bed*] *side* Anon. conj.

Sec. Hun. It would seem strange unto him when he waked.

Lord. Even as a flattering dream or worthless fancy.
Then take him up and manage well the jest:
Carry him gently to my fairest chamber
And hang it round with all my wanton pictures:
Balm his foul head in warm distilled waters
And burn sweet wood to make the lodging sweet:
Procure me music ready when he wakes,
To make a dulcet and a heavenly sound;
And if he chance to speak, be ready straight
And with a low submissive reverence
Say 'What is it your honour will command?'
Let one attend him with a silver basin
Full of rose-water and bestrew'd with flowers;
Another bear the ewer, the third a diaper,
And say 'Will't please your lordship cool your hands?'
Some one be ready with a costly suit
And ask him what apparel he will wear;
Another tell him of his hounds and horse,
And that his lady mourns at his disease:
Persuade him that he hath been lunatic;
And when he says he is, say that he dreams,
For he is nothing but a mighty lord.
This do and do it kindly, gentle sirs:
It will be pastime passing excellent,
If it be husbanded with modesty.

First Hun. My lord, I warrant you we will play our part,
As he shall think by our true diligence
He is no less than what we say he is.

41, 42. *waked.* Lord. *Even... fancy. Then*] *waked, Even...fancy.* Lord. *Then* Anon. conj.

46. *Balm...head*] *Bath...hide* Capell conj.

in] *with* Rowe (ed. 2).

55. *the third*] *a third* Rowe.

62. *And...he is,*] Ff Q. *And when he says he is poor,* Rowe (ed. 1). *And ...he's poor,* Rowe (ed. 2). *And...he is,* —Theobald. *And...he's Sly,* Johnson conj. *And when he says what he is,* Long conj. MS. *When he says what he is,* Collier MS. *And what he says he is,* Jackson conj. *And when he says who he is,* Anon. ap. Halliwell conj. See note (III).

67. *we will*] *we'll* Rowe (ed. 2).

Lord. Take him up gently and to bed with him;
And each one to his office when he wakes.
[*Some bear out Sly. A trumpet sounds.*
Sirrah, go see what trumpet 'tis that sounds:
[*Exit Servingman.*
Belike, some noble gentleman that means,
Travelling some journey, to repose him here.

Re-enter Servingman.

How now! who is it?
Serv. An't please your honour, players
That offer service to your lordship.
Lord. Bid them come near.

Enter Players.

Now, fellows, you are welcome.
Players. We thank your honour.
Lord. Do you intend to stay with me to-night?
A Player. So please your lordship to accept our duty.
Lord. With all my heart. This fellow I remember,
Since once he play'd a farmer's eldest son:
'Twas where you woo'd the gentlewoman so well:
I have forgot your name; but, sure, that part
Was aptly fitted and naturally perform'd.
A Player. I think 'twas Soto that your honour means.
Lord. 'Tis very true: thou didst it excellent.
Well, you are come to me in happy time;
The rather for I have some sport in hand
Wherein your cunning can assist me much.
There is a lord will hear you play to-night:
But I am doubtful of your modesties;

71. [Some bear out Sly.] Theobald. om. Ff Q.
A trumpet sounds.] Sound trumpets. Ff Q.
72. [Exit S.] Ex. Servant. Theobald. om. Ff Q.
75. SCENE III. Pope.
Re-enter...] Enter... Ff Q.
75, 76. *An't...players That*] Ff Q. *Please your honour, players That* Pope. *An it...Players that* Malone.
76. *That offer*] *That come to offer* Capell. *That offer humble* Collier MS.
77. Enter P.] Ff Q, after line 76.
80. A Player.] Edd. 2. Player. Ff Q.
85. *fitted*] *fit* S. Walker conj.
86. A Player.] Sincklo. F_1 Q. Sin. F_2. Sim. F_3 F_4. 1. P. Capell. See note (IV).

Lest over-eyeing of his odd behaviour,—
For yet his honour never heard a play,—
You break into some merry passion
And so offend him; for I tell you, sirs,
If you should smile he grows impatient.

A Player. Fear not, my lord: we can contain ourselves,
Were he the veriest antic in the world.

Lord. Go, sirrah, take them to the buttery,
And give them friendly welcome every one:
Let them want nothing that my house affords.
[*Exit one with the Players.*
Sirrah, go you to Barthol'mew my page,
And see him dress'd in all suits like a lady:
That done, conduct him to the drunkard's chamber;
And call him 'madam,' do him obeisance.
Tell him from me, as he will win my love,
He bear himself with honourable action,
Such as he hath observed in noble ladies
Unto their lords, by them accomplished:
Such duty to the drunkard let him do
With soft low tongue and lowly courtesy,
And say, 'What is't your honour will command,
Wherein your lady and your humble wife
May show her duty and make known her love?'
And then with kind embracements, tempting kisses,
And with declining head into his bosom,
Bid him shed tears, as being overjoy'd
To see her noble lord restored to health,
Who for this seven years hath esteemed him
No better than a poor and loathsome beggar:
And if the boy have not a woman's gift
To rain a shower of commanded tears,

98. A Player.] Plai. F_1 F_2. Play. Q. Pla. F_3 F_4. 1. P. Capell.
99. See note (V).
101. *And...one*] omitted by Rowe.
103. *Barthol'mew*] *Bartholmew* Ff Q. *Bartholomew* Rowe.
108. *bear*] F_3 F_4. *beare* F_1 F_2. *bare* Q.
112. *soft low*] *soft slow* Malone conj.
113. *will*] *doth* Q.
120. *this seven*] *these seven* Rowe (ed. 2). *twice seven* Theobald. *him*] *himself* Rowe.

An onion will do well for such a shift,
Which in a napkin being close convey'd
Shall in despite enforce a watery eye.
See this dispatch'd with all the haste thou canst:
Anon I'll give thee more instructions. [*Exit a Servingman.*
I know the boy will well usurp the grace,
Voice, gait and action of a gentlewoman:
I long to hear him call the drunkard husband,
And how my men will stay themselves from laughter
When they do homage to this simple peasant.
I'll in to counsel them; haply my presence
May well abate the over-merry spleen
Which otherwise would grow into extremes. [*Exeunt.*

SCENE II. *A bedchamber in the* Lord's *house.*

Enter aloft SLY, *with* Attendants; *some with apparel, others with basin and ewer and other appurtenances, and* Lord.

Sly. For God's sake, a pot of small ale.

First Serv. Will't please your lordship drink a cup of sack?

Sec. Serv. Will't please your honour taste of these conserves?

Third Serv. What raiment will your honour wear to-day?

Sly. I am Christophero Sly; call not me 'honour' nor 'lordship:' I ne'er drank sack in my life; and if you give me any conserves, give me conserves of beef: ne'er ask me what raiment I'll wear; for I have no more doublets than

125. *being...convey'd*] (*being...convei'd*) Ff Q.

133. *peasant.*] Johnson. *peasant,* Ff Q. *peasant;* Rowe.

135. *the*] *their* Collier (Collier MS.).

SCENE II.] Capell. SCENE IV. Pope.

A...house.] Theobald.

Enter aloft SLY...] Enter aloft the drunkard... Ff Q. A stately Room in the Lord's House: In it a Stage and other Appurtenances, for the Play: and, in another Part, a Bed; SLY, in a rich Night-dress, sitting on it; surrounded by Servants, bearing Apparel, Bason, Ewer, &c. a Side-board being by. Enter, at lower End, the Lord, himself habited like a Servant. Capell.

1. Sly.] Beg. Ff Q, and elsewhere in the scene.

5. *Christophero*] *Christopher* Warburton.

backs, no more stockings than legs, nor no more shoes than feet; nay, sometime more feet than shoes, or such shoes as my toes look through the overleather.

Lord. Heaven cease this idle humour in your honour!
O, that a mighty man of such descent,
Of such possessions and so high esteem,
Should be infused with so foul a spirit!

Sly. What, would you make me mad? Am not I Christopher Sly, old Sly's son of Burton-heath, by birth a pedlar, by education a card-maker, by transmutation a bear-herd, and now by present profession a tinker? Ask Marian Hacket, the fat ale-wife of Wincot, if she know me not: if she say I am not fourteen pence on the score for sheer ale, score me up for the lyingest knave in Christendom. What! I am not bestraught: here's—

Third Serv. O, this it is that makes your lady mourn!

Sec. Serv. O, this is it that makes your servants droop!

Lord. Hence comes it that your kindred shuns your house,
As beaten hence by your strange lunacy.
O noble lord, bethink thee of thy birth,
Call home thy ancient thoughts from banishment
And banish hence these abject lowly dreams.
Look how thy servants do attend on thee,
Each in his office ready at thy beck.
Wilt thou have music? hark! Apollo plays, [*Music.*
And twenty caged nightingales do sing:
Or wilt thou sleep? we'll have thee to a couch

10. *sometime*] *sometimes* F_3F_4.
12. *idle*] *evil* Collier MS.
17. *Christopher*] F_1QF_2. *Christophero* F_3F_4.
Sly's] *Sies* F_1.
Burton-heath] *Barton-heath* Steevens conj.
18. *card-maker*] *cart-maker* or *cord-maker* or *crate-maker* or *cord-wainer* Anon. conj.
21. *fourteen pence*] xiiii. d. F_1QF_2. xiv. d. F_3F_4.
score] *sorce* F_2.
22. *sheer*] F_4. *sheere* $F_1QF_2F_3$. *shear* Jordan conj. *Warwickshire* Collier MS.
23. *What!*] *What* Ff Q. *What?—* Hanmer.
bestraught] *distraught* Steevens conj. (withdrawn).
here's—] Ff. *here's* Q.
24. Third Serv.] 3. Man. $F_1Q\ F_2$. 1. Man. $F_3\ F_4$.
25. *is it*] *it is* Rowe.
26. *shuns*] *shun* Rowe.

Softer and sweeter than the lustful bed
On purpose trimm'd up for Semiramis.
Say thou wilt walk; we will bestrew the ground:
Or wilt thou ride? thy horses shall be trapp'd,
Their harness studded all with gold and pearl.
Dost thou love hawking? thou hast hawks will soar
Above the morning lark: or wilt thou hunt?
Thy hounds shall make the welkin answer them,
And fetch shrill echoes from the hollow earth.

First Serv. Say thou wilt course; thy greyhounds are as swift
As breathed stags, ay, fleeter than the roe.

Sec. Serv. Dost thou love pictures? we will fetch thee straight
Adonis painted by a running brook
And Cytherea all in sedges hid
Which seem to move and wanton with her breath,
Even as the waving sedges play with wind.

Lord. We'll show thee Io as she was a maid
And how she was beguiled and surprised,
As lively painted as the deed was done.

Third Serv. Or Daphne roaming through a thorny wood,
Scratching her legs that one shall swear she bleeds,
And at that sight shall sad Apollo weep,
So workmanly the blood and tears are drawn.

Lord. Thou art a lord and nothing but a lord:
Thou hast a lady far more beautiful
Than any woman in this waning age.

First Serv. And till the tears that she hath shed for thee
Like envious floods o'er-run her lovely face,
She was the fairest creature in the world;
And yet she is inferior to none.

Sly. Am I a lord? and have I such a lady?
Or do I dream? or have I dream'd till now?
I do not sleep: I see, I hear, I speak;
I smell sweet savours and I feel soft things:
Upon my life, I am a lord indeed

43. *hounds*] *bounds* Q.
47. Sec. Serv.] 2. M. Ff Q.
51. *with*] *with th'* Anon. conj.
63. *o'er-run*] *o'er-ran* Theobald.

And not a tinker nor Christophero Sly.
Well, bring our lady hither to our sight;
And once again, a pot o' the smallest ale.

Sec. Serv. Will't please your mightiness to wash your hands?
O, how we joy to see your wit restored!
O, that once more you knew but what you are!
These fifteen years you have been in a dream;
Or when you waked, so waked as if you slept.

Sly. These fifteen years! by my fay, a goodly nap.
But did I never speak of all that time?

First Serv. O, yes, my lord, but very idle words:
For though you lay here in this goodly chamber,
Yet would you say ye were beaten out of door;
And rail upon the hostess of the house;
And say you would present her at the leet,
Because she brought stone jugs and no seal'd quarts:
Sometimes you would call out for Cicely Hacket.

Sly. Ay, the woman's maid of the house.

Third Serv. Why, sir, you know no house nor no such maid,
Nor no such men as you have reckon'd up,
As Stephen Sly and old John Naps of Greece
And Peter Turph and Henry Pimpernell
And twenty more such names and men as these
Which never were nor no man ever saw.

Sly. Now Lord be thanked for my good amends!

All. Amen.

Sly. I thank thee: thou shalt not lose by it.

Enter the Page *as a lady, attended.*

Page. How fares my noble lord?

71. *Christophero*] $F_2F_3F_4$. *Christopher* F_1 Q.
74. [presenting the Ewer, &c. Capell.
75. *wit*] *wits* F_3F_4.
78. *so*] *you* Rowe.
84. *rail*] *rail'd* Rowe.
86. *no*] *not* Collier MS.
91. *of Greece*] *o' th' Green* Hanmer (L. H. apud Theobald conj.). *of Greys* or *of Greete* Halliwell conj.
92. *Henry*] *Harry* Capell conj.
96. See note (VI).
97. SCENE V. Pope.
Enter...] Capell. Enter Lady with Attendants. Ff Q (after line 96).
98—100. Capell prints as two lines *How...well; For...wife?*

Sly. Marry, I fare well; for here is cheer enough.
Where is my wife?
Page. Here, noble lord: what is thy will with her?
Sly. Are you my wife and will not call me husband?
My men should call me 'lord:' I am your good-man.
Page. My husband and my lord, my lord and husband;
I am your wife in all obedience.
Sly. I know it well. What must I call her?
Lord. Madam.
Sly. Al'ce madam, or Joan madam?
Lord. 'Madam,' and nothing else: so lords call ladies.
Sly. Madam wife, they say that I have dream'd
And slept above some fifteen year or more.
Page. Ay, and the time seems thirty unto me,
Being all this time abandon'd from your bed.
Sly. 'Tis much. Servants, leave me and her alone.
Madam, undress you and come now to bed.
Page. Thrice-noble lord, let me entreat of you
To pardon me yet for a night or two;
Or, if not so, until the sun be set:
For your physicians have expressly charged,
In peril to incur your former malady,
That I should yet absent me from your bed:
I hope this reason stands for my excuse.
Sly. Ay, it stands so that I may hardly tarry so long. But I would be loath to fall into my dreams again: I will therefore tarry in despite of the flesh and the blood.

Enter a Messenger.

Mess. Your honour's players, hearing your amendment,
Are come to play a pleasant comedy;

99, 100. *Marry...wife?*] Printed as prose by Pope.
108. *Al'ce*] Capell. *Alce* Ff.
110. See note (VII).
Madam] *Humph madam* Capell conj. *Madam, my* S. Walker conj.
110, 111. *Madam...more*] As prose in Pope.
111. *above*] F_1 Q F_2. *about* F_3 F_4.
year or] *year and* F_4. *years and* Rowe.
114, 115. *'Tis much...bed*] As prose in Pope.
120. *In*] *On* Capell.
your] *you* Q.
124. *dreams*] *dream* Rowe.
126. SCENE VI. Pope.
Enter...] Ff. Enter another servant. Capell.

For so your doctors hold it very meet,
Seeing too much sadness hath congeal'd your blood,
And melancholy is the nurse of frenzy:
Therefore they thought it good you hear a play
And frame your mind to mirth and merriment,
Which bars a thousand harms and lengthens life.

Sly. Marry, I will, let them play it. Is not a comonty a Christmas gambold or a tumbling-trick?

Page. No, my good lord; it is more pleasing stuff.

Sly. What, household stuff?

Page. It is a kind of history.

Sly. Well, we'll see't. Come, madam wife, sit by my side and let the world slip: we shall ne'er be younger.

Flourish.

ACT I.

SCENE I. *Padua. A public place.*

Enter LUCENTIO *and his man* TRANIO.

Luc. Tranio, since for the great desire I had
To see fair Padua, nursery of arts,
I am arrived for fruitful Lombardy,
The pleasant garden of great Italy;
And by my father's love and leave am arm'd

129. *too much*] *so much* Rowe.

134. *Marry...Is not*] Capell (*play't*). *Marrie I will let them play, it is not* F_1 Q F_2. *Marry I will, let them play, it is not* F_3. *Marry I will, let them play, is it not* F_4.

comonty] *commodity?* Pope, from (Q).

134—140. *Marry...younger*] Capell prints as six lines of verse.

135. *gambold*] Ff Q. *gambol* Pope.

140. *and...younger*] *We shall ne'er be younger, and let the world slide* Collier (Collier MS.), reading 139, 140 as rhyme.

[Seating her for the Play. Capell. They sit down. Malone.

Flourish.] Ff Q. om. Capell.

ACT I. SC. I.] Pope. See note (I).

Padua] Pope.

A public place.] Capell. A street in Padua. Theobald.

...Tranio.] Triano. F_1 Q F_2.

3. *for*] *from* Theobald. *in* Capell (Heath conj.).

With his good will and thy good company,
My trusty servant, well approved in all,
Here let us breathe and haply institute
A course of learning and ingenious studies.
Pisa renowned for grave citizens
Gave me my being and my father first,
A merchant of great traffic through the world,
Vincentio, come of the Bentivolii.
Vincentio's son brought up in Florence
It shall become to serve all hopes conceived,
To deck his fortune with his virtuous deeds:
And therefore, Tranio, for the time I study,
Virtue and that part of philosophy
Will I apply that treats of happiness
By virtue specially to be achieved.
Tell me thy mind; for I have Pisa left
And am to Padua come, as he that leaves
A shallow plash to plunge him in the deep
And with satiety seeks to quench his thirst.

Tra. *Mi perdonato,* gentle master mine,
I am in all affected as yourself;
Glad that you thus continue your resolve
To suck the sweets of sweet philosophy.
Only, good master, while we do admire
This virtue and this moral discipline,
Let's be no stoics nor no stocks, I pray;
Or so devote to Aristotle's checks
As Ovid be an outcast quite abjured:
Balk logic with acquaintance that you have

8. *haply*] F_1 Q. *happly* F_2 F_3 F_4. *happily* Pope. *happ'ly* Capell.

9. *ingenious*] *ingenuous* Johnson conj.

13. *Vincentio, come*] Hanmer. *Vincentio's come* Ff Q. *Vincentio's son come* Malone conj. *Vincentio comes* Collier MS.

14. *Vincentio's*] Ff Q. *Vincentio his* Pope. *Lucentio his* Hanmer.

brought] *brough* F_1.

18. *Virtue*] *To virtue* Hanmer.

25. *Mi perdonato*] *Me pardonato* Ff. *Me pardinato* Q. *Mi perdonate* Capell (Heath conj.).

28. *sweet*] *fair* Anon. conj.

32. *checks*] Ff Q. *ethicks* Rann (Blackstone conj.). See note (VIII).

33. *Ovid*] F_3 F_4. *Ovid;* F_1 Q F_2.

34. *Balk*] *Talk* Rowe. *Chop* Capell conj. *Hack* Anon. conj.

with] *with'* Hunter conj.

And practise rhetoric in your common talk;
Music and poesy use to quicken you;
The mathematics and the metaphysics,
Fall to them as you find your stomach serves you;
No profit grows where is no pleasure ta'en:
In brief, sir, study what you most affect.
Luc. Gramercies, Tranio, well dost thou advise.
If, Biondello, thou wert come ashore,
We could at once put us in readiness,
And take a lodging fit to entertain
Such friends as time in Padua shall beget.
But stay a while: what company is this?
Tra. Master, some show to welcome us to town.

Enter BAPTISTA, KATHARINA, BIANCA, GREMIO, *and* HORTENSIO. LUCENTIO *and* TRANIO *stand by.*

Bap. Gentlemen, importune me no farther,
For how I firmly am resolved you know;
That is, not to bestow my youngest daughter
Before I have a husband for the elder:
If either of you both love Katharina,
Because I know you well and love you well,
Leave shall you have to court her at your pleasure.
Gre. [*Aside*] To cart her rather: she's too rough for me.
There, there, Hortensio, will you any wife?
Kath. I pray you, sir, is it your will
To make a stale of me amongst these mates?
Hor. Mates, maid! how mean you that? no mates for you,
Unless you were of gentler, milder mould.
Kath. I'faith, sir, you shall never need to fear:

38. *you find*] om. F_4.
serves you] *serves* Anon. conj.
41. *Gramercies*] *Gramercy* Hanmer.
42. *thou wert*] *now were* Dyce (Collier MS.). *then were* Delius conj.
47. ...Gremio...] ...Gremio a Pantelowne... F_1.
...Hortensio...] ...Hortentio sister to Bianca... F_1 Q. ...H. a shuiter to B.... F_2. ...H. a suitor to B... F_3 F_4.
48. *Gentlemen*] *Gentlemen both* Theobald.
no] *not* Rowe (ed. 2).
57. *will*] *will and pleasure* Hanmer. *gracious will* Collier (Collier MS.). See note (IX).
58. *these*] F_1 Q F_2. *those* F_3 F_4.
59. As two lines in Ff Q, ending *that?...you.*
60. *mould*] *mood* Collier MS.

I wis it is not half way to her heart;
But if it were, doubt not her care should be
To comb your noddle with a three-legg'd stool
And paint your face and use you like a fool.

Hor. From all such devils, good Lord deliver us!

Gre. And me too, good Lord!

Tra. Husht, master! here's some good pastime toward:
That wench is stark mad or wonderful froward.

Luc. But in the other's silence do I see
Maid's mild behaviour and sobriety.
Peace, Tranio!

Tra. Well said, master; mum! and gaze your fill.

Bap. Gentlemen, that I may soon make good
What I have said, Bianca, get you in:
And let it not displease thee, good Bianca,
For I will love thee ne'er the less, my girl.

Kath. A pretty peat! it is best
Put finger in the eye, an she knew why.

Bian. Sister, content you in my discontent.
Sir, to your pleasure humbly I subscribe:
My books and instruments shall be my company,
On them to look and practise by myself.

Luc. Hark, Tranio! thou may'st hear Minerva speak.

Hor. Signior Baptista, will you be so strange?
Sorry am I that our good will effects
Bianca's grief.

Gre. Why will you mew her up,
Signior Baptista, for this fiend of hell,
And make her bear the penance of her tongue?

Bap. Gentlemen, content ye; I am resolved:
Go in, Bianca: [*Exit Bianca.*

62. *I wis*] F_4. *I-wis* $F_1 Q F_2 F_3$.

63. *should*] F_1 Q F_2. *shall* F_3 F_4.

66. *us*] *me* Hanmer.

67. *good*] *O good* Hanmer.

68. *Husht*] F_1 Q F_2. *Hush'd* F_3 F_4. *Hush* Rowe (ed. 2).

here's] F_4. *heres* F_1 Q F_2 F_3. *here is* Hanmer.

72. *Peace, Tranio!*] *Peace!* Anon. conj.

73. *Well*] *Why, well* Hanmer.

74. *Gentlemen*] *Come, gentlemen* Hanmer. *Well, gentlemen* Capell.

78, 79. *A pretty...why*] Printed as prose in Ff Q.

86. *our*] *your* Hanmer (ed. 2), a misprint.

90. *Gentlemen, content ye*] *Content ye, gentlemen* Hanmer.

91. Exit Bianca.] Theobald. om. Ff Q.

And for I know she taketh most delight
In music, instruments and poetry,
Schoolmasters will I keep within my house,
Fit to instruct her youth. If you, Hortensio,
Or Signior Gremio, you, know any such,
Prefer them hither; for to cunning men
I will be very kind, and liberal
To mine own children in good bringing-up:
And so farewell. Katharina, you may stay;
For I have more to commune with Bianca. [*Exit.*

Kath. Why, and I trust I may go too, may I not?
What, shall I be appointed hours; as though, belike,
I knew not what to take, and what to leave, ha? [*Exit.*

Gre. You may go to the devil's dam: your gifts are so good, here's none will hold you. Their love is not so great, Hortensio, but we may blow our nails together, and fast it fairly out: our cake's dough on both sides. Farewell: yet, for the love I bear my sweet Bianca, if I can by any means light on a fit man to teach her that wherein she delights, I will wish him to her father.

Hor. So will I, Signior Gremio: but a word, I pray. Though the nature of our quarrel yet never brooked parle, know now, upon advice, it toucheth us both, that we may yet again have access to our fair mistress, and be happy rivals in Bianca's love, to labour and effect one thing specially.

Gre. What's that, I pray?

Hor. Marry, sir, to get a husband for her sister.

Gre. A husband! a devil.

Hor. I say, a husband.

Gre. I say, a devil. Thinkest thou, Hortensio, though her father be very rich, any man is so very a fool to be married to hell?

Hor. Tush, Gremio, though it pass your patience and

98. *liberal*] *liberal,* Ff Q.

102—104. Printed in Ff Q as four lines, ending *not?...though...take,... Ha;* as prose by Pope; by Capell as three lines, ending *not?...belike,...ha!*

102. *and*] om. Rowe.

106. *here's*] *here is* F_4.

Their] $F_1 F_2$. *There* Q. *Our* $F_3 F_4$. *Your* Malone conj. *There;* Collier. *This* Collier MS. *Her* Bubier conj.

113. *yet never*] *never yet* Pope.

parle] F_1 Q F_2. *parlee* $F_3 F_4$. *parly* Capell.

122. *any*] *any a* F_2.

mine to endure her loud alarums, why, man, there be good fellows in the world, an a man could light on them, would take her with all faults, and money enough.

Gre. I cannot tell; but I had as lief take her dowry with this condition, to be whipped at the high-cross every morning.

Hor. Faith, as you say, there's small choice in rotten apples. But come; since this bar in law makes us friends, it shall be so far forth friendly maintained till by helping Baptista's eldest daughter to a husband we set his youngest free for a husband, and then have to't afresh. Sweet Bianca! Happy man be his dole! He that runs fastest gets the ring. How say you, Signior Gremio?

Gre. I am agreed; and would I had given him the best horse in Padua to begin his wooing that would thoroughly woo her, wed her and bed her and rid the house of her! Come on. [*Exeunt Gremio and Hortensio.*

Tra. I pray, sir, tell me, is it possible
That love should of a sudden take such hold?

Luc. O Tranio, till I found it to be true,
I never thought it possible or likely;
But see, while idly I stood looking on,
I found the effect of love in idleness:
And now in plainness do confess to thee,
That art to me as secret and as dear
As Anna to the Queen of Carthage was,
Tranio, I burn, I pine, I perish, Tranio,
If I achieve not this young modest girl.
Counsel me, Tranio, for I know thou canst;
Assist me, Tranio, for I know thou wilt.

Tra. Master, it is no time to chide you now;
Affection is not rated from the heart:
If love have touch'd you, nought remains but so,

125. *loud*] *lowd* F_1 Q. *lewd* F_2 F_3 F_4.
alarums] *alarms* Rowe.
127. *all*] *all her* F_4.
130. *small*] *a small* Theobald.
131. *But come*] F_1 Q. *come* F_2 F_3 F_4.
138. *his wooing*] *the wooing* Rowe (ed. 2).
thoroughly] F_1 Q. *throughly* F_2 F_3 F_4.
140. Exeunt...] Exeunt ambo. Manet Tranio and Lucentio. Ff Q.
142. *of*] F_1 Q F_2. *on* F_3 F_4.
156. *have*] F_1 Q. om. F_2 F_3 F_4. *has* Rowe (ed. 1). *hath* Rowe (ed. 2).
touch'd] *toyl'd* Warburton.
nought] $F_2 F_3 F_4$. *naught* F_1Q.

'Redime te captum quam queas minimo.'
Luc. Gramercies, lad, go forward; this contents:
The rest will comfort, for thy counsel's sound.
Tra. Master, you look'd so longly on the maid,
Perhaps you mark'd not what's the pith of all.
Luc. O yes, I saw sweet beauty in her face,
Such as the daughter of Agenor had,
That made great Jove to humble him to her hand,
When with his knees he kiss'd the Cretan strond.
Tra. Saw you no more? mark'd you not how her sister
Began to scold and raise up such a storm
That mortal ears might hardly endure the din?
Luc. Tranio, I saw her coral lips to move
And with her breath she did perfume the air:
Sacred and sweet was all I saw in her.
Tra. Nay, then, 'tis time to stir him from his trance.
I pray, awake, sir: if you love the maid,
Bend thoughts and wits to achieve her. Thus it stands:
Her eldest sister is so curst and shrewd
That till the father rid his hands of her,
Master, your love must live a maid at home;
And therefore has he closely mew'd her up,
Because she will not be annoy'd with suitors.
Luc. Ah, Tranio, what a cruel father's he!
But art thou not advised, he took some care
To get her cunning schoolmasters to instruct her?
Tra. Ay, marry, am I, sir; and now 'tis plotted.
Luc. I have it, Tranio.
Tra. Master, for my hand,

157. *captum*] $F_2F_3F_4$. *captam* F_1Q.
158. *Gramercies*] *Gramercy* Rowe.
159. *counsel's*] $F_2F_3F_4$. *counsels* F_1 Q.
163. *Agenor had*] *Agenor's race* Collier MS.
165. *strond*] F_1Q F_2F_3. *strand* F_4.
168. *hardly*] *scarce* Collier MS.
endure] *dure* S. Walker conj.
173. *pray*] *pray you* Q.
[Shaking him. Capell.
174. *wits*] *wit* Rowe (ed. 2).
175. *eldest*] *elder* Q.
176. *rid*] *rids* Rowe.
179. *she*] *he* Singer conj.
will] *shall* Rowe.
182. *To get her*] *Together* F_2. *To gather* Long conj. MS.
schoolmasters] *masters* Collier (Collier MS.).

Both our inventions meet and jump in one.
Luc. Tell me thine first.
Tra. You will be schoolmaster
And undertake the teaching of the maid:
That's your device.
Luc. It is: may it be done?
Tra. Not possible; for who shall bear your part,
And be in Padua here Vincentio's son;
Keep house and ply his book, welcome his friends,
Visit his countrymen and banquet them?
Luc. Basta; content thee, for I have it full.
We have not yet been seen in any house,
Nor can we be distinguish'd by our faces
For man or master; then it follows thus;
Thou shalt be master, Tranio, in my stead,
Keep house and port and servants, as I should:
I will some other be; some Florentine,
Some Neapolitan, or meaner man of Pisa.
'Tis hatch'd and shall be so: Tranio, at once
Uncase thee; take my colour'd hat and cloak:
When Biondello comes, he waits on thee;
But I will charm him first to keep his tongue.
Tra. So had you need.
In brief, sir, sith it your pleasure is,
And I am tied to be obedient;
For so your father charged me at our parting,
'Be serviceable to my son,' quoth he,
Although I think 'twas in another sense;
I am content to be Lucentio,
Because so well I love Lucentio.
Luc. Tranio, be so, because Lucentio loves:

189. *part*] *port* Anon. conj.

200. *meaner*] *mean* Capell.

201. *'Tis*] *It is* Hanmer, ending lines 200—205 at *man...so...take... comes ..first...need.*

202. *take*] *and here take* Hanmer.
colour'd] F_3 F_4. *Conlord* F_1 Q. *Coulord* F_2. om. Hanmer.

205. *So*] *And so, sir* Hanmer.
[They exchange habits. Theobald.

206. *In brief, sir*] *In brief, good sir* Pope; omitted by Capell. *In brief then, sir* Malone. *Be brief then, sir.* Collier MS.
it your pleasure is] *it is your pleasure thus* Anon. conj.

And let me be a slave, to achieve that maid
Whose sudden sight hath thrall'd my wounded eye.
Here comes the rogue.

Enter BIONDELLO.

Sirrah, where have you been?

Bion. Where have I been! Nay, how now! where are you? Master, has my fellow Tranio stolen your clothes? Or you stolen his? or both? pray, what's the news?

Luc. Sirrah, come hither: 'tis no time to jest,
And therefore frame your manners to the time.
Your fellow Tranio here, to save my life,
Puts my apparel and my countenance on,
And I for my escape have put on his;
For in a quarrel since I came ashore
I kill'd a man and fear I was descried:
Wait you on him, I charge you, as becomes,
While I make way from hence to save my life:
You understand me?

Bion. I, sir! ne'er a whit.

Luc. And not a jot of Tranio in your mouth:
Tranio is changed into Lucentio.

Bion. The better for him: would I were so too!

Tra. So could I, faith, boy, to have the next wish after,
That Lucentio indeed had Baptista's youngest daughter.
But, sirrah, not for my sake, but your master's, I advise
You use your manners discreetly in all kind of companies:
When I am alone, why, then I am Tranio;
But in all places else your master Lucentio.

Luc. Tranio, let's go: one thing more rests, that thy-

214. *to*] *t'* Ff Q.

215. *wounded*] *wond'ring* Collier MS.

216. ...Biondello.] ...Binodello. F_2.

218. *my fellow*] om. Hanmer, who reads 217—219 as three lines, ending *you?...cloaths,...news?*

has] F_4. *ha's* F_1 Q F_2 F_3.

225. *ashore*] *a shore* F_1.

226. *was*] *am* F_3 F_4.

229. *I, sir! ne'er*] *Ay, sir, ne'er* Rowe. *Ay, sir.—Ne'er* Dyce conj.

233—238. Printed as prose in Ff Q, as verse first by Capell.

233. *could*] *would* F_3 F_4.

faith] *'faith* Ff Q. *i' faith* Johnson.

235, 236. *advise You use...companies*] *advise you, Use...company* Capell.

238. *your*] *you* F_1 Q.

239—241. Printed as four lines in Ff, ending *go....execute....why.... weighty;* first as prose by Pope.

self execute, to make one among these wooers: if thou ask me why, sufficeth, my reasons are both good and weighty. [*Exeunt.*

The presenters above speak.

First Serv. My lord, you nod; you do not mind the play.

Sly. Yes, by Saint Anne, do I. A good matter, surely: comes there any more of it?

Page. My lord, 'tis but begun.

Sly. 'Tis a very excellent piece of work, madam lady: would 'twere done! [*They sit and mark.*

SCENE II. *Padua. Before* HORTENSIO'S *house.*

Enter PETRUCHIO *and his man* GRUMIO.

Pet. Verona, for a while I take my leave,
To see my friends in Padua, but of all
My best beloved and approved friend,
Hortensio; and I trow this is his house.
Here, sirrah Grumio; knock, I say.

Gru. Knock, sir! whom should I knock? is there any man has rebused your worship?

Pet. Villain, I say, knock me here soundly.

Gru. Knock you here, sir! why, sir, what am I, sir, that I should knock you here, sir?

Pet. Villain, I say, knock me at this gate
And rap me well, or I'll knock your knave's pate.

Gru. My master is grown quarrelsome. I should knock you first,

240. *among*] *'mong* F_2.

241. The presenters above speak.] ...speakes. Ff Q.

242—247. Transferred by Pope to the end of the Act.

247. *'twere*] *it were* Capell.

[They...mark.] Ff Q. om. Pope.

SCENE II.] Capell. ACT II. SCENE I. Rowe. SCENE V. Pope.

Before...house.] Pope.

2. *but of all*] *best of all* Anon. conj.

4. *his*] *the* $F_3 F_4$.

6—24. *Knock, sir!...may I say*] Placed in the margin as spurious by Pope.

6. *knock?*] *knock, sir?* Capell.

7. *has*] F_4. *ha's* $F_1 Q F_2 F_3$. *That has* Capell.

rebused] *rebsu'd* Q. *abused* Tyrwhitt conj.

And then I know after who comes by the worst.

Pet. Will it not be?
Faith, sirrah, an you'll not knock, I'll ring it;
I'll try how you can *sol, fa,* and sing it.

[*He wrings him by the ears.*

Gru. Help, masters, help! my master is mad.

Pet. Now, knock when I bid you, sirrah villain!

Enter HORTENSIO.

Hor. How now! what's the matter? My old friend Grumio! and my good friend Petruchio! How do you all at Verona?

Pet. Signior Hortensio, come you to part the fray?
'Con tutto il core ben trovato,' may I say.

Hor. 'Alla nostra casa ben venuto, molto honorato signor mio Petrucio.'
Rise, Grumio, rise: we will compound this quarrel.

Gru. Nay, 'tis no matter, sir, what he 'leges in Latin. If this be not a lawful cause for me to leave his service, look you, sir, he bid me knock him and rap him soundly, sir: well, was it fit for a servant to use his master so, being perhaps, for aught I see, two-and-thirty, a pip out?
Whom would to God I had well knock'd at first,
Then had not Grumio come by the worst.

Pet. A senseless villain! Good Hortensio,
I bade the rascal knock upon your gate
And could not get him for my heart to do it.

16. *ring*] *wring* Malone.

17. ...wrings...] ...rings... Ff Q.

18. *masters*] Theobald. *mistris* Ff Q.

19. *sirrah villain!*] *sirrah! villain!* Theobald.

24. *Con tutto...trovato*] Theobald. *Contutti le core bene trobatto* Ff Q (*trovatto* $F_2 F_3 F_4$).

25. *ben*] $F_2 F_3 F_4$. *bene* F_1 Q.
molto] Theobald. *multo* Ff Q.
honorato] *honorata* F_1 Q.

26. *signor*] Theobald. *signior* Ff Q.

27—45. *Rise, Grumio...Grumio*] Put in the margin as spurious by Pope.

27. *Grumio, rise*] F_1 Q F_2. *Grumio* $F_3 F_4$.

28. *sir*] om. Rowe.
he 'leges] Capell. *he leges* Ff Q. *be leges* Rann (Tyrwhitt conj.). *he alledges* Long conj. MS.

32. *pip*] Rowe (ed. 2). *peepe* F_1 Q F_2. *peep* $F_3 F_4$.
out] *mo* Collier MS.

33, 34. *Whom...worst*] Printed as prose in Ff Q, as verse first by Rowe (ed. 2).

Gru. Knock at the gate! O heavens! Spake you not these words plain, 'Sirrah, knock me here, rap me here, knock me well, and knock me soundly'? And come you now with, 'knocking at the gate'?

Pet. Sirrah, be gone, or talk not, I advise you.

Hor. Petruchio, patience; I am Grumio's pledge:
Why, this's a heavy chance 'twixt him and you,
Your ancient, trusty, pleasant servant Grumio.
And tell me now, sweet friend, what happy gale
Blows you to Padua here from old Verona?

Pet. Such wind as scatters young men through the world
To seek their fortunes farther than at home
Where small experience grows. But in a few,
Signior Hortensio, thus it stands with me:
Antonio, my father, is deceased;
And I have thrust myself into this maze,
Haply to wive and thrive as best I may:
Crowns in my purse I have and goods at home
And so am come abroad to see the world.

Hor. Petruchio, shall I then come roundly to thee
And wish thee to a shrewd ill-favour'd wife?
Thou'ldst thank me but a little for my counsel:
And yet I'll promise thee she shall be rich
And very rich: but thou'rt too much my friend,
And I'll not wish thee to her.

Pet. Signior Hortensio, 'twixt such friends as we
Few words suffice; and therefore, if thou know
One rich enough to be Petruchio's wife,

38—41. *Knock......gate?*] Capell prints as four lines, ending *heavens! ...here,...soundly?...gate?*

44. *this's*] *this* Ff Q. *this is* Rowe. *this so* Mason conj. *this'* Dyce (S. Walker conj.). *this?* Collier.

48. *young men*] F_3F_4. *yong men* Q. *yongmen* F_1F_2.

50. *grows. But in a few,*] *grows; but in a few,* Hanmer. *grows but in a few.* Ff Q. *grows, but in a few.* Theobald. *grows but in a mew.* Warburton.

53. *have*] *must* Rowe (ed. 2).

54. *Haply*] Malone. *Happily* Ff Q. *Happly* Rowe (ed. 2). *Happ'ly* Hanmer.

59. *Thou'ldst*] *Thou'lt* Hanmer.

61. *thou'rt*] Rowe. *th' art* Ff Q.

63. *Signior*] om. Q.
we] *us* Rowe (ed. 2).

64. *thou*] *you* Rowe (ed. 2).

As wealth is burden of my wooing dance,
Be she as foul as was Florentius' love,
As old as Sibyl, and as curst and shrewd
As Socrates' Xanthippe, or a worse,
She moves me not, or not removes, at least,
Affection's edge in me, were she as rough
As are the swelling Adriatic seas:
I come to wive it wealthily in Padua;
If wealthily, then happily in Padua.

Gru. Nay, look you, sir, he tells you flatly what his mind is: why, give him gold enough and marry him to a puppet or an aglet-baby; or an old trot with ne'er a tooth in her head, though she have as many diseases as two and fifty horses: why, nothing comes amiss, so money comes withal.

Hor. Petruchio, since we are stepp'd thus far in,
I will continue that I broach'd in jest.
I can, Petruchio, help thee to a wife
With wealth enough and young and beauteous,
Brought up as best becomes a gentlewoman:
Her only fault, and that is faults enough,
Is that she is intolerable curst
And shrewd and froward, so beyond all measure,
That, were my state far worser than it is,
I would not wed her for a mine of gold.

Pet. Hortensio, peace! thou know'st not gold's effect:
Tell me her father's name and 'tis enough;
For I will board her, though she chide as loud
As thunder when the clouds in autumn crack.

Hor. Her father is Baptista Minola,

66. *burden*] *guerdon* Becket conj.
dance] *song* Johnson conj.
67. *Florentius'*] *Florentio's* Hanmer conj.
68. *Sibyl*] *Sibell* F_1 Q F_2 F_3. *Sibel* F_4.
69. *Xanthippe*] *Zentippe* F_1 Q. *Zantippe* F_2 F_3 F_4. *Xantippe* Theobald.
a worse] *even worse* Collier MS.
71. *Affection's...me*] F_1 Q. *Affection's edge in time* F_2 F_3 F_4. *Affection sieg'd in coin* Warburton.
as] *is as* F_1.
78. *as two and fifty*] *too as fifty* Rann.
79. *horses*] *houses* Becket conj.
85. *and that*] *as that* Capell.
faults] F_1 Q. *fault* F_2 F_3 F_4.
86. *intolerable*] *intolerably* Hanmer.
87. *shrewd*] *shrow'd* F_1 Q. *shrew'd* F_2 F_3 F_4.
froward] *forward* Warburton.
94. *is*] om. Q.

An affable and courteous gentleman:
Her name is Katharina Minola,
Renown'd in Padua for her scolding tongue.

Pet. I know her father, though I know not her;
And he knew my deceased father well.
I will not sleep, Hortensio, till I see her;
And therefore let me be thus bold with you
To give you over at this first encounter,
Unless you will accompany me thither.

Gru. I pray you, sir, let him go while the humour lasts. O' my word, an she knew him as well as I do, she would think scolding would do little good upon him: she may perhaps call him half a score knaves or so: why, that's nothing; an he begin once, he'll rail in his rope-tricks. I'll tell you what, sir, an she stand him but a little, he will throw a figure in her face and so disfigure her with it that she shall have no more eyes to see withal than a cat. You know him not, sir.

Hor. Tarry, Petruchio, I must go with thee;
For in Baptista's keep my treasure is:
He hath the jewel of my life in hold,
His youngest daughter, beautiful Bianca;
And her withholds from me and other more,
Suitors to her and rivals in my love;
Supposing it a thing impossible,
For those defects I have before rehearsed,
That ever Katharina will be woo'd;
Therefore this order hath Baptista ta'en,
That none shall have access unto Bianca
Till Katharine the curst have got a husband.

Gru. Katharine the curst!
A title for a maid of all titles the worst.

105. *O'*] Rowe (ed. 2). *A* Ff Q.
108. *begin*] *begins* Q.
his] *her* Anon. conj.
rope-tricks] *trope-tricks* Theobald conj. *rhetorick* Hanmer. *rhetoricks* Capell. *roop tricks* Anon conj.
113. *keep*] Ff Q. *house* Rowe.
116. *And her*] *Her he* Rann.
withholds from me and other more] Capell (Thirlby conj.). *with-holds from me. Other more* F_1 Q. *with-holds he from me. Other more* $F_2F_3F_4$ (*hee* F_2). *with-holds he from me, and others more* Theobald. *with-holds he from me, and other more* Hanmer.
119. *For*] *From* Hanmer.

Hor. Now shall my friend Petruchio do me grace;
And offer me disguised in sober robes
To old Baptista as a schoolmaster
Well seen in music, to instruct Bianca;
That so I may, by this device, at least
Have leave and leisure to make love to her
And unsuspected court her by herself.

Gru. Here's no knavery! See, to beguile the old folks, how the young folks lay their heads together!

Enter GREMIO, *and* LUCENTIO *disguised.*

Master, master, look about you: who goes there, ha?

Hor. Peace, Grumio! it is the rival of my love.
Petruchio, stand by a while.

Gru. A proper stripling and an amorous!

Gre. O, very well; I have perused the note.
Hark you, sir; I'll have them very fairly bound:
All books of love, see that at any hand;
And see you read no other lectures to her:
You understand me: over and beside
Signior Baptista's liberality,
I'll mend it with a largess. Take your paper too,
And let me have them very well perfumed:
For she is sweeter than perfume itself
To whom they go to. What will you read to her?

Luc. Whate'er I read to her, I'll plead for you
As for my patron, stand you so assured,
As firmly as yourself were still in place:
Yea, and perhaps with more successful words

132. *herself*] *myself* Capell.
133. SCENE VI. Pope.
Gru.] Gru. [aside.] Dyce.
134. *their heads*] *theirs head* F_2.
...disguised.] Ff Q (after line 131). ...disguised, with books under his arm. Capell.
135. *Master, master*] *Master* Rowe.
ha?] om. Q.
136. *it is*] *'tis* Pope.
137. *Petruchio, stand...*] *Petruchio, stand we by a little while* Capell. Petruchio. *Stand...* Edd. conj.
a while] *a whilt* F_2.
140. *Hark you*] *Hark* S. Walker conj.
very] om. Anon. conj.
145. *Take your paper too,*] *Take your papers too* Pope. *Take your papers* Hanmer. *Here, take your papers too* Capell. See note (X).
148. *go to*] *go* Rowe.

Than you, unless you were a scholar, sir.
Gre. O this learning, what a thing it is!
Gru. O this woodcock, what an ass it is!
Pet. Peace, sirrah!
Hor. Grumio, mum! God save you, Signior Gremio.
Gre. And you are well met, Signior Hortensio.
Trow you whither I am going? To Baptista Minola.
I promised to inquire carefully
About a schoolmaster for the fair Bianca:
And by good fortune I have lighted well
On this young man, for learning and behaviour
Fit for her turn, well read in poetry
And other books, good ones, I warrant ye.
Hor. 'Tis well; and I have met a gentleman
Hath promised me to help me to another,
A fine musician to instruct our mistress;
So shall I no whit be behind in duty
To fair Bianca, so beloved of me.
Gre. Beloved of me; and that my deeds shall prove.
Gru. And that his bags shall prove.
Hor. Gremio, 'tis now no time to vent our love:
Listen to me, and if you speak me fair,
I'll tell you news indifferent good for either.
Here is a gentleman whom by chance I met,
Upon agreement from us to his liking,
Will undertake to woo curst Katharine,
Yea, and to marry her, if her dowry please.
Gre. So said, so done, is well.
Hortensio, have you told him all her faults?

157. Hor. *Grumio, mum!*] Hor. *Grumio mum:* F_1Q. Hor. *Gru. mum:* F_2 F_3 F_4.

158—167. Printed as prose by Pope.

158. *And you are*] *And you're* Steevens.

158, 159. *And you......Trow you whither*] *You......trow you Whither* Capell.

158—161. Malone prints as five lines, ending *Hortensio...whither...Minola...about...Bianca.*

160. *promised*] *promis'd him* Capell.

161. *schoolmaster*] *master* Collier (Collier MS.).

the fair] *fair* Steevens.

165. *ye*] *you* Steevens.

167. *help me*] Rowe. *help one* Ff Q.

171. *deeds*] *deed* Warburton.

Pet. I know she is an irksome brawling scold:
If that be all, masters, I hear no harm.

Gre. No, say'st me so, friend? What countryman?

Pet. Born in Verona, old Antonio's son:
My father dead, my fortune lives for me;
And I do hope good days and long to see.

Gre. O sir, such a life, with such a wife, were strange!
But if you have a stomach, to't i' God's name:
You shall have me assisting you in all.
But will you woo this wild-cat?

Pet. Will I live?

Gru. Will he woo her? ay, or I'll hang her.

Pet. Why came I hither but to that intent?
Think you a little din can daunt mine ears?
Have I not in my time heard lions roar?
Have I not heard the sea puff'd up with winds
Rage like an angry boar chafed with sweat?
Have I not heard great ordnance in the field,
And heaven's artillery thunder in the skies?
Have I not in a pitched battle heard
Loud 'larums, neighing steeds, and trumpets' clang?
And do you tell me of a woman's tongue,
That gives not half so great a blow to hear
As will a chestnut in a farmer's fire?
Tush, tush! fear boys with bugs.

Gru. For he fears none.

Gre. Hortensio, hark:
This gentleman is happily arrived,
My mind presumes, for his own good and ours.

Hor. I promised we would be contributors

184. *What*] *pray, what* Hanmer.

185. *Antonio's*] Rowe. *Butonios* F_1QF_2. *Butonio's* F_3F_4.

186. *father*] *father's* Rowe.

188. *O sir, such*] *Oh, such* Hanmer. *Sir, such* Capell.

189. *stomach, to't...name:*] *stomach to't,...name,* Bubier conj.

a stomach] *stomacke* Q.

to't i'] Edd. *too 't a* $F_1QF_2F_3$. *to 't a* F_4. *to 't o'* Theobald.

192. *or*] om. Rann.

194. *mine*] *my* Rowe (ed. 2).

197. *sweat*] *pursuit* Theobald conj.

201. *trumpets' clang*] *trumpets clangue* Ff Q. *trumpets' clangue* Capell.

203. *hear*] *th' ear* Hanmer (Warburton).

208. *ours*] Theobald (Thirlby conj.). *yours* Ff Q.

And bear his charge of wooing, whatsoe'er.
Gre. And so we will, provided that he win her.
Gru. I would I were as sure of a good dinner.

Enter TRANIO *brave, and* BIONDELLO.

Tra. Gentlemen, God save you. If I may be bold,
Tell me, I beseech you, which is the readiest way
To the house of Signior Baptista Minola?
Bion. He that has the two fair daughters: is't he you mean?
Tra. Even he, Biondello.
Gre. Hark you, sir; you mean not her to—
Tra. Perhaps, him and her, sir: what have you to do?
Pet. Not her that chides, sir, at any hand, I pray.
Tra. I love no chiders, sir. Biondello, let's away.
Luc. Well begun, Tranio.
Hor. Sir, a word ere you go;
Are you a suitor to the maid you talk of, yea or no?
Tra. And if I be, sir, is it any offence?
Gre. No; if without more words you will get you hence.
Tra. Why, sir, I pray, are not the streets as free
For me as for you?
Gre. But so is not she.
Tra. For what reason, I beseech you?
Gre. For this reason, if you'll know,
That she's the choice love of Signior Gremio.
Hor. That she's the chosen of Signior Hortensio.
Tra. Softly, my masters! if you be gentlemen,

213. SCENE VII. Pope.
...brave,] ...bravely apparelled, Pope.
you. If...bold,] *you, if...bold.* Edd. conj.
213—215. Printed as prose by Pope.
216. Bion.] Gre. Capell (Tyrwhitt and Heath conj.).
is 't he] *is 't* [aside to Tranio] *he* Malone.
218. *Even he, Biondello.*] *Even he Biondello.* FfQ. *Even he, sir.* Capell. *Even he. Biondello!* Steevens (Tyrwhitt and Heath conj.). *Even he.* Rann.
219. *her to—*] Ff Q. *her too.* Tyrwhitt conj. *her to woo.* Halliwell (Malone conj.).
221. *Not*] *Nor* Rowe (ed. 2).
226. *And if*] Ff. *And* Q. *An if* Hanmer.
228. *I pray*] Ff. *I pray you* Q.
232. *That she's*] *She's* Hanmer.
233. *That she's*] Ff. *That she is* Q. *She is* Hanmer.
Signior] om. Hanmer.

Do me this right; hear me with patience.
Baptista is a noble gentleman,
To whom my father is not all unknown;
And were his daughter fairer than she is,
She may more suitors have and me for one.
Fair Leda's daughter had a thousand wooers;
Then well one more may fair Bianca have:
And so she shall; Lucentio shall make one,
Though Paris came in hope to speed alone.

Gre. What, this gentleman will out-talk us all!

Luc. Sir, give him head: I know he'll prove a jade.

Pet. Hortensio, to what end are all these words?

Hor. Sir, let me be so bold as ask you,
Did you yet ever see Baptista's daughter?

Tra. No, sir; but hear I do that he hath two,
The one as famous for a scolding tongue
As is the other for beauteous modesty.

Pet. Sir, sir, the first's for me; let her go by.

Gre. Yea, leave that labour to great Hercules;
And let it be more than Alcides' twelve.

Pet. Sir, understand you this of me in sooth:
The youngest daughter whom you hearken for
Her father keeps from all access of suitors;
And will not promise her to any man
Until the elder sister first be wed:
The younger then is free and not before.

Tra. If it be so, sir, that you are the man
Must stead us all and me amongst the rest;
And if you break the ice and do this feat,
Achieve the elder, set the younger free
For our access, whose hap shall be to have her
Will not so graceless be to be ingrate.

235. *with patience*] Ff. *patience* Q.
239. *suitors*] *sutore* F_2.
244. *What,*] *What, what,* Capell.
245. *Sir, give*] Ff. *Give* Q.
247. *as ask you*] F_1 Q. *as to ask you* F_2 F_3 F_4. *as ask you this* Capell.
251. *As is the other*] *As the other is* Pope.
259. *the elder*] *the eldest* Rowe (ed. 2). *her elder* Capell. See note (XI).
262. *stead*] Capell. *steed* Ff Q.
263. *And if*] *An if* Capell. *feat*] Rowe. *seeke* F_1 Q F_2. *seek* F_3 F_4.

Hor. Sir, you say well and well you do conceive;
And since you do profess to be a suitor,
You must, as we do, gratify this gentleman,
To whom we all rest generally beholding.
Tra. Sir, I shall not be slack: in sign whereof,
Please ye we may contrive this afternoon,
And quaff carouses to our mistress' health,
And do as adversaries do in law,
Strive mightily, but eat and drink as friends.
Gru. Bion. O excellent motion! Fellows, let's be gone.
Hor. The motion's good indeed and be it so,
Petruchio, I shall be your ben venuto. [*Exeunt.*

ACT II.

SCENE I. *Padua. A room in* BAPTISTA'S *house.*

Enter KATHARINA *and* BIANCA.

Bian. Good sister, wrong me not, nor wrong yourself,
To make a bondmaid and a slave of me;
That I disdain: but for these other gawds,
Unbind my hands, I'll pull them off myself,
Yea, all my raiment, to my petticoat;
Or what you will command me will I do,
So well I know my duty to my elders.
Kath. Of all thy suitors, here I charge thee, tell
Whom thou lovest best: see thou dissemble not.
Bian. Believe me, sister, of all the men alive
I never yet beheld that special face

270. *beholding*] *beholden* Rowe.
272. *contrive*] *convive* Theobald.
273. *mistress'*] *mistress'* (for *mistresses'*) S. Walker conj.
276. Gru.] Gre. Ritson conj.
Bion.] om. Capell.
278. *I shall*] *I'll* Capell.
ben venuto] $F_2 F_3 F_4$. *been venuto* F_1 Q. See note (XII).
3. *gawds*] Theobald. *goods* Ff Q. *gards* Collier (Collier MS.).
4. *pull*] *put* Boswell.
8. *charge thee*] $F_2 F_3 F_4$. *charge* F_1 Q.
10. *the*] om. S. Walker conj.

Which I could fancy more than any other.
Kath. Minion, thou liest. Is't not Hortensio?
Bian. If you affect him, sister, here I swear
I'll plead for you myself, but you shall have him.
Kath. O then, belike, you fancy riches more:
You will have Gremio to keep you fair.
Bian. Is it for him you do envy me so?
Nay then you jest, and now I well perceive
You have but jested with me all this while:
I prithee, sister Kate, untie my hands.
Kath. If that be jest, then all the rest was so.
[*Strikes her.*

Enter BAPTISTA.

Bap. Why, how now, dame! whence grows this insolence?
Bianca, stand aside. Poor girl! she weeps.
Go ply thy needle; meddle not with her.
For shame, thou hilding of a devilish spirit,
Why dost thou wrong her that did ne'er wrong thee?
When did she cross thee with a bitter word?
Kath. Her silence flouts me, and I'll be revenged.
[*Flies after Bianca.*
Bap. What, in my sight? Bianca, get thee in.
[*Exit Bianca.*
Kath. What, will you not suffer me? Nay, now I see
She is your treasure, she must have a husband;
I must dance bare-foot on her wedding day
And for your love to her lead apes in hell.
Talk not to me: I will go sit and weep
Till I can find occasion of revenge. [*Exit.*
Bap. Was ever gentleman thus grieved as I?
But who comes here?

13. *Is't*] F_1 F_2 F_3. *It's* Q. *is it* F_4.
14. *you*] Ff. *thou* Q.
17. *you fair*] *you fine* Johnson conj. *your fair* Halliwell conj.
18. *envy me so*] *so envy me* Pope.
21. *untie*] Ff. *unite* Q.
25. *thy*] Ff. *the* Q.
29. [Flies after B.] Ff Q. Flies at B. Hanmer.
30. [Exit B.] Exit. Ff Q.
31. *What*] om. Pope.
37. *ever*] *never* F_2.

Enter GREMIO, LUCENTIO *in the habit of a mean man;* PETRUCHIO, *with* HORTENSIO *as a musician; and* TRANIO, *with* BIONDELLO *bearing a lute and books.*

Gre. Good morrow, neighbour Baptista.

Bap. Good morrow, neighbour Gremio. God save you, gentlemen!

Pet. And you, good sir! Pray, have you not a daughter
Call'd Katharina, fair and virtuous?

Bap. I have a daughter, sir, called Katharina.

Gre. You are too blunt: go to it orderly.

Pet. You wrong me, Signior Gremio: give me leave.
I am a gentleman of Verona, sir,
That, hearing of her beauty and her wit,
Her affability and bashful modesty,
Her wondrous qualities and mild behaviour,
Am bold to show myself a forward guest
Within your house, to make mine eye the witness
Of that report which I so oft have heard.
And, for an entrance to my entertainment,
I do present you with a man of mine, [*Presenting Hortensio.*
Cunning in music and the mathematics,
To instruct her fully in those sciences,
Whereof I know she is not ignorant:
Accept of him, or else you do me wrong:
His name is Licio, born in Mantua.

Bap. You're welcome, sir; and he, for your good sake.
But for my daughter Katharine, this I know,
She is not for your turn, the more my grief.

Pet. I see you do not mean to part with her,
Or else you like not of my company.

39. SCENE II. Pope.
Petruchio.......books] Rowe. Petruchio with Tranio, with his boy bearing a Lute and Bookes. Ff Q.

40. *God save*] *Save* Capell conj.

42, 43. *And you...virtuous*] Printed as prose in Ff Q as verse first by Capell.

43. *fair*] om. Q

45. *too*] *to* Q.

50. *wondrous*] *woman's* Collier MS.

60. *Licio*] F_2 F_3 F_4. *Litio* F_1 Q.

61. *You're*] Warburton. *Y'are* Ff Q. *You 'are* Theobald.

62. *Katharine*] *Katerine* F_1 Q F_2. *Katerina* F_3. *Katherina* F_4.

63. *the more*] F_1 Q F_2. *the more's* F_3 F_4.

Bap. Mistake me not; I speak but as I find.
Whence are you, sir? what may I call your name?

Pet. Petruchio is my name; Antonio's son,
A man well known throughout all Italy.

Bap. I know him well: you are welcome for his sake.

Gre. Saving your tale, Petruchio, I pray,
Let us, that are poor petitioners, speak too:
Baccare! you are marvellous forward.

Pet. O, pardon me, Signior Gremio; I would fain be doing.

Gre. I doubt it not, sir; but you will curse your wooing.

Neighbour, this is a gift very grateful, I am sure of it. To express the like kindness, myself, that have been more kindly beholding to you than any, freely give unto you this young scholar [*presenting Lucentio*], that hath been long studying at Rheims; as cunning in Greek, Latin, and other languages, as the other in music and mathematics: his name is Cambio; pray, accept his service.

Bap. A thousand thanks, Signior Gremio. Welcome, good Cambio. But, gentle sir [*to Tranio*], methinks you walk like a stranger: may I be so bold to know the cause of your coming?

66. *as*] F_1Q. *what* $F_2F_3F_4$.

71—73. *Saving...forward*] Steevens. Printed as prose in Ff Q; first as three lines of verse by Capell, ending *let...too...forward, sir.*

71. *I pray*] *pray* S. Walker conj.

73. *Baccare*] $F_2F_3F_4$. *Bacare* F_1 Q. *Baccalare* Theobald (Warburton).

75—82. *I doubt...service*] Printed first as prose by Pope; in Ff Q as ten lines, ending *curse...gift...express...been....any....hath....cunning....languages,...mathematics:...service:* by Capell as ten lines, ending *wooing. ...Neighbour,...it:...myself,...any,—...scholar,....cunning....languages,....mathematicks:...service.*

75, 76. *wooing. Neighbour, this*] Theobald. *wooing neighbors: this* F_1 Q. *wooing neighbours: this* $F_2F_3F_4$. *wooing, neighbours. This* Rowe (ed. 1). *wooing. Neighbours this* Rowe (ed. 2).

76. *Neighbour*] *Neighbour* [to Baptista] Capell.

To] *And—to* Capell.

78. *kindly*] om. Capell.

beholding] *beholden* Pope.

freely give unto you] Edd. (Glover conj.). *I freely give unto you* Capell (Tyrwhitt conj.). *Freely give unto* F_1QF_2. *Free leave give unto* F_3F_4.

79. [presenting Lucentio] Rowe.

80. *Rheims*] *Rhemes* Ff Q.

Greek, Latin] *Latin, Greek* Capell.

81. *mathematics*] *the mathematics* Capell.

82. *pray*] *pray you* Q.

83—86. *A thousand......coming?*]

Tra. Pardon me, sir, the boldness is mine own;
That, being a stranger in this city here,
Do make myself a suitor to your daughter,
Unto Bianca, fair and virtuous.
Nor is your firm resolve unknown to me,
In the preferment of the eldest sister.
This liberty is all that I request,
That, upon knowledge of my parentage,
I may have welcome 'mongst the rest that woo
And free access and favour as the rest:
And, toward the education of your daughters,
I here bestow a simple instrument,
And this small packet of Greek and Latin books:
If you accept them, then their worth is great.

Bap. Lucentio is your name; of whence, I pray?

Tra. Of Pisa, sir; son to Vincentio.

Bap. A mighty man of Pisa; by report
I know him well: you are very welcome, sir.
Take you the lute, and you the set of books;
You shall go see your pupils presently.
Holla, within!

Enter a Servant.

Sirrah, lead these gentlemen
To my daughters; and tell them both,

Printed first as prose by Pope; as four lines in Ff Q, ending *Gremio:...sir, ...stranger,...coming?*

83, 85. *Signior...walk...so bold... cause*] *good signior...walk here...bold... cause too* Capell, ending line 85, *may I.*

89. *myself*] $F_1QF_3F_4$. *thy selfe* F_2.

99. *packet*] *pack* S. Walker conj.

100. [They greet privately. Theobald.

101. Bap. *Lucentio is your name; of whence, I pray?*] *Lucentio is my name.* Bap. *Of whence, I pray?* Theobald conj.

103. *Pisa; by report*] Rowe. *Pisa by report,* Ff Q.

104. *know*] *knew* Rann (Capell conj.).

you are] *you're* Capell.

107. *within*] *within there* Capell.

lead] *shew* Capell, corrected in MS.

107, 108. *Sirrah...both*] Steevens. prints as two lines, ending *lead...both.*

108. *To...both*] *In to my daughters; tell them both from me* Capell conj.

daughters] F_1 Q. *two daughters* $F_2 F_3 F_4$.

tell] F_1 Q. *then tell* $F_2F_3F_4$.

These are their tutors: bid them use them well.
[Exit Servant, with Luc. and Hor., Bio. following.
We will go walk a little in the orchard,
And then to dinner. You are passing welcome,
And so I pray you all to think yourselves.
Pet. Signior Baptista, my business asketh haste,
And every day I cannot come to woo.
You knew my father well, and in him me,
Left solely heir to all his lands and goods,
Which I have better'd rather than decreased:
Then tell me, if I get your daughter's love,
What dowry shall I have with her to wife?
Bap. After my death the one half of my lands,
And in possession twenty thousand crowns.
Pet. And, for that dowry, I'll assure her of
Her widowhood, be it that she survive me,
In all my lands and leases whatsoever:
Let specialties be therefore drawn between us,
That covenants may be kept on either hand.
Bap. Ay, when the special thing is well obtain'd,
That is, her love; for that is all in all.
Pet. Why, that is nothing; for I tell you, father,
I am as peremptory as she proud-minded;
And where two raging fires meet together
They do consume the thing that feeds their fury:
Though little fire grows great with little wind,
Yet extreme gusts will blow out fire and all:
So I to her and so she yields to me;
For I am rough and woo not like a babe.
Bap. Well mayst thou woo, and happy be thy speed!
But be thou arm'd for some unhappy words.
Pet. Ay, to the proof; as mountains are for winds,
That shake not, though they blow perpetually.

109. [Exit...Hor.] Theobald. Bio...] Capell.
115. *knew*] F_1 Q. *know* $F_2 F_3 F_4$.
116. *solely*] Rowe. *solie* F_1 Q $F_2 F_3$. *soly* F_4.
122. *of*] *for* Hanmer. *on* Steevens conj.
124. *whatsoever*] *whosoever* F_2.
140. *shake*] $F_2 F_3 F_4$. *shakes* F_1 Q.

Re-enter HORTENSIO, *with his head broke.*

Bap. How now, my friend! why dost thou look so pale?
Hor. For fear, I promise you, if I look pale.
Bap. What, will my daughter prove a good musician?
Hor. I think she'll sooner prove a soldier:
Iron may hold with her, but never lutes.
Bap. Why, then thou canst not break her to the lute?
Hor. Why, no; for she hath broke the lute to me.
I did but tell her she mistook her frets,
And bow'd her hand to teach her fingering;
When, with a most impatient devilish spirit,
'Frets, call you these?' quoth she; 'I'll fume with them:'
And, with that word, she struck me on the head,
And through the instrument my pate made way;
And there I stood amazed for a while,
As on a pillory, looking through the lute;
While she did call me rascal fiddler
And twangling Jack; with twenty such vile terms,
As had she studied to misuse me so.
Pet. Now, by the world, it is a lusty wench;
I love her ten times more than e'er I did:
O, how I long to have some chat with her!
Bap. Well, go with me and be not so discomfited:
Proceed in practice with my younger daughter;
She's apt to learn and thankful for good turns.
Signior Petruchio, will you go with us,
Or shall I send my daughter Kate to you?
Pet. I pray you do; I will attend her here,
[*Exeunt Baptista, Gremio, Tranio, and Hortensio.*
And woo her with some spirit when she comes.
Say that she rail; why then I'll tell her plain
She sings as sweetly as a nightingale:

141. SCENE III. Pope.
144. *sooner*] om. Q.
147. *to me*] *on me* Hanmer.
150. *most*] *moist* Q.
151. *these*] *them* Rowe.
156. *rascal fiddler*] Capell. *rascal, fidler* Ff Q.
158. *had she*] Ff Q. *she had* Rowe.
162. *discomfited*] *discomforted* Capell conj.
167. *I will*] Rowe. *Ile* F_1 Q. *I* $F_2 F_3 F_4$.
[Exeunt...] Exit. Manet Petruchio. Ff Q.

Say that she frown; I'll say she looks as clear
As morning roses newly wash'd with dew:
Say she be mute and will not speak a word;
Then I'll commend her volubility,
And say she uttereth piercing eloquence:
If she do bid me pack, I'll give her thanks,
As though she bid me stay by her a week:
If she deny to wed, I'll crave the day
When I shall ask the banns, and when be married.
But here she comes; and now, Petruchio, speak.

Enter KATHARINA.

Good morrow, Kate; for that's your name, I hear.
Kath. Well have you heard, but something hard of hearing:
They call me Katharine that do talk of me.
Pet. You lie, in faith; for you are call'd plain Kate,
And bonny Kate, and sometimes Kate the curst;
But Kate, the prettiest Kate in Christendom,
Kate of Kate-Hall, my super-dainty Kate,
For dainties are all Kates, and therefore, Kate,
Take this of me, Kate of my consolation;
Hearing thy mildness praised in every town,
Thy virtues spoke of, and thy beauty sounded,
Yet not so deeply as to thee belongs,
Myself am moved to woo thee for my wife.
Kath. Moved! in good time: let him that moved you hither
Remove you hence: I knew you at the first
You were a moveable.
Pet. Why, what's a moveable?
Kath. A join'd-stool.
Pet. Thou hast hit it: come, sit on me.
Kath. Asses are made to bear, and so are you.
Pet. Women are made to bear, and so are you.

179. *banns*] Johnson. *banes* Ff Q.
185. *bonny*] F4. *bony* F_1Q F_2F_3.
188. *Kates*] *cates* Pope.
191. *sounded*] *founded* F_2.
197. *join'd*] *joint* Capell.

Kath. No such jade as you, if me you mean.
Pet. Alas, good Kate, I will not burden thee!
For, knowing thee to be but young and light,—
Kath. Too light for such a swain as you to catch;
And yet as heavy as my weight should be.
Pet. Should be! should—buzz!
Kath. Well ta'en, and like a buzzard.
Pet. O slow-wing'd turtle! shall a buzzard take thee?
Kath. Ay, for a turtle, as he takes a buzzard.
Pet. Come, come, you wasp; i' faith, you are too angry.
Kath. If I be waspish, best beware my sting.
Pet. My remedy is then, to pluck it out.
Kath. Ay, if the fool could find it where it lies.
Pet. Who knows not where a wasp does wear his sting?
In his tail.
Kath. In his tongue.
Pet. Whose tongue?
Kath. Yours, if you talk of tails: and so farewell.
Pet. What, with my tongue in your tail? nay, come again,
Good Kate; I am a gentleman.
Kath. That I'll try. [*She strikes him.*
Pet. I swear I'll cuff you, if you strike again.
Kath. So may you lose your arms:
If you strike me, you are no gentleman;

200. *jade as you*] F_1 Q. *jade, sir, as you* F_2 F_3 F_4. *jack, sir, as you* Farmer conj. *jade as you—bear!* Jackson conj. *load, sir, as you* Singer. *jade to bear you* Collier MS. *jade as bear you* Dyce. *jade as to bear you* Collier (ed. 2). *load as you* Grant White. *a jade as you* S. Walker conj.

205—232. *Should be......care not*] Put in the margin as spurious by Pope.

205. *Should......buzz!*] *Shold be, should: buzze.* F_1 Q. *Should be, should: buzze.* F_2 F_3. *Should be, should: buz.* F_4. *Should be! should! buz.* Rowe. *Should bee;—should buz.—* Theobald. *Should! Bee: should!...buz.* Hanmer.

209. *best*] *'best* F_3 F_4.

211. *Ay*] *Ah* Theobald.
find it] *find out* Collier MS.

212. *does*] *doth* Rowe (ed. 2).

212, 213. *Who...tail*] Printed as prose in Ff Q.

213. Kath. *In his tongue.* Pet. *Whose tongue?*] Cat. *In his tail! in his tongue.* Pet. *In his tongue? whose tongue?* Capell.

214. *tails*] Rowe (ed. 2). *tailes* Q. *tales* Ff.

215, 216. *nay...gentleman*] Pope. Printed as one line in Ff Q.

218—222. *So...coxcomb?*] Printed by Capell as four lines, ending *me... gentlemen...put...coxcomb?*

And if no gentleman, why then no arms.
Pet. A herald, Kate? O, put me in thy books!
Kath. What is your crest? a coxcomb?
Pet. A combless cock, so Kate will be my hen.
Kath. No cock of mine; you crow too like a craven.
Pet. Nay, come, Kate, come; you must not look so sour.
Kath. It is my fashion, when I see a crab.
Pet. Why, here's no crab; and therefore look not sour.
Kath. There is, there is.
Pet. Then show it me.
Kath. Had I a glass, I would.
Pet. What, you mean my face?
Kath. Well aim'd of such a young one.
Pet. Now, by Saint George, I am too young for you.
Kath. Yet you are wither'd.
Pet. 'Tis with cares.
Kath. I care not.
Pet. Nay, hear you, Kate: in sooth you scape not so.
Kath. I chafe you, if I tarry: let me go.
Pet. No, not a whit: I find you passing gentle.
'Twas told me you were rough and coy and sullen,
And now I find report a very liar;
For thou art pleasant, gamesome, passing courteous,
But slow in speech, yet sweet as spring-time flowers:
Thou canst not frown, thou canst not look askance,
Nor bite the lip, as angry wenches will,
Nor hast thou pleasure to be cross in talk,
But thou with mildness entertain'st thy wooers,
With gentle conference, soft and affable.
Why does the world report that Kate doth limp?
O slanderous world! Kate like the hazel-twig
Is straight and slender and as brown in hue
As hazel-nuts and sweeter than the kernels.
O, let me see thee walk: thou dost not halt.

227. *sour*] *so sour* Theobald.
240. *askance*] Capell. *a sconce* F_1 Q *a scance* F_2 F_3 F_4. *ascance* Rowe (ed. 2).
245. *does*] *doth* Rowe.

Kath. Go, fool, and whom thou keep'st command.
Pet. Did ever Dian so become a grove
As Kate this chamber with her princely gait?
O, be thou Dian, and let her be Kate;
And then let Kate be chaste and Dian sportful!
Kath. Where did you study all this goodly speech?
Pet. It is extempore, from my mother-wit.
Kath. A witty mother! witless else her son.
Pet. Am I not wise?
Kath. Yes; keep you warm.
Pet. Marry, so I mean, sweet Katharine, in thy bed:
And therefore, setting all this chat aside,
Thus in plain terms: your father hath consented
That you shall be my wife; your dowry 'greed on;
And, will you, nill you, I will marry you.
Now, Kate, I am a husband for your turn;
For, by this light, whereby I see thy beauty,
Thy beauty, that doth make me like thee well,
Thou must be married to no man but me;
For I am he am born to tame you Kate,
And bring you from a wild Kate to a Kate
Conformable as other household Kates.
Here comes your father: never make denial;
I must and will have Katharine to my wife.

Re-enter BAPTISTA, GREMIO, *and* TRANIO.

Bap. Now, Signior Petruchio, how speed you with my daughter?
Pet. How but well, sir? how but well?
It were impossible I should speed amiss.
Bap. Why, how now, daughter Katharine! in your dumps?

250. *keep'st*] *keepest, those* Hanmer.
257. *witless*] *witness* Capell.
else] *elfe* Theobald conj.
258. *keep*] *to keep* Rann.
259. *Marry*] *Why* Pope.
269. *wild Kate*] *wilde Kate* F_1 Q. *wild Kat* $F_2 F_3 F_4$. *wild cat* Rowe.
270. *Kates*] *cats* Theobald conj.
273. SCENE V. Pope.
Re-enter...] Enter... Pope. Enter... Ff Q (after line 267).
...Tranio.] Q. Trayno. Ff.
Now] om. Hanmer.

Kath. Call you me daughter? now, I promise you
You have show'd a tender fatherly regard,
To wish me wed to one half lunatic;
A mad-cap ruffian and a swearing Jack,
That thinks with oaths to face the matter out.

Pet. Father, 'tis thus: yourself and all the world,
That talk'd of her, have talk'd amiss of her:
If she be curst, it is for policy,
For she's not froward, but modest as the dove;
She is not hot, but temperate as the morn;
For patience she will prove a second Grissel,
And Roman Lucrece for her chastity:
And to conclude, we have 'greed so well together,
That upon Sunday is the wedding-day.

Kath. I'll see thee hang'd on Sunday first.

Gre. Hark, Petruchio; she says she'll see thee hang'd first.

Tra. Is this your speeding? nay, then, good night our part!

Pet. Be patient, gentlemen; I choose her for myself:
If she and I be pleased, what's that to you?
'Tis bargain'd 'twixt us twain, being alone,
That she shall still be curst in company.
I tell you, 'tis incredible to believe
How much she loves me: O, the kindest Kate!
She hung about my neck; and kiss on kiss
She vied so fast, protesting oath on oath,
That in a twink she won me to her love.
O, you are novices! 'tis a world to see,
How tame, when men and women are alone,
A meacock wretch can make the curstest shrew.
Give me thy hand, Kate: I will unto Venice,

277. Kath.] Pet. Theobald.
278. *You have*] *You've* Pope.
286. *morn*] *moon* Collier MS.
287. *Grissel*] *Grizelde* Capell.
289. *we have*] *we've* Pope.
291. *on*] *o'* Capell.
292. *Hark*] *Hark, hark* Hanmer. *hang'd*] *hang'd o' Sunday* Capell.
293. *nay*] om. Hanmer. *part*] *pact* Collier (Collier MS.).
294. *gentlemen*] *sirs* Pope.
301. *vied*] *ply'd* Johnson conj. *vent* Bubier conj.

To buy apparel 'gainst the wedding-day.
Provide the feast, father, and bid the guests;
I will be sure my Katharine shall be fine.
Bap. I know not what to say: but give me your hands;
God send you joy, Petruchio! 'tis a match.
Gre. Tra. Amen, say we: we will be witnesses.
Pet. Father, and wife, and gentlemen, adieu;
I will to Venice; Sunday comes apace:
We will have rings, and things, and fine array;
And, kiss me, Kate, we will be married o' Sunday.
[*Exeunt Petruchio and Katharina severally.*
Gre. Was ever match clapp'd up so suddenly?
Bap. Faith, gentlemen, now I play a merchant's part,
And venture madly on a desperate mart.
Tra. 'Twas a commodity lay fretting by you:
'Twill bring you gain, or perish on the seas.
Bap. The gain I seek is, quiet in the match.
Gre. No doubt but he hath got a quiet catch.
But now, Baptista, to your younger daughter:
Now is the day we long have looked for:
I am your neighbour, and was suitor first.
Tra. And I am one that love Bianca more
Than words can witness, or your thoughts can guess.
Gre. Youngling, thou canst not love so dear as I.
Tra. Greybeard, thy love doth freeze.
Gre. But thine doth fry.
Skipper, stand back: 'tis age that nourisheth.
Tra. But youth in ladies' eyes that flourisheth.
Bap. Content you, gentlemen: I will compound this strife:
'Tis deeds must win the prize; and he, of both,
That can assure my daughter greatest dower
Shall have my Bianca's love.

308. *Provide the feast, father*] *Father, provide the feast*, Pope.

310. *me*] om. Pope.

316. *we will be married*] *we'll marry* Hanmer.

o' Sunday] Hanmer. *a sonday* F_1 Q F_2. *a Sunday* F_3 F_4.

[Exeunt P. and K. severally] Theobald. [Exit P. and K. Ff Q.

317. SCENE VI. Pope.

322. *in*] Rowe (ed. 2). *me* Ff Q.

336. *my Bianca's love.*] F_1 Q. *Bianca's love.* F_2 F_3 F_4. *Bianca's love.—And, first, to you;* Capell.

Say, Signior Gremio, what can you assure her?
Gre. First, as you know, my house within the city
Is richly furnished with plate and gold;
Basins and ewers to lave her dainty hands;
My hangings all of Tyrian tapestry;
In ivory coffers I have stuff'd my crowns;
In cypress chests my arras counterpoints,
Costly apparel, tents, and canopies,
Fine linen, Turkey cushions boss'd with pearl,
Valance of Venice gold in needlework,
Pewter and brass and all things that belong
To house or housekeeping: then, at my farm
I have a hundred milch-kine to the pail,
Sixscore fat oxen standing in my stalls,
And all things answerable to this portion.
Myself am struck in years, I must confess;
And if I die to-morrow, this is hers,
If whilst I live she will be only mine.
Tra. That 'only' came well in. Sir, list to me:
I am my father's heir and only son:
If I may have your daughter to my wife,
I'll leave her houses three or four as good,
Within rich Pisa walls, as any one
Old Signior Gremio has in Padua;
Besides two thousand ducats by the year
Of fruitful land, all which shall be her jointure.
What, have I pinch'd you, Signior Gremio?
Gre. Two thousand ducats by the year of land!
My land amounts not to so much in all:
That she shall have; besides an argosy
That now is lying in Marseilles' road.

343. *arras*] Ff Q. *arras*, Rowe (ed. 2).
counterpoints] *counterpanes* Rowe (ed. 2).
346. *Valance*] Pope. *Vallens* Ff Q.
347. *belong*] Rowe. *belongs* Ff Q.
351. *portion*] *proportion* Theobald conj.
352. *struck*] F_3 F_4. *strooke* F_1 Q F_2. *stuck* Rowe (ed. 1).
362. *jointure*] Rowe. *ioynter* F_1 Q. *joynter* F_2 F_3 F_4.
365. *not to*] *but to* Warburton. *yet to* Staunton conj.
367. *Marseilles'*] *Marcellus* F_1 Q. *Marsellis* F_2 F_3 F_4.

What, have I choked you with an argosy?
Tra. Gremio, 'tis known my father hath no less
Than three great argosies; besides two galliasses,
And twelve tight galleys: these I will assure her,
And twice as much, whate'er thou offer'st next.
Gre. Nay, I have offer'd all, I have no more;
And she can have no more than all I have:
If you like me, she shall have me and mine.
Tra. Why, then the maid is mine from all the world,
By your firm promise: Gremio is out-vied.
Bap. I must confess your offer is the best;
And, let your father make her the assurance,
She is your own; else, you must pardon me,
If you should die before him, where's her dower?
Tra. That's but a cavil: he is old, I young.
Gre. And may not young men die, as well as old?
Bap. Well, gentlemen,
I am thus resolved: on Sunday next you know
My daughter Katharine is to be married:
Now, on the Sunday following, shall Bianca
Be bride to you, if you make this assurance;
If not, to Signior Gremio:
And so, I take my leave, and thank you both.
Gre. Adieu, good neighbour. [*Exit Baptista.*
Now I fear thee not:
Sirrah young gamester, your father were a fool
To give thee all, and in his waning age
Set foot under thy table: tut, a toy!
An old Italian fox is not so kind, my boy. [*Exit.*
Tra. A vengeance on your crafty wither'd hide!
Yet I have faced it with a card of ten.

384—389. *Well...Gremio*] Printed by Hanmer as five lines, ending *resolv'd:....Catharine...following...if you...Gremio.*

384, 385. *Well...resolved*] Capell; as one line in Ff Q.

384. *gentlemen*] *gentlemen, then* Pope, ending lines 384, 385 *resolv'd... know.*

387. *the*] om. Hanmer.

shall Bianca] *Bianca shall* Hanmer.

388. *to you*] *to you, Lucentio* Capell.

make this assurance] *Th' assurance make* Hanmer.

'Tis in my head to do my master good:
I see no reason but supposed Lucentio
Must get a father, call'd—supposed Vincentio;
And that's a wonder: fathers commonly
Do get their children; but in this case of wooing,
A child shall get a sire, if I fail not of my cunning. [*Exit.*

ACT III.

SCENE I. *Padua.* BAPTISTA'S *house.*

Enter LUCENTIO, HORTENSIO, *and* BIANCA.

Luc. Fiddler, forbear; you grow too forward, sir:
Have you so soon forgot the entertainment
Her sister Katharine welcomed you withal?
Hor. But, wrangling pedant, this is
The patroness of heavenly harmony:
Then give me leave to have prerogative;
And when in music we have spent an hour,
Your lecture shall have leisure for as much.
Luc. Preposterous ass, that never read so far
To know the cause why music was ordain'd!
Was it not to refresh the mind of man
After his studies or his usual pain?
Then give me leave to read philosophy,

400. *Must*] *May* Rowe.

401. *wonder*] *wonders* Q.

402. *wooing*] *winning* Collier (Capell conj.).

403. *cunning*] *doing* Rann (Steevens conj.). See note (XIII).

ACT III. SCENE I.] Actus Tertia. F_1 Q. Actus Tertius. $F_2F_3F_4$. ACT II. SCENE II. Capell.

Baptista's house.] Theobald. Another room. Capell.

4. *But...this is*] *Wrangling pedant, this* Pope. *She is a shrew, but, wrangling pedant, this is* Theobald. *But, wrangling pedant, know this lady is* Hanmer. *But, wrangling pedant, this lady is* Malone conj. *Tut, wrangling pedant, I avouch this is* Collier (Collier MS.). See note (IX).

this is] *this'* S. Walker conj. ending lines 4—6 with *patroness... leave...prerogative.*

And while I pause, serve in your harmony.
Hor. Sirrah, I will not bear these braves of thine.
Bian. Why, gentlemen, you do me double wrong,
To strive for that which resteth in my choice:
I am no breeching scholar in the schools;
I'll not be tied to hours nor 'pointed times,
But learn my lessons as I please myself.
And, to cut off all strife, here sit we down:
Take you your instrument, play you the whiles;
His lecture will be done ere you have tuned.
Hor. You'll leave his lecture when I am in tune?
Luc. That will be never: tune your instrument.
Bian. Where left we last?
Luc. Here, madam:
'Hic ibat Simois; hic est Sigeia tellus;
Hic steterat Priami regia celsa senis.'
Bian. Construe them.

Luc. 'Hic ibat,' as I told you before,—'Simois,' I am Lucentio,—'hic est,' son unto Vincentio of Pisa,—'Sigeia tellus,' disguised thus to get your love;—'Hic steterat,' and that Lucentio that comes a-wooing,—'Priami,' is my man Tranio,—'regia,' bearing my port,—'celsa senis,' that we might beguile the old pantaloon.

Hor. Madam, my instrument's in tune.
Bian. Let's hear. O fie! the treble jars.
Luc. Spit in the hole, man, and tune again.
Bian. Now let me see if I can construe it:
'Hic ibat Simois,' I know you not,—'hic est Sigeia tellus,'

14. *while*] *when* Capell (corrected in note).

15. *not*] om. Q.

19. *'pointed*] Hanmer. *pointed* Ff Q.

22. *your*] *the* Q.

play you the whiles] *play you the while* Pope. *stay you a while* Hanmer.

24. [Hortensio retires. Pope. [To Bianca, taking up his lute. Capell.

26. [Sitting to a table with Luc. Capell.

27. [Shewing a book. Capell.

28, 31, 41. *Hic*] Ff Q. *Hac* Theobald.

Sigeia] F_3 F_4. *sigeria* F_1 Q. *sigeia* F_2.

30, 40. *Construe*] F_4. *Conster* F_1 Q F_2 F_3.

32. *Sigeia*] $F_2F_3F_4$. *Sigeria* F_1 Q.

37. Hor.] Hor. [returning] Pope.

38. [Hortensio plays. Capell.

41. *ibat*] *that* F_3 F_4.

Sigeia] *sigeia* $F_2F_3F_4$. *sigeria* F_1 Q.

I trust you not;—'Hic steterat Priami,' take heed he hear us not,—'regia,' presume not,—'celsa senis,' despair not.

Hor. Madam, 'tis now in tune.

Luc. All but the base.

Hor. The base is right; 'tis the base knave that jars.
[*Aside*] How fiery and forward our pedant is!
Now, for my life, the knave doth court my love:
Pedascule, I'll watch you better yet.

Bian. In time I may believe, yet I mistrust.

Luc. Mistrust it not; for, sure, Æacides
Was Ajax, call'd so from his grandfather.

Bian. I must believe my master; else, I promise you,
I should be arguing still upon that doubt:
But let it rest. Now, Licio, to you:
Good masters, take it not unkindly, pray,
That I have been thus pleasant with you both.

Hor. You may go walk, and give me leave a while:
My lessons make no music in three parts.

Luc. Are you so formal, sir? well, I must wait,
[*Aside*] And watch withal; for, but I be deceived,
Our fine musician groweth amorous.

Hor. Madam, before you touch the instrument,
To learn the order of my fingering,
I must begin with rudiments of art;
To teach you gamut in a briefer sort,
More pleasant, pithy, and effectual,

42. *steterat*] F_2 F_3 F_4. *staterat* F_1 Q.

44. [Hortensio plays. Edd. conj.

46. *How...is!*] Luc. *How fiery and forward our pedant is,* F_1 Q F_2. Luc. *How...froward...is,* F_2 F_3 F_4 (*is!* F_4). *How fiery and froward our pedant is!* Rowe (ed. 2). *How fiery and how froward is our pedant!* Pope. *How fiery and how forward is our pedant!* Capell.

47. *the*] F_1 Q. *that* F_2 F_3 F_4.

48. *Pedascule*] *Pedascale* Warburton. *Didascule* Harness conj.

49. *In...mistrust*] Continued to Luc. in Ff Q. Given to Bian. by Pope (ed. 2).
[Seeing Hor. listen. Capell.

50. Luc.] Pope (ed. 2). Bian. FfQ.

52. Bian.] Pope (ed. 2). Hort. FfQ.

54. [rising. Capell.

55. *masters*] Rowe (ed. 2). *master* Ff Q.

57. Hor.] Hort. F_1 Q. Bian. F_2 F_3 F_4.

59—61. [Aside. Johnson.

60. [Aside] Edd.

65. *gamut*] Rowe. *gamoth* Ff Q.

Than hath been taught by any of my trade:
And there it is in writing, fairly drawn.

Bian. Why, I am past my gamut long ago.

Hor. Yet read the gamut of Hortensio.

Bian. [*reads*] "'Gamut' I am, the ground of all accord,
'A re,' to plead Hortensio's passion;
'B mi,' Bianca, take him for thy lord,
'C fa ut,' that loves with all affection:
'D sol re,' one clef, two notes have I:
'E la mi,' show pity, or I die."
Call you this gamut? tut, I like it not:
Old fashions please me best; I am not so nice,
To change true rules for old inventions.

Enter a Servant.

Serv. Mistress, your father prays you leave your books,
And help to dress your sister's chamber up:
You know to morrow is the wedding-day.

Bian. Farewell, sweet masters both; I must be gone.
[*Exeunt Bianca and Servant.*

Luc. Faith, mistress, then I have no cause to stay.
[*Exit.*

Hor. But I have cause to pry into this pedant:
Methinks he looks as though he were in love:
Yet if thy thoughts, Bianca, be so humble,
To cast thy wandering eyes on every stale,
Seize thee that list: if once I find thee ranging,
Hortensio will be quit with thee by changing. [*Exit.*

69, 70, 71, 77. *gamut*] Rowe. *gamouth* F_1 Q. *gamoth* F_2 F_3 F_4.

72. *A re*] Q. *Are* Ff.

73. *B mi*] Pope. *Beeme* Ff Q.

74. *C fa ut*] Q. *Cfavt* F_1 F_2. *Cfaut* F_3 F_4.

loves] *loves thee* Hanmer.

75. *clef*] *cliffe* F_1 Q F_2 F_3. *cliff* F_4.

two] *but two* Pope. *not two* Capell.

76. *show*] *show me* Hanmer.

78. *I am*] *I'm* Pope.

79. *change*] F_2 F_3 F_4. *charge* F_1 Q.

true...old] Ff Q. *true...new* Rowe (ed. 2). *true...odd* Theobald. *old...new* Long conj. MS. *new...old* Malone conj.

Enter a Servant.] Rowe. Enter a Messenger. Ff Q.

80. Serv.] Rowe. Nicke. F_1 Q F_2. Nick. F_3 F_4. See note (IV).

83. [Exeunt B. and S.] Capell. Ex. Rowe. Exit. Pope.

84. [Exit.] Rowe.

86. *were*] *was* Q.

89. *that*] *who* Pope.

SCENE II. *Padua. Before* BAPTISTA'S *house.*

Enter BAPTISTA, GREMIO, TRANIO, KATHARINA, BIANCA, LUCENTIO, *and* others, attendants.

Bap. Signior Lucentio [*to Tranio*], this is the 'pointed day.
That Katharine and Petruchio should be married,
And yet we hear not of our son-in-law.
What will be said? what mockery will it be,
To want the bridegroom when the priest attends
To speak the ceremonial rites of marriage!
What says Lucentio to this shame of ours?

Kath. No shame but mine: I must, forsooth, be forced
To give my hand, opposed against my heart,
Unto a mad-brain rudesby, full of spleen;
Who woo'd in haste, and means to wed at leisure.
I told you, I, he was a frantic fool,
Hiding his bitter jests in blunt behaviour:
And, to be noted for a merry man,
He'll woo a thousand, 'point the day of marriage,
Make friends, invite, and proclaim the banns;
Yet never means to wed where he hath woo'd.
Now must the world point at poor Katharine,
And say, 'Lo, there is mad Petruchio's wife,
If it would please him come and marry her!'

Tra. Patience, good Katharine, and Baptista too.
Upon my life, Petruchio means but well,
Whatever fortune stays him from his word:

SCENE II.] Pope. ACT III. SCENE I. Capell.

Before B.'s house.] Malone. Court before the house. Capell.

Lucentio] Rowe. om. Ff Q.

attendants.] attendants; Lucentio, and Hortensio among them. Capell.

1. Bap.] Bap. [to Tra.] Capell.

'*pointed*] Pope. *pointed* Ff Q.

14. *man,*] Rowe. *man;* F_1 Q F_2 F_3. *man:* F_4.

15. '*point*] Pope. *point* Ff Q.

16. *Make friends, invite,*] F_1 Q. *Make friends, invite, yes* F_2 F_3 F_4. *Make friends, invite them* Malone. *Make friends invite, yes* Singer. *Make friends invited* Grant White. *Make friends invite guests* Dyce conj. *Make feasts, invite friends* Anon. conj.

banns] Johnson. *banes* Ff Q.

18. *Katharine*] *Katharina* Rowe.

Though he be blunt, I know him passing wise;
Though he be merry, yet withal he's honest.

Kath. Would Katharine had never seen him though!
[*Exit weeping, followed by Bianca and others.*

Bap. Go, girl; I cannot blame thee now to weep;
For such an injury would vex a very saint,
Much more a shrew of thy impatient humour.

Enter BIONDELLO.

Bion. Master, master! news, old news, and such news as you never heard of!

Bap. Is it new and old too? how may that be?

Bion. Why, is it not news, to hear of Petruchio's coming?

Bap. Is he come?

Bion. Why, no, sir.

Bap. What then?

Bion. He is coming.

Bap. When will he be here?

Bion. When he stands where I am and sees you there.

Tra. But say, what to thine old news?

Bion. Why, Petruchio is coming in a new hat and an old jerkin, a pair of old breeches thrice turned, a pair of boots that have been candle-cases, one buckled, another laced, an old rusty sword ta'en out of the town-armoury, with a broken hilt, and chapeless; with two broken points: his horse hipped with an old mothy saddle and stirrups of no

24. *know*] Ff. *knew* Q.

26. *him*] om. Q.

[Exit...others.] Exit weeping. Ff Q. Exit weeping: is follow'd by Bianca, Gremio, Hortensio, and Others. Capell.

28. *a very saint*] F_1 Q. *a saint* $F_2F_3F_4$.

29. *thy*] F_2 F_3 F_4. om. F_1 Q.

Enter B.] Enter B., hastily. Capell.

30. SCENE III. Pope.

news, old news, and such news] Capell. *news, and such news* Ff Q. *old news, and such news* Rowe. *news, and such old news* Collier (Collier MS.).

33. *hear*] *heard* F_1. *heare* Q.

40. *what to*] *what be* Capell. *what:—to* Malone. *what is* Collier MS.

thine] F_1 Q F_2. *thy* F_3 F_4.

41. *a new*] *an old* Anon. conj.

43, 45. *laced; an......points*] *laced with two broken points; an...chapeless* Rann (Johnson conj.).

45—47. *his horse...kindred;*] *with an old mothy saddle, the stirrups of no kindred: his horse hip'd*, Rann.

46. *hipped*] *hip'd* Ff Q. *heaped* Collier MS.

and] F_1 Q. *the* $F_2F_3F_4$. *with the* Hanmer (ed. 2).

kindred; besides, possessed with the glanders and like to mose in the chine; troubled with the lampass, infected with the fashions, full of windgalls, sped with spavins, rayed with the yellows, past cure of the fives, stark spoiled with the staggers, begnawn with the bots, swayed in the back and shoulder-shotten; near-legged before and with a half-checked bit and a head-stall of sheep's leather which, being restrained to keep him from stumbling, hath been often burst and now repaired with knots; one girth six times pieced and a woman's crupper of velure, which hath two letters for her name fairly set down in studs, and here and there pieced with packthread.

Bap. Who comes with him?

Bion. O, sir, his lackey, for all the world caparisoned like the horse; with a linen stock on one leg, and a kersey boot-hose on the other, gartered with a red and blue list; an old hat, and 'the humour of forty fancies' pricked in't for a feather: a monster, a very monster in apparel, and not like a Christian footboy or a gentleman's lackey.

Tra. 'Tis some odd humour pricks him to this fashion;
Yet oftentimes he goes but mean-apparell'd.

Bap. I am glad he's come, howsoe'er he comes.

Bion. Why, sir, he comes not.

Bap. Didst thou not say he comes?

Bion. Who? that Petruchio came?

Bap. Ay, that Petruchio came.

Bion. No, sir; I say his horse comes, with him on his back.

Bap. Why, that's all one.

48. *mose*] *mourn* Hanmer.

49. *fashions*] *farcin* Hanmer. *farcy* Long conj. MS.

50. *fives*] *vives* Hanmer.

51. *swayed*] Hanmer. *waid* Ff Q.

52. *near-legged*] *neere leg'd* F_1QF_2. *neer leg'd* F_3F_4. *ne'er legg'd* Malone.

55. *now repaired*] *new-repaired* S. Walker conj.

girth] *girt* Rowe (ed. 2).

57. *down*] *dower* F_2.

63. *the humour of*] *the amours or* Collier MS. See note (XIV).

pricked] *prickt up* F_3F_4.

65. *or a*] F_1Q. *or* F_3F_4.

66. *odd*] *old* Q.

66, 67. *'Tis...apparell'd* Printed as prose in Q.

68. *he's come*] *he is come* Johnson. *he's come though* Capell.

howsoe'er] *howsoere* F_1Q. *howsoever* $F_2F_3F_4$.

71. *that Petruchio*] *that that Petruchio* F_3F_4.

came] *came not* Warburton.

73. *say*] *say, that* Capell.

Bion. Nay, by Saint Jamy,
I hold you a penny,
A horse and a man
Is more than one,
And yet not many.

Enter PETRUCHIO *and* GRUMIO.

Pet. Come, where be these gallants? who's at home?
Bap. You are welcome, sir.
Pet. And yet I come not well.
Bap. And yet you halt not.
Tra. Not so well apparell'd
As I wish you were.
Pet. Were it better, I should rush in thus.
But where is Kate? where is my lovely bride?
How does my father? Gentles, methinks you frown:
And wherefore gaze this goodly company,
As if they saw some wondrous monument,
Some comet or unusual prodigy?
Bap. Why, sir, you know this is your wedding-day:
First were we sad, fearing you would not come;
Now sadder, that you come so unprovided.
Fie, doff this habit, shame to your estate,
An eye-sore to our solemn festival!
Tra. And tell us, what occasion of import

76—80. *Nay...many.*] Printed as prose in Ff Q; as five lines of verse by Collier; as two lines by Rowe (ed. 2).

81. SCENE IV. Pope.

Enter P. and G.] Enter P. and G. fantastically habited. Rowe.

Come] *Come, come* S. Walker conj.

gallants?] *gallants here?* Capell.

who's] *who is* Pope.

81—84. *Come...were*] Verse as in Capell. Printed as prose in Ff Q. See note (XV).

81, 83, 85. *Come...Not so well...Were it...thus.*] *Come, come...Nor so ...Were it not...thus?* Lettsom conj., ending lines 83, 84 at *halt not...were.*

82. *you are*] *you're* Pope.

82, 83. *sir.* Pet. *And yet I come not well.* Bap. *And yet you halt not*] *sir: and yet you come not well.* Pet. *And yet I halt not* Capell conj.

83. *apparell'd*] *'parell'd* Pope, reading as one verse *Not...were.*

84. *wish*] *could wish* Capell.

85. *Were*] *Why, were* Hanmer. *Tut! were* Capell. *Wer't* S. Walker conj.

better] *much better* Collier MS.

thus.] *thus?* Rann.

86. *is my*] *is is my* Q.

95. *An*] *And* Anon. conj.

Hath all so long detain'd you from your wife,
And sent you hither so unlike yourself?

Pet. Tedious it were to tell, and harsh to hear:
Sufficeth, I am come to keep my word,
Though in some part enforced to digress;
Which, at more leisure, I will so excuse
As you shall well be satisfied withal.
But where is Kate? I stay too long from her:
The morning wears, 'tis time we were at church.

Tra. See not your bride in these unreverent robes:
Go to my chamber; put on clothes of mine.

Pet. Not I, believe me: thus I'll visit her.

Bap. But thus, I trust, you will not marry her.

Pet. Good sooth, even thus; therefore ha' done with words:
To me she's married, not unto my clothes:
Could I repair what she will wear in me,
As I can change these poor accoutrements,
'Twere well for Kate and better for myself.
But what a fool am I to chat with you,
When I should bid good morrow to my bride,
And seal the title with a lovely kiss!

[*Exeunt Petruchio and Grumio.*

Tra. He hath some meaning in his mad attire:
We will persuade him, be it possible,
To put on better ere he go to church.

Bap. I'll after him, and see the event of this.

[*Exeunt Baptista, Gremio, and attendants.*

Tra. But to her love concerneth us to add

103. *withal*] *with all* F_1 F_2.

110. *ha'*] F_4. *ha* F_1Q $F_2$$F_3$. *have* Capell.

113. *can*] F_1QF_2. *could* $F_3$$F_4$.

117. *lovely*] *loving* Collier (Collier MS.).

[Exeunt P. and G.] Dyce. [Exit. Ff Q. [Exeunt Pet. Gru. and Bio. Capell.

121. [Exeunt B., G., and attendants.] Exit. Ff Q. [Exeunt Bap. and Attendants. Tranio follows; but is beckon'd back by Lucentio, who converses a while apart. Capell.

122. SCENE V. Pope.

But to her love] Grant White. *But sir, Love* Ff Q. *But, sir, our love* Pope. *But to her love, sir* Capell. *But sir, her love* Rann (Ritson conj.). *But, sir, to her love* Malone (Tyrwhitt conj.). *But to our love* Collier MS. *But, sir, to love* Knight.

Her father's liking: which to bring to pass,
As I before imparted to your worship,
I am to get a man,—whate'er he be,
It skills not much, we'll fit him to our turn,—
And he shall be Vincentio of Pisa;
And make assurance here in Padua
Of greater sums than I have promised.
So shall you quietly enjoy your hope,
And marry sweet Bianca with consent.
Luc. Were it not that my fellow-schoolmaster
Doth watch Bianca's steps so narrowly,
'Twere good, methinks, to steal our marriage;
Which once perform'd, let all the world say no,
I'll keep mine own, despite of all the world.
Tra. That by degrees we mean to look into,
And watch our vantage in this business:
We'll over-reach the greybeard, Gremio,
The narrow-prying father, Minola,
The quaint musician, amorous Licio;
All for my master's sake, Lucentio.

Re-enter GREMIO.

Signior Gremio, came you from the church?
Gre. As willingly as e'er I came from school.
Tra. And is the bride and bridegroom coming home?
Gre. A bridegroom say you? 'tis a groom indeed,
A grumbling groom, and that the girl shall find.
Tra. Curster than she? why, 'tis impossible.
Gre. Why, he's a devil, a devil, a very fiend.
Tra. Why, she's a devil, a devil, the devil's dam.
Gre. Tut, she's a lamb, a dove, a fool to him!
I'll tell you, Sir Lucentio: when the priest

124. *I before*] Pope. *before* F_1 Q. *before I* F_2 F_3 F_4.

126. *our turn*] *turn* Capell (corrected in MS).

140. *narrow-prying*] Pope. *narrow prying* Ff Q.

143. SCENE VI. Pope.

Re-enter Gremio.] Re-enter G. laughing. Capell.

Signior] *Now, signior* Pope.

145. *is*] *are* Hanmer.

147. *grumbling*] *grumlling* F_1. *grumling* Q.

148. *she?*] F_4. *she* F_1 Q F_2 F_3.

Should ask, if Katharine should be his wife,
'Ay, by gogs-wouns,' quoth he; and swore so loud,
That, all amazed, the priest let fall the book;
And, as he stoop'd again to take it up,
The mad-brain'd bridegroom took him such a cuff,
That down fell priest and book, and book and priest:
'Now take them up,' quoth he, 'if any list.'

Tra. What said the wench when he rose again?

Gre. Trembled and shook; for why he stamp'd and swore,
As if the vicar meant to cozen him.
But after many ceremonies done,
He calls for wine: 'A health!' quoth he; as if
He had been aboard, carousing to his mates
After a storm: quaff'd off the muscadel,
And threw the sops all in the sexton's face;
Having no other reason
But that his beard grew thin and hungerly
And seem'd to ask him sops as he was drinking.
This done, he took the bride about the neck
And kiss'd her lips with such a clamorous smack
That at the parting all the church did echo:
And I seeing this came thence for very shame;
And after me, I know, the rout is coming.
Such a mad marriage never was before:
Hark, hark! I hear the minstrels play. [*Music.*

153. *Should ask*] *Did ask* Hanmer.

160. *wench*] *wretch* Capell conj. *rose*] F_1 Q. *rose up* $F_2F_3F_4$. *arose* Reed (1803).

161—177. *Trembled......play*] Arranged as in Reed (1803). Printed as prose in F_1 Q; as verse first in F_2, making 16 lines, ending *swore...him ...done...if...mates...muscadell...face... beard...aske...tooke...lips...parting... this...me...marryage...play.*

164—168. *He calls...reason*] Printed by Capell as five lines, ending *wine... aboard...storm...sops...reason.*

164. *if*] om. Capell.

165. *He had*] *H'ad* Pope.

168. *reason*] *cause* Pope.

170. *him*] *His* F_3 F_4.

173. *all*] om. Long conj. MS. *did echo*] *echo'd* Pope.

174. *And I*] *I* Capell.

175. *I know*] om. Hanmer.

176. *never*] *Ne'er* Theobald.

177. *I hear*] om. Hanmer. *play*] om. Theobald.

Re-enter PETRUCHIO, KATHARINA, BIANCA, BAPTISTA, HORTENSIO, GRUMIO, *and Train.*

Pet. Gentlemen and friends, I thank you for your pains:
I know you think to dine with me to-day,
And have prepared great store of wedding cheer;
But so it is, my haste doth call me hence,
And therefore here I mean to take my leave.
Bap. Is't possible you will away to-night?
Pet. I must away to-day, before night come:
Make it no wonder; if you knew my business,
You would entreat me rather go than stay.
And, honest company, I thank you all,
That have beheld me give away myself
To this most patient, sweet, and virtuous wife:
Dine with my father, drink a health to me;
For I must hence; and farewell to you all.
Tra. Let us entreat you stay till after dinner.
Pet. It may not be.
Gre. Let me entreat you.
Pet. It cannot be.
Kath. Let me entreat you.
Pet. I am content.
Kath. Are you content to stay?
Pet. I am content you shall entreat me stay;
But yet not stay, entreat me how you can.
Kath. Now, if you love me, stay.
Pet. Grumio, my horse.
Gru. Ay, sir, they be ready: the oats have eaten the horses.
Kath. Nay, then,

178. SCENE VII. Pope.
Petruchio, Katharina...] P. and C. as marry'd... Capell.
Grumio, and Train.] Capell.
183. *will*] *must* Hanmer.
193. *you*] *you, sir* Hanmer. *you stay* Steevens conj.
194. *you,*] *you, sir* Hanmer. *you then* Capell. *you stay* Steevens conj.
198. *horse*] *horses* Rowe (ed. 2).
199. *Ay, sir*] *Sir* Hanmer.
oats] *bots* Grey conj.
eaten] *eaten up* Capell.

Do what thou canst, I will not go to-day;
No, nor to-morrow, not till I please myself.
The door is open, sir; there lies your way;
You may be jogging whiles your boots are green;
For me, I'll not be gone till I please myself:
'Tis like you'll prove a jolly surly groom,
That take it on you at the first so roundly.
Pet. O Kate, content thee; prithee, be not angry.
Kath. I will be angry: what hast thou to do?
Father, be quiet: he shall stay my leisure.
Gre. Ay, marry, sir, now it begins to work.
Kath. Gentlemen, forward to the bridal dinner:
I see a woman may be made a fool,
If she had not a spirit to resist.
Pet. They shall go forward, Kate, at thy command.
Obey the bride, you that attend on her;
Go to the feast, revel and domineer,
Carouse full measure to her maidenhead,
Be mad and merry, or go hang yourselves:
But for my bonny Kate, she must with me.
Nay, look not big, nor stamp, nor stare, nor fret;
I will be master of what is mine own:
She is my goods, my chattels; she is my house,
My household stuff, my field, my barn,
My horse, my ox, my ass, my any thing;
And here she stands, touch her whoever dare;
I'll bring mine action on the proudest he
That stops my way in Padua. Grumio,
Draw forth thy weapon, we are beset with thieves;
Rescue thy mistress, if thou be a man.
Fear not, sweet wench, they shall not touch thee, Kate:

203. *not till*] F_1 Q F_2 F_3. *nor till* F_4.
205. *whiles*] *while* Pope.
206. *be gone*] *go* Hanmer.
till I] *till* Capell.
214. *made*] *maide* Q.
220. *yourselves*] *you selves* F_2.
224. *she is my house*] *and my house* Hanmer. *and she is My house* Mitford conj.
225. *My*] *She is my* Hanmer.
my barn] *my barn, my stable* Capell. *my barn, my grange* S. Walker conj. *my barn, my garner* Edd. conj.
228. *mine*] *my* Rowe.
230. *we are*] *we're* Pope.

I'll buckler thee against a million.

[*Exeunt Petruchio, Katharina, and Grumio.*

Bap. Nay, let them go, a couple of quiet ones.

Gre. Went they not quickly, I should die with laughing.

Tra. Of all mad matches never was the like.

Luc. Mistress, what's your opinion of your sister?

Bian. That, being mad herself, she's madly mated.

Gre. I warrant him, Petruchio is Kated.

Bap. Neighbours and friends, though bride and bridegroom wants
For to supply the places at the table,
You know there wants no junkets at the feast.
Lucentio, you shall supply the bridegroom's place;
And let Bianca take her sister's room.

Tra. Shall sweet Bianca practise how to bride it?

Bap. She shall, Lucentio. Come, gentlemen, let's go.

[*Exeunt.*

ACT IV.

SCENE I. PETRUCHIO'S *country house.*

Enter GRUMIO.

Gru. Fie, fie on all tired jades, on all mad masters, and all foul ways! Was ever man so beaten? was ever man so rayed? was ever man so weary? I am sent before to make a fire, and they are coming after to warm them. Now, were not I a little pot, and soon hot, my very lips might freeze to my teeth, my tongue to the roof of my mouth, my heart in my belly, ere I should come by a fire

233. [Exeunt P. K. and G.] Exeunt P. Ka. Ff Q. [Exit, hurrying Catherine out; Grumio, with his sword drawn, bringing up the rear. Capell.

237. Luc. *Mistress...sister?*] Continued to Tranio by Capell.

240. *wants*] *want* Pope.

242. *wants*] *want* Grant White.

243. *shall supply*] *supply* Pope. *shall have* Rann (Capell conj.).

246. *Come*] om. Pope. See note (XVI).

ACT IV. SCENE I.] Pope.

P.'s country house.] Pope. A hall in... Capell.

2, 3. *Was...beaten? was...rayed? was...weary?*] *was...weary? was... beaten? was...raied?* Hanmer.

3. *rayed*] *'wray'd* Capell.

to thaw me: but I, with blowing the fire, shall warm myself; for, considering the weather, a taller man than I will take cold. Holla, ho! Curtis!

Enter CURTIS.

Curt. Who is that calls so coldly?

Gru. A piece of ice: if thou doubt it, thou mayst slide from my shoulder to my heel with no greater a run but my head and my neck. A fire, good Curtis.

Curt. Is my master and his wife coming, Grumio?

Gru. O, ay, Curtis, ay: and therefore fire, fire; cast on no water.

Curt. Is she so hot a shrew as she's reported?

Gru. She was, good Curtis, before this frost: but, thou knowest, winter tames man, woman, and beast; for it hath tamed my old master, and my new mistress, and myself, fellow Curtis.

Curt. Away, you three-inch fool! I am no beast.

Gru. Am I but three inches? why, thy horn is a foot; and so long am I at the least. But wilt thou make a fire, or shall I complain on thee to our mistress, whose hand, she being now at hand, thou shalt soon feel, to thy cold comfort, for being slow in thy hot office?

Curt. I prithee, good Grumio, tell me, how goes the world?

Gru. A cold world, Curtis, in every office but thine; and therefore fire: do thy duty, and have thy duty; for my master and mistress are almost frozen to death.

Curt. There's fire ready; and therefore, good Grumio, the news.

Gru. Why, 'Jack, boy! ho! boy!' and as much news as thou wilt.

Curt. Come, you are so full of cony-catching!

11. *is*] *is 't* Anon. conj.

16. *Curtis*] *Burtis* Q.

19. *this*] *the* Rowe (ed. 2).

21. *myself*] *thyself* Hanmer (Warburton).

23. *three-inch*] *three-inch'd* Rowe.

24. *thy*] *my* Theobald.

34. *There's*] *There is* Hanmer.

37. *thou wilt*] *wilt thou* F_1. *will thaw* Anon. conj.

Gru. Why, therefore fire; for I have caught extreme cold. Where's the cook? is supper ready, the house trimmed, rushes strewed, cobwebs swept; the serving-men in their new fustian, their white stockings, and every officer his wedding-garment on? Be the jacks fair within, the jills fair without, the carpets laid, and every thing in order?

Curt. All ready; and therefore, I pray thee, news.

Gru. First, know, my horse is tired; my master and mistress fallen out.

Curt. How?

Gru. Out of their saddles into the dirt; and thereby hangs a tale.

Curt. Let's ha't, good Grumio.

Gru. Lend thine ear.

Curt. Here.

Gru. There. [*Strikes him.*

Curt. This is to feel a tale, not to hear a tale.

Gru. And therefore 'tis called a sensible tale: and this cuff was but to knock at your ear, and beseech listening. Now I begin: *Imprimis*, we came down a foul hill, my master riding behind my mistress,—

Curt. Both of one horse?

Gru. What's that to thee?

Curt. Why, a horse.

Gru. Tell thou the tale: but hadst thou not crossed me, thou shouldst have heard how her horse fell and she under her horse; thou shouldst have heard in how miry a place, how she was bemoiled, how he left her with the horse upon her, how he beat me because her horse stumbled, how she waded through the dirt to pluck him off me, how he swore, how she prayed, that never prayed before, how I cried, how the horses ran away, how her bridle was burst, how I lost my crupper, with many things of worthy me-

42. *their*] F_3F_4. *the* F_1QF_2. *the —in their* S. Walker conj., supposing an omission.

43, 44. *within...without*] *without... within* Hanmer.

44. *the carpets*] *carpets* F_3F_4.

45. *news*] *what news* $F_2F_3F_4$. *thy news* Malone conj.

54. [Strikes him.] Rowe.

55. *is*] Rowe (ed. 2). *'tis* FfQ.

60. *of*] *on* Rowe.

71. *of worthy*] *worthy of* S. Walker conj.

mory, which now shall die in oblivion and thou return unexperienced to thy grave.

Curt. By this reckoning he is more shrew than she.

Gru. Ay; and that thou and the proudest of you all shall find when he comes home. But what talk I of this? Call forth Nathaniel, Joseph, Nicholas, Philip, Walter, Sugarsop and the rest: let their heads be sleekly combed, their blue coats brushed and their garters of an indifferent knit: let them curtsy with their left legs and not presume to touch a hair of my master's horse-tail till they kiss their hands. Are they all ready?

Curt. They are.

Gru. Call them forth.

Curt. Do you hear, ho? you must meet my master to countenance my mistress!

Gru. Why, she hath a face of her own.

Curt. Who knows not that?

Gru. Thou, it seems, that calls for company to countenance her.

Curt. I call them forth to credit her.

Gru. Why, she comes to borrow nothing of them.

Enter four or five serving-men.

Nath. Welcome home, Grumio!

Phil. How now, Grumio!

Jos. What, Grumio!

Nich. Fellow Grumio!

Nath. How now, old lad?

Gru. Welcome, you;—how now, you;—what, you;—fellow, you;—and thus much for greeting. Now, my spruce companions, is all ready, and all things neat?

73. *thy*] *the* Q.

74. *is*] om. Q.

77. *Walter, Sugarsop*] *Walter Sugarsop* S. Walker conj.

Sugarsop] corrupt, Id. conj.

78. *sleekly*] *slickely* F_1QF_2. *slickly* F_3F_4.

79. *indifferent*] *different* Malone conj.

80. *knit*] *knot* Capell.

89. *calls*] Ff Q. *call'st* Rowe (ed. 2).

92. Enter...] Ff Q (after line 90).

97. Nath.] Walt. Edd. conj.

Nath. All things is ready. How near is our master?

Gru. E'en at hand, alighted by this; and therefore be not—Cock's passion, silence! I hear my master.

Enter PETRUCHIO *and* KATHARINA.

Pet. Where be these knaves? What, no man at door
To hold my stirrup nor to take my horse!
Where is Nathaniel, Gregory, Philip?

All Serv. Here, here, sir; here, sir.

Pet. Here, sir! here, sir! here, sir! here, sir!
You logger-headed and unpolish'd grooms!
What, no attendance? no regard? no duty?
Where is the foolish knave I sent before?

Gru. Here, sir; as foolish as I was before.

Pet. You peasant swain! you whoreson malt-horse drudge!
Did I not bid thee meet me in the park,
And bring along these rascal knaves with thee?

Gru. Nathaniel's coat, sir, was not fully made,
And Gabriel's pumps were all unpink'd i' the heel;
There was no link to colour Peter's hat,
And Walter's dagger was not come from sheathing:
There were none fine but Adam, Ralph, and Gregory;
The rest were ragged, old, and beggarly;
Yet, as they are, here are they come to meet you.

Pet. Go, rascals, go, and fetch my supper in.
[*Exeunt Servants.*

[*Singing*] Where is the life that late I led—

Where are those—Sit down, Kate, and welcome.—

101. *is ready*] F_1 Q. *are ready* $F_2 F_3 F_4$.

104. SCENE II. Pope.

104—106. *Where...Philip*] Printed as prose in $F_3 F_4$.

104. *door*] *the door* Capell.

106—108. *Where is...here, sir!*] Printed by Capell as two lines, ending the first at *Here, here, sir.*

110. *attendance*] *attendants* Q.

113. *peasant*] *pleasant* Pope (ed. 2).

115. *these*] F_1 Q. *the* $F_2 F_3 F_4$.

122. *here are*] F_1 Q. om. $F_2 F_3 F_4$.

123. [Exeunt Servants] Ex. Ser. Ff Q. Exeunt some of the servants. Cloth lay'd. Capell.

124. [Singing.] Theobald. See note (XVII).

led—] *led, say they:—* Capell.

125. *those—*] *those villains?* Capell.

Soud, soud, soud, soud!

Re-enter Servants *with supper.*

Why, when, I say? Nay, good sweet Kate, be merry.
Off with my boots, you rogues! you villains, when?
[*Sings.*

It was the friar of orders grey,
As he forth walked on his way:—

Out, you rogue! you pluck my foot awry:
Take that, and mend the plucking off the other.
[*Strikes him.*
Be merry, Kate. Some water, here; what, ho!
Where's my spaniel Troilus? Sirrah, get you hence,
And bid my cousin Ferdinand come hither:
One, Kate, that you must kiss, and be acquainted with.
Where are my slippers? Shall I have some water?

Enter one with water.

Come, Kate, and wash, and welcome heartily.
You whoreson villain! will you let it fall? [*Strikes him.*

Kath. Patience, I pray you; 'twas a fault unwilling.

Pet. A whoreson beetle-headed, flap-ear'd knave!
Come, Kate, sit down; I know you have a stomach.
Will you give thanks, sweet Kate; or else shall I?
What's this? mutton?

First Serv. Ay.

Pet. Who brought it?

Peter. I.

Pet. 'Tis burnt; and so is all the meat.
What dogs are these! Where is the rascal cook?

126. *Soud...soud*] *Sü...sü.* A. A. (N. and Q.) conj.
[Humming. Hanmer. [Wipes himself. Capell.
128. *rogues*] *rogue* Hanmer.
[Sings.] Rowe.
131. *Out*] *Out, out* Pope.
132. *mend*] *mind* Hanmer.
[Strikes him.] Rowe.
134. *my*] *by* Hanmer (a misprint).
137. [Water presented. Capell.
[Enter...] Ff Q (after line 133). om. Capell.
138. [Servant lets the ewer fall. Capell.
141. *flap-ear'd*] *flatear'd* Rowe.
144. *What's*] *What is* Hanmer.
Ay] *Yes* Rowe.
Peter.] F_1Q. Ser. $F_2F_3F_4$.
145. *all the*] *all the rest o'the* Capell.

How durst you, villains, bring it from the dresser,
And serve it thus to me that love it not?
There, take it to you, trenchers, cups, and all:
[*Throws the meat, &c. about the stage.*
You heedless joltheads and unmanner'd slaves!
What, do you grumble? I'll be with you straight.
Kath. I pray you, husband, be not so disquiet:
The meat was well, if you were so contented.
Pet. I tell thee, Kate, 'twas burnt and dried away;
And I expressly am forbid to touch it,
For it engenders choler, planteth anger;
And better 'twere that both of us did fast,
Since, of ourselves, ourselves are choleric,
Than feed it with such over-roasted flesh.
Be patient; to-morrow 't shall be mended,
And, for this night, we'll fast for company:
Come, I will bring thee to thy bridal chamber. [*Exeunt.*

Re-enter Servants *severally.*

Nath. Peter, didst ever see the like?
Peter. He kills her in her own humour.

Re-enter CURTIS.

Gru. Where is he?
Curt. In her chamber, making a sermon of continency to her;
And rails, and swears, and rates, that she, poor soul,
Knows not which way to stand, to look, to speak,
And sits as one new-risen from a dream.
Away, away! for he is coming hither. [*Exeunt.*

Re-enter PETRUCHIO.

Pet. Thus have I politicly begun my reign,

149. [Throws...] Rowe.
160. *to-morrow*] *for to-morrow* Pope.
162. [Exeunt.] Ff Q. [Exit, leading out Cat. Cur. follows. Capell.
163—166. *Peter...chamber*] As two lines in Capell, ending *kills her... chamber*.
164. [Re-enter Curtis.] Enter Curtis a servant. Ff Q (after line 165).
166—171. *In her...hither*] Pope. Printed as prose in Ff Q.
168. *swears*] *sweare* F_2.
that she] *and she* Rowe.
171. [Exeunt.] Pope. om. Ff Q.
172. SCENE III. Pope.

And 'tis my hope to end successfully.
My falcon now is sharp and passing empty;
And till she stoop she must not be full-gorged,
For then she never looks upon her lure.
Another way I have to man my haggard,
To make her come and know her keeper's call,
That is, to watch her, as we watch these kites
That bate and beat and will not be obedient.
She eat no meat to-day, nor none shall eat;
Last night she slept not, nor to-night she shall not;
As with the meat, some undeserved fault
I'll find about the making of the bed;
And here I'll fling the pillow, there the bolster,
This way the coverlet, another way the sheets:
Ay, and amid this hurly I intend
That all is done in reverend care of her;
And in conclusion she shall watch all night:
And if she chance to nod I'll rail and brawl
And with the clamour keep her still awake.
This is a way to kill a wife with kindness;
And thus I'll curb her mad and headstrong humour.
He that knows better how to tame a shrew,
Now let him speak: 'tis charity to show. [*Exit.*

SCENE II. *Padua. Before* BAPTISTA'S *house.*

Enter TRANIO *and* HORTENSIO.

Tra. Is't possible, friend Licio, that Mistress Bianca
Doth fancy any other but Lucentio?

180. *bate...beat*] *baite...beate* F_1Q F_2. *bait...beat* F_3F_4.

182. *she shall*] *shall* F_3F_4.

186. *another*] *that* Pope.

187. *I intend*] *I'll pretend* Rowe (ed. 2).

SCENE II.] Steevens. ACT V. SCENE I. Pope. SCENE IV. Hanmer. ACT IV. SCENE I. Capell. See note (XVIII).

Padua] Pope.

Before B's house.] Theobald.

Enter T. and H.] FfQ. Enter Lucentio and Bianca courting; and, on the opposite side, Tranio and Hortensio. Capell.

1. *that*] om. S. Walker conj.

Mistress] om. Pope.

I tell you, sir, she bears me fair in hand.
Hor. Sir, to satisfy you in what I have said,
Stand by and mark the manner of his teaching.

Enter BIANCA *and* LUCENTIO.

Luc. Now, mistress, profit you in what you read?
Bian. What, master, read you? first resolve me that.
Luc. I read that I profess, the Art to Love.
Bian. And may you prove, sir, master of your art!
Luc. While you, sweet dear, prove mistress of my heart!
Hor. Quick proceeders, marry! Now, tell me, I pray,
You that durst swear that your mistress Bianca
Loved none in the world so well as Lucentio.
Tra. O despiteful love! unconstant womankind!
I tell thee, Licio, this is wonderful.
Hor. Mistake no more: I am not Licio,
Nor a musician, as I seem to be;
But one that scorn to live in this disguise,
For such a one as leaves a gentleman,
And makes a god of such a cullion:
Know, sir, that I am call'd Hortensio.
Tra. Signior Hortensio, I have often heard
Of your entire affection to Bianca;
And since mine eyes are witness of her lightness,
I will with you, if you be so contented,
Forswear Bianca and her love for ever.
Hor. See, how they kiss and court! Signior Lucentio,

4. Hor.] $F_2F_3F_4$. Luc. F_1Q.
Sir, to satisfy you] FfQ. *To satisfy you, sir* Pope. *Signior, to satisfy you* Anon conj.
have] om. Pope.

5. [They stand by. Theobald.
...and Lucentio] Rowe.

6, 8. Luc.] $F_2F_3F_4$. Hor. F_1Q.

7. *What, master, read you? first*] Theobald. *What master read you first,* FfQ.

8. *to*] *of* Rowe (ed. 2).

10. [They retire backward. Theobald. [Court apart. Capell.

11. *Quick proceeders, marry*] *Marry, quick proceeders* Capell.
Now, tell me] *Tell me now* Capell.

11—13. *Quick...Lucentio*] F_1QF_2. As prose in F_3F_4.

12. *that your mistress*] *your mistress fair* Capell.

13. *none*] Rowe. *me* FfQ.
in the] *i'the* Capell.
as] *as her* Capell.

14. *O*] om. Capell.

Here is my hand, and here I firmly vow
Never to woo her more, but do forswear her,
As one unworthy all the former favours
That I have fondly flatter'd her withal.

Tra. And here I take the like unfeigned oath,
Never to marry with her though she would entreat:
Fie on her! see, how beastly she doth court him!

Hor. Would all the world but he had quite forsworn!
For me, that I may surely keep mine oath,
I will be married to a wealthy widow,
Ere three days pass, which hath as long loved me
As I have loved this proud disdainful haggard.
And so farewell, Signior Lucentio.
Kindness in women, not their beauteous looks,
Shall win my love: and so I take my leave,
In resolution as I swore before. [*Exit.*

Tra. Mistress Bianca, bless you with such grace
As 'longeth to a lover's blessed case!
Nay, I have ta'en you napping, gentle love,
And have forsworn you with Hortensio.

Bian. Tranio, you jest: but have you both forsworn me?

Tra. Mistress, we have.

Luc. Then we are rid of Licio.

Tra. I'faith, he'll have a lusty widow now,
That shall be woo'd and wedded in a day.

Bian. God give him joy!

Tra. Ay, and he'll tame her.

Bian. He says so, Tranio.

Tra. Faith, he is gone unto the taming-school.

Bian. The taming-school! what, is there such a place?

29. *Never ... forswear her*] om. Rowe.
31. *her*] F_3F_4. *them* F_1 Q F_2.
33. *Never*] *Ne'er* Steevens.
with her] *her* Pope. *wi'her* S. Walker conj.
she would] *she* Pope. *she'ld* S. Walker conj.
35. *forsworn*] *forsworn her* Rowe (ed. 2).
36. *oath,*] Rowe. *oath.* Ff Q.
38. *hath*] *has* F_4.
42. *so*] om. F_2. *thus* Collier MS.
44. Tra.] Tra. [passing to the other side]. Capell.
45. *'longeth*] Hanmer. *longeth* Ff Q.
53. *her*] *her too* S. Walker conj.
54. *unto*] Ff Q. *into* Warburton. *to* Heath conj.

Tra. Ay, mistress, and Petruchio is the master;
That teacheth tricks eleven and twenty long,
To tame a shrew and charm her chattering tongue.

Enter BIONDELLO.

Bion. O master, master, I have watch'd so long
That I am dog-weary! but at last I spied
An ancient angel coming down the hill,
Will serve the turn.

Tra. What is he, Biondello?

Bion. Master, a mercatantè, or a pedant,
I know not what; but formal in apparel,
In gait and countenance surely like a father.

Luc. And what of him, Tranio?

Tra. If he be credulous and trust my tale,
I'll make him glad to seem Vincentio,
And give assurance to Baptista Minola,
As if he were the right Vincentio.
Take in your love, and then let me alone.
[*Exeunt Lucentio and Bianca.*

Enter a Pedant.

Ped. God save you, sir!

Tra. And you, sir! you are welcome.
Travel you far on, or are you at the farthest?

Ped. Sir, at the farthest for a week or two:

59. ACT V. SCENE II. Pope. SCENE V. Hanmer.

Enter B.] Enter B. running. Theobald.

60. *I am*] *I'm* Pope.

61. *ancient angel*] *angel-merchant* Steevens conj.

angel] *Angel* $F_1F_3F_4$. *Angell* QF_2. *engle* Theobald. *ayeul* Becket conj. *gentleman* or *gentle* Mitford conj. *morsel* Staunton conj. *ambler* Collier (Collier MS.). *antick* Anon. conj. *uncle* Bubier conj.

coming] *going* Pope (ed. 2).

63. *mercatantè, or*] Capell. *marcantant, or* Ff Q. *mercantant, or else* Pope.

65. *surely*] F_1Q. *surly* $F_2F_3F_4$.

66. *And*] om. Capell.

Tranio] om. S. Walker conj.

69. *give*] *give him* Theobald.

71. *Take in*] Theobald. Par. *Take me* F_1Q. *Take me,* $F_2F_3F_4$. *Partake* or *Take on* Anon. conj.

Take...and then] *Partake your love within;* Anon. conj.

[Exeunt L. and B.] Rowe.

But then up farther, and as far as Rome;
And so to Tripoli, if God lend me life.
Tra. What countryman, I pray?
Ped. Of Mantua.
Tra. Of Mantua, sir? marry, God forbid!
And come to Padua, careless of your life?
Ped. My life, sir! how, I pray? for that goes hard.
Tra. 'Tis death for any one in Mantua
To come to Padua. Know you not the cause?
Your ships are stay'd at Venice; and the Duke,
For private quarrel 'twixt your duke and him,
Hath publish'd and proclaim'd it openly:
'Tis marvel, but that you are but newly come,
You might have heard it else proclaim'd about.
Ped. Alas, sir, it is worse for me than so!
For I have bills for money by exchange
From Florence, and must here deliver them.
Tra. Well, sir, to do you courtesy,
This will I do, and this I will advise you:
First, tell me, have you ever been at Pisa?
Ped. Ay, sir, in Pisa have I often been;
Pisa renowned for grave citizens.
Tra. Among them know you one Vincentio?
Ped. I know him not, but I have heard of him;
A merchant of incomparable wealth.
Tra. He is my father, sir; and, sooth to say,
In countenance somewhat doth resemble you.
Bion. As much as an apple doth an oyster, and all one.
[*Aside.*
Tra. To save your life in this extremity,
This favour will I do you for his sake;
And think it not the worst of all your fortunes

75. *and*] *e'en* Theobald conj.
78. *sir? marry*] *sir?* Pope. *sir, say you?* Hanmer. *sir? marry now* Capell.
81. *in*] *of* Hanmer.
86. *you are*] *you're* Pope.
91. *courtesy*] *courtesy herein* Capell.
92. *I will*] *will I* Pope.
100. *countenance*] *count'nance* F_1 Q F_3F_4. *countnance* F_2.
101. [Aside.] Rowe.

That you are like to Sir Vincentio.
His name and credit shall you undertake,
And in my house you shall be friendly lodged:
Look that you take upon you as you should;
You understand me, sir: so shall you stay
Till you have done your business in the city:
If this be courtesy, sir, accept of it.
Ped. O sir, I do; and will repute you ever
The patron of my life and liberty.
Tra. Then go with me to make the matter good.
This, by the way, I let you understand;
My father is here look'd for every day,
To pass assurance of a dower in marriage
'Twixt me and one Baptista's daughter here:
In all these circumstances I'll instruct you:
Go with me to clothe you as becomes you. [*Exeunt.*

SCENE III. *A room in* PETRUCHIO'S *house.*

Enter KATHARINA *and* GRUMIO.

Gru. No, no, forsooth; I dare not for my life.
Kath. The more my wrong, the more his spite appears:
What, did he marry me to famish me?
Beggars, that come unto my father's door,
Upon entreaty have a present alms;
If not, elsewhere they meet with charity:
But I, who never knew how to entreat,
Nor never needed that I should entreat,
Am starved for meat, giddy for lack of sleep;
With oaths kept waking, and with brawling fed:

105. *like to Sir*] *so like to* Collier MS. *like, sir, to* Staunton conj.
110. *the city*] *this city* Capell conj.
111. *courtesy*] *court'sie* Ff Q.
117. *dower*] Warburton. *dowre* Ff Q. *dowry* Rowe.
120. *me*] F_1Q. *me, sir* $F_2F_3F_4$. See note (XIX).

SCENE III.] Steevens. Actus Quartus. Scæna Prima. Ff Q. ACT IV. SCENE IV. Pope. ACT V. SCENE I. Hanmer. ACT IV. SCENE VI. Warburton. ACT IV. SCENE II. Capell.
8. *Nor...entreat*] omitted in Reed (1803, 1813), Boswell (1821), &c.

And that which spites me more than all these wants,
He does it under name of perfect love;
As who should say, if I should sleep or eat,
'Twere deadly sickness or else present death.
I prithee go and get me some repast;
I care not what, so it be wholesome food.

Gru. What say you to a neat's foot?

Kath. 'Tis passing good: I prithee let me have it.

Gru. I fear it is too choleric a meat.
How say you to a fat tripe finely broil'd?

Kath. I like it well: good Grumio, fetch it me.

Gru. I cannot tell; I fear 'tis choleric.
What say you to a piece of beef and mustard?

Kath. A dish that I do love to feed upon.

Gru. Ay, but the mustard is too hot a little.

Kath. Why then, the beef, and let the mustard rest.

Gru. Nay then, I will not: you shall have the mustard,
Or else you get no beef of Grumio.

Kath. Then both, or one, or any thing thou wilt.

Gru. Why then, the mustard without the beef.

Kath. Go, get thee gone, thou false deluding slave, [*Beats him.*
That feed'st me with the very name of meat:
Sorrow on thee and all the pack of you
That triumph thus upon my misery!
Go, get thee gone, I say.

Enter PETRUCHIO *and* HORTENSIO *with meat.*

Pet. How fares my Kate? What, sweeting, all amort?

Hor. Mistress, what cheer?

Kath. Faith, as cold as can be.

Pet. Pluck up thy spirits; look cheerfully upon me.
Here, love; thou see'st how diligent I am

11. *wants*] *wrongs* Capell (corrected in MS.).

19. *choleric*] F_1Q. *phlegmatic* $F_2F_3F_4$.

22. *'tis*] *it is* Rowe. *it's* Pope.

27. *Nay then*] *Nay, that* Collier (Collier MS.).

30. *without*] *e'en without* Hanmer. *now without* Capell.

36. SCENE V. Pope. SCENE VII. Warburton.

37. *Faith*] *I'faith* Capell.

To dress thy meat myself and bring it thee:
I am sure, sweet Kate, this kindness merits thanks.
What, not a word? Nay, then thou lovest it not;
And all my pains is sorted to no proof.
Here, take away this dish.
Kath. I pray you, let it stand.
Pet. The poorest service is repaid with thanks;
And so shall mine, before you touch the meat.
Kath. I thank you, sir.
Hor. Signior Petruchio, fie! you are to blame.
Come, Mistress Kate, I'll bear you company.
Pet. Eat it up all, Hortensio, if thou lovest me. [*Aside.*
Much good do it unto thy gentle heart!
Kate, eat apace: and now, my honey love,
Will we return unto thy father's house,
And revel it as bravely as the best,
With silken coats and caps and golden rings,
With ruffs and cuffs and fardingales and things;
With scarfs and fans and double change of bravery,
With amber bracelets, beads and all this knavery.
What, hast thou dined? The tailor stays thy leisure,
To deck thy body with his ruffling treasure.

Enter Tailor.

Come, tailor, let us see these ornaments;
Lay forth the gown.

Enter Haberdasher.

What news with you, sir?

40. [Sets the dish on a table. Capell (after line 39).

41. *I am*] *I'm* Pope.

43. *is*] *are* Halliwell.

44. *this*] *the* F_3F_4.

I pray you] *Pray* Hanmer.

49. [Sits to table along with her. Capell.

50. *me.*] *me:* FfQ. *me,* Rowe. [Aside.] Theobald.

51. *Much*] *Now much* Capell.

55, 56. *rings ... things*] *things ... rings* Johnson conj. (withdrawn).

56. *fardingales*] F_1QF_2F_3. *fardingals* F_4.

59. *What*] F_1Q. *With* $F_2F_3F_4$.

60. *To*] *The* F_2.

ruffling] *rustling* Pope.

61. SCENE VI. Pope. ACT V. SCENE III. Hanmer. SCENE VIII. Warburton.

62. Enter...] FfQ (after line 61).

sir?] *sir? ha!* Hanmer.

Hab. Here is the cap your worship did bespeak.
Pet. Why, this was moulded on a porringer;
A velvet dish: fie, fie! 'tis lewd and filthy:
Why, 'tis a cockle or a walnut-shell,
A knack, a toy, a trick, a baby's cap:
Away with it! come, let me have a bigger.
Kath. I'll have no bigger: this doth fit the time
And gentlewomen wear such caps as these.
Pet. When you are gentle, you shall have one too,
And not till then.
Hor. That will not be in haste. [*Aside.*
Kath. Why, sir, I trust I may have leave to speak;
And speak I will; I am no child, no babe:
Your betters have endured me say my mind,
And if you cannot, best you stop your ears.
My tongue will tell the anger of my heart,
Or else my heart concealing it will break;
And rather than it shall, I will be free
Even to the uttermost, as I please, in words.
Pet. Why, thou say'st true; it is a paltry cap,
A custard-coffin, a bauble, a silken pie:
I love thee well, in that thou likest it not.
Kath. Love me or love me not, I like the cap;
And it I will have, or I will have none. [*Exit Haberdasher.*
Pet. Thy gown? why, ay: come, tailor, let us see't.
O mercy, God! what masquing stuff is here?
What's this? a sleeve? 'tis like a demi-cannon:
What, up and down, carved like an apple-tart?
Here's snip and nip and cut and slish and slash,
Like to a censer in a barber's shop:
Why, what, i' devil's name, tailor, call'st thou this?
Hor. I see she's like to have neither cap nor gown. [*Aside.*
Tai. You bid me make it orderly and well,

63. Hab.] Rowe. Fel. FfQ.
72. [Aside.] Hanmer.
80. *uttermost*] *utmost* Pope.
81. *a*] om. F_1.
85. *it I will have*] *I will have it* Pope. [Exit Haberdasher] Edd.
87. *God*] *Heav'n* Rowe (ed. 2).
88. *What's this?*] F_1 Q. *What this?* F_2. *What? this* F_3F_4. *like a*] *like* F_1.
92. *i'*] Edd. *a* FfQ. *o'* Capell. *tailor*] *trilor* F_4.
93. *to have*] *to've* Pope. [Aside.] Theobald.

According to the fashion and the time.
Pet. Marry, and did; but if you be remember'd,
I did not bid you mar it to the time.
Go, hop me over every kennel home,
For you shall hop without my custom, sir:
I'll none of it: hence! make your best of it.
Kath. I never saw a better-fashion'd gown,
More quaint, more pleasing, nor more commendable:
Belike you mean to make a puppet of me.
Pet. Why, true; he means to make a puppet of thee.
Tai. She says your worship means to make a puppet of her.
Pet. O monstrous arrogance! Thou liest, thou thread, thou thimble,
Thou yard, three-quarters, half-yard, quarter, nail!
Thou flea, thou nit, thou winter-cricket thou!
Braved in mine own house with a skein of thread?
Away, thou rag, thou quantity, thou remnant;
Or I shall so be-mete thee with thy yard,
As thou shalt think on prating whilst thou livest!
I tell thee, I, that thou hast marr'd her gown.
Tai. Your worship is deceived; the gown is made
Just as my master had direction:
Grumio gave order how it should be done.
Gru. I gave him no order; I gave him the stuff.
Tai. But how did you desire it should be made?
Gru. Marry, sir, with needle and thread.
Tai. But did you not request to have it cut?
Gru. Thou hast faced many things.
Tai. I have.

Gru. Face not me: thou hast braved many men; brave not me; I will neither be faced nor braved. I say unto thee, I bid thy master cut out the gown; but I did not bid him cut it to pieces: ergo, thou liest.

95. *and*] *of* Rowe (ed. 2).
96. *and did*] *I did* Long conj. MS.
106, 107. As two lines in Ff Q, ending *arrogance:...thimble.* As one line in Capell. As two lines ending *liest,...thimble* Malone. As two ending *thread...thimble* Knight.
106. *monstrous*] F_1Q. *most monstrous* $F_2F_3F_4$.
liest] *list* Anon conj.
thou thread] om. Ritson conj.
107. *thimble,*] *thimble thou! thou liest,* Hanmer.
108. *yard,*] $F_2F_3F_4$. *yard* F_1Q.

Tai. Why, here is the note of the fashion to testify.

Pet. Read it.

Gru. The note lies in's throat, if he say I said so.

Tai. [*reads*] 'Imprimis, a loose-bodied gown:'

Gru. Master, if ever I said loose-bodied gown, sew me in the skirts of it, and beat me to death with a bottom of brown thread: I said a gown.

Pet. Proceed.

Tai. [*reads*] 'With a small compassed cape:'

Gru. I confess the cape.

Tai. [*reads*] 'With a trunk sleeve:'

Gru. I confess two sleeves.

Tai. [*reads*] 'The sleeves curiously cut.'

Pet. Ay, there's the villany.

Gru. Error i' the bill, sir; error i' the bill. I commanded the sleeves should be cut out, and sewed up again; and that I'll prove upon thee, though thy little finger be armed in a thimble.

Tai. This is true that I say: an I had thee in place where, thou shouldst know it.

Gru. I am for thee straight: take thou the bill, give me thy mete-yard, and spare not me.

Hor. God-a-mercy, Grumio! then he shall have no odds.

Pet. Well, sir, in brief, the gown is not for me.

Gru. You are i' the right, sir: 'tis for my mistress.

Pet. Go, take it up unto thy master's use.

Gru. Villain, not for thy life: take up my mistress' gown for thy master's use!

Pet. Why, sir, what's your conceit in that?

Gru. O, sir, the conceit is deeper than you think for:
Take up my mistress' gown to his master's use!
O, fie, fie, fie!

Pet. Hortensio, say thou wilt see the tailor paid. [*Aside.*

131, 136, 138, 140. [reads] Capell.

131. *Imprimis*] F_3F_4. *Inprimis* F_1QF_2.

132. *loose-bodied*] *loose body's* Steevens conj. from (Q).

sew me] *sow me up* Pope.

146. *an*] Pope. *and* Ff Q.

147. *where, thou shouldst*] QF_3F_4. *where thou shouldst* F_1. *where thou should* F_2.

149. *not me*] *me not* Hanmer.

150. Pet.] Kath. Daniel conj.

154, 158. *mistress'*] *mistress's* Rowe.

158. *to*] *unto* F_3F_4.

160. [Aside.] Rowe.

Go take it hence; be gone, and say no more.
Hor. Tailor, I'll pay thee for thy gown to-morrow:
Take no unkindness of his hasty words:
Away! I say; commend me to thy master. [*Exit Tailor.*
Pet. Well, come, my Kate; we will unto your father's
Even in these honest mean habiliments:
Our purses shall be proud, our garments poor;
For 'tis the mind that makes the body rich;
And as the sun breaks through the darkest clouds,
So honour peereth in the meanest habit.
What is the jay more precious than the lark,
Because his feathers are more beautiful?
Or is the adder better than the eel,
Because his painted skin contents the eye?
O, no, good Kate; neither art thou the worse
For this poor furniture and mean array.
If thou account'st it shame, lay it on me;
And therefore frolic: we will hence forthwith,
To feast and sport us at thy father's house.
Go, call my men, and let us straight to him;
And bring our horses unto Long-lane end;
There will we mount, and thither walk on foot.
Let's see; I think 'tis now some seven o'clock,
And well we may come there by dinner-time.
Kath. I dare assure you, sir, 'tis almost two;
And 'twill be supper-time ere you come there.
Pet. It shall be seven ere I go to horse:
Look, what I speak, or do, or think to do,
You are still crossing it. Sirs, let't alone:
I will not go to-day; and ere I do,
It shall be what o'clock I say it is.
Hor. Why, so this gallant will command the sun. [*Exeunt.*

164. [Exit Tailor.] Exit Tail. Ff Q. Exeunt Tailor and Haberdasher. Collier.

170. *peereth*] *'peareth* Grant White (Capell conj.).

171. *What is*] FfQ. *What; is* Pope.

171, 172. *lark, ...beautiful?*] $F_2F_3F_4$. *larke?...beautifull.* F_1Q.

175. *good*] om. Q.

177. *account'st*] Rowe. *accountedst* $F_1Q F_2$. *accounted'st* F_3F_4.

182. *on foot*] *afoot* Capell.

190. *and*] *or*, Capell.

192. *Why, so*] *Why so* F_1Q. *Why so:* $F_2F_3F_4$. *Why, so!* Capell. See note (XIX).

SCENE IV. *Padua. Before* BAPTISTA'S *house.*

Enter TRANIO, *and the* Pedant *dressed like* VINCENTIO.

Tra. Sir, this is the house: please it you that I call?
Ped. Ay, what else? and but I be deceived
Signior Baptista may remember me,
Near twenty years ago, in Genoa,
Where we were lodgers at the Pegasus.
Tra. 'Tis well; and hold your own, in any case,
With such austerity as 'longeth to a father.
Ped. I warrant you.

Enter BIONDELLO.

But, sir, here comes your boy;
'Twere good he were school'd.
Tra. Fear you not him. Sirrah Biondello,
Now do your duty throughly, I advise you:
Imagine 'twere the right Vincentio.
Bion. Tut, fear not me.
Tra. But hast thou done thy errand to Baptista?
Bion. I told him that your father was at Venice;
And that you look'd for him this day in Padua.
Tra. Thou'rt a tall fellow: hold thee that to drink.
Here comes Baptista: set your countenance, sir.

SCENE IV.] Steevens. ACT V. SCENE II. Pope (ed. 1). ACT V. SCENE III. Pope (ed. 2). ACT V. SCENE IV. Hanmer. SCENE IX. Warburton. SCENE III. Capell. ACT V. SCENE I. Johnson conj.

Before B's house.] Capell.

...Pedant dressed...] Pedant, booted, and drest... Capell.

1. *Sir*] Theobald. *Sirs* Ff Q.

2. *Ay,*] *I* Ff Q. *Ay, ay,* Hanmer. *Ay, sir;* Capell.

4, 5. *Genoa, Where we*] *Genoa, where We* Steevens. *Genoa When we* Halliwell.

5, 6. *Where we*...Tra. *'Tis*] Theobald. Tra. *Where we ... Tis* Ff Q. Tra. *Where you...Tis* Capell.

7. *'longeth to a*] Hanmer. *longeth to a* Ff Q. *'longs t' a* S. Walker conj.

9. *good*] *good that* Hanmer.

11. *Now*] om. Hanmer.

throughly] *thoroughly* Steevens.

I advise you] om. Hanmer.

15. *at*] *in* F_3F_4.

17. *Thou'rt*] Capell. *Th'art* F_1 QF_2. *That's* F_3F_4.

Enter BAPTISTA *and* LUCENTIO.

Signior Baptista, you are happily met.
[*To the Pedant*] Sir, this is the gentleman I told you of:
I pray you, stand good father to me now,
Give me Bianca for my patrimony.
Ped. Soft, son!
Sir, by your leave: having come to Padua
To gather in some debts, my son Lucentio
Made me acquainted with a weighty cause
Of love between your daughter and himself:
And, for the good report I hear of you,
And for the love he beareth to your daughter,
And she to him, to stay him not too long,
I am content, in a good father's care,
To have him match'd; and, if you please to like
No worse than I, upon some agreement
Me shall you find ready and willing
With one consent to have her so bestow'd;
For curious I cannot be with you,
Signior Baptista, of whom I hear so well.
Bap. Sir, pardon me in what I have to say:
Your plainness and your shortness please me well.
Right true it is, your son Lucentio here
Doth love my daughter, and she loveth him,
Or both dissemble deeply their affections:
And therefore, if you say no more than this,
That like a father you will deal with him,
And pass my daughter a sufficient dower,

19. SCENE III. Pope (ed. 1). SCENE IV. Pope (ed. 2). ACT V. SCENE V. Hanmer. ACT IV. SCENE X. Warburton.

Enter B. and L.] Enter B. and L.: Pedant booted and bare headed. Ff Q. (and Pedant $F_2F_3F_4$.)

20. [To the Pedant] Capell.

Sir, this is] *Sir, This is* Capell. *Sir, this 's* Edd. conj.

21. *stand good father to*] *stand, good father, to* Rowe.

23, 24. As in Hanmer. As one line in Ff Q.

33. *I, upon*] F_1. *I upon* Q. *I sir upon* $F_2F_3F_4$.

34. *ready and willing*] F_1Q. *most ready and most willing* $F_2F_3F_4$.

38. *to say*] *say* Steevens (1778), a misprint.

45. *dower*] F_1 Q F_2. *dowre* F_3F_4. *dowry* Rowe.

The match is made, and all is done:
Your son shall have my daughter with consent.

Tra. I thank you, sir. Where then do you know best
We be affied and such assurance ta'en
As shall with either part's agreement stand?

Bap. Not in my house, Lucentio; for, you know,
Pitchers have ears, and I have many servants:
Besides, old Gremio is hearkening still;
And happily we might be interrupted.

Tra. Then at my lodging, an it like you:
There doth my father lie; and there, this night,
We'll pass the business privately and well.
Send for your daughter by your servant here;
My boy shall fetch the scrivener presently.
The worst is this, that, at so slender warning,
You are like to have a thin and slender pittance.

Bap. It likes me well. Cambio, hie you home,
And bid Bianca make her ready straight;
And, if you will, tell what hath happened,
Lucentio's father is arrived in Padua,
And how she's like to be Lucentio's wife.

Bion. I pray the gods she may with all my heart!

Tra. Dally not with the gods, but get thee gone.
[*Exit Bion*

Signior Baptista, shall I lead the way?

46. *made*] *fully made* Hanmer. *done*] *done with me* Capell. *happily done* Collier (Collier MS.).

48, 49. *Where then do you ... We be*] *Then where you do ... Be we* Becket conj.

48. *do you know*] *do you trow is* Hanmer. *you do know* Johnson conj. *do you trow* Rann (Johnson conj.). *do you hold* Collier (Collier MS.).

49. *We be*] *Be we* Rowe (ed. 2).

54. *And happily*] *And happilie* F_1 Q. *Ann haply* F_2. *And haply* F_3F_4. *And haply then* Pope. *And hapily* Capell. *And happely* Grant White. *might*] Ff. *may* Q.

55. *like you*] F_1Q. *like you, sir* $F_2F_3F_4$. *liketh you* Anon conj.

60. *You are*] *You're* Pope.

62, 63. As in Steevens. As two lines ending *well:...straight* in Ff Q.

62. *Cambio*] *Go, Cambio* Pope. *Biondello* Edd. conj. See note (XX).

64. *And, if you will, tell*] Rowe. *And if you will tell* Ff Q. *happened*] Capell. *hapned* Ff Q. *happen'd here* Pope.

67. Bion.] $F_2F_3F_4$. Biond. F_1Q. Luc. Rowe.

68. [Exit Bion.] Exit. Ff Q, after line 67. om. Capell. See note (XX). Enter Peter. Ff Q.

Welcome! one mess is like to be your cheer:
Come, sir; we will better it in Pisa.

Bap. I follow you.

[*Exeunt Tranio, Pedant, and Baptista.*

Re-enter BIONDELLO.

Bion. Cambio.

Luc. What sayest thou, Biondello?

Bion. You saw my master wink and laugh upon you?

Luc. Biondello, what of that?

Bion. Faith, nothing; but has left me here behind, to expound the meaning or moral of his signs and tokens.

Luc. I pray thee, moralize them.

Bion. Then thus. Baptista is safe, talking with the deceiving father of a deceitful son.

Luc. And what of him?

Bion. His daughter is to be brought by you to the supper.

Luc. And then?

Bion. The old priest at Saint Luke's church is at your command at all hours.

Luc. And what of all this?

Bion. I cannot tell; expect they are busied about a counterfeit assurance: take you assurance of her, 'cum privilegio ad imprimendum solum:' to the church; take the priest, clerk, and some sufficient honest witnesses:
If this be not that you look for, I have no more to say,
But bid Bianca farewell for ever and a day.

70. *Welcome*] F_1Q. *We come* $F_2F_3F_4$. See note (XXI).

70, 71. *Welcome...Come, sir; we will*] *Come, sir; one mess...cheer; We'll* Capell.

71. *Come*] *But come* Hanmer.

72. Exeunt T. P. and B] Exeunt. Ff Q.

Re-enter Biondello.] Edd. Enter Lucentio and Biondello. Ff Q.

73. ACT V. SCENE IV. Pope (ed. 1). SCENE V. Pope (ed. 2). ACT V. SCENE VI. Hanmer. ACT IV. SCENE XI. Warburton.

75. *wink and laugh*] *laugh, and wink* Capell conj.

77. *has*] *'has* Rowe. *ha's* Theobald. *h'as* Hanmer. *he's* Johnson. *he has* Steevens.

79. *them*] *then* Anon conj.

84. *then?*] $F_2F_3F_4$. *then.* F_1Q.

87. *this?*] $F_2F_3F_4$. *this.* F_1Q.

88. *expect*] F_1Q. *except* $F_2F_3F_4$. *expect,* Warburton. *except, while* Capell. *expect;—* Malone. *except—* Tyrwhitt conj.

90. *imprimendum solum*] $F_2F_3F_4$. *impremendum solem* F_1Q.

church;] Rann (Tyrwhitt conj.). *church* Ff Q.

93. [Going. Capell.

Luc. Hearest thou, Biondello?

Bion. I cannot tarry: I knew a wench married in an afternoon as she went to the garden for parsley to stuff a rabbit; and so may you, sir: and so, adieu, sir. My master hath appointed me to go to Saint Luke's, to bid the priest be ready to come against you come with your appendix. [*Exit.*

Luc. I may, and will, if she be so contented:
She will be pleased; then wherefore should I doubt?
Hap what hap may, I'll roundly go about her:
It shall go hard if Cambio go without her. [*Exit.*

SCENE V. *A public road.*

Enter PETRUCHIO, KATHARINA, HORTENSIO, *and* Servants.

Pet. Come on, i' God's name; once more toward our father's.
Good Lord, how bright and goodly shines the moon!

Kath. The moon! the sun: it is not moonlight now.

Pet. I say it is the moon that shines so bright.

Kath. I know it is the sun that shines so bright.

Pet. Now, by my mother's son, and that's myself,
It shall be moon, or star, or what I list,
Or ere I journey to your father's house.
Go on, and fetch our horses back again.
Evermore cross'd and cross'd; nothing but cross'd!

Hor. Say as he says, or we shall never go.

Kath. Forward, I pray, since we have come so far,

101. *I doubt*] *we doubt* Rowe. *I doubt her* Pope.

SCENE V.] Steevens. ACT V. SCENE V. Pope (ed. 1). SCENE VI. Pope. (ed. 2). ACT V. SCENE VII. Hanmer. ACT IV. SCENE XII. Warburton. ACT V. SCENE I. Capell.

A public road.] Capell. The street before Lucentio's house. Pope. A green lane. Theobald. The road to Padua. Hanmer.

...and Servants.] Edd. om. Ff Q.

1. *i'*] Edd. *a* Ff Q. *o'* Theobald. *toward*] $F_1F_2F_3$. *towards* Q F_4. *tow'rds* Pope.

5. *shines*] *shine*, Q_1.

7. *I list*] *I I list* F_2.

9. *Go on*] *Go one* Rann (Capell conj.).

And be it moon, or sun, or what you please:
An if you please to call it a rush-candle,
Henceforth I vow it shall be so for me.

Pet. I say it is the moon.

Kath. I know it is the moon.

Pet. Nay, then you lie: it is the blessed sun.

Kath. Then, God be bless'd, it is the blessed sun:
But sun it is not, when you say it is not;
And the moon changes even as your mind.
What you will have it named, even that it is;
And so it shall be so for Katharine.

Hor. Petruchio, go thy ways; the field is won.

Pet. Well, forward, forward! thus the bowl should run,
And not unluckily against the bias.
But, soft! company is coming here.

Enter VINCENTIO.

[*To Vincentio*] Good morrow, gentle mistress: where away?
Tell me, sweet Kate, and tell me truly too,
Hast thou beheld a fresher gentlewoman?
Such war of white and red within her cheeks!
What stars do spangle heaven with such beauty,
As those two eyes become that heavenly face?
Fair lovely maid, once more good day to thee.
Sweet Kate, embrace her for her beauty's sake.

Hor. A' will make the man mad, to make a woman of him.

Kath. Young budding virgin, fair and fresh and sweet,
Whither away, or where is thy abode?

13. *you*] *your* F_2.

14. *An*] Collier. *And* Ff Q.

16. *I know it is the moon.*] *I know it is.* Steevens.

18. *is*] *in* F_1.

22. *so it shall be so*] *so it shall be, sir,* Capell. *so it shall be still* Singer (Ritson conj.). *so it shall be 'sol'* Becket conj.

24. *should*] *shall* Harness.

26. *company*] *some company* Pope. *what company* Steevens (Ritson conj.).

ACT V. SCENE VI. Pope. ACT V. SCENE VIII. Hanmer. ACT IV. SCENE XIII. Warburton.

Enter V.] Enter V. journeying. Capell. Enter V. in a travelling dress. Malone.

27. [To Vincentio] Rowe.

where] *whither* Capell.

31, 32. *do.... such.... those two*] *so ...their...do those* Seymour conj.

35. *A'*] *A* Ff Q. *He* Rowe.

a woman] $F_2F_3F_4$. *the woman* F_1Q.

37. *Whither...where*] F_2 F_3 F_4. *Whether...whether* F_1Q.

Happy the parents of so fair a child;
Happier the man, whom favourable stars
Allot thee for his lovely bed-fellow!
Pet. Why, how now, Kate! I hope thou art not mad:
This is a man, old, wrinkled, faded, wither'd;
And not a maiden, as thou say'st he is.
Kath. Pardon, old father, my mistaking eyes,
That have been so bedazzled with the sun,
That every thing I look on seemeth green:
Now I perceive thou art a reverend father;
Pardon, I pray thee, for my mad mistaking.
Pet. Do, good old grandsire; and withal make known
Which way thou travellest: if along with us,
We shall be joyful of thy company.
Vin. Fair sir, and you my merry mistress,
That with your strange encounter much amazed me,
My name is call'd Vincentio; my dwelling Pisa;
And bound I am to Padua; there to visit
A son of mine, which long I have not seen.
Pet. What is his name?
Vin. Lucentio, gentle sir.
Pet. Happily met; the happier for thy son.
And now by law, as well as reverend age,
I may entitle thee my loving father:
The sister to my wife, this gentlewoman,
Thy son by this hath married. Wonder not,
Nor be not grieved: she is of good esteem,
Her dowry wealthy, and of worthy birth;
Beside, so qualified as may beseem
The spouse of any noble gentleman.
Let me embrace with old Vincentio,
And wander we to see thy honest son,
Who will of thy arrival be full joyous.

39. *whom*] *whose* Capell conj.

40. *Allot*] Pope. *A lots* F_1. *Alots* QF_2F_3. *Allots* F_4.

44 *mistaking*] *mistaken* Rowe.

49. *withal*] *withall* Ff. *with all* Q.

52. *mistress*] *mistress too* Hanmer. *mistress here* Capell.

54. *name is call'd Vincentio*] *name's Vincentio call'd* Anon conj.

my dwelling] *dwelling* Hanmer.

66. *gentleman*] *gentlewoman* Q.

67. *with*] *thee,* Capell conj.

Vin. But is this true? or is it else your pleasure,
Like pleasant travellers, to break a jest
Upon the company you overtake?

Hor. I do assure thee, father, so it is.

Pet. Come, go along, and see the truth hereof;
For our first merriment hath made thee jealous.
[*Exeunt all but Hortensio.*

Hor. Well, Petruchio, this has put me in heart.
Have to my widow! and if she be froward,
Then hast thou taught Hortensio to be untoward. [*Exit.*

ACT V.

SCENE I. *Padua. Before* LUCENTIO'S *house.*

GREMIO *discovered. Enter behind* BIONDELLO, LUCENTIO, *and* BIANCA.

Bion. Softly and swiftly, sir; for the priest is ready.

Luc. I fly, Biondello: but they may chance to need thee at home; therefore leave us.

Bion. Nay, faith, I'll see the church o' your back; and then come back to my master's as soon as I can.
[*Exeunt Lucentio, Bianca, and Biondello.*

Gre. I marvel Cambio comes not all this while.

70. *is it else*] *else is it* Anon. conj.

75. Exeunt...] Exeunt. Ff Q.

76. *Well, Petruchio,*] *Petruchio, well!* Hanmer. *Well, sir Petruchio* Capell. *Well done, Petruchio* Anon conj.
has] *hath* Hanmer.

77. *be*] $F_2F_3F_4$. om. F_1Q.

78. *to be*] *be* Capell.

ACT V. Theobald. SCENE I. Warburton. ACT V. SCENE VII. Pope. ACT V. SCENE IX. Hanmer. ACT V. SCENE II. Capell.

Before L's house] Pope. Before Tranio's house. Capell.

Gremio...] Edd. Enter Bion. Luc. and Bianca, Gremio is out before. Ff Q. Enter B. L. and B., Gremio walking on one side. Rowe. Enter Bion. with Luc. and Bian., hastily; Gremio is seen ent'ring, behind. Capell.

4. *o'*] Rowe (ed. 2). *a* Ff Q.

5. *master's*] Capell. *mistris* Ff Q. *master* Theobald. *business* Hanmer.
Exeunt...] Rowe. Exit. Ff Q (after line 3).

Enter PETRUCHIO, KATHARINA, VINCENTIO, GRUMIO, *with* Attendants.

Pet. Sir, here's the door, this is Lucentio's house:
My father's bears more toward the market-place;
Thither must I, and here I leave you, sir.

Vin. You shall not choose but drink before you go:
I think I shall command your welcome here,
And, by all likelihood, some cheer is toward. [*Knocks.*

Gre. They're busy within; you were best knock louder.

Pedant *looks out of the window.*

Ped. What's he that knocks as he would beat down the gate?

Vin. Is Signior Lucentio within, sir?

Ped. He's within, sir, but not to be spoken withal.

Vin. What if a man bring him a hundred pound or two, to make merry withal?

Ped. Keep your hundred pounds to yourself: he shall need none, so long as I live.

Pet. Nay, I told you your son was well beloved in Padua. Do you hear, sir?—to leave frivolous circumstances,—I pray you, tell Signior Lucentio, that his father is come from Pisa, and is here at the door to speak with him.

Ped. Thou liest: his father is come from Padua, and here looking out at the window.

Vin. Art thou his father?

Ped. Ay, sir; so his mother says, if I may believe her.

Pet. [*To Vincentio*] Why, how now, gentleman! why, this is flat knavery, to take upon you another man's name.

Ped. Lay hands on the villain: I believe a' means to cozen somebody in this city under my countenance.

8. *toward*] *towards* Rowe (ed. 2).

12. [Knocks.] Knock. Ff Q. Noise within. Knocks. Capell.

21. *so*] F_1 Q F_2. *as* F_3F_4.

22. *well*] om. Q.

26. *from Padua*] Ff Q. *to Padua* Pope. *from—Mantua* [aside] Capell. *from Pisa* Malone (Tyrwhitt conj.). See note (XXII).

27. *out at*] *out of* Q.

30. [To Vincentio] Capell.

32. *a'*] *a* F_1QF_2. *he* F_3F_4.

Re-enter BIONDELLO.

Bion. I have seen them in the church together: God send 'em good shipping! But who is here? mine old master Vincentio! now we are undone, and brought to nothing.

Vin. [*Seeing Biondello*] Come hither, crack-hemp.

Bion. I hope I may choose, sir.

Vin. Come hither, you rogue. What, have you forgot me?

Bion. Forgot you! no, sir: I could not forget you, for I never saw you before in all my life.

Vin. What, you notorious villain, didst thou never see thy master's father, Vincentio?

Bion. What, my old worshipful old master? yes, marry, sir: see where he looks out of the window.

Vin. Is't so, indeed? [*Beats Biondello.*

Bion. Help, help, help! here's a madman will murder me. [*Exit.*

Ped. Help, son! help, Signior Baptista! [*Exit from above.*

Pet. Prithee, Kate, let's stand aside, and see the end of this controversy. [*They retire.*

Re-enter Pedant *below;* TRANIO, BAPTISTA, *and* Servants.

Tra. Sir, what are you, that offer to beat my servant?

Vin. What am I, sir! nay, what are you, sir? O immortal gods! O fine villain! A silken doublet! a velvet hose! a scarlet cloak! and a copatain hat! O, I am undone! I am undone! while I play the good husband at home, my son and my servant spend all at the university.

34. SCENE VIII. Pope. SCENE X. Hanmer. SCENE II. Warburton.

35. [drawing backward. Capell.

36. *brought*] *brough* F_1.

37. [Seeing Biondello.] Rowe.

45. *master's*] $F_2F_3F_4$. *mistris* F_1 Q.

46. *my old worshipful*] *my worshipfull* Q.

48. [Beats B.] He beates B. Ff Q.

50. [Exit.] Exit, crying out. Capell. om. Ff Q.

51. [Exit...] Capell. om. Ff Q.

53. [They retire.] Theobald. Re-enter...] Capell. Enter Pedant with servants, Baptista, Tranio. Ff Q.

59. *servant*] *servants* Rowe.

Tra. How now! what's the matter?

Bap. What, is the man lunatic?

Tra. Sir, you seem a sober ancient gentleman by your habit, but your words show you a madman. Why, sir, what 'cerns it you if I wear pearl and gold? I thank my good father, I am able to maintain it.

Vin. Thy father! O villain! he is a sail-maker in Bergamo.

Bap. You mistake, sir, you mistake, sir. Pray, what do you think is his name?

Vin. His name! as if I knew not his name: I have brought him up ever since he was three years old, and his name is Tranio.

Ped. Away, away, mad ass! his name is Lucentio; and he is mine only son, and heir to the lands of me, Signior Vincentio.

Vin. Lucentio! O, he hath murdered his master! Lay hold on him, I charge you, in the Duke's name. O, my son, my son! Tell me, thou villain, where is my son Lucentio?

Tra. Call forth an officer.

Enter one with an Officer.

Carry this mad knave to the gaol. Father Baptista, I charge you see that he be forthcoming.

Vin. Carry me to the gaol!

Gre. Stay, officer: he shall not go to prison.

Bap. Talk not, Signior Gremio: I say he shall go to prison.

Gre. Take heed, Signior Baptista, lest you be cony-catched in this business: I dare swear this is the right Vincentio.

Ped. Swear, if thou darest.

60. *matter?*] *matter now?* Capell.

61. *the man*] *this man* Rowe.

64. *'cerns*] Collier. *cernes* F_1Q. *concerns* $F_2F_3F_4$.

72. *Tranio*] $F_2F_3F_4$. *Tronio* F_1Q.

80. Enter one with an Officer.] Capell. om. Ff Q.

81, 83, 94, 118. *gaol*] *Iaile* F_1QF_2. *Jayle* F_3. *Goal* F_4.

83. *the gaol*] *goal* Rowe (ed. 1). *jail* Id. (ed. 2).

Gre. Nay, I dare not swear it.

Tra. Then thou wert best say that I am not Lucentio.

Gre. Yes, I know thee to be Signior Lucentio.

Bap. Away with the dotard! to the gaol with him!

Vin. Thus strangers may be haled and abused:
O monstrous villain!

Re-enter BIONDELLO, *with* LUCENTIO *and* BIANCA.

Bion. O, we are spoiled! and—yonder he is: deny him, forswear him, or else we are all undone.

Luc. Pardon, sweet father. [*Kneeling.*

Vin. Lives my sweet son?

[*Exeunt Biondello, Tranio, and Pedant, as fast as may be.*

Bian. Pardon, dear father.

Bap. How hast thou offended?
Where is Lucentio?

Luc. Here's Lucentio,
Right son to the right Vincentio;
That have by marriage made thy daughter mine,
While counterfeit supposes blear'd thine eyne.

Gre. Here's packing, with a witness, to deceive us all!

Vin. Where is that damned villain Tranio,
That faced and braved me in this matter so?

Bap. Why, tell me, is not this my Cambio?

Bian. Cambio is changed into Lucentio.

Luc. Love wrought these miracles. Bianca's love
Made me exchange my state with Tranio,

94. *to the*] *to* Rowe (ed. 1).

95. *haled*] *haild* F_1QF_2. *hal'd* F_3F_4. *handled* Collier MS.

96. *villain*] F_3F_4. *villaine* F_1Q F_2. *villany* Dyce conj.

97. Re-enter...] Enter... Ff Q (after line 94). Enter Luc. and Bianca. Rowe.

and—] Capell. *and* Ff Q.

98. *undone*] *done* F_2.

99. SCENE IX. Pope. SCENE XI. Hanmer. SCENE III. Warburton.

[Kneeling.] Kneele. F_1Q.

[Exeunt...] Exit... FfQ (after line 95).

100. [Kneels to Bap. Capell.

100—102. *Pardon...Vincentio*] Arranged as in Capell: as prose in FfQ.

102. *Right son to*] Ff Q. *Right son unto* Capell. *The right son to* Anon. conj.

104. *supposes*] *supposers* Rowe (ed. 2). *eyne*] *eyes* Pope.

105. *all*] om. Hanmer.

106. *damned*] *damn'd* Rowe.

111. *exchange*] *exchangr* F_2.

While he did bear my countenance in the town;
And happily I have arrived at the last
Unto the wished haven of my bliss.
What Tranio did, myself enforced him to;
Then pardon him, sweet father, for my sake.

Vin. I'll slit the villain's nose, that would have sent me to the gaol.

Bap. But do you hear, sir? have you married my daughter without asking my good will?

Vin. Fear not, Baptista; we will content you, go to: but I will in, to be revenged for this villany. [*Exit.*

Bap. And I, to sound the depth of this knavery. [*Exit.*

Luc. Look not pale, Bianca; thy father will not frown.
[*Exeunt Lucentio and Bianca.*

Gre. My cake is dough: but I'll in among the rest;
Out of hope of all, but my share of the feast. [*Exit.*

Kath. Husband, let's follow, to see the end of this ado.

Pet. First kiss me, Kate, and we will.

Kath. What, in the midst of the street?

Pet. What, art thou ashamed of me?

Kath. No, sir, God forbid; but ashamed to kiss.

Pet. Why, then let's home again. Come, sirrah, let's away.

Kath. Nay, I will give thee a kiss: now pray thee, love, stay.

Pet. Is not this well? Come, my sweet Kate:
Better once than never, for never too late. [*Exeunt.*

113. *arrived at the*] F_1Q. *arriv'd at* $F_2F_3F_4$.

122. *for this villany*] *for this villanie* F_1Q. *for this villaine* F_2. *on this villain* F_3F_4. *on this vallain* Rowe (ed. 1).

124. [Exeunt L. and B.] Capell. [Exeunt. FfQ.

126. [Exit.] Rowe.

127. P. and C. advancing. Theobald.

131. *No*] *Mo* F_1.

133. *pray thee*] *pray* Q.

135. *once*] *late* Hanmer. *at once* Anon. conj.

never] *never's* Anon. conj. See note (XIX).

SCENE II. *Padua.* LUCENTIO'S *house.*

Enter BAPTISTA, VINCENTIO, GREMIO, *the* Pedant, LUCENTIO, BIANCA, PETRUCHIO, KATHARINA, HORTENSIO, *and* Widow, TRANIO, BIONDELLO, *and* GRUMIO: *the Serving-men with Tranio bringing in a banquet.*

Luc. At last, though long, our jarring notes agree:
And time it is, when raging war is done,
To smile at scapes and perils overblown.
My fair Bianca, bid my father welcome,
While I with self-same kindness welcome thine.
Brother Petruchio, sister Katharina,
And thou, Hortensio, with thy loving widow,
Feast with the best, and welcome to my house:
My banquet is to close our stomachs up,
After our great good cheer. Pray you, sit down;
For now we sit to chat, as well as eat.

Pet. Nothing but sit and sit, and eat and eat!

Bap. Padua affords this kindness, son Petruchio.

Pet. Padua affords nothing but what is kind.

Hor. For both our sakes, I would that word were true.

Pet. Now, for my life, Hortensio fears his widow.

Wid. Then never trust me, if I be afeard.

Pet. You are very sensible, and yet you miss my sense:
I mean, Hortensio is afeard of you.

Wid. He that is giddy thinks the world turns round.

Pet. Roundly replied.

Kath. Mistress, how mean you that?

SCENE II.] Steevens. Actus Quintus. $F_1QF_2F_3$. Scena Quarta. F_4. ACT V. SCENE I. Rowe. SCENE IV. Warburton. SCENE III. Capell.

...Petruchio, Katharina, Hortensio...] om. FfQ. Enter...Tranio's servants bringing in a banquet. Rowe. Musick. A banquet set out. Enter ...Tranio, Grumio, Biondello and others, attending. Capell.

1—62. *At last...outright*] Put in the margin as spurious by Pope.

2. *done*] Rowe. *come* FfQ. *calm* Malone conj. *gone* Collier (Collier MS.).

6. *Katharina*] *Katharine* Rowe.

8. *best*] *rest* Anon conj.

9. *banquet*] F_3F_4. *banket* F_1QF_2.

11. [Company sit to table. Capell.

14. *nothing*] *no thing* S. Walker conj.

17. Wid.] F_1Q. Hor. $F_2F_3F_4$.

18. *very*] om. Steevens.
and yet] *yet* Anon conj.

Wid. Thus I conceive by him.
Pet. Conceives by me! How likes Hortensio that?
Hor. My widow says, thus she conceives her tale.
Pet. Very well mended. Kiss him for that, good widow.
Kath. 'He that is giddy thinks the world turns round:'
I pray you, tell me what you meant by that.
Wid. Your husband, being troubled with a shrew,
Measures my husband's sorrow by his woe:
And now you know my meaning.
Kath. A very mean meaning.
Wid. Right, I mean you.
Kath. And I am mean, indeed, respecting you.
Pet. To her, Kate!
Hor. To her, widow!
Pet. A hundred marks, my Kate does put her down.
Hor. That's my office.
Pet. Spoke like an officer: ha' to thee, lad.
[*Drinks to Hortensio.*
Bap. How likes Gremio these quick-witted folks?
Gre. Believe me, sir, they butt together well.
Bian. Head, and butt! an hasty-witted body
Would say your head and butt were head and horn.
Vin. Ay, mistress bride, hath that awaken'd you?
Bian. Ay, but not frighted me; therefore I'll sleep again.
Pet. Nay, that you shall not: since you have begun,
Have at you for a bitter jest or two!
Bian. Am I your bird? I mean to shift my bush;
And then pursue me as you draw your bow.

22—37. *Thus I...lad*] Verses differently arranged in Capell.
23. *Conceives*] *Conceive* Capell.
27. *meant*] *mean* Anon conj.
35. *does*] F_1Q. *doe* F_2. *do* F_3F_4.
37. *ha' to thee, lad*] *ha to the lad* F_1. *ha to thee lad* $QF_2F_3F_4$. *here's to thee, lad* Collier MS.
38. *How likes*] *And how likes* Capell. *How liketh* Anon. conj.
39. *they*] *they'ld* Anon conj.
butt together well] *butt heads together well* Rowe (ed. 2). *but heads well together* Capell.
40. *Head*] *How! head* Capell.
45. *bitter*] Capell (Theobald conj.). *better* Ff Q.
two] F_3F_4. *too* F_1QF_2.
47. *your*] *my* Q.
[Rising. Capell.

You are welcome all.
[*Exeunt Bianca, Katharina, and Widow.*
Pet. She hath prevented me. Here, Signior Tranio,
This bird you aim'd at, though you hit her not;
Therefore a health to all that shot and miss'd.
Tra. O, sir, Lucentio slipp'd me like his greyhound,
Which runs himself, and catches for his master.
Pet. A good swift simile, but something currish.
Tra. 'Tis well, sir, that you hunted for yourself:
'Tis thought your deer does hold you at a bay.
Bap. O ho, Petruchio! Tranio hits you now.
Luc. I thank thee for that gird, good Tranio.
Hor. Confess, confess, hath he not hit you here?
Pet. A' has a little gall'd me, I confess;
And, as the jest did glance away from me,
'Tis ten to one it maim'd you two outright.
Bap. Now, in good sadness, son Petruchio,
I think thou hast the veriest shrew of all.
Pet. Well, I say no: and therefore for assurance
Let's each one send unto his wife;
And he whose wife is most obedient
To come at first when he doth send for her,
Shall win the wager which we will propose.
Hor. Content. What is the wager?
Luc. Twenty crowns.
Pet. Twenty crowns!
I'll venture so much of my hawk or hound,

48. [Exeunt B., K., and Widow.] Exit... Rowe. [Exit B. FfQ. [Exit. Cat. and Wid. follow. Capell.

49. [Filling. Capell.

50. *her*] *it* Rowe.

51. [Drinks. Capell.

57. *O ho*] Capell. *Oh, Oh* FfQ.

60. *A' has*] *A has* FfQ. *He has* Rowe.

62. *two*] Rowe. *too* FfQ.

63. SCENE X. Pope. SCENE XII. Hanmer.

65. *therefore for*] $F_2F_3F_4$. *therefore sir* F_1. *therefore sir,* Q. *for assurance*] *sir, as surance* Staunton conj.

66—69. *Let's...wager*] Printed by Pope as three lines ending *he...first... wager.*

66. *Let's*] *Please you, let's* Capell. *wife*] *several wife* Collier MS.

68. *at first*] *first* Pope.

69. *which we will propose*] omitted by Pope.

70. *What is the*] Steevens. *what's the* FfQ. *what* Pope. *the* Capell.

72. *of*] *on* Rowe.

But twenty times so much upon my wife.
Luc. A hundred then.
Hor. Content.
Pet. A match! 'tis done.
Hor. Who shall begin?
Luc. That will I.
Go, Biondello, bid your mistress come to me.
Bion. I go. [*Exit.*
Bap. Son, I'll be your half, Bianca comes.
Luc. I'll have no halves; I'll bear it all myself.

Re-enter BIONDELLO.

How now! what news?
Bion. Sir, my mistress sends you word
That she is busy, and she cannot come.
Pet. How! she is busy, and she cannot come!
Is that an answer?
Gre. Ay, and a kind one too:
Pray God, sir, your wife send you not a worse.
Pet. I hope, better.
Hor. Sirrah Biondello, go and entreat my wife
To come to me forthwith. [*Exit Biondello.*
Pet. O, ho! entreat her!
Nay, then she must needs come.
Hor. I am afraid, sir,
Do what you can, yours will not be entreated.

Re-enter BIONDELLO.

Now, where's my wife?
Bion. She says you have some goodly jest in hand:
She will not come; she bids you come to her.
Pet. Worse and worse; she will not come! O vile,

75. *begin?*] *begin, Lucentio?* Anon. conj.

That will I.] *That will I.—Here, where are you?* Capell.

78. *I'll*] *Ile* F_1QF_2. *I'le* F_3F_4. *I will* Capell.

your half] Ff (*yonr* F_4). *you halfe* Q.

80. *Sir*] om. S. Walker conj.

81, 82. *she cannot*] *cannot* F_3F_4.

82—88. *How!...come*] Printed as prose in FfQ.

82. *she is*] Capell. *she's* FfQ.

85. *better*] *a better* S. Walker conj.

88. *must needs*] *needs must* Steevens.

93, 94. *Worse...endured*] As two lines in FfQ, ending *come...indur'd.*

Intolerable, not to be endured!
Sirrah Grumio, go to your mistress;
Say, I command her come to me. [*Exit Grumio.*

Hor. I know her answer.

Pet. What?

Hor. She will not.

Pet. The fouler fortune mine, and there an end.

Bap. Now, by my holidame, here comes Katharina!

Re-enter KATHARINA.

Kath. What is your will, sir, that you send for me?

Pet. Where is your sister, and Hortensio's wife?

Kath. They sit conferring by the parlour fire.

Pet. Go, fetch them hither: if they deny to come,
Swinge me them soundly forth unto their husbands:
Away, I say, and bring them hither straight.
[*Exit Katharina.*

Luc. Here is a wonder, if you talk of a wonder.

Hor. And so it is: I wonder what it bodes.

Pet. Marry, peace it bodes, and love, and quiet life,
An awful rule, and right supremacy;
And, to be short, what not, that's sweet and happy?

Bap. Now, fair befal thee, good Petruchio!
The wager thou hast won; and I will add
Unto their losses twenty thousand crowns;
Another dowry to another daughter,
For she is changed, as she had never been.

Pet. Nay, I will win my wager better yet,
And show more sign of her obedience,
Her new-built virtue and obedience.

95. *Sirrah*] *Here, sirrah* Capell.

96. *come*] *to come* F_3F_4.

97. *She*] *That she* Capell.
not] *not come* Steevens.

98. *there*] *there's* Rowe.

99. *Katharina*] *Katharine* Rowe.
Re-enter K.] Enter K. FfQ (after line 98).

105. *them*] *then* F_2.

106. *of a wonder*] *of wonder* S. Walker conj.

109. *An awful*] *And awful* Rowe (ed. 2). *And lawful* Rawlinson conj.

117. *her obedience*] *her submission* S. Walker conj.

118. *and obedience*] *of obedience* Capell. *and her gentleness* or *and her patience* Edd. conj.

See where she comes and brings your froward wives
As prisoners to her womanly persuasion.

Re-enter KATHARINA, *with* BIANCA *and* Widow.

Katharine, that cap of yours becomes you not:
Off with that bauble, throw it under-foot.
Wid. Lord, let me never have a cause to sigh,
Till I be brought to such a silly pass!
Bian. Fie, what a foolish duty call you this?
Luc. I would your duty were as foolish too:
The wisdom of your duty, fair Bianca,
Hath cost me an hundred crowns since supper-time.
Bian. The more fool you, for laying on my duty.
Pet. Katharine, I charge thee, tell these headstrong women
What duty they do owe their lords and husbands.
Wid. Come, come, you're mocking: we will have no telling.
Pet. Come on, I say; and first begin with her.
Wid. She shall not.
Pet. I say she shall: and first begin with her.
Kath. Fie, fie! unknit that threatening unkind brow;
And dart not scornful glances from those eyes,
To wound thy lord, thy king, thy governor:
It blots thy beauty as frosts do bite the meads,
Confounds thy fame as whirlwinds shake fair buds,
And in no sense is meet or amiable.
A woman moved is like a fountain troubled,
Muddy, ill-seeming, thick, bereft of beauty;

120\. Re-enter K. with B. and Widow] Enter Kate, B. and Widdow. Ff Q (after line 118).

122\. [She pulls off her cap, and throws it down. Rowe.

128\. *Hath cost me an*] Rowe. *Hath cost me five* Ff Q. *Cost me an* Pope. *Cost me a* Capell. *Hath cost one* Singer (ed. 1). *Cost me one* Collier MS.

130, 131. *Katharine....husbands*] Printed as prose in Ff Q; as verse by Rowe (ed. 2).

131\. *do owe*] *owe to* F_3F_4.

132\. *you're*] F_3F_4. *your* F_1QF_2.

133\. *begin with her*] *begin*— Capell, ending the verse with *shall not.*

136\. *threatening*] *thretaning* F_1. *threating* F_2.

139\. *do bite*] F_1Q. *bite* $F_2F_3F_4$.

140\. *fame*] *frame* Grey conj.

And while it is so, none so dry or thirsty
Will deign to sip or touch one drop of it.
Thy husband is thy lord, thy life, thy keeper,
Thy head, thy sovereign; one that cares for thee,
And for thy maintenance commits his body
To painful labour both by sea and land,
To watch the night in storms, the day in cold,
Whilst thou liest warm at home, secure and safe;
And craves no other tribute at thy hands
But love, fair looks and true obedience;
Too little payment for so great a debt.
Such duty as the subject owes the prince
Even such a woman oweth to her husband;
And when she is froward, peevish, sullen, sour,
And not obedient to his honest will,
What is she but a foul contending rebel,
And graceless traitor to her loving lord?
I am ashamed that women are so simple
To offer war where they should kneel for peace;
Or seek for rule, supremacy and sway,
When they are bound to serve, love and obey.
Why are our bodies soft and weak and smooth,
Unapt to toil and trouble in the world,
But that our soft conditions and our hearts
Should well agree with our external parts?
Come, come, you froward and unable worms!
My mind hath been as big as one of yours,
My heart as great, my reason haply more,
To bandy word for word and frown for frown;
But now I see our lances are but straws,
Our strength as weak, our weakness past compare,
That seeming to be most which we indeed least are.
Then vail your stomachs, for it is no boot,

145. *one*] *a* Rowe (ed. 2).
157. *she is*] *she's* Pope.
169. *you*] Ff Q. *you'ar* Rowe (ed. 1). *you're* Rowe (ed. 2).
171. *as*] F_1Q. *is* $F_2F_3F_4$.
174. *as*] *is* Rowe.
175. *to be*] om. Collier MS. *indeed*] om. Steevens.
176—189. *Then vail...tamed so*] Put in the margin as spurious by Pope. See note (XXIII).

And place your hands below your husband's foot:
In token of which duty, if he please,
My hand is ready, may it do him ease.
Pet. Why, there's a wench! Come on, and kiss me,
Kate.
Luc. Well, go thy ways, old lad; for thou shalt ha't.
Vin. 'Tis a good hearing, when children are toward.
Luc. But a harsh hearing, when women are froward.
Pet. Come, Kate, we'll to bed.
We three are married, but you two are sped.
'Twas I won the wager, though you hit the white;
[*To Lucentio.*
And, being a winner, God give you good night!
[*Exeunt Petruchio and Katharina.*
Hor. Now, go thy ways; thou hast tamed a curst shrew.
Luc. 'Tis a wonder, by your leave, she will be tamed so.
[*Exeunt.*

181. Luc.] Bap. Capell conj.
185. *three*] *two* Rowe.
186. *won*] *one* Capell (corrected in note). [To Lucentio.] Malone.
187. [.....and Katharina] ......and Kath. Rowe.
189. *be*] om. Q.

NOTES.

NOTE I.

IND. The Folios and the Quarto have here *Actus Primus. Scæna Prima*, making no separation between the play and the Induction. The play is divided into Acts, but not into Scenes. The second Act, however, is not marked in any of the old copies. The arrangement which we have followed is that of Steevens, which all subsequent editors have adopted, and which is therefore the most convenient for purposes of reference.

NOTE II.

IND. I. 7. The phrase 'Go by, Jeronimy,' quoted from Kyd's 'Spanish Tragedy,' was used in popular 'slang,' derisively. It occurs frequently in the dramatic literature of the time, for example, in Beaumont and Fletcher's *Captain*, Act III. Sc. 5. The 'S' of the Folios may have been derived from a note of exclamation in the MS., written, as it is usually printed, like a note of interrogation.

NOTE III.

IND. I. 62. Mr Lettsom's suggestion that a line has been lost between 61 and 62 seems the most probable solution of the difficulties presented by this passage in its present form.

NOTE IV.

IND. I. 86. 'Sincklo,' the stage direction of the first Folio, was the name of an actor in Shakespeare's company, not mentioned in the list of 'Principall Actors' at the beginning of the first Folio. He was one of the actors in the Second Part of *Henry IV.*, as appears from the 4to. edition of that play, published in 1600, where the stage direction to Act v. Scene 4 is, "Enter Sincklo and three or foure officers," and the part taken by Sincklo is that usually assigned to the 'Officer.' In the Third Part of *Henry VI.* Act III. Scene 1, the stage direction in the first Folio is, 'Enter Sinklo, and Humfrey, with crosse-bowes in their hands.' Sinklo also appears as an actor in the Induction to Marston's play of *The Malcontent.* In the present play he probably took the part of Lucentio.

In III. 1. 80, '*Nicke.*' is supposed by Steevens to mean Nicholas Tooley, who at a later period became one of the 'Principall Actors.'

NOTE V.

IND. 1. 99. Pope inserts here the following speech from the old play:

'2 *Player* [*to the other*]. Go get a dishclout to make clean your shoes, and I'll speak for the properties. [*Exit Player.*] My lord, we must have a shoulder of mutton for a property, and a little vinegar to make our devil roar.'

This insertion is repeated by all subsequent editors, till Capell struck it out of the text and Steevens placed it in a note.

NOTE VI.

IND. 2. 96. The following speeches are here inserted by Pope from the same source:

'*Sly.* By th' mass I think I am a lord indeed.
What's thy name?

Man. Simon, an't please your honour.

Sly. Sim? that's as much as to say Simeon or Simon; put forth thy hand and fill the pot.'

Capell was the first to strike it out of the text.

NOTE VII.

IND. 2. 110. Pope prefixed to Sly's speech the following words from the old play, without giving any indication that they were not Shakespeare's: 'Come sit down on my knee. Sim, drink to her.' They are repeated in all subsequent editions, till Capell restored the true text. After line 115, Pope again added, 'Sim, drink to her.'

Note VIII.

I. 1. 32. The old play (Q) after the Induction, commences thus:

'*Polidor.* Welcome to Athens, my beloved friend,
To Plato's school and Aristotle's walks...'

but this affords us no hint as to the true reading of the passage in question, whether 'checks' or 'ethics.' When Mr Halliwell conjectured that we should read 'works' for 'walks,' he had not observed that the allusion was to the gardens of the Lyceum, the favourite haunt of the Peripatetics.

Note IX.

I. 1. 57. We have often observed that as in this line and in III. I. 4, and Ind. 2. 110, the metre may be completed by pronouncing the name of the speaker at the beginning. This is one indication among many, of the haste with which parts of Shakespeare's plays were thrown off.

Note X.

I. 2. 145. Considering the carelessness with which a plural demonstrative pronoun was used with reference to a singular noun and *vice versa*, we have not altered the reading of the old editions in order to accommodate the construction to modern rule. See note (IV) to *Love's Labour's Lost.*

Note XI.

I. 2. 259. The misprint in Rowe's second edition remained uncorrected by Pope, Theobald, Hanmer, Warburton, and Johnson. Capell in correcting the error made another by writing 'her' for 'the.' He printed his edition not from any former text, but from a manuscript of his own writing.

Another instance of the facility with which a misprint which makes sense escapes correction is found in II. I. 4, where 'put,' a misprint for 'pull' in the Variorum of 1821, was retained by many subsequent editors, Mr Collier, Mr Singer, &c.

Note XII.

I. 2. 278. Mr Grant White believes the whole of the foregoing scene to be by some other hand than Shakespeare's. Coleridge and Sidney

Walker also held that large portions of the play were not from the master's hand. It appears to us impossible to discriminate, as in *Henry the Eighth* and *The Two Noble Kinsmen*, what parts were due to Shakespeare and what to another hand. The feeblest scenes of this play seem to have been touched by him. The probability is that he worked, in this case, not with, but after, another.

NOTE XIII.

II. I. 403. Pope inserts from the old play:

'[*Sly speaks to one of the servants.*

Sly. Sim, when will the fool come again?

Sim. Anon, my lord.

Sly. Give's some more drink here—where's the tapster? here Sim, eat some of these things.

Sim. So I do, my lord.

Sly. Here Sim, I drink to thee.'

These lines were repeated by all subsequent editors down to Capell, who inserted them at a different place. See note (XVI).

NOTE XIV.

III. 2. 63. Mr Collier says that the Quarto reads 'the humor *or* fourty fancies...' If so, his copy differs from ours, which reads 'the humor *of* fourty fancies...'

NOTE XV.

III. 2. 81—84. It is not always clear from the way in which Capell's text is printed whether he meant a passage where there is a rapid change of speakers to be read as prose or verse. In the Edition before us, this is always explained by certain conventional symbols inserted with his own hand in red ink. This he probably did with a view to a second edition, which he never lived to bring out. 'Tulit alter honores.'

NOTE XVI.

III. 2. 245. Capell here inserted the lines which Pope put after II. I. 403. See note (XIII).

Note XVII.

IV. I. 124. Theobald first printed 'Where is the life that late I led?' as part of a song. He printed also the following words, 'Where are those —' in italics, as if they were a continuation of the song. He was followed by Hanmer, Warburton, and Johnson, but not by Capell. As the song is lost, the question must remain doubtful.

Note XVIII.

IV. 2. Pope made a bold transposition, and placed here the scene which in our Edition stands as the third scene of the fourth Act, beginning:

'*Gra.* No, no, forsooth, I dare not for my life,'

and ending:

'*Hor.* Why so this gallant will command the sun.'

The scene thus in Pope's edition counted as the 4th, 5th, and 6th scenes of Act IV.

Our Scene 2 of Act IV. is in Pope's edition Scenes I and 2 of Act V.

Theobald restored the old arrangement, which, as he proves in a note, is indisputably the right one.

Note XIX.

IV. 2. 120. Hanmer inserts from the old play the following lines, which are placed by Pope after IV. 3. 192, and by Capell after V. I. 132.

'*Lord.* Who's within there? [*Sly sleeps.*

Enter Servants.

Asleep again! go take him easily up, and put him in his own apparel again. But see you wake him not in any case.

Serv. It shall be done, my lord: come help to bear him hence.

[*They carry off Sly.*'

Note XX.

IV. 4. 62. There is evidently some mistake here. On the whole it seems better to change 'Cambio' to 'Biondello' in line 62, than '*Bion.*' to 'Luc.' in line 66. The supposed Cambio was not acting as Baptista's servant, and, moreover, had he been sent on such an errand he would have 'flown on the wings of love' to perform it. We must suppose that Biondello apparently makes his exit, but really waits till the stage is clear for an interview with his disguised master. The line 67 is as suitable to the faithful servant as to the master himself.

NOTE XXI.

IV. 4. 70. Mr Dyce says that in some copies of the first Folio the 'l' in welcome is scarcely visible. It was from one of these copies, doubtless, that the later Folios were printed. The 'l' is clear enough in Capell's copy of F_1.

NOTE XXII.

V. 1. 26. We have retained 'from Padua,' which is the reading of the old Edition, and probably right. The Pedant has been staying some time at Padua, and that is all he means when he contradicts the newly arrived traveller from Pisa.

NOTE XXIII.

V. 2. 176—189. The following speeches are added by Pope from the old play, and remained as part of the text till Capell's time:

'*Enter two Servants bearing* Sly *in his own apparel, and leave him on the stage. Then enter a* Tapster.

Sly awaking.] Sim, give 's some more wine—what, all the Players gone? am not I a lord?

Tap. A lord with a murrain! Come, art thou drunk still?

Sly. Who's this? Tapster! oh, I have had the bravest dream that ever thou heardst in all thy life.

Tap. Yea marry, but thou hadst best get thee home, for your wife will course you for dreaming here all night.

Sly. Will she? I know how to tame a Shrew. I dreamt upon it all this night, and thou hast wak'd me out of the best dream that ever I had. But I'll to my wife, and tame her too, if she anger me.'

ALL'S WELL THAT ENDS WELL.

DRAMATIS PERSONÆ[1].

KING OF FRANCE.
DUKE OF FLORENCE.
BERTRAM, Count of Rousillon[2].
LAFEU[3], an old lord.
PAROLLES[4], a follower of Bertram.
Steward, } servants to the Countess of Rousillon.
LAVACHE, a Clown, } servants to the Countess of Rousillon.
A Page.

COUNTESS OF ROUSILLON, mother to Bertram.
HELENA, a gentlewoman protected by the Countess.
An old Widow of Florence.
DIANA, daughter to the Widow.
VIOLENTA, } neighbours and friends to the Widow.
MARIANA, } neighbours and friends to the Widow.

Lords, Officers, Soldiers, &c., French and Florentine.

SCENE: *Rousillon; Paris; Florence; Marseilles.*

[1] DRAMATIS PERSONÆ] First given by Rowe. See note (I).

[2] *Rousillon*] Pope. *Rossilion.* Rowe. *Rosillion* Capell.

[3] LAFEU] LEFEU Steevens conj.

[4] PAROLLES] PAROLES Steevens conj.

ALL'S WELL THAT ENDS WELL.

ACT I.

SCENE I. *Rousillon. The* Count's *palace.*

Enter BERTRAM, *the* COUNTESS of ROUSILLON, HELENA, *and* LAFEU, *all in black.*

Count. In delivering my son from me, I bury a second husband.

Ber. And I in going, madam, weep o'er my father's death anew: but I must attend his majesty's command, to whom I am now in ward, evermore in subjection.

Laf. You shall find of the king a husband, madam; you, sir, a father: he that so generally is at all times good, must of necessity hold his virtue to you; whose worthiness would stir it up where it wanted, rather than lack it where there is such abundance.

Count. What hope is there of his majesty's amendment?

Laf. He hath abandoned his physicians, madam; under whose practices he hath persecuted time with hope, and

ACT I. SCENE I.] Actus Primus. Scæna Prima. Ff.

Enter......] Enter yong Bertram, Count of Rossillion, his Mother, and Helena, Lord Lafew, all in blacke. Ff.

1. Count.] Mother. Ff, and afterwards Mo.

delivering] *delivering up* Hanmer. *dissevering* Warburton.

son from me,] *son, for me* or *son, 'fore me,* Becket conj.

3. *And I in going, madam*] F_1. *And in going Madam* F_2 F_3 F_4. *And in going, madam, I* Rowe.

9. *lack*] *slack* Theobald (Warburton).

13. *persecuted*] *prosecuted* Hanmer.

finds no other advantage in the process but only the losing of hope by time.

Count. This young gentlewoman had a father,—O, that 'had'! how sad a passage 'tis!—whose skill was almost as great as his honesty; had it stretched so far, would have made nature immortal, and death should have play for lack of work. Would, for the king's sake, he were living! I think it would be the death of the king's disease.

Laf. How called you the man you speak of, madam?

Count. He was famous, sir, in his profession, and it was his great right to be so,—Gerard de Narbon.

Laf. He was excellent indeed madam: the king very lately spoke of him admiringly and mourningly: he was skilful enough to have lived still, if knowledge could be set up against mortality.

Ber. What is it, my good lord, the king languishes of?

Laf. A fistula, my lord.

Ber. I heard not of it before.

Laf. I would it were not notorious. Was this gentlewoman the daughter of Gerard de Narbon?

Count. His sole child, my lord; and bequeathed to my overlooking. I have those hopes of her good that her education promises; her dispositions she inherits, which makes fair gifts fairer; for where an unclean mind carries virtuous qualities, there commendations go with pity; they are virtues and traitors too: in her they are the better for their simpleness; she derives her honesty and achieves her goodness.

Laf. Your commendations, madam, get from her tears.

Count. 'Tis the best brine a maiden can season her praise in. The remembrance of her father never approaches her heart but the tyranny of her sorrows takes all livelihood from

17. *passage*] *preface* Hanmer. *presage* Warburton. *pesage* Becket conj.
was] om. Collier (Collier MS.).

18. *would*] *it would* Rowe. *'t would* Singer.

19. *have*] *have had* Hanmer.
play] *play'd* Warburton.

29, 31, 52. Ber.] Ros. Ff.

35. *hopes of her good that her*] *good hopes of her that her* or *hopes of her that her good* Anon. conj.

36. *promises; her*] Rowe. *promises her* Ff. *promises her;* Pope.
her dispositions] *the honesty of her dispositions* Staunton conj.
dispositions] *disposition* Rowe.

39. *their*] *her* Hanmer (Warburton).

41. *from her tears*] *tears from her* Pope.

her cheek. No more of this, Helena, go to, no more; lest it be rather thought you affect a sorrow than to have—

Hel. I do affect a sorrow, indeed, but I have it too.

Laf. Moderate lamentation is the right of the dead; excessive grief the enemy to the living.

Count. If the living be enemy to the grief, the excess makes it soon mortal.

Ber. Madam, I desire your holy wishes.

Laf. How understand we that?

Count. Be thou blest, Bertram, and succeed thy father
In manners, as in shape! thy blood and virtue
Contend for empire in thee, and thy goodness
Share with thy birthright! Love all, trust a few,
Do wrong to none: be able for thine enemy
Rather in power than use; and keep thy friend
Under thy own life's key: be check'd for silence,
But never tax'd for speech. What heaven more will,
That thee may furnish, and my prayers pluck down,
Fall on thy head! Farewell, my lord;
'Tis an unseason'd courtier; good my lord,
Advise him.

Laf. He cannot want the best
That shall attend his love.

Count. Heaven bless him! Farewell, Bertram. [*Exit.*

Ber. [*To Helena*] The best wishes that can be forged in your thoughts be servants to you! Be comfortable to my mother, your mistress, and make much of her.

46. *it be rather thought you*] *you be rather thought to* Hanmer.
to have—] Ff. *to have it.* Warburton. *have it.* Capell. *to have.* Steevens.

48. *lamentation*] F_1. *lamentations* F_2 F_3 F_4.

50. Count.] Hel. Tieck.
be] *be not* Theobald (Warburton).

52, 53. Ber. *Madam,*... Laf. *How* ...] Laf. *How*... Ber. *Madam,*... Theobald conj.

63. *head*] F_1. *hand* F_2 F_3 F_4.
Farewell, my lord;] *Farewell my Lord,* Ff. *Farewel.—My lord Lafeu,* Capell. *Farewell. My lord,* Steevens.

63—67. Hanmer ends the lines *'tis an*...*advise him*...*attend*...*Bertram.* S. Walker would end them *My lord Lafeu,* ... *my lord*...*that shall*...*Bertram,* reading *can't* for *cannot* in line 65.

64. *Advise him.*] *Advise him you.* Capell.

65—87. Laf. *He cannot*......*draw*] Omitted in F_4.

67. *Heaven*] *May heaven* Hanmer.

68. [To Helena] Rowe.

Laf. Farewell, pretty lady: you must hold the credit of your father. [*Exeunt Bertram and Lafeu.*

Hel. O, were that all! I think not on my father;
And these great tears grace his remembrance more
Than those I shed for him. What was he like?
I have forgot him: my imagination
Carries no favour in 't but Bertram's.
I am undone: there is no living, none,
If Bertram be away. 'Twere all one
That I should love a bright particular star
And think to wed it, he is so above me:
In his bright radiance and collateral light
Must I be comforted, not in his sphere.
The ambition in my love thus plagues itself:
The hind that would be mated by the lion
Must die for love. 'Twas pretty, though a plague,
To see him every hour; to sit and draw
His arched brows, his hawking eye, his curls,
In our heart's table; heart too capable
Of every line and trick of his sweet favour:
But now he's gone, and my idolatrous fancy
Must sanctify his reliques. Who comes here?

Enter PAROLLES.

[*Aside*] One that goes with him: I love him for his sake;
And yet I know him a notorious liar,
Think him a great way fool, solely a coward;
Yet these fix'd evils sit so fit in him,
That they take place, when virtue's steely bones

71. *must hold*] *uphold* Rann (Mason conj.).

72. [Exeunt...] Rowe. om. Ff.

73. SCENE II. Pope.

75. *those I*] *they are* Hanmer.

77. *in't but Bertram's*] *in it but my Bertram's* Pope. *in it, but of Bertram* Capell. *in 't but only Bertram's* Collier (Collier MS.).

79. *'Twere*] $F_1F_2F_3$. *It were* Pope.

80. *particular*] $F_1F_2F_3$. *partic'lar* Pope.

81. *me:*] Rowe. *me* F_1 F_2 F_3.

84. *The*] *Th'* $F_1F_2F_3$.

88. *brows*] *browes* F_1 F_2. *arrows* F_3F_4.

89. *our*] *my* Collier MS.

90. *trick*] *trait* Becket conj.

92. *reliques*] F_1 F_2. *relick* F_3F_4.
Enter Parolles.] Ff. Dyce transfers to line 99.

93. [Aside] Edd.

95. *solely*] F_3F_4. *solie* F_1F_2. *wholly* Hanmer.

97. *steely*] *seely* Williams conj.

Look bleak i' the cold wind: withal, full oft we see
Cold wisdom waiting on superfluous folly.

Par. Save you, fair queen!

Hel. And you, monarch!

Par. No.

Hel. And no.

Par. Are you meditating on virginity?

Hel. Ay. You have some stain of soldier in you: let me ask you a question. Man is enemy to virginity; how may we barricado it against him?

Par. Keep him out.

Hel. But he assails; and our virginity, though valiant, in the defence yet is weak: unfold to us some warlike resistance.

Par. There is none: man, sitting down before you, will undermine you and blow you up.

Hel. Bless our poor virginity from underminers and blowers up! Is there no military policy, how virgins might blow up men?

Par. Virginity being blown down, man will quicklier be blown up: marry, in blowing him down again, with the breach yourselves made, you lose your city. It is not politic in the commonwealth of nature to preserve virginity. Loss of virginity is rational increase and there was never virgin got till virginity was first lost. That you were made of is metal to make virgins. Virginity by being once lost may be ten times found; by being ever kept, it is ever lost: 'tis too cold a companion; away with 't!

98. *Look*] Rowe. *Lookes* F_1 F_2. *Looks* F_3 F_4.
i'the] *in the* Pope.
withal] om. Pope.
99. *Cold*] S. Walker conjectures that this is corrupt.
folly] F_3 F_4. *follie* F_1 F_2.
100. SCENE III. Pope.
Save] *'Save* Hanmer.
105. *stain*] *strain* Halliwell conj.
107. *barricado*] Rowe. *barracedo* F_1. *barrocado* F_2 F_3 F_4.
107—109. *him?* Par. *Keep him out.* Hel. *But*] *him to keep him out? for* Hanmer.
109. *assails*] *assails us* S. Walker conj.
109, 110. *valiant, in the defence yet*] Ff. *valiant in the defence, yet* Steevens.
110. *to us*] F_1. *us* F_2 F_3 F_4.
112. *sitting*] Johnson. *setting* Ff.
114. *Bless*] *'Bless* Capell conj. MS.
121. *rational*] *national* Hanmer (Theobald conj.). *natural* Anon. ap. Halliwell conj.
122. *got*] F_2 F_3 F_4. *goe* F_1.

Hel. I will stand for 't a little, though therefore I die a virgin.

Par. There's little can be said in 't; 'tis against the rule of nature. To speak on the part of virginity, is to accuse your mothers; which is most infallible disobedience. He that hangs himself is a virgin: virginity murders itself; and should be buried in highways out of all sanctified limit, as a desperate offendress against nature. Virginity breeds mites, much like a cheese; consumes itself to the very paring, and so dies with feeding his own stomach. Besides, virginity is peevish, proud, idle, made of self-love, which is the most inhibited sin in the canon. Keep it not; you cannot choose but lose by 't: out with 't! within ten year it will make itself ten, which is a goodly increase; and the principal itself not much the worse: away with 't!

Hel. How might one do, sir, to lose it to her own liking?

Par. Let me see: marry, ill, to like him that ne'er it likes. 'Tis a commodity will lose the gloss with lying; the longer kept, the less worth: off with 't while 'tis vendible; answer the time of request. Virginity, like an old courtier, wears her cap out of fashion; richly suited, but unsuitable: just like the brooch and the tooth-pick, which wear not now. Your date is better in your pie and your porridge than in your cheek: and your virginity, your old virginity, is like one of our French withered pears, it looks ill, it eats drily; marry, 'tis a withered pear; it was formerly better; marry, yet 'tis a withered pear: will you any thing with it?

130. *mothers*] *mother* Rowe.

130, 131. *He...is*] *He...is like* Hanmer. *As he...so is* Warburton.

135. *his*] *its* Rowe. *on its* Hanmer.

137. *inhibited*] F_1. *inhabited* F_2 F_3 F_4. *prohibited* Pope.

138, 139. *ten year...ten,*] *ten years ...ten* Hanmer. *ten yeare...two* F_1. *ten yeares...two* F_2 F_3. *ten years...two* F_4. *two years...two* Collier, ed. 2 (Steevens conj.). *ten years......twelve* Tollet conj. *ten months...two* Singer (Malone conj.). *one year...two* Grant White. *the year...two* Anon. conj.

142, 143. *it likes*] *likes it* S. Walker conj.

143. *'Tis*] *And 'tis* Hanmer.

147. *wear*] Capell. *were* Ff. *we wear* Rowe.

152. *yet*] *yes,* Hanmer.

will you] *will you do* Collier MS.

with it?] *with me?* Johnson conj. *with us?* Tyrwhitt conj. *with it? I am now bound for the court.* Malone conj. *with it? We are for the Court.* Staunton conj.

Hel. Not my virginity yet......
There shall your master have a thousand loves,
A mother and a mistress and a friend,
A phœnix, captain and an enemy,
A guide, a goddess, and a sovereign,
A counsellor, a traitress, and a dear;
His humble ambition, proud humility,
His jarring concord, and his discord dulcet,
His faith, his sweet disaster; with a world
Of pretty, fond, adoptious christendoms,
That blinking Cupid gossips. Now shall he—
I know not what he shall. God send him well!
The court's a learning place, and he is one—

Par. What one, i' faith?

Hel. That I wish well. 'Tis pity—

Par. What's pity?

Hel. That wishing well had not a body in't,
Which might be felt; that we, the poorer born,
Whose baser stars do shut us up in wishes,
Might with effects of them follow our friends,
And show what we alone must think, which never
Returns us thanks.

Enter Page.

Page. Monsieur Parolles, my lord calls for you. [*Exit.*

Par. Little Helen, farewell: if I can remember thee, I will think of thee at court.

153. *Not*] *Not with* Collier MS.
yet.] *yet. You're for the Court:* Hanmer. See note (II).
153, 154. *Not...your*] *No!—my virginity! yet There shall its* Jackson conj.
154. *shall*] *should* Steevens conj.
155. *A mother*] *Another* Rowe (ed. 2).
156—163. *A phœnix......shall he*] Put in brackets as spurious by Warburton.
156. *captain*] *captor* Anon. conj.
159. *humble*] F_1. *humblest* $F_2F_3F_4$.
162. *pretty*] *petty* Harness.
fond, adoptious] *fond-adoptious* S. Walker conj.
163. *he—*] Rowe. *he:* Ff.
165. *learning place*] *learning-place* Steevens.
one—] Rowe. *one.* Ff.
167. *pity—*] Rowe. *pitty.* $F_1F_2F_3$. *pity.* F_4.
168. Par. *What's pity?*] Omitted in Pope (ed. 2).
170. *the*] F_1. om. $F_2F_3F_4$.
176. Exit.] Theobald.

Hel. Monsieur Parolles, you were born under a charitable star.

Par. Under Mars, I.

Hel. I especially think, under Mars.

Par. Why under Mars?

Hel. The wars have so kept you under, that you must needs be born under Mars.

Par. When he was predominant.

Hel. When he was retrograde, I think, rather.

Par. Why think you so?

Hel. You go so much backward when you fight.

Par. That's for advantage.

Hel. So is running away, when fear proposes the safety: but the composition that your valour and fear makes in you is a virtue of a good wing, and I like the wear well.

Par. I am so full of businesses, I cannot answer thee acutely. I will return perfect courtier; in the which, my instruction shall serve to naturalize thee, so thou wilt be capable of a courtier's counsel, and understand what advice shall thrust upon thee; else thou diest in thine unthankfulness, and thine ignorance makes thee away: farewell. When thou hast leisure, say thy prayers; when thou hast none, remember thy friends: get thee a good husband, and use him as he uses thee: so, farewell. [*Exit.*

Hel. Our remedies oft in ourselves do lie,
Which we ascribe to heaven: the fated sky
Gives us free scope; only doth backward pull
Our slow designs when we ourselves are dull.
What power is it which mounts my love so high;
That makes me see, and cannot feed mine eye?

183. *wars have*] Pope. *warres hath* F_1F_2. *waters hath* F_3F_4. *waters have* Rowe.

190. *So...safety*] Printed as two lines in Ff, the first ending *away*.

the safety] *safety* F_3F_4.

191. *makes*] *make* Hanmer.

192. *wing*] *ming* Warburton.

I like the wear] *is like to wear* Mason conj.

193. *businesses*] $F_1F_2F_3$. *business* F_4. *businesses, as* Theobald.

195. *instruction*] *instrument* Rowe (ed. 2).

196. *of a*] F_1. *of the* $F_2F_3F_4$. *of* Pope.

202. SCENE IV. Pope.

207. *That*] *Which* Capell.

The mightiest space in fortune nature brings
To join like likes and kiss like native things.
Impossible be strange attempts to those
That weigh their pains in sense, and do suppose
What hath been cannot be: who ever strove
To show her merit, that did miss her love?
The king's disease—my project may deceive me,
But my intents are fix'd, and will not leave me. [*Exit.*

SCENE II. *Paris. The* KING'S *palace.*

Flourish of cornets. Enter the KING OF FRANCE *with letters, and divers Attendants.*

King. The Florentines and Senoys are by the ears;
Have fought with equal fortune, and continue
A braving war.

First Lord. So 'tis reported, sir.

King. Nay, 'tis most credible; we here receive it
A certainty, vouch'd from our cousin Austria,
With caution, that the Florentine will move us
For speedy aid; wherein our dearest friend
Prejudicates the business, and would seem
To have us make denial.

First Lord. His love and wisdom,
Approved so to your majesty, may plead
For amplest credence.

King. He hath arm'd our answer,
And Florence is denied before he comes:

208. *The mightiest space*] *The mighty and base* Mason conj. *The wid'st apart* Staunton conj.
fortune nature] *nature fortune* Malone conj. (withdrawn).
brings] *springs* Anon. (Fras. Mag.) conj.
208, 209. *The...To join like likes*] *Through...Likes to join likes* Johnson conj. *The...Like to join like* Long MS.
212. *hath been cannot be*] *hath not been ca'nt be* Hanmer. *ha'nt been cannot be* Mason conj. *n' ath been cannot be* Staunton conj.
214. *The king's disease—*] Rowe. (*The Kings disease*) Ff.
SCENE II.] Capell. SCENE V. Pope.
Flourish of cornets.] Flourish cornets. Ff.
1. *Senoys*] *Siennois* or *Siennese* Lloyd conj.
the ears] Capell. *th' eares* Ff.
3, 9, 18. First Lord.] 1. Lord. Rowe. 1. Lo. G. Ff.

Yet, for our gentlemen that mean to see
The Tuscan service, freely have they leave
To stand on either part.
Sec. Lord. It well may serve
A nursery to our gentry, who are sick
For breathing and exploit.
King. What's he comes here?

Enter BERTRAM, LAFEU, *and* PAROLLES.

First Lord. It is the Count Rousillon, my good lord,
Young Bertram.
King. Youth, thou bear'st thy father's face;
Frank nature, rather curious than in haste,
Hath well composed thee. Thy father's moral parts
Mayst thou inherit too! Welcome to Paris.
Ber. My thanks and duty are your majesty's.
King. I would I had that corporal soundness now,
As when thy father and myself in friendship
First tried our soldiership! He did look far
Into the service of the time, and was
Discipled of the bravest: he lasted long;
But on us both did haggish age steal on,
And wore us out of act. It much repairs me
To talk of your good father. In his youth
He had the wit, which I can well observe
To-day in our young lords; but they may jest
Till their own scorn return to them unnoted
Ere they can hide their levity in honour:
So like a courtier, contempt nor bitterness
Were in his pride or sharpness; if they were,

15, 67. Sec. Lord.] 2. Lord. Rowe. 2. Lo. E. Ff.

15. *well may*] *may well* $F_3 F_4$.

18. *It is*] $F_1 F_4$. *It 'tis* $F_2 F_3$. *Rousillon*] Pope. *Rosignoll* F_1. *Rosillion* F_2. *Rossillion* $F_3 F_4$.

21. *Hath well composed thee*] *Compos'd thee well* Pope.

28. *bravest*] *brav'st* Pope.

32. *well*] *ill* Long MS.

35. *hide their levity in honour*] *vye their levity with his honour* Hanmer. *hide their levity in humour* Long MS.

35, 36. *honour: So like a courtier,*] Ff. *honour, So like a courtier:* Capell (Blackstone conj.). *honour: No courtier-like* Lloyd conj.

36. *contempt nor*] *no contempt nor* Rowe (ed. 1). *no contempt or* Rowe (ed. 2).

37. *in his pride or sharpness;*] *in him; pride or sharpness,* Theobald

His equal had awaked them; and his honour,
Clock to itself, knew the true minute when
Exception bid him speak, and at this time
His tongue obey'd his hand: who were below him
He used as creatures of another place;
And bow'd his eminent top to their low ranks,
Making them proud of his humility,
In their poor praise he humbled. Such a man
Might be a copy to these younger times;
Which, follow'd well, would demonstrate them now
But goers backward.

Ber. His good remembrance, sir,
Lies richer in your thoughts than on his tomb;
So in approof lives not his epitaph
As in your royal speech.

King. Would I were with him! He would always say—
Methinks I hear him now; his plausive words
He scatter'd not in ears, but grafted them,
To grow there and to bear,—'Let me not live,'—
This his good melancholy oft began,
On the catastrophe and heel of pastime,
When it was out,—'Let me not live,' quoth he,
'After my flame lacks oil, to be the snuff
Of younger spirits, whose apprehensive senses
All but new things disdain; whose judgements are
Mere fathers of their garments; whose constancies
Expire before their fashions. This he wish'd:

(Warburton). *in him, pride or sharpness;* Capell.

if they were] *if there were* Theobald (Warburton).

39. *Clock*] *Block* Rowe (ed. 2).

40. *Exception*] *Exceptions* Theobald.

this] *that* Rowe.

41. *his hand*] *the hand* Johnson conj. *it's hand* Capell. *his head* Long MS.

42. *another place*] *a brother-race* Hanmer.

44. *proud of*] *proud; and* Warburton.

44, 45. *humility, In...praise he humbled*] *humility: He, in...praise, humbled* Becket conj.

45. *he humbled*] *be-humbled* Staunton conj.

47. *demonstrate them now*] *now demonstrate them* Pope.

50. *So in approof lives not his*] *Approof so lives not in his* Johnson conj. *So his approof lives not in* Capell.

56. *This*] Ff. *Thus* Pope.

58. *it*] *wit* Staunton conj.

62. *fathers*] *feathers* Tyrwhitt conj. *parcels* Williams conj.

I after him do after him wish too,
Since I nor wax nor honey can bring home,
I quickly were dissolved from my hive,
To give some labourers room.

Sec. Lord. You are loved, sir;
They that least lend it you shall lack you first.

King. I fill a place, I know't. How long is't, count,
Since the physician at your father's died?
He was much famed.

Ber. Some six months since, my lord.

King. If he were living, I would try him yet.
Lend me an arm; the rest have worn me out
With several applications: nature and sickness
Debate it at their leisure. Welcome, count;
My son's no dearer.

Ber. Thank your majesty.

[*Exeunt. Flourish.*

SCENE III. *Rousillon. The* COUNT'S *palace.*

Enter COUNTESS, Steward, *and* Clown.

Count. I will now hear; what say you of this gentlewoman?

Stew. Madam, the care I have had to even your content, I wish might be found in the calendar of my past endeavours; for then we wound our modesty and make foul the clearness of our deservings, when of ourselves we publish them.

Count. What does this knave here? Get you gone, sirrah: the complaints I have heard of you I do not all believe: 'tis my slowness that I do not; for I know you

67. *labourers*] *labourer* Warburton.
You are] Capell. *You'r* F_1 F_2. *You 're* F_3 F_4.
76. *Thank*] *Thanks to* Rowe.
[Exeunt.] Exit. Ff.
SCENE III.] SCENE VI. Pope.
1. *hear; what say you*] Theobald. *heare, what say you* Ff. *hear what you say* Capell.
gentlewoman?] F_4. *gentlewoman.* $F_1F_2F_3$.
3. *even*] *win* Collier conj.
6. *foul*] *out* Rowe (ed. 2).
10. *'tis*] *it is* S. Walker conj., reading lines 9—12 as verse, ending *complaints...believe...them...make...yours.*

lack not folly to commit them, and have ability enough to make such knaveries yours.

Clo. 'Tis not unknown to you, madam, I am a poor fellow.

Count. Well, sir.

Clo. No, madam, 'tis not so well that I am poor, though many of the rich are damned: but, if I may have your ladyship's good will to go to the world, Isbel the woman and I will do as we may.

Count. Wilt thou needs be a beggar?

Clo. I do beg your good will in this case.

Count. In what case?

Clo. In Isbel's case and mine own. Service is no heritage: and I think I shall never have the blessing of God till I have issue o' my body; for they say barnes are blessings.

Count. Tell me thy reason why thou wilt marry.

Clo. My poor body, madam, requires it: I am driven on by the flesh; and he must needs go that the devil drives.

Count. Is this all your worship's reason?

Clo. Faith, madam, I have other holy reasons, such as they are.

Count. May the world know them?

Clo. I have been, madam, a wicked creature, as you and all flesh and blood are; and, indeed, I do marry that I may repent.

Count. Thy marriage, sooner than thy wickedness.

Clo. I am out o' friends, madam; and I hope to have friends for my wife's sake.

Count. Such friends are thine enemies, knave.

Clo. You're shallow, madam, in great friends; for the

12. *yours*] *yare* Warburton conj.

13. *I am*] *that I am* Capell.

17. *may have*] F_1. *have* $F_2 F_3 F_4$.

18. *to go to*] *to go into* Long MS.

18, 19. *the woman*] *your woman* Grant White.

19. *and I will*] $F_2 F_3 F_4$. *and w will* F_1. *and we will* Collier.

25. *o'*] Rowe (ed. 2). *a* Ff. *of* Rann.

barnes] F_1. *bearns* F_2. *barns* $F_3 F_4$.

38. *out o'*] Capell. *out a* $F_1F_2F_3$. *out of* F_4.

41. *You're*] Capell. *Y'are* Ff. *You are* Steevens.

madam, in] *madam; e'en* Hanmer. *madam, my* Tyrwhitt conj.

knaves come to do that for me, which I am aweary of. He that ears my land spares my team, and gives me leave to in the crop; if I be his cuckold, he's my drudge: he that comforts my wife is the cherisher of my flesh and blood; he that cherishes my flesh and blood loves my flesh and blood; he that loves my flesh and blood is my friend: ergo, he that kisses my wife is my friend. If men could be contented to be what they are, there were no fear in marriage; for young Charbon the puritan and old Poysam the papist, howsome'er their hearts are severed in religion, their heads are both one; they may joul horns together, like any deer i' the herd.

Count. Wilt thou ever be a foul-mouthed and calumnious knave?

Clo. A prophet I, madam; and I speak the truth the next way:

For I the ballad will repeat,
  Which men full true shall find;
Your marriage comes by destiny,
  Your cuckoo sings by kind.

Count. Get you gone, sir; I'll talk with you more anon.

Stew. May it please you, madam, that he bid Helen come to you: of her I am to speak.

Count. Sirrah, tell my gentlewoman I would speak with her; Helen I mean.

Clo. Was this fair face the cause, quoth she,
  Why the Grecians sacked Troy?
Fond done, done fond,
  Was this King Priam's joy?

42. *aweary*] *weary* Rowe.

43. *to in*] F_4. *to Inne* $F_1F_2F_3$.

46. *cherishes*] F_1. *cherisheth* $F_2F_3F_4$.

50. *Charbon...Poysam*] See note (III).

howsome'er] *how somere* F_1F_2. *howsomeere* F_3. *howsomere* F_4. *howsoe'er* Pope.

57—60. *For I...kind*] Printed as verse first in Rowe (ed. 2).

66. *the cause, quoth she*] *quoth she, the cause* Collier (Collier MS.).

68. *Fond done, done fond*] omitted by Pope.

68, 69. *done fond...joy?*] *done, fond ...joy,* F_1F_2. *fond done;—for Paris he...joy.* Theobald (Warburton). *fond done! but Paris he...joy,* Capell conj. *done fond, good sooth, it was:...joy?* Collier (Collier MS.). *For it undone, undone, quoth he,...joy.* Rann (Heath conj.).

With that she sighed as she stood,
With that she sighed as she stood,
And gave this sentence then;
Among nine bad if one be good,
Among nine bad if one be good,
There's yet one good in ten.

Count. What, one good in ten? you corrupt the song, sirrah.

Clo. One good woman in ten, madam; which is a purifying o' the song: would God would serve the world so all the year! we'd find no fault with the tithe-woman, if I were the parson: one in ten, quoth a'! an we might have a good woman born but one every blazing star, or at an earthquake, 'twould mend the lottery well: a man may draw his heart out, ere a' pluck one.

Count. You'll be gone, sir knave, and do as I command you.

Clo. That man should be at woman's command, and yet no hurt done! Though honesty be no puritan, yet it will do no hurt; it will wear the surplice of humility over the black gown of a big heart. I am going, forsooth: the business is for Helen to come hither. [*Exit.*

Count. Well, now.

Stew. I know, madam, you love your gentlewoman entirely.

Count. Faith, I do: her father bequeathed her to me; and she herself, without other advantage, may lawfully make

70, 71. *With...stood*] *With...stood*, bis. Ff (bis in italics).

71. Omitted by Pope.

72—75. *And gave...ten*] Printed first as verse in Rowe (ed. 2).

73, 74. *one*] *none* Capell conj.

74. Omitted by Pope.

78. *a*] $F_1 F_2$. *the* $F_3 F_4$.

79. *o' the*] Capell. *o' th'* Rowe (ed. 2). *ath'* $F_1 F_2$. *a'th* $F_3 F_4$.

song] *song and mending of the sex* Collier (Collier MS. *o' the*).

82. *one*] Collier (Collier MS.). *ore* $F_1 F_2$. *o're* $F_3 F_4$. *o'er* Rowe. om. Pope. *or* Capell. *on* Rann. *ere* Collier (ed. 1). *for* Harness. *'fore* Staunton. *at* Halliwell conj.

83. *well*] *wheel* Malone conj.

draw] *pray* Rowe.

84. *a'*] *he* Rowe (ed. 2).

86. *you.*] Pope. *you?* Ff.

87. *woman's*] F_1. *a woman's* $F_2 F_3 F_4$.

87, 88. *and yet*] $F_1 F_2$. *and get* $F_3 F_4$.

88. *no puritan*] *a puritan* Rann (Tyrwhitt conj.).

89. *do no hurt*] *do what is enjoined* Malone conj.

96. *advantage*] *advantages* Rowe.

title to as much love as she finds: there is more owing her than is paid; and more shall be paid her than she'll demand.

Stew. Madam, I was very late more near her than I think she wished me: alone she was, and did communicate to herself her own words to her own ears; she thought, I dare vow for her, they touched not any stranger sense. Her matter was, she loved your son: Fortune, she said, was no goddess, that had put such difference betwixt their two estates; Love no god, that would not extend his might, only where qualities were level; . . . . queen of virgins, that would suffer her poor knight surprised, without rescue in the first assault, or ransom afterward. This she delivered in the most bitter touch of sorrow that e'er I heard virgin exclaim in: which I held my duty speedily to acquaint you withal; sithence, in the loss that may happen, it concerns you something to know it.

Count. You have discharged this honestly; keep it to yourself: many likelihoods informed me of this before, which hung so tottering in the balance, that I could neither believe nor misdoubt. Pray you, leave me: stall this in your bosom; and I thank you for your honest care: I will speak with you further anon. [*Exit Steward.*

Enter HELENA.

Even so it was with me when I was young:
If ever we are nature's, these are ours; this thorn
Doth to our rose of youth rightly belong;
Our blood to us, this to our blood is born;

105. *would*] *should* Capell.
not] om. Long MS.
might, only] F_4. *might onelie*, F_1 F_2. *might onely* F_3.
106. *level;...queen*] *levell, Queene* F_1 F_2. *levell: Queen* F_3 F_4. *level: Complain'd against the Queen* Rowe. *level; Diana no queen* Theobald. See note (IV).
107. *knight*] *spright* Warburton conj.
surprised] *to be surpris'd* Rowe.
107, 108. *without rescue in the first assault,*] *in the first assault, without rescue* Capell.
109. *virgin*] *a virgin* Pope.
110. *held*] *held it* Rowe.
113. *honestly*] *honesty* F_3 F_4.
115. *neither*] F_1. *never* F_2 F_3 F_4.
118. Enter H.] Enter Hellen. Ff. Enter H. Singer (after line 126). See note (V).
119. SCENE VII. Pope.
Even] Old Cou. *Even* Ff.
120. *ever*] om. Pope. *e'er* Edd. conj.

It is the show and seal of nature's truth,
Where love's strong passion is impress'd in youth:
By our remembrances of days foregone,
Such were our faults, or then we thought them none.
Her eye is sick on't: I observe her now.

Hel. What is your pleasure, madam?

Count. You know, Helen,
I am a mother to you.

Hel. Mine honourable mistress.

Count. Nay, a mother:
Why not a mother? When I said 'a mother,'
Methought you saw a serpent: what's in 'mother,'
That you start at it? I say, I am your mother;
And put you in the catalogue of those
That were enwombed mine: 'tis often seen
Adoption strives with nature; and choice breeds
A native slip to us from foreign seeds:
You ne'er oppress'd me with a mother's groan,
Yet I express to you a mother's care:
God's mercy, maiden! does it curd thy blood
To say I am thy mother? What's the matter,
That this distemper'd messenger of wet,
The many-colour'd Iris, rounds thine eye?
Why? that you are my daughter?

Hel. That I am not.

Count. I say, I am your mother.

Hel. Pardon, madam;
The Count Rousillon cannot be my brother:
I am from humble, he from honour'd name;
No note upon my parents, his all noble:
My master, my dear lord he is; and I

126. *Such were our faults, or*] Ff. *Such were our faults, tho'* Hanmer. *Such were our faults,—O!* Johnson (Warburton conj.). *Search we out faults, for* Collier MS.

then...them] *them...then* Staunton.

128. *You know, Helen*] *Helen, you know* Pope.

130, 131. *Nay...said 'a mother'*] As one line in Ff.

131. *said 'a mother'*] *said mother* F_3 F_4.

133. *I am*] Ff. *I'm* Pope.

137. *seeds*] *soil* Anon. conj.

143. *The*] *This* S. Walker conj.

eye] *eyes* Pope.

144. *Why?*] —*Why*, Ff. *Why,*— Rowe.

are] *art* F_2.

His servant live, and will his vassal die:
He must not be my brother.

Count. Nor I your mother?

Hel. You are my mother, madam; would you were,—
So that my lord your son were not my brother,—
Indeed my mother! or were you both our mothers,
I care no more for than I do for heaven,
So I were not his sister. Can't no other,
But I your daughter, he must be my brother?

Count. Yes, Helen, you might be my daughter-in-law:
God shield you mean it not! daughter and mother
So strive upon your pulse. What, pale again?
My fear hath catch'd your fondness: now I see
The mystery of your loneliness, and find
Your salt tears' head: now to all sense 'tis gross
You love my son; invention is ashamed,
Against the proclamation of thy passion,
To say thou dost not: therefore tell me true;
But tell me then, 'tis so; for, look, thy cheeks
Confess it, th' one to th' other; and thine eyes
See it so grossly shown in thy behaviours,
That in their kind they speak it: only sin
And hellish obstinacy tie thy tongue,
That truth should be suspected. Speak, is't so?
If it be so, you have wound a goodly clew;
If it be not, forswear't: howe'er, I charge thee,
As heaven shall work in me for thine avail,

151. *mother?*] Rowe (ed. 2). *mother.* Ff.

155. *I care...heaven*] *I cannot ask for more than that of heav'n* Hanmer. *I can no more fear, than I do fear heav'n* Warburton. *I cannot more fear than I do fear heav'n* Heath conj. *I'd care no more for't than I do for heaven* Capell. *I care would...heaven* or *I crave would...heaven* Mason conj. *I care no more for than you do, 'fore heaven* Becket conj. [Aside] *I care no more for than I do for heaven* Staunton conj.

156, 157. *Can't no other, But I... he......brother?*] Theobald. *Cant no other, But I...he...brother.* Ff. *Can't no other? But I...he...brother.* Pope. *Can't be no other Way I...but he... brother?* Hanmer.

162. *loneliness*] Theobald. *loveliness* Ff. *lowliness* Hall conj. *liveliness* Becket conj.

168. *th' one to th'*] Knight. *'ton tooth to th'* F_1. *'ton to th'* F_2. *'tone to th'* F_3 F_4. *one to th'* Rowe.

169. *it*] *it is* F_2.
behaviours] *behaviour* F_3F_4.

173. *you have*] *you've* Pope.

175. *thine*] F_1. *mine* F_2 F_3 F_4.

To tell me truly.
Hel. Good madam, pardon me!
Count. Do you love my son?
Hel. Your pardon, noble mistress!
Count. Love you my son?
Hel. Do not you love him, madam?
Count. Go not about; my love hath in't a bond,
Whereof the world takes note: come, come, disclose
The state of your affection; for your passions
Have to the full appeach'd.
Hel. Then, I confess,
Here on my knee, before high heaven and you,
That before you, and next unto high heaven,
I love your son.
My friends were poor, but honest; so's my love:
Be not offended; for it hurts not him
That he is loved of me: I follow him not
By any token of presumptuous suit;
Nor would I have him till I do deserve him;
Yet never know how that desert should be.
I know I love in vain, strive against hope;
Yet, in this captious and intenible sieve,
I still pour in the waters of my love,
And lack not to lose still: thus, Indian-like,
Religious in mine error, I adore
The sun, that looks upon his worshipper,
But knows of him no more. My dearest madam,
Let not your hate encounter with my love
For loving where you do: but if yourself,
Whose aged honour cites a virtuous youth,
Did ever in so true a flame of liking
Wish chastely and love dearly, that your Dian

176. *truly*] *true* Hanmer.

180. *disclose*] F_3F_4. *disclose:* F_1F_2.

184. *heaven*] F_1. *heavens* $F_2F_3F_4$.

184, 185. *That...son*] As in Pope. Printed as one line in Ff.

193. *captious*] *carious* Johnson conj. *cap'cious* Farmer conj. *copious* Jackson conj.

intenible] *intemible* F_1. *inteemible* Nicholson conj.

194. *waters*] *water* Rowe.

195. *lose*] F_4. *loose* $F_1F_2F_3$. *love* Tyrwhitt conj.

202. *liking*] F_1. *living* F_2. *loving* F_3F_4.

203. *Wish......dearly*] *Love dearly and wish chastely* Malone conj.

Was both herself and love; O, then, give pity
To her, whose state is such, that cannot choose
But lend and give where she is sure to lose;
That seeks not to find that her search implies,
But riddle-like lives sweetly where she dies!
Count. Had you not lately an intent,—speak truly,—
To go to Paris?
Hel. Madam, I had.
Count. Wherefore? tell true.
Hel. I will tell truth; by grace itself I swear.
You know my father left me some prescriptions
Of rare and proved effects, such as his reading
And manifest experience had collected
For general sovereignty; and that he will'd me
In heedfull'st reservation to bestow them,
As notes, whose faculties inclusive were,
More than they were in note: amongst the rest,
There is a remedy, approved, set down,
To cure the desperate languishings whereof
The king is render'd lost.
Count. This was your motive
For Paris, was it? speak.
Hel. My lord your son made me to think of this;
Else Paris, and the medicine, and the king,
Had from the conversation of my thoughts
Haply been absent then.
Count. But think you, Helen,
If you should tender your supposed aid,
He would receive it? he and his physicians
Are of a mind; he, that they cannot help him,
They, that they cannot help: how shall they credit

205. *that*] *she* Hanmer.

207. *her*] F_1. om. $F_2F_3F_4$. *which* Rowe.

210. *tell true*] om. Steevens conj.

211. *tell truth*] F_1. *tell true* $F_2F_3F_4$. *tell you true* Capell (corrected in note).

214. *manifest*] *manifold* Collier (Long MS.).

220. *languishings*] Ff. *languishes* Reed (1803).

226. *Haply*] Pope. *Happily* Ff.

229. *that they cannot help him*] *that he can't be help'd* Hanmer. *that they cannot help* Capell conj. *that they cannot heal him* S. Walker conj.

230. *cannot help*] *can't help him* Capell conj. *cannot cure* Bailey conj.

A poor unlearned virgin, when the schools,
Embowell'd of their doctrine, have left off
The danger to itself?
Hel. There's something in't,
More than my father's skill, which was the greatest
Of his profession, that his good receipt
Shall for my legacy be sanctified
By the luckiest stars in heaven: and, would your honour
But give me leave to try success, I'd venture
The well-lost life of mine on his Grace's cure
By such a day and hour.
Count. Dost thou believe't?
Hel. Ay, madam, knowingly.
Count. Why, Helen, thou shalt have my leave and love,
Means and attendants and my loving greetings
To those of mine in court: I'll stay at home
And pray God's blessing into thy attempt:
Be gone to-morrow; and be sure of this,
What I can help thee to, thou shalt not miss. [*Exeunt.*

233. *in't*] *hints* Hanmer (Warburton).
237. *By the*] *Byth'* $F_1 F_2 F_3$. *By th'* F_4.
238. *to try*] F_1. *to* $F_2 F_3 F_4$. *for the* Rowe.
239. *The*] *This* Hanmer.
on his] *on's* S. Walker conj.
240. *and*] *an* F_1.
243. *attendants*] *attendance* S. Walker conj.
245. *into*] $F_1 F_2$. *unto* $F_3 F_4$. *upon* Hanmer.
246. *Be gone*] $F_3 F_4$. *Begon* $F_1 F_2$.

ACT II.

SCENE I. *Paris. The* KING'S *palace.*

Flourish of cornets. Enter the KING, *attended with divers young* Lords *taking leave for the Florentine war;* BERTRAM, *and* PAROLLES.

King. Farewell, young lords; these warlike principles
Do not throw from you: and you, my lords, farewell:
Share the advice betwixt you; if both gain, all
The gift doth stretch itself as 'tis received,
And is enough for both.

First Lord. 'Tis our hope, sir,
After well-enter'd soldiers, to return
And find your Grace in health.

King. No, no, it cannot be; and yet my heart
Will not confess he owes the malady
That doth my life besiege. Farewell, young lords;
Whether I live or die, be you the sons
Of worthy Frenchmen: let higher Italy,—
Those bated that inherit but the fall
Of the last monarchy,—see that you come
Not to woo honour, but to wed it; when
The bravest questant shrinks, find what you seek,
That fame may cry you loud: I say, farewell.

Sec. Lord. Health, at your bidding, serve your majesty!

ACT II.] Actus Secundus. Ff (Sæcundus F_2).

Enter...attended...] Capell. Enter ...warre: Count Rosse, and Parolles. Florish Cornets. Ff.

divers] two Hanmer. om. Steevens.

1, 2. *lords...lords*] Ff. *lord...lord* Hanmer. See note (VI).

2. *and you*] *you* Pope.

3. *both gain, all*] Ff. *both gain,* Pope. *both gain, well!* Hanmer. *both gain all,* Johnson. *back again,* Jackson conj. *both gain, All* Anon. conj. See note (VII).

5. First Lord] 1. Lord. Rowe. Lord G. Ff.

'Tis] Ff. *It is* Steevens.

9. *he owes*] *it owns* Pope. *he owns* Long MS.

12. *higher*] *hired* Coleridge conj.

13. *bated*] *bastards* Hanmer. *'bated ones* Capell conj.

15, 16. *wed it; when...shrinks,*] Pope. *wed it, when...shrinkes:* $F_1F_2F_3$. *wed it, when...shrinks;* F_4.

16. *questant*] F_1. *question* $F_2F_3F_4$. *questor* Collier MS.

18. Sec. Lord.] 2. Lord. Rowe (ed. 2). L. G. Ff. 1. Lord. Rowe (ed. 1).

King. Those girls of Italy, take heed of them:
They say, our French lack language to deny,
If they demand: beware of being captives,
Before you serve.

Both. Our hearts receive your warnings.

King. Farewell. Come hither to me. [*Exit.*

First Lord. O my sweet lord, that you will stay behind us!

Par. 'Tis not his fault, the spark.

Sec. Lord. O, 'tis brave wars!

Par. Most admirable: I have seen those wars.

Ber. I am commanded here, and kept a coil with
'Too young,' and 'the next year,' and ''tis too early.'

Par. An thy mind stand to't, boy, steal away bravely.

Ber. I shall stay here the forehorse to a smock,
Creaking my shoes on the plain masonry,
Till honour be bought up, and no sword worn
But one to dance with! By heaven, I'll steal away.

First Lord. There's honour in the theft.

Par. Commit it, count.

Sec. Lord. I am your accessary; and so, farewell.

Ber. I grow to you, and our parting is a tortured body.

First Lord. Farewell, captain.

Sec. Lord. Sweet Monsieur Parolles!

22. Both.] Rowe. Bo. Ff.

23. *Come......me*] *Come......me* [to Bert.] Pope. om. Hanmer. *Come...me* [to Attendants]. Theobald.

Exit.] Pope. om. Ff. Retires to a Couch; Attendants leading him. Capell. See note (VIII).

24, 34, 37. First Lord.] 1. Lord. Rowe. 1. Lo. G. Ff.

25. *fault, the spark.*] F_3F_4. *fault the spark.* F_1F_2. *fault, the spark—* Rowe. *fault; the spark—* Theobald.

25, 35, 38. Sec. Lord.] 2. Lord. Rowe. 2. Lo. E. Ff.

27. *a coil*] *acoyle* F_2.

27, 28. *with 'Too young'*] Pope. *with, Too young* Ff. *with; 'Too young'* Capell.

29. *An...to't, boy,...bravely*] Theobald. *And...too 't boy, Steale away bravely* $F_1F_2F_3$. *And...to it...* F_4. *And thy mind—stand to it, boy; steal away bravely.* Pope.

30. *I shall stay*] *I stay* Rowe. *Shall I stay* Pope.

36. *I...our...a tortured body*] *I...this our...A tortur'd body* Hanmer. *I...our...the parting of a tortured body* Johnson conj. *I...our...a torture* Capell. *I...our...as a tortured body* S. Walker conj., reading lines 34—37 *Commit...captain.* as three lines, ending *accessary...parting...captain.*

to you] *t' ye* S. Walker conj.

37. *captain*] *worthy captain* Hanmer.

Par. Noble heroes, my sword and yours are kin. Good sparks and lustrous, a word, good metals: you shall find in the regiment of the Spinii one Captain Spurio, with his cicatrice, an emblem of war, here on his sinister cheek; it was this very sword entrenched it: say to him, I live; and observe his reports for me.

First Lord. We shall, noble captain. [*Exeunt Lords.*

Par. Mars dote on you for his novices! what will ye do?

Ber. Stay: the king.

Re-enter KING.

Par. [*Aside to Ber.*] Use a more spacious ceremony to the noble lords; you have restrained yourself within the list of too cold an adieu: be more expressive to them: for they wear themselves in the cap of the time, there do muster true gait, eat, speak, and move under the influence of the most received star; and though the devil lead the measure, such are to be followed: after them, and take a more dilated farewell.

Ber. And I will do so.

Par. Worthy fellows; and like to prove most sinewy sword-men. [*Exeunt Bertram and Parolles.*

Enter LAFEU.

Laf. [*Kneeling*] Pardon, my lord, for me and for my tidings.

39. *yours*] *yours* [measuring swords with them] Capell.

40. *a word*] *in a word* Long MS.

41, 42. *with his cicatrice, an emblem*] Theobald. *his cicatrice, with an emblem* Ff (*sicatrice* F_1). *he's cicatriced with an emblem* Rann conj.

44. *for*] F_1 F_2. *of* F_3 F_4.

45. First Lord.] 1. Lord. Rowe. Lo. G. F_1F_2. L. G. F_3F_4. 2. Lord. Warburton. Both. Edd. conj.

46. *novices! what will ye do?*] *novices, what will ye do?* Ff (*doe* F_1F_2). See note (IX).

ye] *you* Hanmer.

47. *Stay: the king.*] F_2 F_3 F_4. *Stay the king.* F_1. *Stay; the king—* Pope. *Stay with the king* Grant White (Collier conj.).

Re-enter King.] Edd. See note (VIII).

51. *there do muster*] *there, to muster* Warburton. *they do muster with the* Johnson conj. *there do master* Heath conj. *they do master* Collier conj. *there demonstrate* Anon. conj.

51, 52. *there...gait*] *do muster your true gaité* Becket conj. om. Collier MS.

true gait] *together* Hanmer.

52. *eat*] *dress* Hanmer. *they eat* Singer conj.

move] F_1. *more* $F_2F_3F_4$.

57. Exeunt B. and P.] Exeunt. Ff.

58. SCENE II. Pope.

Enter L.] Enter the King and L. Pope. Enter L. hastily. Capell.

Kneeling] Johnson. om. Ff.

King. I'll fee thee to stand up.

Laf. Then here's a man stands, that has brought his pardon.
I would you had kneel'd, my lord, to ask me mercy;
And that at my bidding you could so stand up.

King. I would I had; so I had broke thy pate,
And ask'd thee mercy for't.

Laf. Good faith, across: but, my good lord, 'tis thus;
Will you be cured of your infirmity?

King. No.

Laf. O, will you eat no grapes, my royal fox?
Yes, but you will my noble grapes, an if
My royal fox could reach them: I have seen a medicine
That's able to breathe life into a stone,
Quicken a rock, and make you dance canary
With spritely fire and motion; whose simple touch
Is powerful to araise King Pepin, nay,
To give great Charlemain a pen in's hand,
And write to her a love-line.

King. What 'her' is this?

Laf. Why, Doctor She: my lord, there's one arrived,
If you will see her: now, by my faith and honour,
If seriously I may convey my thoughts
In this my light deliverance, I have spoke
With one that, in her sex, her years, profession,

59. *I'll fee*] Theobald. *Ile see* Ff. *I'll sue* Staunton. *I'll free* Anon. ap. Halliwell conj. *I beseech* Keightley conj.

59—62. Capell ends the lines *man ...I would you...mercy; and...up.*

60. *has*] F_1. *hath* F_2 F_3 F_4.

brought] Ff. *bought* Theobald.

63, 64. *I would...for't*] *You would ...for't?* Anon. conj.

64—70. Capell ends the lines *across:...cur'd...eat...will...fox...medicine.*

65. *across*] *a cross* F_4.

69. *my noble grapes*] omitted by Hanmer, ending the line at *fox.* *aye, noble grapes* Collier MS.

70. *seen a medicine*] *seen A medicine* Anon. conj.

medicine] *med'cin* (in italics) Theobald. *medecin* Steevens.

74. *araise*] *raise* Pope. *upraise* Collier MS.

Pepin] Theobald. *Pippen* Ff.

75. *To give*] *And give* Capell.

in's] *in his* Capell. Malone supposes a line to be lost after this.

76. *And write*] *To write* Hanmer. *And cause him write* Singer conj.

to her a love-line] *a love-line to her* Hanmer.

77. *Doctor She*] Grant White. *doctor she* Ff. *Doctor-she* Theobald.

79. *convey*] *convay* F_1. *convoy* F_2 F_3 F_4.

Wisdom and constancy, hath amazed me more
Than I dare blame my weakness: will you see her,
For that is her demand, and know her business?
That done, laugh well at me.

King. Now, good Lafeu,
Bring in the admiration; that we with thee
May spend our wonder too, or take off thine
By wondering how thou took'st it.

Laf. Nay, I'll fit you,
And not be all day neither. [*Exit.*

King. Thus he his special nothing ever prologues.

Re-enter LAFEU, *with* HELENA.

Laf. Nay, come your ways.

King. This haste hath wings indeed.

Laf. Nay, come your ways;
This is his majesty, say your mind to him:
A traitor you do look like; but such traitors
His majesty seldom fears: I am Cressid's uncle,
That dare leave two together; fare you well. [*Exit.*

King. Now, fair one, does your business follow us?

Hel. Ay, my good lord.
Gerard de Narbon was my father;
In what he did profess, well found.

King. I knew him.

Hel. The rather will I spare my praises towards him;
Knowing him is enough. On's bed of death
Many receipts he gave me; chiefly one,

83. *Than...weakness*] *Than* (*blame my weakness*) *I dare—* Becket conj.
blame] *blaze* Theobald conj.
89. Exit] Theobald. om. Ff.
90. *nothing*] *nothings* Hanmer.
Re-enter L. with H.] Enter Hellen. Ff (after line 91 *come your ways*).
91. Laf. *Nay,...ways*] Laf. [Returns.] *Nay...ways* [Bringing in Helena. Theobald.
95. *I am*] *I'm* Pope.
96. Exit] Ff. Exit. Attendants retire. Capell. See note (VIII).
97. SCENE III.] Pope.
98—100. *Ay...him*] As in Ff. As three lines, ending *was...found...him.* Hanmer. As two, ending *father... him.* Capell.
99. *Gerard de Narbon*] *Gerardo of Narbona* Anon. conj.
100. *In*] *One in* S. Walker conj.
101. *praises*] *praise* Theobald.
102. *On's*] *On his* Capell.
103. *receipts*] Rowe. *receits* Ff.

Which, as the dearest issue of his practice,
And of his old experience the only darling,
He bade me store up, as a triple eye,
Safer than mine own two, more dear; I have so:
And, hearing your high majesty is touch'd
With that malignant cause, wherein the honour
Of my dear father's gift stands chief in power,
I come to tender it and my appliance,
With all bound humbleness.

King. We thank you, maiden;
But may not be so credulous of cure,
When our most learned doctors leave us, and
The congregated college have concluded
That labouring art can never ransom nature
From her inaidible estate; I say we must not
So stain our judgement, or corrupt our hope,
To prostitute our past-cure malady
To empirics, or to dissever so
Our great self and our credit, to esteem
A senseless help, when help past sense we deem.

Hel. My duty, then, shall pay me for my pains:
I will no more enforce mine office on you;
Humbly entreating from your royal thoughts
A modest one, to bear me back again.

King. I cannot give thee less, to be call'd grateful:
Thou thought'st to help me; and such thanks I give
As one near death to those that wish him live:
But, what at full I know, thou know'st no part;
I knowing all my peril, thou no art.

Hel. What I can do can do no hurt to try,
Since you set up your rest 'gainst remedy
He that of greatest works is finisher,
Oft does them by the weakest minister:

105. *the*] *th'* Ff.

107. *two, more dear*] Steevens. *two: more dear* Ff.

109, 110. *honour...power*] *power ...honour* Rann (Johnson conj.).

116. *ransom*] *answer* Steevens (1778).

117. *inaidible*] *inaydible* $F_1 F_2$. *unaydible* $F_3 F_4$. *unaidable* Rowe. *inaidable* Capell.

estate] *state* S. Walker conj.

I say] om. Pope.

118. *stain*] *strain* Anon. conj.

124. *mine*] F_1. *my* $F_2 F_3 F_4$.

So holy writ in babes hath judgement shown,
When judges have been babes; great floods have flown
From simple sources; and great seas have dried,
When miracles have by the greatest been denied.
Oft expectation fails, and most oft there
Where most it promises; and oft it hits
Where hope is coldest, and despair most fits.

King. I must not hear thee; fare thee well, kind maid;
Thy pains not used must by thyself be paid:
Proffers not took reap thanks for their reward.

Hel. Inspired merit so by breath is barr'd:
It is not so with Him that all things knows,
As 'tis with us that square our guess by shows;
But most it is presumption in us when
The help of heaven we count the act of men.
Dear sir, to my endeavours give consent;
Of heaven, not me, make an experiment.
I am not an impostor, that proclaim
Myself against the level of mine aim;
But know I think, and think I know most sure,
My art is not past power, nor you past cure.

King. Art thou so confident? within what space
Hopest thou my cure?

Hel. The great'st grace lending grace,
Ere twice the horses of the sun shall bring
Their fiery torcher his diurnal ring;
Ere twice in murk and occidental damp
Moist Hesperus hath quench'd his sleepy lamp;
Or four and twenty times the pilot's glass
Hath told the thievish minutes how they pass;
What is infirm from your sound parts shall fly,
Health shall live free, and sickness freely die.

King. Upon thy certainty and confidence

139. *miracles...greatest*] *miracles... great'st* Ff. *mir'cles...greatest* Theobald. Johnson supposes a line lost after this.

142. *fits*] Collier (Theobald conj.). *shifts* Ff. *sits* Pope. See note (x).

153. *impostor*] F_3 F_4. *impostrue* F_1 F_2. *imposture* Capell.

158. *The great'st grace lending*] Capell. *The greatest grace lending* Ff. *The Greatest lending* Rowe.

162. *his*] Rowe. *her* Ff.

What darest thou venture?
Hel. Tax of impudence,
A strumpet's boldness, a divulged shame
Traduced by odious ballads: my maiden's name
Sear'd otherwise, ne worse of worst extended,
With vilest torture let my life be ended.
King. Methinks in thee some blessed spirit doth speak
His powerful sound within an organ weak:
And what impossibility would slay
In common sense, sense saves another way.
Thy life is dear; for all, that life can rate
Worth name of life, in thee hath estimate,
Youth, beauty, wisdom, courage, all
That happiness and prime can happy call:
Thou this to hazard needs must intimate
Skill infinite or monstrous desperate.
Sweet practiser, thy physic I will try,
That ministers thine own death if I die.
Hel. If I break time, or flinch in property
Of what I spoke, unpitied let me die,
And well deserved: not helping, death's my fee;

169, 170. *shame......ballads: my maiden's name*] Ff. *shame;...ballads my maiden's name,* Theobald conj. *shame;...ballads: my maiden's name* Id. conj. *shame,...ballads my maiden name* Johnson conj.

171. *Sear'd otherwise, ne worse of...*] F_1. *Seard otherwise, no worse of...* $F_2 F_3 F_4$. *Sear'd otherwise no worse of worst: extended* Theobald conj. *Sear'd, otherwise no worse of worst extended;* Id. conj. *Sear'd: otherwise, the worst of...* Hanmer. *Sear'd otherwise, to worst of...* Johnson conj. *Fear otherwise to worst of...* Id. conj. *Sear'd; otherwise the worst to...* Id. conj. *Fear, otherwise, to worst of worse* Heath conj. *Sear'd otherwise; or, worse to...* Capell. *Sear'd otherwise, as worse of...* Long MS. *Fear'd o' the wise no worse if...* Mason conj. *Sear'd otherwise; nay, worst of...* Malone conj. *Sear'd otherwise; the worst of...* Id. conj. *Sear'd otherwise; the worst of...* Rann. *Sear'd otherwise; nay, worse of...* Singer.

ne...extended] *and worse, if worse, attended* Becket conj. *and, worse of worst expended* Staunton conj. *on worst of racks extended* Anon. conj. *nay, worse, if worse, extended* Anon. conj.

173, 174. *speak His powerful sound*] *speak, It powerful sounds* Hanmer. *speak: His power full sounds* Warburton. *O powerful sound* Becket conj. (transposing lines 173, 174).

174. *within*] F_1. *wherein* $F_2F_3F_4$.

179. *courage*] *courage, virtue* Theobald. *courage, honour* Collier (Collier MS.).

180. *and prime*] *and pride* Tyrwhitt conj. *in prime* Rann (Mason conj.).

But, if I help, what do you promise me?
King. Make thy demand.
Hel. But will you make it even?
King. Ay, by my sceptre and my hopes of heaven.
Hel. Then shalt thou give me with thy kingly hand
What husband in thy power I will command:
Exempted be from me the arrogance
To choose from forth the royal blood of France,
My low and humble name to propagate
With any branch or image of thy state;
But such a one, thy vassal, whom I know
Is free for me to ask, thee to bestow.
King. Here is my hand; the premises observed,
Thy will by my performance shall be served:
So make the choice of thy own time; for I,
Thy resolved patient, on thee still rely.
More should I question thee, and more I must,
Though more to know could not be more to trust,
From whence thou camest, how tended on: but rest
Unquestion'd welcome, and undoubted blest.
Give me some help here, ho! If thou proceed
As high as word, my deed shall match thy deed.
[*Flourish. Exeunt.*

SCENE II. *Rousillon. The* COUNT'S *palace.*

Enter COUNTESS *and* CLOWN.

Count. Come on, sir; I shall now put you to the height of your breeding.

Clo. I will show myself highly fed and lowly taught: I know my business is but to the court.

190. *heaven*] Theobald (Thirlby conj.). *helpe* F_1 F_2. *help* F_3 F_4.
196. *image*] *impage* Warburton.
201. *make the*] *make thee* Anon. conj.
thy] F_1. *thine* F_2 F_3 F_4.
208. *thy deed*] *thy meed* Anon. conj.
[Flourish. Exeunt.] Florish. Exit. F_1. Exeunt. F_2 F_3 F_4.
SCENE II.] SCENE IV. Pope.
1. Count.] Lady. Ff (and Lady. or La. throughout the scene).

Count. To the court! why, what place make you special, when you put off that with such contempt? But to the court!

Clo. Truly, madam, if God have lent a man any manners, he may easily put it off at court: he that cannot make a leg, put off's cap, kiss his hand, and say nothing, has neither leg, hands, lip, nor cap; and, indeed, such a fellow, to say precisely, were not for the court; but for me, I have an answer will serve all men.

Count. Marry, that's a bountiful answer that fits all questions.

Clo. It is like a barber's chair, that fits all buttocks, the pin-buttock, the quatch-buttock, the brawn-buttock, or any buttock.

Count. Will your answer serve fit to all questions?

Clo. As fit as ten groats is for the hand of an attorney, as your French crown for your taffeta punk, as Tib's rush for Tom's forefinger, as a pancake for Shrove Tuesday, a morris for May-day, as the nail to his hole, the cuckold to his horn, as a scolding quean to a wrangling knave, as the nun's lip to the friar's mouth, nay, as the pudding to his skin.

Count. Have you, I say, an answer of such fitness for all questions?

Clo. From below your duke to beneath your constable, it will fit any question.

Count. It must be an answer of most monstrous size that must fit all demands.

Clo. But a trifle neither, in good faith, if the learned should speak truth of it: here it is, and all that belongs to't. Ask me if I am a courtier: it shall do you no harm to learn.

Count. To be young again, if we could: I will be a fool in question, hoping to be the wiser by your answer. I pray you, sir, are you a courtier?

5. *To the court*] *But to the court* Theobald.

6. *contempt?...court!*] Pope. *contempt,...Court?* Ff.

11. *court; but for me,*] Rowe. *court, but for me,* Ff. *court, but for me:* Pope.

18. *serve fit*] *sir, fit* Anon. conj. *fit* Anon. conj.

20, 21. *Tib's...Tom's*] *Tom's...Tib's* Hawkins conj.

36. *I pray...*] F_3. La. *I pray...* F_1 F_2. Lady. *I pray...* F_4.

Clo. O Lord, sir! There's a simple putting off. More, more, a hundred of them.

Count. Sir, I am a poor friend of yours, that loves you.

Clo. O Lord, sir! Thick, thick, spare not me.

Count. I think, sir, you can eat none of this homely meat.

Clo. O Lord, sir! Nay, put me to't, I warrant you.

Count. You were lately whipped, sir, as I think.

Clo. O Lord, sir! spare not me.

Count. Do you cry, 'O Lord, sir!' at your whipping, and 'spare not me'? Indeed your 'O Lord, sir!' is very sequent to your whipping: you would answer very well to a whipping, if you were but bound to't.

Clo. I ne'er had worse luck in my life in my 'O Lord, sir!' I see things may serve long, but not serve ever.

Count. I play the noble housewife with the time,
To entertain 't so merrily with a fool.

Clo. O Lord, sir! why, there't serves well again.

Count. An end, sir; to your business. Give Helen this,
And urge her to a present answer back:
Commend me to my kinsmen and my son:
This is not much.

Clo. Not much commendation to them.

Count. Not much employment for you: you understand me?

Clo. Most fruitfully: I am there before my legs.

Count. Haste you again. [*Exeunt severally.*

50. *but*] *and* Hanmer.

51, 52. Printed as prose in Ff. As verse first by Knight.

51. *housewife*] *huswife* Ff.

52. *entertain 't*] Edd. (S. Walker conj.). *entertain it* Ff.

54. *An end, sir; to*] Rowe (ed. 2). *And end sir to* F_1 F_2. *And end; sir to* F_3 F_4.

57. *is not*] *isn't* Hanmer.

62. [Exeunt severally] Capell. Exeunt. Ff.

SCENE III. *Paris. The* KING'S *palace.*

Enter BERTRAM, LAFEU, *and* PAROLLES.

Laf. They say miracles are past; and we have our philosophical persons, to make modern and familiar, things supernatural and causeless. Hence is it that we make trifles of terrors; ensconcing ourselves into seeming knowledge, when we should submit ourselves to an unknown fear.

Par. Why, 'tis the rarest argument of wonder that hath shot out in our latter times.

Ber. And so 'tis.

Laf. To be relinquished of the artists,—

Par. So I say; both of Galen and Paracelsus.

Laf. Of all the learned and authentic fellows,—

Par. Right; so I say.

Laf. That gave him out incurable,—

Par. Why, there 'tis; so say I too.

Laf. Not to be helped,—

Par. Right; as 'twere, a man assured of a—

Laf. Uncertain life, and sure death.

Par. Just, you say well; so would I have said.

Laf. I may truly say, it is a novelty to the world.

Par. It is, indeed: if you will have it in showing, you shall read it in—what do ye call there?

Laf. A showing of a heavenly effect in an earthly actor.

Par. That's it; I would have said the very same.

SCENE III.] SCENE V. Pope.
1. Laf.] Ol. Laf. Ff (and throughout the scene).
and] *yet* Anon. apud Halliwell.
2. *persons*] *person* F_3F_4. *reasons* Long MS.
familiar, things] Theobald. *familiar things* Ff. *familiar things,* Steevens.
6. Par.] Ber. S. Walker conj.
7. *latter*] *later* Hanmer.
8. Ber.] Par. S. Walker conj.
10, 11. Par. *So...Paracelsus.* Laf. *Of all...*] Par. *So I say.* Laf. *Both... Paracelsus, of all...* Johnson conj. Par. *So I say.* Laf. *Both...Paracelsus.* Par. *So I say.* Laf. *Of all...* Edd. conj.
11. Laf.] Ol. Laf. $F_1F_3F_4$. Ol. Fal. F_2.
16. *a*—] *an*— Rowe.
20. *in showing*] *in shewing* F_1F_2. *in the shewing* F_3F_4. *a showing* Rann (Tyrwhitt conj.).
23. *it;...said the*] *it,...said the* F_4. *it,...said, the* $F_1F_2F_3$. *it,...said; the* Capell.

Laf. Why, your dolphin is not lustier: 'fore me, I speak in respect—

Par. Nay, 'tis strange, 'tis very strange, that is the brief and the tedious of it; and he's of a most facinerious spirit that will not acknowledge it to be the—

Laf. Very hand of heaven.

Par. Ay, so I say.

Laf. In a most weak—

Par. And debile minister, great power, great transcendence: which should, indeed, give us a further use to be made than alone the recovery of the king, as to be—

Laf. Generally thankful.

Par. I would have said it; you say well. Here comes the king.

Enter KING, HELENA, *and* Attendants.

Laf. Lustig, as the Dutchman says: I'll like a maid the better, whilst I have a tooth in my head: why, he's able to lead her a coranto.

Par. Mort du vinaigre! is not this Helen?

Laf. 'Fore God, I think so.

King. Go, call before me all the lords in court.
Sit, my preserver, by thy patient's side;
And with this healthful hand, whose banish'd sense
Thou hast repeal'd, a second time receive
The confirmation of my promised gift,
Which but attends thy naming.

24. *dolphin*] *Dauphin* Theobald conj. (withdrawn).

'fore] Capell. *fore* F_1. *for* $F_2 F_3 F_4$.

27. *facinerious*] Ff. *facinorous* Steevens.

31—34. Laf. *In a most weak*— Par. *And...king, as to be*—] Laf. *In a most...king.* Par. *As to be*— Rann (Johnson conj.). Laf. *In....weak*— Par. *Ay, so I say.* Laf. *And debile... king, as to be* [after a pause] *generally thankful* Edd. conj.

33. *give us a further*] *give us* * * * *a further* Warburton.

34. *alone*] F_1. *only* $F_2 F_3 F_4$.

36. SCENE VI. Pope.

say] F_1. *said* $F_2 F_3 F_4$.

37. Enter...] Ff (after line 35).

38. *Lustig*] *Lustique* $F_1 F_2$. *Lustick* $F_3 F_4$. *Lustigh* Capell.

39. *whilst*] F_1. *while* $F_2 F_3 F_4$.

40. *coranto*] *carranto* Ff. *corranto* Rowe.

41. *Mort du vinaigre*] *Mor du vinager* Ff. *Mort du vainqueur* Collier.

43. [Exeunt some attendants. Capell.

Enter three or four Lords.

Fair maid, send forth thine eye: this youthful parcel
Of noble bachelors stand at my bestowing,
O'er whom both sovereign power and father's voice
I have to use: thy frank election make;
Thou hast power to choose, and they none to forsake.

Hel. To each of you one fair and virtuous mistress
Fall, when Love please! marry, to each, but one!

Laf. I'd give bay Curtal and his furniture,
My mouth no more were broken than these boys',
And writ as little beard.

King. Peruse them well:
Not one of those but had a noble father.

Hel. Gentlemen,
Heaven hath through me restored the king to health.

All. We understand it, and thank heaven for you.

Hel. I am a simple maid; and therein wealthiest,
That I protest I simply am a maid.
Please it your majesty, I have done already:
The blushes in my cheeks thus whisper me,
'We blush that thou shouldst choose; but, be refused,
Let the white death sit on thy cheek for ever;
We'll ne'er come there again.'

King. Make choice; and, see,
Who shuns thy love shuns all his love in me.

Hel. Now, Dian, from thy altar do I fly;
And to imperial Love, that god most high,

51. *sovereign*] *sovereign's* Collier MS.

54, 55. *mistress Fall,*] Rowe. *mistress; Fall* Ff.

54. [coming from her Seat, and addressing herself to the Lords. Capell.

55. *marry...one!*] Par. *Marry... one!* Tyrwhitt conj.

58. *writ*] *with* Collier MS.

60. [She addresses her to a Lord. Ff.

60, 61. *Gentlemen......health*] Arranged as in Capell. Printed as prose in Ff; as two lines by Theobald, ending *restor'd...health.*

67. *choose; but, be refused,*] Rann. *choose, but be refused;* Ff. *chuse: but being refused* Hanmer.

67—69. *We blush...again*] Kin. *We blush...again* F_3 F_4.

68. *Let the*] *Let not* F_3 F_4.
death] *dearth* Warburton conj.
cheek] *cheeks* F_3 F_4.

69. King.] om. F_3 F_4.

72. *imperial Love*] *imperiall loue* F_1. *imperiall Iove* F_2. *impartiall Jove* F_3. *impartial Jove* F_4. *impartial love* Warburton.

Do my sighs stream. Sir, will you hear my suit?
First Lord. And grant it.
Hel. Thanks, sir; all the rest is mute.
Laf. I had rather be in this choice than throw
Ames-ace for my life.
Hel. The honour, sir, that flames in your fair eyes,
Before I speak, too threateningly replies:
Love make your fortunes twenty times above
Her that so wishes and her humble love!
Sec. Lord. No better, if you please.
Hel. My wish receive,
Which great Love grant! and so, I take my leave.

Laf. Do all they deny her? An they were sons of mine, I'd have them whipped; or I would send them to the Turk, to make eunuchs of.

Hel. Be not afraid that I your hand should take;
I'll never do you wrong for your own sake:
Blessing upon your vows! and in your bed
Find fairer fortune, if you ever wed!

Laf. These boys are boys of ice, they'll none have her: sure, they are bastards to the English; the French ne'er got 'em.

Hel. You are too young, too happy, and too good,
To make yourself a son out of my blood.
Fourth Lord. Fair one, I think not so.

Laf. There's one grape yet; I am sure thy father drunk wine: but if thou be'st not an ass, I am a youth of fourteen; I have known thee already.

Hel. [*To Bertram*] I dare not say I take you; but I give

73. *stream*] *steam* Collier MS.
74. *is mute*] *are mute* Pope.
75. Laf.] Par. Theobald conj.
76. *Ames-ace*] F_1. *A deaus-ace* F_2 F_3 F_4.
78. *threateningly*] *threatingly* F_2.
82. *Love*] F_1 F_2. *Jove* F_3 F_4.
83. *all they*] *they all* Capell conj. *An*] Capell. *And* Ff. *If* Pope.
84, 85. *to the*] *to'th* Ff.
89. *fairer*] *fair* Rann. *ever*] F_1. *ere* F_2 F_3 F_4.
90, 91. *have her*] *haue heere* F_1. *of her* Rowe.
90—92. S. Walker would read as three lines of verse, ending *her...English...got 'em.*
92. *'em*] *them* Capell.
93. Hel.] F_3 F_4. La. F_1 F_2.
96, 98. Laf. *There's...already*] Laf. *There's...yet,*— Par. *I am sure...wine.* — Laf. *But...already* Theobald.
96. *thy*] F_1. *my* F_2 F_3 F_4.
99. [To Bertram] Rowe.

Me and my service, ever whilst I live,
Into your guiding power. This is the man.

King. Why, then, young Bertram, take her; she's thy wife.

Ber. My wife, my liege! I shall beseech your highness,
In such a business give me leave to use
The help of mine own eyes.

King. Know'st thou not, Bertram,
What she has done for me?

Ber. Yes, my good lord;
But never hope to know why I should marry her.

King. Thou know'st she has raised me from my sickly bed.

Ber. But follows it, my lord, to bring me down
Must answer for your raising? I know her well:
She had her breeding at my father's charge.
A poor physician's daughter my wife! Disdain
Rather corrupt me ever!

King. 'Tis only title thou disdain'st in her, the which
I can build up. Strange is it, that our bloods,
Of colour, weight, and heat, pour'd all together,
Would quite confound distinction, yet stand off
In differences so mighty. If she be
All that is virtuous, save what thou dislikest,
A poor physician's daughter, thou dislikest
Of virtue for the name: but do not so:
From lowest place when virtuous things proceed,
The place is dignified by the doer's deed:
Where great additions swell's, and virtue none,
It is a dropsied honour. Good alone

105, 107. *Know'st thou not...her*] Arranged as in Pope; printed as prose in Ff.

106. *has*] *h'as* $F_1 F_2$. *hath* $F_3 F_4$.

112. *my wife! Disdain Rather*] *she my wife! Disdain rather* Hanmer.

114. *only title*] *But title* Hanmer. *only lack of title* S. Walker conj.

116. *Of colour*] *Alike of colour* Capell.

117. *stand*] Rowe (ed. 2). *stands* Ff.

118. *so*] F_1. *of* $F_2 F_3 F_4$. om. Long MS.

121. *the name*] *a name* Collier conj.

122. *place when*] Theobald (Thirlby conj). *place, whence* Ff.

123. *by the*] *by th'* Ff.

124. *additions swell's*] F_1. *addition swell's* F_2. *addition swells* $F_3 F_4$. *additions swell* Malone.

125. *honour.*] *honour,* Ff.

125, 126. *Good...so:*] *Good a lone,*

Is good without a name. Vileness is so:
The property by what it is should go,
Not by the title. She is young, wise, fair;
In these to nature she's immediate heir,
And these breed honour: that is honour's scorn,
Which challenges itself as honour's born,
And is not like the sire: honours thrive,
When rather from our acts we them derive
Than our foregoers: the mere word's a slave
Debosh'd on every tomb, on every grave
A lying trophy; and as oft is dumb
Where dust and damn'd oblivion is the tomb
Of honour'd bones indeed. What should be said?
If thou canst like this creature as a maid,
I can create the rest: virtue and she
Is her own dower; honour and wealth from me.

Ber. I cannot love her, nor will strive to do't.

King. Thou wrong'st thyself, if thou shouldst strive to choose.

Hel. That you are well restored, my lord, I'm glad:
Let the rest go.

King. My honour's at the stake; which to defeat,
I must produce my power. Here, take her hand,
Proud scornful boy, unworthy this good gift;
That dost in vile misprision shackle up
My love and her desert; that canst not dream,
We, poising us in her defective scale,

Is good without a name? Vilenesse is so: F_1 F_2. *Good alone,...name? Vileness is so:* F_3. *Good alone,...name. Vileness is so:* F_4. *good...name, in't self is so:* Hanmer. *good alone Is good; and, with a name, vileness is so:* Warburton. *good alone Is good, without a name vileness is so:* Johnson. *Virtue alone Is good without a name; Helen is so;* Johnson conj. *good alone Is good, without a name; in vileness is so* Steevens conj. *good alone Is good;—without a name, vileness is so* Mason conj.

127. *it is*] *is is* F_1.

128. *young*] *good* Warburton. *sprung* Becket conj.

131. *honour's born*] *honour-born* Hanmer.

132. *thrive*] F_1. *best thrive* F_2 F_3 F_4.

134. *word's*] $F_2F_3F_4$. *words*, F_1.

135. *grave*] *grave:* Ff.

137, 138. *tomb Of...indeed.*] Theobald (Thirlby conj.). *tomb. Of...indeed,* Ff.

146. *defeat,*] Ff. *defend* Theobald. *defeat,—* Id. conj.

Shall weigh thee to the beam; that wilt not know,
It is in us to plant thine honour where
We please to have it grow. Check thy contempt:
Obey our will, which travails in thy good:
Believe not thy disdain, but presently
Do thine own fortunes that obedient right
Which both thy duty owes and our power claims;
Or I will throw thee from my care for ever
Into the staggers and the careless lapse
Of youth and ignorance; both my revenge and hate
Loosing upon thee, in the name of justice,
Without all terms of pity. Speak; thine answer.

Ber. Pardon, my gracious lord; for I submit
My fancy to your eyes: when I consider
What great creation and what dole of honour
Flies where you bid it, I find that she, which late
Was in my nobler thoughts most base, is now
The praised of the king; who, so ennobled,
Is as 't were born so.

King. Take her by the hand,
And tell her she is thine: to whom I promise
A counterpoise; if not to thy estate,
A balance more replete.

Ber. I take her hand.

King. Good fortune and the favour of the king
Smile upon this contract; whose ceremony
Shall seem expedient on the now-born brief,
And be perform'd to-night: the solemn feast
Shall more attend upon the coming space,
Expecting absent friends. As thou lovest her,

155. *travails*] *trauailes* F_1. *travailes* F_2. *travells* F_3. *travels* F_4.
159. *throw*] *through* F_2.
care] F_1F_2. *cares* F_3F_4.
160. *staggers and the*] *staggering and* Long MS.
the careless] F_1. *careless* F_2. *the cureless* S. Walker conj.
161. *both*] om. Theobald.
162. *Loosing*] *Let loose* Hanmer.
163. *Speak; thine*] *Speak, thine* $F_1F_2F_3$. *Speak thine* F_4.
167. *bid it*] Ff. *bid* Rowe.
169. *praised*] *prised* Warburton.
who, so] *who's so* Long MS.
172. *to*] F_1. *in* $F_2F_3F_4$.
175. *this*] F_1. *the* $F_2F_3F_4$.
175—177. *whose...And be*] *what...Shall be* Johnson conj.
176. *now-born*] *now born* F_3F_4. *now borne* F_1F_2. *new-born* Warburton.

Thy love's to me religious; else, does err.

[Exeunt all but Lafeu and Parolles.

Laf. Do you hear, monsieur? a word with you.

Par. Your pleasure, sir?

Laf. Your lord and master did well to make his recantation.

Par. Recantation! My lord! my master!

Laf. Ay; is it not a language I speak?

Par. A most harsh one, and not to be understood without bloody succeeding. My master!

Laf. Are you companion to the Count Rousillon?

Par. To any count, to all counts, to what is man.

Laf. To what is count's man: count's master is of another style.

Par. You are too old, sir; let it satisfy you, you are too old.

Laf. I must tell thee, sirrah, I write man; to which title age cannot bring thee.

Par. What I dare too well do, I dare not do.

Laf. I did think thee, for two ordinaries, to be a pretty wise fellow; thou didst make tolerable vent of thy travel; it might pass: yet the scarfs and the bannerets about thee did manifoldly dissuade me from believing thee a vessel of too great a burthen. I have now found thee; when I lose thee again, I care not: yet art thou good for nothing but taking up; and that thou'rt scarce worth.

Par. Hadst thou not the privilege of antiquity upon thee,—

Laf. Do not plunge thyself too far in anger, lest thou hasten thy trial; which if—Lord have mercy on thee for a hen! So, my good window of lattice, fare thee well: thy casement I need not open, for I look through thee. Give me thy hand.

Par. My lord, you give me most egregious indignity.

180. [Exeunt...] Exeunt. Parolles and Lafew stay behind, commenting of this wedding. Ff.

181. SCENE VII. Pope.

199. *thou*] F_1F_2. *if thou* F_3F_4.

200. *bannerets*] F_1F_2. *banners* F_3F_4.

208. *if—*] Theobald. *if,* F_1F_2. *is,* F_3F_4.

209. *lattice*] F_3F_4. *lettice* F_1F_2.

210. *for*] om. F_3F_4.

Laf. Ay, with all my heart; and thou art worthy of it.

Par. I have not, my lord, deserved it.

Laf. Yes, good faith, every dram of it; and I will not bate thee a scruple.

Par. Well, I shall be wiser.

Laf. Ev'n as soon as thou canst, for thou hast to pull at a smack o' the contrary. If ever thou be'st bound in thy scarf and beaten, thou shalt find what it is to be proud of thy bondage. I have a desire to hold my acquaintance with thee, or rather my knowledge, that I may say in the default, he is a man I know.

Par. My lord, you do me most insupportable vexation.

Laf. I would it were hell-pains for thy sake, and my poor doing eternal: for doing I am past; as I will by thee, in what motion age will give me leave. [*Exit.*

Par. Well, thou hast a son shall take this disgrace off me; scurvy, old, filthy, scurvy lord! Well, I must be patient; there is no fettering of authority. I'll beat him, by my life, if I can meet him with any convenience, an he were double and double a lord. I'll have no more pity of his age than I would have of—I'll beat him, an if I could but meet him again.

Re-enter LAFEU.

Laf. Sirrah, your lord and master's married; there's news for you: you have a new mistress.

Par. I most unfeignedly beseech your lordship to make some reservation of your wrongs: he is my good lord: whom I serve above is my master.

Laf. Who? God?

Par. Ay, sir.

217. *wiser.*] *wiser—* Theobald.

219. *o' the*] Rowe (ed. 2). *a' th* Ff.

220. *shalt*] *shall* F_1.

222, 223. *in the default*] *on thy defaults* Hanmer.

226, 227. *for doing...leave*] Put in the margin as spurious by Hanmer.

226. *past; as I will*] *past; * * * as I will* Warburton, who supposes a line to be lost. *past; as I will be* Capell conj. *past, so I will by thee* Staunton conj.

229. *scurvy lord*] *scabby lord* Collier conj.

238, 239. *he...whom*] *he my good lord, whom* Rowe (ed. 2). *he, my good lord, whom* Pope.

239. *whom*] *he whom* Capell.

Laf. The devil it is that's thy master. Why dost thou garter up thy arms o' this fashion? dost make hose of thy sleeves? do other servants so? Thou wert best set thy lower part where thy nose stands. By mine honour, if I were but two hours younger, I'd beat thee: methinks't, thou art a general offence, and every man should beat thee: I think thou wast created for men to breathe themselves upon thee.

Par. This is hard and undeserved measure, my lord.

Laf. Go to, sir; you were beaten in Italy for picking a kernel out of a pomegranate; you are a vagabond, and no true traveller: you are more saucy with lords and honourable personages than the commission of your birth and virtue gives you heraldry. You are not worth another word, else I'd call you knave. I leave you. [*Exit.*

Par. Good, very good; it is so then: good, very good; let it be concealed awhile.

Re-enter BERTRAM.

Ber. Undone, and forfeited to cares for ever!

Par. What's the matter, sweet-heart?

Ber. Although before the solemn priest I have sworn,
I will not bed her.

Par. What, what, sweet-heart?

Ber. O my Parolles, they have married me!
I'll to the Tuscan wars, and never bed her.

Par. France is a dog-hole, and it no more merits
The tread of a man's foot: to the wars!

Ber. There's letters from my mother: what the import is, I know not yet.

Par. Ay, that would be known. To the wars, my boy, to the wars!

243. *o'*] Rowe (ed. 2). *a* Ff.
246. *methinks't*] Dyce (S. Walker conj.). *methink'st* Ff. *methinks* Rowe (ed. 2).
253, 254. *commission...heraldry*] Ff. *heraldry...commission* Hanmer. *condition......heraldry* Collier (Collier MS.).
256. SCENE VIII. Pope.
257. Re-enter B.] Enter Count Rossillion. Ff (after line 255).
259. *What's*] *What is* F_4.
260, 261. *Although...her*] Printed as prose in Ff, as verse first by Rowe (ed. 2).
265, 266. *France...wars*] Printed as verse in Ff, as prose by Pope.
266. *wars!*] *wars, Bertram!* or *wars, Rousillon!* Anon. conj.

He wears his honour in a box unseen,
That hugs his kicky-wicky here at home,
Spending his manly marrow in her arms,
Which should sustain the bound and high curvet
Of Mars's fiery steed. To other regions
France is a stable; we that dwell in't jades;
Therefore, to the war!

Ber. It shall be so: I'll send her to my house,
Acquaint my mother with my hate to her,
And wherefore I am fled; write to the king
That which I durst not speak: his present gift
Shall furnish me to those Italian fields,
Where noble fellows strike: war is no strife
To the dark house and the detested wife.

Par. Will this capriccio hold in thee, art sure?

Ber. Go with me to my chamber, and advise me.
I'll send her straight away: to-morrow
I'll to the wars, she to her single sorrow.

Par. Why, these balls bound; there's noise in it. 'Tis hard:
A young man married is a man that's marr'd:
Therefore away, and leave her bravely; go:
The king has done you wrong: but, hush, 'tis so. [*Exeunt.*

SCENE IV. *Paris. The King's Palace.*

Enter HELENA *and* CLOWN.

Hel. My mother greets me kindly: is she well?

Clo. She is not well; but yet she has her health: she's

271. *kicky-wicky*] *kickie wickie* F_1. *kicksie wicksie* F_2F_3. *kicksy wicksy* F_4. *kicksy-winsy* Collier conj.

274, 275. *regions France*] Pope. *regions, France* Ff. *regions! France* Capell.

282. *war*] *warres* F_1.

283. *detested*] Rowe. *detected* Ff. See note (XI).

286. *to-morrow*] *even to-morrow* Hanmer. *betimes to-morrow* Steevens conj.

290. *her bravely; go*] *her; bravely go* Delius.

SCENE IV.] SCENE IX. Pope.

The King's Palace.] Another room in the same. Capell.

2—5. S. Walker would read as four lines of verse, ending *health...not well...wants...well.*

very merry; but yet she is not well: but thanks be given, she's very well and wants nothing i' the world; but yet she is not well.

Hel. If she be very well, what does she ail, that she's not very well?

Clo. Truly, she's very well indeed, but for two things.

Hel. What two things?

Clo. One, that she's not in heaven, whither God send her quickly! the other, that she's in earth, from whence God send her quickly!

Enter PAROLLES.

Par. Bless you, my fortunate lady!

Hel. I hope, sir, I have your good will to have mine own good fortunes.

Par. You had my prayers to lead them on; and to keep them on, have them still. O, my knave, how does my old lady?

Clo. So that you had her wrinkles, and I her money, I would she did as you say.

Par. Why, I say nothing.

Clo. Marry, you are the wiser man; for many a man's tongue shakes out his master's undoing: to say nothing, to do nothing, to know nothing, and to have nothing, is to be a great part of your title; which is within a very little of nothing.

Par. Away! thou'rt a knave.

Clo. You should have said, sir, before a knave thou'rt a knave; that's, before me thou'rt a knave: this had been truth, sir.

Par. Go to, thou art a witty fool; I have found thee.

3. *but thanks*] *thanks* Hanmer.
10. *she's*] F_1. *she is* $F_2 F_3 F_4$.
11. *in earth*] *on earth* Hanmer.
from whence] *whence* Rowe (ed. 2).
15. *fortunes*] Capell (Heath conj.). *fortune* Ff.
23. *shakes out*] *speaks out* Warburton. *shapes out* Anon. conj. *shakes to* Anon. conj.
27. *thou'rt*] Rowe. *th' art* Ff. *Before God thou'rt* Anon. conj.
28, 29. *knave...knave;...me thou'rt*] *knave,...knave,...me th' art* $F_1 F_2$. *knave,...knave,...th' art* $F_3 F_4$. *knave; thou art a knave; and I am before thee that art* Hanmer.
28. *thou'rt*] Capell. *th' art* Ff.

Clo. Did you find me in yourself, sir? or were you taught to find me? The search, sir, was profitable; and much fool may you find in you, even to the world's pleasure and the increase of laughter.

Par. A good knave, i' faith, and well fed.
Madam, my lord will go away to-night;
A very serious business calls on him.
The great prerogative and rite of love,
Which, as your due, time claims, he does acknowledge;
But puts it off to a compell'd restraint;
Whose want, and whose delay, is strew'd with sweets,
Which they distil now in the curbed time,
To make the coming hour o'erflow with joy,
And pleasure drown the brim.

Hel. What's his will else?

Par. That you will take your instant leave o' the king,
And make this haste as your own good proceeding,
Strengthen'd with what apology you think
May make it probable need.

Hel. What more commands he?

Par. That, having this obtain'd, you presently
Attend his further pleasure.

Hel. In every thing I wait upon his will.

Par. I shall report it so.

Hel. I pray you. [*Exit Parolles.*]
Come, sirrah. [*Exeunt.*

33. *find me? The search*] Rowe. *find me?* Clo. *The search* Ff. *find me?* Par. *Go to, I say: I have found thee: no more; I have found thee, a witty fool.* Clo. *The search* Collier (Collier MS.).

39. *rite*] *right* Capell.

40. *due, time claims*] *duteous claim* or *duty's claim* Anon. conj.

41. *to*] F_1 F_2. *by* F_3 F_4. *on* Capell.

42. *is*] *are* Hanmer.

43. *curbed*] *cup of* Collier conj.

46. *o'*] Rowe. *a'* Ff.

53. [Exit Par.] Ff (after *so*).
you. Come] Theobald. *you come* Ff.
[Exeunt.] Exit. Ff.

SCENE V. *Paris. The King's Palace.*

Enter LAFEU *and* BERTRAM.

Laf. But I hope your lordship thinks not him a soldier.

Ber. Yes, my lord, and of very valiant approof.

Laf. You have it from his own deliverance.

Ber. And by other warranted testimony.

Laf. Then my dial goes not true: I took this lark for a bunting.

Ber. I do assure you, my lord, he is very great in knowledge, and accordingly valiant.

Laf. I have then sinned against his experience and transgressed against his valour; and my state that way is dangerous, since I cannot yet find in my heart to repent. Here he comes: I pray you, make us friends; I will pursue the amity.

Enter PAROLLES.

Par. These things shall be done, sir. [*To Bertram.*

Laf. Pray you, sir, who's his tailor?

Par. Sir?

Laf. O, I know him well, I, sir; he, sir, 's a good workman, a very good tailor.

Ber. Is she gone to the king? [*Aside to Parolles.*

Par. She is.

Ber. Will she away to-night?

Par. As you'll have her.

Ber. I have writ my letters, casketed my treasure,
Given order for our horses; and to-night,

SCENE V.] SCENE X. Pope.
The King's Palace.] Another room in the same. Capell.
11. *yet*] F_1. om. $F_2F_3F_4$.
14. [To Bertram.] Capell.
15. *Pray you*] *I pray you* Rowe. *who's*] *whose* F_1.
17. *sir, 's*] Theobald. *sir's* $F_2F_3F_4$. *sirs* F_1. *sits* Pope.
19. [Aside...] Rowe.
23—26. *I have...begin*] Printed as prose by Pope.
24. *horses*] F_1. *horse* $F_2 F_3 F_4$.

When I should take possession of the bride,
End ere I do begin.

Laf. A good traveller is something at the latter end of a dinner; but one that lies three thirds, and uses a known truth to pass a thousand nothings with, should be once heard, and thrice beaten. God save you, captain.

Ber. Is there any unkindness between my lord and you, monsieur?

Par. I know not how I have deserved to run into my lord's displeasure.

Laf. You have made shift to run into't, boots and spurs and all, like him that leaped into the custard; and out of it you'll run again, rather than suffer question for your residence.

Ber. It may be you have mistaken him, my lord.

Laf. And shall do so ever, though I took him at's prayers. Fare you well, my lord; and believe this of me, there can be no kernel in this light nut; the soul of this man is his clothes. Trust him not in matter of heavy consequence; I have kept of them tame, and know their natures. Farewell, monsieur: I have spoken better of you than you have or will to deserve at my hand; but we must do good against evil. [*Exit.*

Par. An idle lord, I swear.

Ber. I think so.

Par. Why, do you not know him?

Ber. Yes, I do know him well, and common speech
Gives him a worthy pass. Here comes my clog.

Enter HELENA.

Hel. I have, sir, as I was commanded from you,

25, 26. *bride, End...begin.*] Collier (Egerton MS.). *bride, And...begin* Ff. *bride—And...begin—* Rowe.

28. *one that*] Rowe (ed. 2). *on that* Ff. *if on that he* Rowe (ed. 1).

30. *heard*] *hard* F_1.

you] *your* F_2.

36. *leaped*] *leapt* F_1. *leapes* F_2. *leaps* F_3 F_4.

custard] See note (XII).

46. *or will*] *qualities or will* Malone conj. *wit or will* Singer conj.

to] F_1. om. F_2 F_3 F_4.

hand] F_1 F_2. *hands* F_3 F_4.

47. [Exit.] Rowe.

49. *so*] *not so* Long MS.

51, 52. *Yes......clog*] As prose in Hanmer.

53. SCENE XI. Pope.

Spoke with the king, and have procured his leave
For present parting; only he desires
Some private speech with you.

Ber. I shall obey his will.
You must not marvel, Helen, at my course,
Which holds not colour with the time, nor does
The ministration and required office
On my particular. Prepared I was not
For such a business; therefore am I found
So much unsettled: this drives me to entreat you,
That presently you take your way for home,
And rather muse than ask why I entreat you;
For my respects are better than they seem,
And my appointments have in them a need
Greater than shows itself at the first view
To you that know them not. This to my mother:
[*Giving a letter.*
'Twill be two days ere I shall see you; so,
I leave you to your wisdom.

Hel. Sir, I can nothing say,
But that I am your most obedient servant.

Ber. Come, come, no more of that.

Hel. And ever shall
With true observance seek to eke out that
Wherein toward me my homely stars have fail'd
To equal my great fortune.

Ber. Let that go:
My haste is very great: farewell; hie home.

Hel. Pray, sir, your pardon.

Ber. Well, what would you say?

Hel. I am not worthy of the wealth I owe;
Nor dare I say 'tis mine, and yet it is;
But, like a timorous thief, most fain would steal
What law does vouch mine own.

Ber. What would you have?

57. *must*] *must must* F_2.

64. *ask why I*] *ask why, I* Hanmer.

entreat you] *dismiss you* S. Walker conj. *request it* Bailey conj.

68. [Giving a letter.] Rowe.

75, 76. *Let...home*] Printed as prose in Ff.

Hel. Something; and scarce so much: nothing, indeed.
I would not tell you what I would, my lord: faith, yes;
Strangers and foes do sunder, and not kiss.
Ber. I pray you, stay not, but in haste to horse.
Hel. I shall not break your bidding, good my lord.
Ber. Where are my other men, monsieur? Farewell.
[*Exit Helena.*
Go thou toward home; where I will never come,
Whilst I can shake my sword, or hear the drum.
Away, and for our flight.
Par. Bravely, coragio! [*Exeunt.*

ACT III.

SCENE I. *Florence. The* DUKE'S *palace.*

Flourish. Enter the DUKE *of Florence, attended; the two Frenchmen with a troop of soldiers.*

Duke. So that from point to point now have you heard
The fundamental reasons of this war,
Whose great decision hath much blood let forth
And more thirsts after.
First Lord. Holy seems the quarrel
Upon your Grace's part; black and fearful
On the opposer.
Duke. Therefore we marvel much our cousin France
Would in so just a business shut his bosom
Against our borrowing prayers.

83, 84. *I would...kiss*] Arranged as in Ff. As three lines, ending *lord ...yes...kiss.* Dyce conj.

83. *my lord*] om. Hanmer.

87. Ber. *Where are......Farewell*] Hanmer (Theobald conj.): continued to Helena in Ff.

men, monsieur?] Hanmer (Theobald conj.). *men? Monsieur:* Ff.

[Exit H.] Hanmer. [Exit. Ff. [Exit Hel. Warburton (after line 86).

90. [Exeunt.] om. Ff.

...attended] Capell. om. Ff.

5. *part*] *party* S. Walker conj. *black*] *but black* Pope.

6. *opposer*] *opposer's* Hanmer.

Sec. Lord. Good my lord,
The reasons of our state I cannot yield,
But like a common and an outward man,
That the great figure of a council frames
By self-unable motion: therefore dare not
Say what I think of it, since I have found
Myself in my incertain grounds to fail
As often as I guess'd.
Duke. Be it his pleasure.
First Lord. But I am sure the younger of our nature,
That surfeit on their ease, will day by day
Come here for physic.
Duke. Welcome shall they be;
And all the honours that can fly from us
Shall on them settle. You know your places well;
When better fall, for your avails they fell:
To-morrow to the field. [*Flourish. Exeunt.*

SCENE II. *Rousillon. The* COUNT'S *Palace.*

Enter COUNTESS *and* CLOWN.

Count. It hath happened all as I would have had it, save that he comes not along with her.

Clo. By my troth, I take my young lord to be a very melancholy man.

Count. By what observance, I pray you?

Clo. Why, he will look upon his boot and sing; mend the ruff and sing; ask questions and sing; pick his teeth

9. Sec. Lord] 2 Lord. Rowe. French E. Ff.
13. *By*] *From* Theobald conj.
motion] *notion* Warburton (Theobald conj.).
17. First Lord] Fren. G. F_1. Fre. G. F_2 F_3 F_4. 2 Lord. Rowe.
nature] *nation* Rowe.
22. *fell*] *fall* Hanmer (Thirlby conj.).
23. *to*] *to 'th* F_1.
[Exeunt.] om. Ff.
7. *the ruff*] *his ruff* Rowe. *the ruffle* Whalley conj.

and sing. I know a man that had this trick of melancholy sold a goodly manor for a song.

Count. Let me see what he writes, and when he means to come. [*Opening a letter.*

Clo. I have no mind to Isbel since I was at court: our old ling and our Isbels o' the country are nothing like your old ling and your Isbels o' the court: the brains of my Cupid's knocked out, and I begin to love, as an old man loves money, with no stomach.

Count. What have we here?

Clo. E'en that you have there. [*Exit.*

Count. [*reads*] I have sent you a daughter-in-law: she hath recovered the king, and undone me. I have wedded her, not bedded her; and sworn to make the 'not' eternal. You shall hear I am run away: know it before the report come. If there be breadth enough in the world, I will hold a long distance. My duty to you.

Your unfortunate son,

BERTRAM.

This is not well, rash and unbridled boy,
To fly the favours of so good a king;
To pluck his indignation on thy head
By the misprising of a maid too virtuous
For the contempt of empire.

Re-enter CLOWN.

Clo. O madam, yonder is heavy news within between two soldiers and my young lady!

Count. What is the matter?

Clo. Nay, there is some comfort in the news, some comfort; your son will not be killed so soon as I thought he would.

Count. Why should he be killed?

Clo. So say I, madam, if he run away, as I hear he does: the danger is in standing to't; that's the loss of men, though

8. *know*] *knew* Rowe.

9. *sold*] F_3F_4. *hold* F_1F_2.
sold...manor for] *holds...manner for* Harness conj. *hold...manor by* Collier conj.

11. [Reads the letter. Theobald.

13. *ling*] $F_2F_3F_4$. *lings* F_1.

14. *old ling*] *youngling* S. Walker conj.
brains] *brain* Pope.

18. *E'en*] Theobald. *In* Ff.

19. Count. [reads] A letter. Ff.

30. *contempt*] $F_1F_2F_3$. *content* F_4.

it be the getting of children. Here they come will tell you more: for my part, I only hear your son was run away.
[*Exit.*

Enter HELENA *and two* Gentlemen.

First Gent. Save you, good madam.
Hel. Madam, my lord is gone, for ever gone.
Sec. Gent. Do not say so.
Count. Think upon patience. Pray you, gentlemen,
I have felt so many quirks of joy and grief,
That the first face of neither, on the start,
Can woman me unto't: where is my son, I pray you?
Sec. Gent. Madam, he's gone to serve the duke of Florence:
We met him thitherward; for thence we came,
And, after some dispatch in hand at court,
Thither we bend again.
Hel. Look on his letter, madam; here's my passport.
[*reads*] When thou canst get the ring upon my finger which never shall come off, and show me a child begotten of thy body that I am father to, then call me husband: but in such a 'then' I write a 'never.'
This is a dreadful sentence.
Count. Brought you this letter, gentlemen?
First Gent. Ay, madam;
And for the contents' sake are sorry for our pains.
Count. I prithee, lady, have a better cheer;
If thou engrossest all the griefs are thine,
Thou robb'st me of a moiety: he was my son;

41. *hear*] *heard* Hanmer.
42. SCENE III. Pope.
First Gent.] 1 Gen. Rowe. French E. Ff. See note (VI).
44. Sec. Gent.] 2 Gen. Rowe. French G. $F_1F_3F_4$. Fren. G. F_2. See note (VI).
45. *patience. Pray you,*] *patience, pray you* F_1F_2. *patience; pray you* F_3. *patience: pray you* F_4. *patience, 'pray you:* Hanmer.
46. *I have*] *I've* Pope.
48. *I pray you*] om. Theobald.
50. *for*] *from* Rowe.
53. *his*] *this* Rowe.
54. [reads.] Capell.
54, 55. *upon my...off*] *from my...off* Hanmer. *upon thy...off mine* Johnson conj. (withdrawn).
59. First Gent.] 1 G. $F_1F_2F_3$. 1 Gen. F_4.
59, 60. *Ay, madam...pains*] Arranged as in Capell; printed as prose in Ff.
62. *are*] *as* Rowe.

But I do wash his name out of my blood,
And thou art all my child. Towards Florence is he?

Sec. Gent. Ay, madam.

Count. And to be a soldier?

Sec. Gent. Such is his noble purpose; and, believe 't,
The Duke will lay upon him all the honour
That good convenience claims.

Count. Return you thither?

First Gent. Ay, madam, with the swiftest wing of speed.

Hel. [*reads*] Till I have no wife, I have nothing in France.
'Tis bitter.

Count. Find you that there?

Hel. Ay, madam.

First Gent. 'Tis but the boldness of his hand, haply, which his heart was not consenting to.

Count. Nothing in France, until he have no wife!
There's nothing here that is too good for him
But only she; and she deserves a lord
That twenty such rude boys might tend upon
And call her hourly mistress. Who was with him?

First Gent. A servant only, and a gentleman
Which I have sometime known.

Count. Parolles, was it not?

First Gent. Ay, my good lady, he.

Count. A very tainted fellow, and full of wickedness.
My son corrupts a well-derived nature
With his inducement.

First Gent. Indeed, good lady,
The fellow has a deal of that too much,
Which holds him much to have.

71. [reads] Reading. Rowe.

72. *bitter*] F_1. *better* $F_2F_3F_4$.

73. *Ay*] *Yes* Rowe.

74. *haply*] F_1. *happily* $F_2F_3F_4$.

81, 82. *A servant...known*] Printed as prose in Ff; as verse first in Pope.

82. *sometime*] F_1F_2. *some times* F_3. *sometimes* F_4. *some time* Pope (ed. 2).

was it] Ff. *was't* Pope.

84—86. *A very......inducement*] Printed as prose by Hanmer.

84. *very*] om. S. Walker conj.

and] om. Pope.

86. *Indeed*] *Why, indeed* Capell.

86—94. *Indeed...affairs*] Printed as prose in Ff; as verse first in Capell.

87. *that too*] Rowe. *that, too* Ff.

88. *holds him much to have*] *soils him much to have* Theobald conj. *'hoves him not much to have* Hanmer.

Count. Y' are welcome, gentlemen.
I will entreat you, when you see my son,
To tell him that his sword can never win
The honour that he loses: more I'll entreat you
Written to bear along.
Sec. Gent. We serve you, madam,
In that and all your worthiest affairs.
Count. Not so, but as we change our courtesies.
Will you draw near? [*Exeunt Countess and Gentlemen.*
Hel. 'Till I have no wife, I have nothing in France.'
Nothing in France, until he has no wife!
Thou shalt have none, Rousillon, none in France;
Then hast thou all again. Poor lord! is 't I
That chase thee from thy country and expose
Those tender limbs of thine to the event
Of the none-sparing war? and is it I
That drive thee from the sportive court, where thou
Wast shot at with fair eyes, to be the mark
Of smoky muskets? O you leaden messengers,
That ride upon the violent speed of fire,
Fly with false aim; move the still-peering air,
That sings with piercing; do not touch my lord.
Whoever shoots at him, I set him there;
Whoever charges on his forward breast,
I am the caitiff that do hold him to 't;
And, though I kill him not, I am the cause
His death was so effected: better 'twere
I met the ravin lion when he roar'd

'hoves him much to leave Collier (Collier MS.). *fouls him much to have* Singer conj.

95. *courtesies.*] Rowe (ed. 2). *courtesies,* Ff.

96. [Exeunt C. and G.] Rowe. [Exit. Ff.

97. SCENE IV. Pope.

107. *violent*] *volant* Collier (Collier MS.).

108. *move the still peering*] F_1. *move the still-piercing* F_2 F_3 F_4 (*still piercing* F_4). *pierce the still-moving* Hanmer (Warburton). *move the still-piecing* Steevens (Anon. conj.). *rove the still-piecing* Tyrwhitt conj. *move the still-pierced* Nares conj. *mow the still-pacing* Jackson conj. *wound the still-piecing* Collier (Collier MS.). *move the still 'pearing* Grant White conj. (withdrawn). *move the still-closing* Bailey conj.

109. *sings*] F_1. *stings* $F_2F_3F_4$.

112. *to't*] *to it* Theobald.

115. *ravin*] Capell. *ravine* $F_1F_2F_3$. *raving* F_4. *rav'ning* Rowe (ed. 2).

With sharp constraint of hunger; better 'twere
That all the miseries which nature owes
Were mine at once. No, come thou home, Rousillon,
Whence honour but of danger wins a scar,
As oft it loses all: I will be gone;
My being here it is that holds thee hence:
Shall I stay here to do't? no, no, although
The air of paradise did fan the house,
And angels officed all: I will be gone,
That pitiful rumour may report my flight,
To consolate thine ear. Come, night; end, day!
For with the dark, poor thief, I'll steal away. [*Exit.*

SCENE III. *Florence. Before the* DUKE'S *palace.*

Flourish. Enter the DUKE *of Florence,* BERTRAM, PAROLLES, Soldiers, Drum, *and* Trumpets.

Duke. The general of our horse thou art; and we,
Great in our hope, lay our best love and credence
Upon thy promising fortune.
Ber. Sir, it is
A charge too heavy for my strength; but yet
We'll strive to bear it for your worthy sake
To the extreme edge of hazard.
Duke. Then go thou forth;
And fortune play upon thy prosperous helm,
As thy auspicious mistress!
Ber. This very day,
Great Mars, I put myself into thy file:
Make me but like my thoughts, and I shall prove
A lover of thy drum, hater of love. [*Exit.*

124. *angels*] *angles* F_1.
126. *consolate*] *consolats* F_2.
SCENE III.] SCENE V. Pope.
Before......palace.] Capell. Scene changes to the Duke's court in Florence. Theobald.
PAROLLES] om. Capell.
3. *Sir, it is*] See note (XIII).
4. *but yet*] F_1. *but* $F_2 F_3 F_4$.
6. *the*] *th'* Ff.
thou] om. Pope.

SCENE IV. *Rousillon. The* COUNT'S *palace.*

Enter COUNTESS *and* Steward.

Count. Alas! and would you take the letter of her?
Might you not know she would do as she has done,
By sending me a letter? Read it again.

Stew. [*reads*] I am Saint Jaques' pilgrim, thither gone:
Ambitious love hath so in me offended,
That barefoot plod I the cold ground upon,
With sainted vow my faults to have amended.
Write, write, that from the bloody course of war
My dearest master, your dear son, may hie:
Bless him at home in peace, whilst I from far
His name with zealous fervour sanctify:
His taken labours bid him me forgive;
I, his despiteful Juno, sent him forth
From courtly friends with camping foes to live,
Where death and danger dogs the heels of worth:
He is too good and fair for death and me;
Whom I myself embrace to set him free.

Count. Ah, what sharp stings are in her mildest words!
Rinaldo, you did never lack advice so much,
As letting her pass so: had I spoke with her,
I could have well diverted her intents,
Which thus she hath prevented.

Stew. Pardon me, madam:
If I had given you this at over-night,
She might have been o'erta'en; and yet she writes,
Pursuit would be but vain.

Count. What angel shall

SCENE IV.] SCENE VI. Pope.
4. Stew. [Reads] Collier. Letter Ff. Ste. Capell.
Saint] *S.* F_1 F_2 F_3. *St.* F_4.
7. *have*] *hane* F_1.
10. *Bless*] *'Bless* Capell conj. MS.
peace, whilst] F_3 F_4. *peace. Whilst* F_1 F_2.
12. *His taken*] *Herculean* Rann conj.
15. *dogs*] *dog* Rowe.
18. Count.] Cou. Capell. om. Ff.
19. *Rinaldo*] *Rynaldo* F_1 F_3 F_4. *Rynardo* F_2.
did never lack] *ne'er lack'd* Hanmer.
22. *me*] om. Pope.

Bless this unworthy husband? he cannot thrive,
Unless her prayers, whom heaven delights to hear
And loves to grant, reprieve him from the wrath
Of greatest justice. Write, write, Rinaldo,
To this unworthy husband of his wife;
Let every word weigh heavy of her worth
That he does weigh too light: my greatest grief,
Though little he do feel it, set down sharply.
Dispatch the most convenient messenger:
When haply he shall hear that she is gone,
He will return; and hope I may that she,
Hearing so much, will speed her foot again,
Led hither by pure love: which of them both
Is dearest to me, I have no skill in sense
To make distinction: provide this messenger:
My heart is heavy and mine age is weak;
Grief would have tears, and sorrow bids me speak. [*Exeunt.*

SCENE V. *Florence. Without the walls. A tucket afar off.*

Enter an old Widow *of Florence,* DIANA, VIOLENTA, *and* MARIANA, *with other* Citizens.

Wid. Nay, come; for if they do approach the city, we shall lose all the sight.

26. *cannot*] *can't* S. Walker conj.

27. *whom*] *which* Hanmer.

29. *Write, write*] $F_1F_3F_4$. *Write and write* F_2. *Write, oh, write* Hanmer.

33. *he do*] *do he* Rowe (ed. 2). *does he* Hanmer.

39. *I have*] *I've* Pope.

skill in sense] *skill or sense* Collier (Collier MS.).

42. *and*] *but* Hanmer.

SCENE V.] SCENE VII. Pope.

Without the walls.] Capell. A public place in Florence. Theobald.

A tucket...] Transferred to line 7 by Dyce.

DIANA] her daughter. Ff.

VIOLENTA] om. Capell.

1—14. As seventeen lines, ending *come...city...sight...done...service...reported ... commander ... slew ... labour ...hark ... trumpets ... again ... of it... earl ... name ... rich ... honesty...neighbour...gentleman...companion* in Ff. First as prose by Pope.

Dia. They say the French count has done most honourable service.

Wid. It is reported that he has taken their greatest commander; and that with his own hand he slew the Duke's brother. [*Tucket.*] We have lost our labour; they are gone a contrary way: hark! you may know by their trumpets.

Mar. Come, let's return again, and suffice ourselves with the report of it. Well, Diana, take heed of this French earl: the honour of a maid is her name; and no legacy is so rich as honesty.

Wid. I have told my neighbour how you have been solicited by a gentleman his companion.

Mar. I know that knave; hang him! one Parolles: a filthy officer he is in those suggestions for the young earl. Beware of them, Diana; their promises, enticements, oaths, tokens, and all these engines of lust, are not the things they go under: many a maid hath been seduced by them; and the misery is, example, that so terrible shows in the wreck of maidenhood, cannot for all that dissuade succession, but that they are limed with the twigs that threaten them. I hope I need not to advise you further; but I hope your own grace will keep you where you are, though there were no further danger known but the modesty which is so lost.

Dia. You shall not need to fear me.

Wid. I hope so.

Enter HELENA, *disguised like a Pilgrim.*

Look, here comes a pilgrim: I know she will lie at my house; thither they send one another: I'll question her. God save you, pilgrim! whither are you bound?

Hel. To Saint Jaques le Grand.
Where do the palmers lodge, I do beseech you?

3. Dia.] Violenta. Edd. conj.

5. *taken*] *ta'en* Rowe.
greatest] *great'st* Ff.

7. [Tucket.] Capell.

18. *not*] *but* Hanmer. om. Warburton.

20. *is, example*] Rowe (ed. 2). *is example* Ff.

22. *threaten*] Pope. *threatens* Ff.

25. *known*] *found* Hanmer (Warburton).
the modesty] *of the modesty* Long MS.

27. Enter...] Rowe. Enter Hellen. Ff.

31. *le*] F_3F_4. *la* F_1F_2.

Wid. At the Saint Francis here beside the port.
Hel. Is this the way?
Wid. Ay, marry, is't. [*A march afar.*] Hark you! they come this way.
If you will tarry, holy pilgrim,
But till the troops come by,
I will conduct you where you shall be lodged;
The rather, for I think I know your hostess
As ample as myself.
Hel. Is it yourself?
Wid. If you shall please so, pilgrim.
Hel. I thank you, and will stay upon your leisure.
Wid. You came, I think, from France?
Hel. I did so.
Wid. Here you shall see a countryman of yours
That has done worthy service.
Hel. His name, I pray you.
Dia. The Count Rousillon: know you such a one?
Hel. But by the ear, that hears most nobly of him:
His face I know not.
Dia. Whatsome'er he is,
He's bravely taken here. He stole from France,
As 'tis reported, for the king had married him
Against his liking: think you it is so?
Hel. Ay, surely, mere the truth: I know his lady.
Dia. There is a gentleman that serves the count
Reports but coarsely of her.
Hel. What's his name?
Dia. Monsieur Parolles.
Hel. O, I believe with him,

33. *here*] om. Theobald.

34—37. Arranged as in Ff; as prose in Pope; as three lines, ending *Hark you!...pilgrim...by* in Capell.

35. *is 't*] *is it* Capell.
A march afar.] Ff. Tucket. Capell.

36. *holy*] om. Capell.

37. *the*] *the the* F_2.

40. *ample*] *amply* Capell conj.

40, 41. *Is it...pilgrim*] As one line in Capell.

43. *I did*] *True, I did* Hanmer.

48. *Whatsome'er he is*] *What somere he is* $F_1 F_3 F_4$. *What somere his is* F_2. *Whatsoe'er he is* Rowe.

52. *mere the*] *the meer* Hanmer. *meerlye* Warburton.

54. *coarsely*] Johnson. *coursely* Ff.

In argument of praise, or to the worth
Of the great count himself, she is too mean
To have her name repeated: all her deserving
Is a reserved honesty, and that
I have not heard examined.
Dia. Alas, poor lady!
'Tis a hard bondage to become the wife
Of a detesting lord.
Wid. I write good creature, wheresoe'er she is,
Her heart weighs sadly: this young maid might do her
A shrewd turn, if she pleased.
Hel. How do you mean?
May be the amorous count solicits her
In the unlawful purpose.
Wid. He does indeed;
And brokes with all that can in such a suit
Corrupt the tender honour of a maid:
But she is arm'd for him, and keeps her guard
In honestest defence.
Mar. The gods forbid else!
Wid. So, now they come:

Drum and Colours.

Enter BERTRAM, PAROLLES, *and the whole army.*

That is Antonio, the Duke's eldest son;
That, Escalus.
Hel. Which is the Frenchman?
Dia. He;
That with the plume: 'tis a most gallant fellow.
I would he loved his wife: if he were honester
He were much goodlier: is't not a handsome gentleman?
Hel. I like him well.

60. *Alas*] *Ah* Pope.

63. *I write good creature,*] F_1. *I right good creature,* $F_2 F_3 F_4$. *Ah! right good creature!* Rowe. *Ah! right; good creature!* Theobald. *Ay, right:—Good creature!* Capell. *A right good creature:* Steevens (Malone conj.). *I weet, good creature,* Steevens conj. *I write, good creature,* Grant White.

68. *brokes*] *brooks* Rowe (ed. 2).

71. SCENE VIII. Pope.

72. Enter Bertram...] Enter Count Rossillion... Ff (after *defence*, line 71).

77. *is't not a*] *but is it not A* Hanmer.

Dia. 'Tis pity he is not honest: yond's that same knave
That leads him to these places: were I his lady,
I would poison that vile rascal.

Hel. Which is he?

Dia. That jack-an-apes with scarfs: why is he melancholy?

Hel. Perchance he's hurt i' the battle.

Par. Lose our drum! well.

Mar. He's shrewdly vexed at something: look, he has spied us.

Wid. Marry, hang you!

Mar. And your courtesy, for a ring-carrier!

[*Exeunt Bertram, Parolles, and army.*

Wid. The troop is past. Come, pilgrim, I will bring you
Where you shall host: of enjoin'd penitents
There's four or five, to great Saint Jaques bound,
Already at my house.

Hel. I humbly thank you:
Please it this matron and this gentle maid
To eat with us to-night, the charge and thanking
Shall be for me; and, to requite you further,
I will bestow some precepts of this virgin
Worthy the note.

Both. We'll take your offer kindly. [*Exeunt.*

SCENE VI. *Camp before Florence.*

Enter BERTRAM *and the two French* Lords.

Sec. Lord. Nay, good my lord, put him to't; let him have his way.

79. *he is*] *he's* Hanmer.

80. *places*] *paces* Theobald. *pranks* Heath conj. *passes* Lettsom conj.

81. *I would*] *I'd* Pope.

82—84. *That...well*] S. Walker reads as three lines, ending *melancholy...drum... Well.*

84. *well*] om. Hanmer.

87. [Parolles bows to them. Capell.

88. Exeunt...] Exit. Ff.

89. *bring you*] Rowe (ed. 2). *bring you,* (*you* in next line) F_1. *bring You,* F_2 F_3 F_4.

96. *of*] F_1. *on* F_2 F_3 F_4.

SCENE VI.] SCENE IX. Pope.

Camp before Florence.] Capell.

Enter...] Rowe. Enter Count Rossillion and the Frenchmen, as at first. Ff.

1. Sec. Lord.] Cap. E. Ff, and

First Lord. If your lordship find him not a hilding, hold me no more in your respect.

Sec. Lord. On my life, my lord, a bubble.

Ber. Do you think I am so far deceived in him?

Sec. Lord. Believe it, my lord, in mine own direct knowledge, without any malice, but to speak of him as my kinsman, he's a most notable coward, an infinite and endless liar, an hourly promise-breaker, the owner of no one good quality worthy your lordship's entertainment.

First Lord. It were fit you knew him; lest, reposing too far in his virtue, which he hath not, he might at some great and trusty business in a main danger fail you.

Ber. I would I knew in what particular action to try him.

First Lord. None better than to let him fetch off his drum, which you hear him so confidently undertake to do.

Sec. Lord. I, with a troop of Florentines, will suddenly surprise him; such I will have, whom I am sure he knows not from the enemy: we will bind and hoodwink him so, that he shall suppose no other but that he is carried into the leaguer of the adversaries, when we bring him to our own tents. Be but your lordship present at his examination: if he do not, for the promise of his life and in the highest compulsion of base fear, offer to betray you and deliver all the intelligence in his power against you, and that with the divine forfeit of his soul upon oath, never trust my judgement in any thing.

First Lord. O, for the love of laughter, let him fetch his drum; he says he has a stratagem for't: when your lordship sees the bottom of his success in't, and to what metal this counterfeit lump of ore will be melted, if you

generally throughout the scene. *1.* Ld. Rowe. Fr. Env. Collier. See note (VI).

3. First Lord.] Cap. G. Ff, and throughout the scene. *2.* Ld. Rowe. Fr. Gent. Collier. See note (VI).

18. Sec. Lord.] C. E. F_1. G. E. F_2. Cap. E. F_3 F_4. Omitted by Capell, who continues the following speech to *1. L.*

22. *leaguer*] F_4. *leager* F_1 F_2 F_3. *adversaries*] *adversary* or *adversary's* Grant White conj.

29, 30. *O...drum*] Omit and insert lines 35, 36, 37. Capell conj.

29. *fetch*] *fetch off* Dyce (Collier MS.).

31. *his*] Rowe. *this* Ff.

32. *ore*] *oar* Theobald. *ours* Ff. *ores* Collier MS.

give him not John Drum's entertainment, your inclining cannot be removed. Here he comes.

Enter PAROLLES.

Sec. Lord. [*Aside to Ber.*] O, for the love of laughter, hinder not the honour of his design: let him fetch off his drum in any hand.

Ber. How now, monsieur! this drum sticks sorely in your disposition.

First Lord. A pox on't, let it go; 'tis but a drum.

Par. 'But a drum'! is't 'but a drum'? A drum so lost! There was excellent command,—to charge in with our horse upon our own wings, and to rend our own soldiers!

First Lord. That was not to be blamed in the command of the service: it was a disaster of war that Cæsar himself could not have prevented, if he had been there to command.

Ber. Well, we cannot greatly condemn our success: some dishonour we had in the loss of that drum; but it is not to be recovered.

Par. It might have been recovered.

Ber. It might; but it is not now.

Par. It is to be recovered: but that the merit of service is seldom attributed to the true and exact performer, I would have that drum or another, or 'hic jacet.'

Ber. Why, if you have a stomach, to't, monsieur: if you think your mystery in stratagem can bring this instrument of honour again into his native quarter, be magnanimous in the enterprise and go on; I will grace the attempt for a worthy exploit: if you speed well in it, the Duke shall both speak of it, and extend to you what further becomes his greatness, even to the utmost syllable of your worthiness.

33. *John*] *Tom* Hanmer (Theobald conj.).
inclining] *incliniug* F_1.
35. SCENE X. Pope.
Enter P.] Dyce (after line 37).
35—37. Marked as 'Aside' by Capell.
36. *honour*] $F_3 F_4$. *honor* $F_1 F_2$. *humour* Theobald.
42. *in*] $F_1 F_2 F_3$. *him* F_4.
44, 45. *command*] *conduct* Collier conj.
55. '*hic jacet.*'] *hic jacet*— Theobald.
57. *mystery*] *mastery* Collier conj.

Par. By the hand of a soldier, I will undertake it.

Ber. But you must not now slumber in it.

Par. I'll about it this evening: and I will presently pen down my dilemmas, encourage myself in my certainty, put myself into my mortal preparation; and by midnight look to hear further from me.

Ber. May I be bold to acquaint his Grace you are gone about it?

Par. I know not what the success will be, my lord; but the attempt I vow.

Ber. I know thou'rt valiant; and, to the possibility of thy soldiership, will subscribe for thee. Farewell.

Par. I love not many words. [*Exit.*

Sec. Lord. No more than a fish loves water. Is not this a strange fellow, my lord, that so confidently seems to undertake this business, which he knows is not to be done; damns himself to do and dares better be damned than to do't?

First Lord. You do not know him, my lord, as we do: certain it is, that he will steal himself into a man's favour and for a week escape a great deal of discoveries; but when you find him out, you have him ever after.

Ber. Why, do you think he will make no deed at all of this that so seriously he does address himself unto?

Sec. Lord. None in the world; but return with an invention and clap upon you two or three probable lies: but we have almost embossed him; you shall see his fall to-night; for indeed he is not for your lordship's respect.

First Lord. We'll make you some sport with the fox ere we case him. He was first smoked by the old lord Lafeu: when his disguise and he is parted, tell me what a sprat you shall find him; which you shall see this very night.

73, 74. As three lines, ending *valiant...souldiership...Farewell* in Ff.
73. *thou'rt*] Capell. *th' art* Ff.
74. *thy*] om. Warburton.
76. SCENE XI. Pope.
79. *do*] *do't* F_4.
79, 80. *to do 't*] *do 't* Rann.
83. *discoveries*] *discovery* S. Walker conj.
88. *probable*] *improbable* S. Walker conj.
92. *case*] *uncase* Hanmer. *uncape* Anon. conj.
93. *is parted*] *are parted* Hanmer. *tell me*] *you'll tell me* Rann conj.

Sec. Lord. I must go look my twigs: he shall be caught.
Ber. Your brother he shall go along with me.
Sec. Lord. As't please your lordship: I'll leave you.
[*Exit.*
Ber. Now will I lead you to the house, and show you
The lass I spoke of.
First Lord. But you say she's honest.
Ber. That's all the fault: I spoke with her but once
And found her wondrous cold; but I sent to her,
By this same coxcomb that we have i' the wind,
Tokens and letters which she did re-send;
And this is all I have done. She's a fair creature:
Will you go see her?
First Lord. With all my heart, my lord. [*Exeunt.*

SCENE VII. *Florence. The* Widow's *house.*

Enter HELENA *and* Widow.

Hel. If you misdoubt me that I am not she,
I know not how I shall assure you further,
But I shall lose the grounds I work upon.
Wid. Though my estate be fallen, I was well born,
Nothing acquainted with these businesses;
And would not put my reputation now
In any staining act.
Hel. Nor would I wish you.
First, give me trust, the count he is my husband,
And what to your sworn counsel I have spoken
Is so from word to word; and then you cannot,

95. *I...caught*] Continued to the former speaker by Capell.
go look] *go and look* Rowe. *go lime* Long MS. *go lack* Jackson conj. *go loop* Anon. conj.
97. Sec. Lord.] 2 Lord. Theobald. Cap. G. Ff.
Sec. Lord. *As't...you*] Fr. Gent. *As't...lordship.* Fr. En. *I'll leave you.* Collier.
99, 105. First Lord.] Cap. E. Ff.
104. *I have*] *I've* Pope.
SCENE VII.] SCENE XII. Pope.
5. *businesses*] *basenesses* Anon. conj.
8, 17. *count he*] *county* Edd. conj.
8. *is*] *his* F_2.

By the good aid that I of you shall borrow,
Err in bestowing it.
Wid. I should believe you;
For you have show'd me that which well approves
You're great in fortune.
Hel. Take this purse of gold,
And let me buy your friendly help thus far,
Which I will over-pay and pay again
When I have found it. The count he wooes your daughter,
Lays down his wanton siege before her beauty,
Resolved to carry her: let her in fine consent,
As we'll direct her how 'tis best to bear it.
Now his important blood will nought deny
That she'll demand: a ring the county wears,
That downward hath succeeded in his house
From son to son, some four or five descents
Since the first father wore it: this ring he holds
In most rich choice; yet in his idle fire,
To buy his will, it would not seem too dear,
Howe'er repented after.
Wid. Now I see
The bottom of your purpose.
Hel. You see it lawful, then: it is no more,
But that your daughter, ere she seems as won,
Desires this ring; appoints him an encounter;
In fine, delivers me to fill the time,
Herself most chastely absent: after this,
To marry her, I'll add three thousand crowns
To what is past already.

14. *You're*] *Y'are* Ff. *You are* Capell.

17. *he*] om. Pope.

19. *Resolved*] Collier (Egerton MS.). *Resolve* F_1. *Resolves* $F_2F_3F_4$.
in fine] om. Rowe (ed 2).

20. *how 'tis*] *how, 'tis* Warburton.

21. *his important*] F_1 F_2. *this important* F_3 F_4. *this importurate* Rowe (ed. 1). *his importunate* Rowe (ed. 2).

22. *county wears*] *countie weares* F_1. *county weares* F_2F_3. *count wears* F_4. *count does wear* Rowe. See note (XIV).

28, 29. *Now...purpose*] As in Capell. As one line in Ff. *Now do I see...purpose* (as one line) Hanmer.

34. *after this*] $F_2F_3F_4$. *after* F_1. *afterwards* Collier conj.

36. *past*] *pact* Anon. conj.

Wid. I have yielded:
Instruct my daughter how she shall persever,
That time and place with this deceit so lawful
May prove coherent. Every night he comes
With musics of all sorts and songs composed
To her unworthiness: it nothing steads us
To chide him from our eaves; for he persists
As if his life lay on't.
Hel. Why then to-night
Let us assay our plot; which, if it speed,
Is wicked meaning in a lawful deed,
And lawful meaning in a lawful act,
Where both not sin, and yet a sinful fact:
But let's about it. [*Exeunt.*

ACT IV.

SCENE I. *Without the Florentine camp.*

Enter Second French Lord, *with five or six other* Soldiers *in ambush.*

Sec. Lord. He can come no other way but by this hedge-corner. When you sally upon him, speak what terrible language you will: though you understand it not yourselves, no matter; for we must not seem to understand him, unless some one among us whom we must produce for an interpreter.

First Sold. Good captain, let me be the interpreter.

Sec. Lord. Art not acquainted with him? knows he not thy voice?

First Sold. No, sir, I warrant you.

40. *musics*] *Musickes* F_1F_2. *Musicks* F_3. *Musick* F_4.
41. *steads*] F_4. *steeds* $F_1F_2F_3$.
42. *eaves*] Hanmer. *eeves* Ff.
46. *And lawful*] *Unlawful* Hanmer.
lawful act] *wicked act* Warburton. *lawless act* Anon. conj.
SCENE I. Without...] Capell. Continues in Florence. Pope. Part of the French camp in Florence. Theobald.
Enter Second French Lord...] Edd. Enter one of the Frenchmen....Ff. Enter First Lord... Capell. Enter French Envoy...Collier. See note(VI).
Sec. Lord.] 1. Lord. E. Ff.
5. *among*] *amongst* Rowe.
7. *captain*] F_3F_4. *captaine* F_1. *captaive* F_2.

Sec. Lord. But what linsey-woolsey hast thou to speak to us again?

First Sold. E'en such as you speak to me.

Sec. Lord. He must think us some band of strangers i' the adversary's entertainment. Now he hath a smack of all neighbouring languages; therefore we must every one be a man of his own fancy, not to know what we speak one to another; so we seem to know, is to know straight our purpose: choughs' language, gabble enough, and good enough. As for you, interpreter, you must seem very politic. But couch, ho! here he comes, to beguile two hours in a sleep, and then to return and swear the lies he forges.

Enter PAROLLES.

Par. Ten o'clock: within these three hours 'twill be time enough to go home. What shall I say I have done? It must be a very plausive invention that carries it: they begin to smoke me; and disgraces have of late knocked too often at my door. I find my tongue is too foolhardy; but my heart hath the fear of Mars before it and of his creatures, not daring the reports of my tongue.

Sec. Lord. This is the first truth that e'er thine own tongue was guilty of.

Par. What the devil should move me to undertake the recovery of this drum, being not ignorant of the impossibility, and knowing I had no such purpose? I must give myself some hurts, and say I got them in exploit: yet slight ones will not carry it; they will say, 'Came you off with so little?' and great ones I dare not give. Wherefore, what's the instance? Tongue, I must put you into a butter-woman's mouth, and buy myself another of Bajazet's mule, if you prattle me into these perils.

15. *adversary's*] Johnson. *adversaries* Ff. *adversaries'* Warburton.

18. *know straight*] *shew straight* Hanmer. *go straight to* Collier (Collier MS.).

19. *choughs'*] *chough's* F_3 F_4. *choughs* F_1F_2.

23. *o'*] Johnson. *a* Ff.

29. *my*] *my own* Mason conj. *mine own* Rann.

39. *myself*] om. Steevens.

Bajazet's] *Baiazeths* F_1. *Bajazeths* $F_2F_3F_4$.

40. *mule*] F_1 F_2. *Mules* F_3 F_4. *mute* Hanmer (Warburton).

Sec. Lord. Is it possible he should know what he is, and be that he is?

Par. I would the cutting of my garments would serve the turn, or the breaking of my Spanish sword.

Sec. Lord. We cannot afford you so.

Par. Or the baring of my beard; and to say it was in stratagem.

Sec. Lord. 'Twould not do.

Par. Or to drown my clothes, and say I was stripped.

Sec. Lord. Hardly serve.

Par. Though I swore I leaped from the window of the citadel—

Sec. Lord. How deep?

Par. Thirty fathom.

Sec. Lord. Three great oaths would scarce make that be believed.

Par. I would I had any drum of the enemy's: I would swear I recovered it.

Sec. Lord. You shall hear one anon.

Par. A drum now of the enemy's,— [*Alarum within.*

Sec. Lord. Throca movousus, cargo, cargo, cargo.

All. Cargo, cargo, cargo, villianda par corbo, cargo.

Par. O, ransom, ransom! do not hide mine eyes.

[*They seize and blindfold him.*

First Sold. Boskos thromuldo boskos.

Par. I know you are the Muskos' regiment;
And I shall lose my life for want of language:
If there be here German, or Dane, low Dutch,
Italian, or French, let him speak to me; I'll
Discover that which shall undo the Florentine.

First Sold. Boskos vauvado: I understand thee, and

57. *enemy's*] Malone. *enemies* Ff. *enemies'* Capell.

60. *enemy's,—*] Edd. *enemy's!* Malone. *enemies!* Theobald. *enemies.* Ff.

62. *cargo, cargo*] *cargo* Hanmer.

63. [They...him.] Rowe. om. Ff.

64. *Boskos...boskos*] F_1. *Baskos... baskos* F_2 F_3 F_4.

65. *Muskos'*] Capell. *Muskos* Ff.

68. *or*] om. Capell.

68, 69. Arranged as in Capell. *Ile...Florentine* (in one line) Ff. *I will...undo The...* Malone.

70—74. *Boskos...pray!*] Printed as verse by Capell.

can speak thy tongue. Kerelybonto, sir, betake thee to thy faith, for seventeen poniards are at thy bosom.

Par. O!

First Sold. O, pray, pray, pray! Manka revania dulche.

Sec. Lord. Oscorbidulchos volivorco.

First Sold. The general is content to spare thee yet;
And, hoodwink'd as thou art, will lead thee on
To gather from thee: haply thou mayst inform
Something to save thy life.

Par. O, let me live!
And all the secrets of our camp I'll show,
Their force, their purposes; nay, I'll speak that
Which you will wonder at.

First Sold. But wilt thou faithfully?

Par. If I do not, damn me.

First Sold. Acordo linta.
Come on; thou art granted space.

[*Exit, with Parolles guarded. A short alarum within.*

Sec. Lord. Go, tell the Count Rousillon, and my brother,
We have caught the woodcock, and will keep him muffled
Till we do hear from them.

Sec. Sold. Captain, I will.

Sec. Lord. A' will betray us all unto ourselves:
Inform on that.

Sec. Sold. So I will, sir.

Sec. Lord. Till then I'll keep him dark and safely lock'd. [*Exeunt.*

73, 74. Par. *O!* First Sold. *O, pray*] Par. *Oh, oh!* 1. S. *Pray.* Capell.

74. *revania*] F_1. *revanta* F_2. *revancha* F_3 F_4.

76. *Oscorbidulchos*] F_1. *Osceorbidulchos* $F_2F_3F_4$.

86. Exit...] Capell. Exit. Ff.

A short alarum within.] Ff. om. Capell.

88. *We have*] *We've* Pope.

90. *A'*] *A* Ff. *He* Rowe.

91. *Inform on that*] *Inform 'em that* Rowe. *Inform 'em too of that* Capell.

SCENE II. *Florence. The* Widow's *house.*

Enter BERTRAM *and* DIANA.

Ber. They told me that your name was Fontibell.
Dia. No, my good lord, Diana.
Ber. Titled goddess;
And worth it, with addition! But, fair soul,
In your fine frame hath love no quality?
If the quick fire of youth light not your mind,
You are no maiden, but a monument:
When you are dead, you should be such a one
As you are now, for you are cold and stern;
And now you should be as your mother was
When your sweet self was got.
Dia. She then was honest.
Ber. So should you be.
Dia. No:
My mother did but duty; such, my lord,
As you owe to your wife.
Ber. No more o' that;
I prithee, do not strive against my vows:
I was compell'd to her; but I love thee
By love's own sweet constraint, and will for ever
Do thee all rights of service.
Dia. Ay, so you serve us
Till we serve you; but when you have our roses,
You barely leave our thorns to prick ourselves,
And mock us with our bareness.
Ber. How have I sworn!
Dia. 'Tis not the many oaths that makes the truth,

Enter...] Enter Bertram and the Maid called Diana. Ff.

2. *Titled goddess*] *Titl'd, goddess* Capell.

8. *stern*] F_3 F_4. *sterne* F_1 F_2. *stone* Collier (Collier MS.).

13. *o'*] Rowe. *a'* Ff.

14. *strive...vows:*] *drive against my vows:* Johnson conj. *shrive—against my voice* Id. conj.

19. *barely*] *basely* Rowe (ed. 2).

21—31. Dia. *'Tis not...opinion*] Dia. *'Tis not...witness.* Ber. *Then... ill?* Dia. *This......opinion* Staunton conj.

21. *makes*] F_1. *make* F_2 F_3 F_4.

But the plain single vow that is vow'd true.
What is not holy, that we swear not by,
But take the High'st to witness: then, pray you, tell me,
If I should swear by Jove's great attributes,
I loved you dearly, would you believe my oaths,
When I did love you ill? This has no holding,
To swear by him whom I protest to love,
That I will work against him: therefore your oaths
Are words and poor conditions, but unseal'd,
At least in my opinion.

Ber. Change it, change it;
Be not so holy-cruel: love is holy;
And my integrity ne'er knew the crafts
That you do charge men with. Stand no more off,
But give thyself unto my sick desires,
Who then recover: say thou art mine, and ever
My love as it begins shall so persever.

Dia. I see that men make rope's in such a scarre
That we'll forsake ourselves. Give me that ring.

Ber. I'll lend it thee, my dear; but have no power
To give it from me.

Dia. Will you not, my lord?

23, 24. *What......me,] But......by?* Jackson conj. (inverting the lines).

What...witness: then, pray] Bert. *What...witness.* Diana. *Then, pray* Johnson conj.

23—29. *What......against him]* Erased in Collier MS.

23. *swear not by,] swear, not 'bides,* Warburton.

24. *pray you] pray* Pope.

25. *Jove's] Joves* $F_3 F_4$. *Ioues* $F_1 F_2$. *love's* Grant White (Johnson conj.). *God's* Edd. conj. See note (XV).

attributes] F_1. *attribute* $F_2 F_3 F_4$.

28. *by] to* Johnson conj.

whom] when Singer.

28, 29. *whom I...him] and to protest I love Whom I will work against* Becket conj.

32. *holy-cruel]* Theobald. *holy cruel* Ff.

love] my love Staunton conj.

35, 36. *desires, Who then recover]* Rowe (ed. 2). *desires, Who then recovers* Ff. *desires, Which then recover* Pope. *desire, Who then recovers* Capell.

38. *rope's...scarre]* $F_1 F_2$. *ropes .. scarre* F_3. *ropes...scar* F_4. *hopes... affairs* Rowe. *hopes...scene* Malone. *mopes in...scar* or *japes of...scathe* Becket conj. *hopes...scare* Henley conj. *hopes..... cause* Mitford conj. *hopes...war* Singer (ed. 1). *hopes... scarre* Singer (Knight conj.). *slopes ... scarre* Collier conj. *ropes...staire* Id. conj. *hopes ... case* Dyce. *hopes ... snare* Staunton. *hopes...suit* Collier (Collier MS.). *may cope's...sorte* Williams conj.

Ber. It is an honour 'longing to our house,
Bequeathed down from many ancestors;
Which were the greatest obloquy i' the world
In me to lose.

Dia. Mine honour's such a ring:
My chastity's the jewel of our house,
Bequeathed down from many ancestors;
Which were the greatest obloquy i' the world
In me to lose: thus your own proper wisdom
Brings in the champion Honour on my part,
Against your vain assault.

Ber. Here, take my ring:
My house, mine honour, yea, my life, be thine,
And I'll be bid by thee.

Dia. When midnight comes, knock at my chamber-window:
I'll order take my mother shall not hear.
Now will I charge you in the band of truth,
When you have conquer'd my yet maiden bed,
Remain there but an hour, nor speak to me:
My reasons are most strong; and you shall know them
When back again this ring shall be deliver'd:
And on your finger in the night I'll put
Another ring, that what in time proceeds
May token to the future our past deeds.
Adieu, till then; then, fail not. You have won
A wife of me, though there my hope be done.

Ber. A heaven on earth I have won by wooing thee. [*Exit.*

Dia. For which live long to thank both heaven and me!
You may so in the end.
My mother told me just how he would woo,
As if she sat in's heart; she says all men
Have the like oaths: he had sworn to marry me
When his wife's dead; therefore I'll lie with him

44. *were*] *'twere* Collier (Collier MS.).

53. *And I'll*] *An I* Collier conj.

65. *done*] *none* Collier MS.

66. *I have*] F_1 F_2. *I've* F_3F_4.

71. *had*] *hath* Capell conj. *has* Grant White.

When I am buried. Since Frenchmen are so braid,
Marry that will, I live and die a maid:
Only in this disguise I think't no sin
To cozen him that would unjustly win. [*Exit.*

SCENE III. *The Florentine camp.*

Enter the two French Lords *and some two or three* Soldiers.

First Lord. You have not given him his mother's letter?

Sec. Lord. I have delivered it an hour since: there is something in't that stings his nature; for on the reading it he changed almost into another man.

First Lord. He has much worthy blame laid upon him for shaking off so good a wife and so sweet a lady.

Sec. Lord. Especially he hath incurred the everlasting displeasure of the king, who had even tuned his bounty to sing happiness to him. I will tell you a thing, but you shall let it dwell darkly with you.

First Lord. When you have spoken it, 'tis dead, and I am the grave of it.

Sec. Lord. He hath perverted a young gentlewoman here in Florence, of a most chaste renown; and this night he fleshes his will in the spoil of her honour: he hath given her his monumental ring, and thinks himself made in the unchaste composition.

First Lord. Now, God delay our rebellion! as we are ourselves, what things are we!

Sec. Lord. Merely our own traitors. And as in the common course of all treasons, we still see them reveal themselves, till they attain to their abhorred ends, so he

73. *Frenchmen*] *men* Hanmer.

74. *Marry*] *Marry 'em* Theobald (Warburton).

74. *I*] F_1F_2. *I'le* F_3 F_4. *I'd* Theobald (Warburton).

Lords] Captains Ff.

1. First Lord.] 1 Ld. Rowe. Cap. G. Ff (and throughout the scene).

2. Sec. Lord.] 2 Ld. Rowe. Cap. E. Ff (and throughout the scene).

16. *made*] *paid* Staunton conj.

18. *delay*] *allay* Hanmer.

22. *till*] *ere* Hanmer. *when* Mason conj.

that in this action contrives against his own nobility, in his proper stream o'erflows himself.

First Lord. Is it not meant damnable in us, to be trumpeters of our unlawful intents? We shall not then have his company to-night?

Sec. Lord. Not till after midnight; for he is dieted to his hour.

First Lord. That approaches apace: I would gladly have him see his company anatomized, that he might take a measure of his own judgements, wherein so curiously he had set this counterfeit.

Sec. Lord. We will not meddle with him till he come; for his presence must be the whip of the other.

First Lord. In the mean time, what hear you of these wars?

Sec. Lord. I hear there is an overture of peace.

First Lord. Nay, I assure you, a peace concluded.

Sec. Lord. What will Count Rousillon do then? will he travel higher, or return again into France?

First Lord. I perceive, by this demand, you are not altogether of his council.

Sec. Lord. Let it be forbid, sir; so should I be a great deal of his act.

First Lord. Sir, his wife some two months since fled from his house: her pretence is a pilgrimage to Saint Jaques le Grand; which holy undertaking with most austere sanctimony she accomplished; and, there residing, the tenderness of her nature became as a prey to her grief; in fine, made a groan of her last breath, and now she sings in heaven.

23, 24. *nobility,...stream*] Theobald. *nobility...stream,* Ff.

25. *meant*] Ff. *most* Hanmer. *meantime* Heath conj. *mean and* Mason conj. *maint* Nicholson conj. *mere* Anon. conj.

26. *trumpeters*] *the trumpeters* Rowe.

30. *apace*] *agace* F_3.

31. *company*] *companion* Hanmer.
anatomized] *anatomiz'd* Rowe. *anathomiz'd* Ff.

32. *judgements*] Ff. *judgement* Pope.
wherein so curiously] *where so incuriously* Badham conj.
curiously] F_1F_2. *seriously* F_3F_4.

33. *this*] F_1F_2. *his* F_3F_4.

36. *these*] F_1. *those* $F_2F_3F_4$.

39. *concluded*] *is concluded* Rowe (ed. 1).

47. *is*] om. Capell.

48. *most*] *a most* Rowe (ed. 2).

49. *the*] *through the* Capell.

50. *as*] om. Long MS.

Sec. Lord. How is this justified?

First Lord. The stronger part of it by her own letters, which makes her story true, even to the point of her death: her death itself, which could not be her office to say is come, was faithfully confirmed by the rector of the place.

Sec. Lord. Hath the count all this intelligence?

First Lord. Ay, and the particular confirmations, point from point, to the full arming of the verity.

Sec. Lord. I am heartily sorry that he'll be glad of this.

First Lord. How mightily sometimes we make us comforts of our losses!

Sec. Lord. And how mightily some other times we drown our gain in tears! The great dignity that his valour hath here acquired for him shall at home be encountered with a shame as ample.

First Lord. The web of our life is of a mingled yarn, good and ill together: our virtues would be proud, if our faults whipped them not; and our crimes would despair, if they were not cherished by our virtues.

Enter a Messenger.

How now! where's your master?

Serv. He met the Duke in the street, sir, of whom he hath taken a solemn leave: his lordship will next morning for France. The Duke hath offered him letters of commendations to the king.

Sec. Lord. They shall be no more than needful there, if they were more than they can commend.

First Lord. They cannot be too sweet for the king's tartness. Here's his lordship now.

53. *stronger*] *stranger* Collier (Collier MS.).

54. *makes*] Ff. *make* Malone.

55. *itself*] *is selfe* F_2. See note (XVI).

56. *was*] *and* Collier (Collier MS.).

58, 59. *point from point*] Ff. *from point to point* Hanmer. *point for point* Capell.

64. *gain*] *gains* Edd. conj.

70. Messenger] Ff. Servant Rowe (ed. 2).

74, 75. *commendations*] *commendation* Rowe (ed. 2).

78. SCENE IV. Pope.

First Lord.] Ber. F_1F_2. Cap.. G. F_3F_4.

Enter BERTRAM.

How now, my lord! is 't not after midnight?

Ber. I have to-night dispatched sixteen businesses, a month's length a-piece, by an abstract of success: I have congied with the Duke, done my adieu with his nearest; buried a wife, mourned for her; writ to my lady mother I am returning; entertained my convoy; and between these main parcels of dispatch effected many nicer needs: the last was the greatest, but that I have not ended yet.

Sec. Lord. If the business be of any difficulty, and this morning your departure hence, it requires haste of your lordship.

Ber. I mean, the business is not ended, as fearing to hear of it hereafter. But shall we have this dialogue between the fool and the soldier? Come, bring forth this counterfeit module, has deceived me, like a double-meaning prophesier.

Sec. Lord. Bring him forth: he has sat i' the stocks all night, poor gallant knave.

Ber. No matter; his heels have deserved it, in usurping his spurs so long. How does he carry himself?

Sec. Lord. I have told your lordship already, the stocks carry him. But to answer you as you would be understood; he weeps like a wench that had shed her milk: he hath confessed himself to Morgan, whom he supposes to be a friar, from the time of his remembrance to this very instant disaster of his setting i' the stocks: and what think you he hath confessed?

Ber. Nothing of me, has a'?

Sec. Lord. His confession is taken, and it shall be read

79. Enter B.] Enter Count Rossillion Ff (after line 77).

83. *congied*] Ff. *conge'd* Capell.

86. *effected*] F_3F_4. *affected* F_1F_2.

94. *module*] Ff. *medal* Hanmer (Warburton). *model* Collier.

module, has] F_2. *module has* F_1. *module; 'has* F_3F_4. *module; h'as* Rowe (ed. 2).

96. *forth*] *forth* [Exeunt Soldiers.] Capell.

he has] *h'as* F_1F_2. *ha's* F_3F_4.

i'the] *i'th* Ff. *in the* Rowe.

100. Sec. Lord.] 2 L. Capell. Cap. E. F_1F_2. Cap. G. F_3F_4. 1 Ld. Rowe.

105. *i'the*] *i'th* Ff.

107. *has a'*] *ha's a* $F_1F_2F_3$. *has a* F_4. *has he* Rowe (ed. 2).

to his face: if your lordship be in't, as I believe you are, you must have the patience to hear it.

Enter PAROLLES *guarded, and* First Soldier.

Ber. A plague upon him! muffled! he can say nothing of me: hush, hush!

First Lord. Hoodman comes! Portotartarosa.

First Sold. He calls for the tortures: what will you say without 'em?

Par. I will confess what I know without constraint: if ye pinch me like a pasty, I can say no more.

First Sold. Bosko chimurcho.

First Lord. Boblibindo chicurmurco.

First Sold. You are a merciful general. Our general bids you answer to what I shall ask you out of a note.

Par. And truly, as I hope to live.

First Sold. [*reads*] First demand of him how many horse the Duke is strong. What say you to that?

Par. Five or six thousand; but very weak and unserviceable: the troops are all scattered, and the commanders very poor rogues, upon my reputation and credit and as I hope to live.

First Sold. Shall I set down your answer so?

Par. Do: I'll take the sacrament on 't, how and which way you will.

Ber. All's one to him. What a past-saving slave is this!

First Lord. You're deceived, my lord: this is Monsieur Parolles, the gallant militarist,—that was his own phrase,—

110. *hear*] *bear* Anon. conj.
Enter...] Enter Parolles with his Interpreter. Ff.

111. SCENE V. Pope.

112. *hush, hush!*] *hush* F_2.

112, 113. *hush, hush!* First Lord. *Hoodman*] 1 Lord. *Hush! hoodman* Hanmer. 1 L. *Hush, hush! hoodman* S. Walker conj.

113. *Hoodman*] *Headsman* Grey conj.

114. First Sold.] Int. Ff (and throughout the scene).

116, 117. *I will...more*] Printed as two lines in Ff, ending ...*constraint*, ...*more*.

132. Ber. *All's one to him. What*] Capell. *All's one to him.* Ber. *What* Ff. *All's one to me.* Ber. *What* Rowe. 1 Lord, or 2. Lord, *All's...him* Ber. *What* Ritson conj. *All's one to me.* Ber. *All's one to him! what* Anon. conj.

132—139, 143—145, 161—163, 176, 177, 181, 182, 193, 194, 206, 217—222, 244—246, 254—256, 264 are marked as 'Asides' by Capell.

133. *You're*] *Y'are* Ff.

that had the whole theoric of war in the knot of his scarf, and the practice in the chape of his dagger.

Sec. Lord. I will never trust a man again for keeping his sword clean, nor believe he can have every thing in him by wearing his apparel neatly.

First Sold. Well, that's set down.

Par. Five or six thousand horse, I said,—I will say true,—or thereabouts, set down, for I'll speak truth.

First Lord. He's very near the truth in this.

Ber. But I con him no thanks for't, in the nature he delivers it.

Par. Poor rogues, I pray you, say.

First Sold. Well, that's set down.

Par. I humbly thank you, sir: a truth's a truth, the rogues are marvellous poor.

First Sold. [*reads*] Demand of him, of what strength they are a-foot. What say you to that?

Par. By my troth, sir, if I were to live this present hour, I will tell true. Let me see: Spurio, a hundred and fifty; Sebastian, so many; Corambus, so many; Jaques, so many; Guiltian, Cosmo, Lodowick, and Gratii, two hundred and fifty each; mine own company, Chitopher, Vaumond, Bentii, two hundred and fifty each: so that the muster-file, rotten and sound, upon my life, amounts not to fifteen thousand poll; half of the which dare not shake the snow from off their cassocks, lest they shake themselves to pieces.

Ber. What shall be done to him?

First Lord. Nothing, but let him have thanks. Demand of him my condition, and what credit I have with the Duke.

First Sold. Well, that's set down. [*Reads*] You shall demand of him, whether one Captain Dumain be i' the camp, a Frenchman; what his reputation is with the Duke; what his valour, honesty, and expertness in wars; or whether he thinks it were not possible,

135. *theoric*] *theory* Rowe.

152. *live*] *die* S. Walker conj. *leave* Staunton conj. *shrive* Anon. conj.

this] *but this* Hanmer. See note (XIV).

155. *Guiltian*] *Julian* S. Walker conj.

155, 156. *and fifty*] Rowe (ed. 2). *fifty* F_1F_2. om. F_3F_4.

157. *and fifty*] Rowe (ed. 2). *fifty* Ff.

163. *condition*] F_1. *conditions* $F_2F_3F_4$.

165. *i' the*] *i'th* $F_1F_3F_4$. *it'h* F_2.

167. *wars*] $F_1F_2F_3$. *war* F_4.

with well-weighing sums of gold, to corrupt him to a revolt. What say you to this? what do you know of it?

Par. I beseech you, let me answer to the particular of the inter'gatories: demand them singly.

First Sold. Do you know this Captain Dumain?

Par. I know him: a' was a botcher's 'prentice in Paris, from whence he was whipped for getting the shrieve's fool with child,—a dumb innocent, that could not say him nay.

Ber. Nay, by your leave, hold your hands; though I know his brains are forfeit to the next tile that falls.

First Sold. Well, is this captain in the Duke of Florence's camp?

Par. Upon my knowledge, he is, and lousy.

First Lord. Nay, look not so upon me; we shall hear of your lordship anon.

First Sold. What is his reputation with the Duke?

Par. The Duke knows him for no other but a poor officer of mine; and writ to me this other day to turn him out o' the band: I think I have his letter in my pocket.

First Sold. Marry, we'll search.

Par. In good sadness, I do not know; either it is there, or it is upon a file with the Duke's other letters in my tent.

First Sold. Here 'tis; here's a paper: shall I read it to you?

Par. I do not know if it be it or no.

Ber. Our interpreter does it well.

First Lord. Excellently.

First Sold. [*reads*] Dian, the count's a fool, and full of gold,—

Par. That is not the Duke's letter, sir; that is an advertisement to a proper maid in Florence, one Diana, to take heed of the allurement of one Count Rousillon, a

170. *particular*] *particulars* Capell.

171. *inter'gatories*] *interrogatories* F_4. *interrogatory* Capell.

173. *a'*] *a* Ff. *he* Rowe.

174. *shrieve's*] *sheriff's* Hanmer.

175. [Dumain lifts up his hand in anger. Johnson.

182. *your lordship*] Pope. *your Lord* Ff. *you Lord* Rowe (ed. 1).

185. *this*] F_1F_2. *the* F_3F_4.

186. *o' the*] *a' th* Ff.

189. *a file*] *the file* Theobald.

195. After this line Johnson supposes one to be lost.

gold] *golden store* or *golden ore* Steevens conj. *gold, I speak it* Jackson conj. (reading lines 208—210 in this order 209, 210, 208).

foolish idle boy, but for all that very ruttish: I pray you, sir, put it up again.

First Sold. Nay, I'll read it first, by your favour.

Par. My meaning in't, I protest, was very honest in the behalf of the maid; for I knew the young count to be a dangerous and lascivious boy, who is a whale to virginity and devours up all the fry it finds.

Ber. Damnable both-sides rogue!

First Sold. [*reads*] When he swears oaths, bid him drop gold, and take it;
After he scores, he never pays the score:
Half won is match well made; match, and well make it;
He ne'er pays after-debts, take it before;
And say a soldier, Dian, told thee this,
Men are to mell with, boys are not to kiss:
For count of this, the count's a fool, I know it,
Who pays before, but not when he does owe it.

Thine, as he vowed to thee in thine ear,
PAROLLES.

Ber. He shall be whipped through the army with this rhyme in's forehead.

Sec. Lord. This is your devoted friend, sir, the manifold linguist and the armipotent soldier.

Ber. I could endure any thing before but a cat, and now he's a cat to me.

First Sold. I perceive, sir, by the general's looks, we shall be fain to hang you.

Par. My life, sir, in any case: not that I am afraid to die; but that, my offences being many, I would repent out

207. First Sold. [reads] Int. Let. Ff. Inter. reads the letter. Rowe.

209. *well made*] *ill made* Capell conj. *half made* Jackson conj.

match, and well] *match well and* Hanmer. *watch, and well* Johnson conj. (who would read the lines 207—210 in the following order, 209, 207, 208, 210).

and well] *an' we'll* Steevens conj.

212. *not*] *but* Pope (ed. 2. Theobald).

213. *count's*] *count* F_2.

214. *when*] *where* Collier (Collier MS.).

218. *in 's*] *in his* Rowe.

222. *now*] F_1. om. $F_2F_3F_4$.

223. *the*] F_3F_4. *your* F_1F_2. *our* Capell.

the remainder of nature: let me live, sir, in a dungeon, i' the stocks, or any where, so I may live.

First Sold. We'll see what may be done, so you confess freely; therefore, once more to this Captain Dumain: you have answered to his reputation with the Duke and to his valour: what is his honesty?

Par. He will steal, sir, an egg out of a cloister: for rapes and ravishments he parallels Nessus: he professes not keeping of oaths; in breaking 'em he is stronger than Hercules: he will lie, sir, with such volubility, that you would think truth were a fool: drunkenness is his best virtue, for he will be swine-drunk; and in his sleep he does little harm, save to his bed-clothes about him; but they know his conditions and lay him in straw. I have but little more to say, sir, of his honesty: he has every thing that an honest man should not have; what an honest man should have, he has nothing.

First Lord. I begin to love him for this.

Ber. For this description of thine honesty? A pox upon him for me, he's more and more a cat.

First Sold. What say you to his expertness in war?

Par. Faith, sir, has led the drum before the English tragedians; to belie him, I will not, and more of his soldiership I know not; except, in that country he had the honour to be the officer at a place there called Mile-end, to instruct for the doubling of files: I would do the man what honour I can, but of this I am not certain.

First Lord. He hath out-villained villany so far, that the rarity redeems him.

Ber. A pox on him, he's a cat still.

First Sold. His qualities being at this poor price, I need not to ask you if gold will corrupt him to revolt.

Par. Sir, for a quart d'écu he will sell the fee-simple of

227. *i' the*] *i' th* Ff.

228. *or*] F_1F_2. om. F_3F_4.

233. *an egg*] *an Ag.* (i. e. *Agnes*) Becket conj.

235. *in breaking*] F_1. *breaking* $F_2F_3F_4$.

'em] *em* $F_1F_2F_3$. *them* F_4.

246. *he's*] *he is* Pope.

248. *has*] *ha's* Ff. *h'as* Rowe.

254. *out-villained*] *out-villanied* S. Walker conj.

259. *quart d'écu*] Pope. *cardceue* F_1. *cardecue* $F_2F_3F_4$.

his salvation, the inheritance of it; and cut the entail from all remainders, and a perpetual succession for it perpetually.

First Sold. What's his brother, the other Captain Dumain?

Sec. Lord. Why does he ask him of me?

First Sold. What's he?

Par. E'en a crow o' the same nest; not altogether so great as the first in goodness, but greater a great deal in evil: he excels his brother for a coward, yet his brother is reputed one of the best that is: in a retreat he outruns any lackey; marry, in coming on he has the cramp.

First Sold. If your life be saved, will you undertake to betray the Florentine?

Par. Ay, and the captain of his horse, Count Rousillon.

First Sold. I'll whisper with the general, and know his pleasure.

Par. [*Aside*] I'll no more drumming; a plague of all drums! Only to seem to deserve well, and to beguile the supposition of that lascivious young boy the count, have I run into this danger. Yet who would have suspected an ambush where I was taken?

First Sold. There is no remedy, sir, but you must die: the general says, you that have so traitorously discovered the secrets of your army and made such pestiferous reports of men very nobly held, can serve the world for no honest use; therefore you must die. Come, headsman, off with his head.

Par. O Lord, sir, let me live, or let me see my death!

First Sold. That shall you, and take your leave of all your friends. [*Unblinding him.*
So, look about you: know you any here?

Ber. Good morrow, noble captain.

Sec. Lord. God bless you, Captain Parolles.

First Lord. God save you, noble captain.

Sec. Lord. Captain, what greeting will you to my Lord Lafeu? I am for France.

261. *for it*] *in it* Hanmer.

266. *o' the*] *o' th* $F_1F_2F_4$. *at'h* F_3.

270. *has*] *ha's* F_1.

276. [Aside] Rowe (ed. 2).

279. *this danger*] *danger* Rowe.

288. [Unblinding him.] Rowe (ed. 1). [Unbinding him. Rowe (ed. 2). [Unmuffling him. Steevens.

291, 293. Sec. Lord.] Lo. E. F_1.

First Lord. Good captain, will you give me a copy of the sonnet you writ to Diana in behalf of the Count Rousillon? an I were not a very coward, I'ld compel it of you: but fare you well. [*Exeunt Bertram and Lords.*

First Sold. You are undone, captain, all but your scarf; that has a knot on't yet.

Par. Who cannot be crushed with a plot?

First Sold. If you could find out a country where but women were that had received so much shame, you might begin an impudent nation. Fare ye well, sir; I am for France too: we shall speak of you there. [*Exit, with Soldiers.*

Par. Yet am I thankful: if my heart were great,
'Twould burst at this. Captain I'll be no more;
But I will eat and drink, and sleep as soft
As captain shall: simply the thing I am
Shall make me live. Who knows himself a braggart,
Let him fear this, for it will come to pass
That every braggart shall be found an ass.
Rust, sword! cool, blushes! and, Parolles, live
Safest in shame! being fool'd, by foolery thrive!
There's place and means for every man alive.
I'll after them. [*Exit.*

SCENE IV. *Florence. The* Widow's *house.*

Enter HELENA, Widow, *and* DIANA.

Hel. That you may well perceive I have not wrong'd you,
One of the greatest in the Christian world
Shall be my surety; 'fore whose throne 'tis needful,
Ere I can perfect mine intents, to kneel:

296. *the sonnet*] $F_1 F_2$. *the same sonnet* F_3 F_4. *that same sonnet* Rowe.

297. *an*] *and* Ff. *if* Pope.

298. [Exeunt B. and Lords.] Exeunt. Ff.

305. [Exit...] Exit. Ff.

306. SCENE VI. Pope. *am I*] *I am* Hanmer.

312. After this S. Walker conjectures that a line has been omitted.

SCENE IV.] SCENE VII. Pope.

3. *'fore*] *for* F_1.

Time was, I did him a desired office,
Dear almost as his life; which gratitude
Through flinty Tartar's bosom would peep forth,
And answer, thanks: I duly am inform'd
His Grace is at Marseilles; to which place
We have convenient convoy. You must know,
I am supposed dead: the army breaking,
My husband hies him home; where, heaven aiding,
And by the leave of my good lord the king,
We'll be before our welcome.

Wid. Gentle madam,
You never had a servant to whose trust
Your business was more welcome.

Hel. Nor you, mistress,
Ever a friend whose thoughts more truly labour
To recompense your love: doubt not but heaven
Hath brought me up to be your daughter's dower,
As it hath fated her to be my motive
And helper to a husband. But, O strange men!
That can such sweet use make of what they hate,
When saucy trusting of the cozen'd thoughts
Defiles the pitchy night: so lust doth play
With what it loathes for that which is away.
But more of this hereafter. You, Diana,
Under my poor instructions yet must suffer
Something in my behalf.

Dia. Let death and honesty
Go with your impositions, I am yours
Upon your will to suffer.

Hel. Yet, I pray you:

6. *which*] *for which* Hanmer.

9. *is at*] *it* F_2.

Marseilles] Rowe (ed. 2). *Marcellæ* F_1. *Marsellis* F_2F_3. *Marselis* F_4.

16. *you*] F_4. *your* $F_1F_2F_3$.

23. *saucy trusting of*] Ff. *fancy trusting in* Hanmer. *fancy trusting of* Warburton.

30, 31. *I pray you: But with the word*] Ff. *I pray you, Bear with the word:* Hanmer. *I pray you, But with the word:* Capell. *I pray you,—But with the word,* Steevens (Henley conj.). *I fray you But with the word:* Collier (Blackstone conj.). *I play you But with the word:* Jackson conj. *I pray you: But with the world* Collier MS. *I pay you But with the word;* Grant White. *I pay you But with the word,* Staunton conj.

But with the word the time will bring on summer,
When briers shall have leaves as well as thorns,
And be as sweet as sharp. We must away;
Our waggon is prepared, and time revives us:
ALL'S WELL THAT ENDS WELL: still the fine's the crown;
Whate'er the course, the end is the renown. [*Exeunt.*

SCENE V. *Rousillon. The* COUNT'S *palace.*

Enter COUNTESS, LAFEU, *and* Clown.

Laf. No, no, no, your son was misled with a snipt-taffeta fellow there, whose villanous saffron would have made all the unbaked and doughy youth of a nation in his colour: your daughter-in-law had been alive at this hour, and your son here at home, more advanced by the king than by that red-tailed humble-bee I speak of.

Count. I would I had not known him; it was the death of the most virtuous gentlewoman that ever nature had praise for creating. If she had partaken of my flesh, and cost me the dearest groans of a mother, I could not have owed her a more rooted love.

Laf. 'Twas a good lady, 'twas a good lady: we may pick a thousand salads ere we light on such another herb.

Clo. Indeed, sir, she was the sweet-marjoram of the salad, or rather, the herb of grace.

Laf. They are not herbs, you knave; they are nose-herbs.

31—33. *But...away*] *But—with the word 'The time...sharp,'—we must away* Anon. conj.

34. *revives*] Ff. *reviles* Hanmer. *revyes* Warburton. *invites* Johnson and Heath conj.

35. *the fine's*] Theobald. *the fines* F_1. *that fines* F_2F_3. *that finds* F_4.

36. *course*] *curse* Rowe (ed. 2).

SCENE V.] SCENE VIII. Pope.

COUNTESS,] Old Lady, Ff.

5. *advanced*] *advantaged* Warburton.

6. *than by that*] *but for that* Hanmer.

7. *I had*] *he had* Hanmer (Theobald conj.).

13. *salads*] *sallets* Ff.

15. *salad*] *sallet* Ff.

16. *herbs*] Ff. *sallet-herbs* Rowe. *pot-herbs* Collier MS.

Clo. I am no great Nebuchadnezzar, sir; I have not much skill in grass.

Laf. Whether dost thou profess thyself, a knave or a fool?

Clo. A fool, sir, at a woman's service, and a knave at a man's.

Laf. Your distinction?

Clo. I would cozen the man of his wife and do his service.

Laf. So you were a knave at his service, indeed.

Clo. And I would give his wife my bauble, sir, to do her service.

Laf. I will subscribe for thee, thou art both knave and fool.

Clo. At your service.

Laf. No, no, no.

Clo. Why, sir, if I cannot serve you, I can serve as great a prince as you are.

Laf. Who's that? a Frenchman?

Clo. Faith, sir, a' has an English name; but his fisnomy is more hotter in France than there.

Laf. What prince is that?

Clo. The black prince, sir; alias, the prince of darkness; alias, the devil.

Laf. Hold thee, there's my purse: I give thee not this to suggest thee from thy master thou talkest of; serve him still.

Clo. I am a woodland fellow, sir, that always loved a great fire; and the master I speak of ever keeps a good fire. But, sure, he is the prince of the world; let his nobility remain in's court. I am for the house with the narrow gate, which I take to be too little for pomp to enter: some that humble themselves may; but the many will be too chill

19. *grass*] Rowe. *grace* Ff.

24. *his wife*] *this wife* F_2.

26. *bauble*] *folly* Hanmer.

34. *Who's*] F_4. *Whose* $F_1F_2F_3$.

35. *a'*] *a* Ff. *he* Rowe (ed. 2).
name] Rowe. *maine* F_1F_2. *main* F_3. *mean* F_4. *mien* Anon. conj.

36. *hotter*] *honour'd* Hanmer (Warburton).
there] F_1F_2. *here* F_3F_4.

41. *suggest*] *seduce* Rowe (ed. 2).

42. *I am*] *I'm* Theobald.

43, 44. *fire. But, sure, he...world;*] *fire, but sure he...world,* Ff. *fire; but since he...world,* Hanmer. *fire. But, for he...world,* Capell.

44. *his*] *the* Collier MS.

and tender, and they'll be for the flowery way that leads to the broad gate and the great fire.

Laf. Go thy ways, I begin to be aweary of thee; and I tell thee so before, because I would not fall out with thee. Go thy ways: let my horses be well looked to, without any tricks.

Clo. If I put any tricks upon 'em, sir, they shall be jades' tricks; which are their own right by the law of nature. [*Exit.*

Laf. A shrewd knave and an unhappy.

Count. So he is. My lord that's gone made himself much sport out of him: by his authority he remains here, which he thinks is a patent for his sauciness; and, indeed, he has no pace, but runs where he will.

Laf. I like him well; 'tis not amiss. And I was about to tell you, since I heard of the good lady's death and that my lord your son was upon his return home, I moved the king my master to speak in the behalf of my daughter; which, in the minority of them both, his majesty, out of a self-gracious remembrance, did first propose: his highness hath promised me to do it: and, to stop up the displeasure he hath conceived against your son, there is no fitter matter. How does your ladyship like it?

Count. With very much content, my lord; and I wish it happily effected.

Laf. His highness comes post from Marseilles, of as able body as when he numbered thirty: he will be here to-morrow, or I am deceived by him that in such intelligence hath seldom failed.

Count. It rejoices me, that I hope I shall see him ere I die. I have letters that my son will be here to-night: I shall beseech your lordship to remain with me till they meet together.

54. *sir*] om. Rowe.
57. *he*] Rowe. *a* Ff.
60. *pace*] *place* Hanmer.
runs] *he runs* F_3F_4.
72. *Marseilles*] Pope. *Marcellus* F_1. *Marsellis* F_2. *Marselles* F_3F_4.
73. *he*] Rowe (ed. 2). *a* Ff. *and* Rowe (ed. 1).
76. *It*] *Ir* F_1. *I* F_2.
that I hope I] *that hope that I* Warburton.

Laf. Madam, I was thinking with what manners I might safely be admitted.

Count. You need but plead your honourable privilege.

Laf. Lady, of that I have made a bold charter; but I thank my God it holds yet.

Re-enter Clown.

Clo. O madam, yonder's my lord your son with a patch of velvet on's face: whether there be a scar under't or no, the velvet knows; but 'tis a goodly patch of velvet: his left cheek is a cheek of two pile and a half, but his right cheek is worn bare.

Laf. A scar nobly got, or a noble scar, is a good livery of honour; so belike is that.

Clo. But it is your carbonadoed face.

Laf. Let us go see your son, I pray you: I long to talk with the young noble soldier.

Clo. Faith, there's a dozen of 'em, with delicate fine hats and most courteous feathers, which bow the head and nod at every man. [*Exeunt.*

ACT V.

SCENE I. *Marseilles. A street.*

Enter HELENA, Widow, *and* DIANA, *with two* Attendants.

Hel. But this exceeding posting day and night
Must wear your spirits low; we cannot help it:
But since you have made the days and nights as one,

90. Laf.] F_1. La. $F_2F_3F_4$. Count Rowe.

90, 91. *A scar...that*] Printed as three lines in Ff, ending *got...honour ...that.*

92. *carbonadoed*] Theobald. *carbinado'd* Ff.

93. Laf.] $F_1F_3F_4$. La. F_2 (and frequently in this scene).

93, 94. *Let us...soldier*] Printed as three lines in Ff, ending *see...talk... soldier.*

Marseilles. A street.] Capell. The Court of France. Pope.

3. *you have*] *you've* Pope.

To wear your gentle limbs in my affairs,
Be bold you do so grow in my requital
As nothing can unroot you. In happy time;

Enter a Gentleman.

This man may help me to his majesty's ear,
If he would spend his power. God save you, sir.
Gent. And you.
Hel. Sir, I have seen you in the court of France.
Gent. I have been sometimes there.
Hel. I do presume, sir, that you are not fallen
From the report that goes upon your goodness;
And therefore, goaded with most sharp occasions,
Which lay nice manners by, I put you to
The use of your own virtues, for the which
I shall continue thankful.
Gent. What's your will?
Hel. That it will please you
To give this poor petition to the king,
And aid me with that store of power you have
To come into his presence.
Gent. The king's not here.
Hel. Not here, sir!
Gent. Not, indeed:
He hence removed last night and with more haste
Than is his use.
Wid. Lord, how we lose our pains!
Hel. ALL'S WELL THAT ENDS WELL yet,
Though time seem so adverse and means unfit.
I do beseech you, whither is he gone?
Gent. Marry, as I take it, to Rousillon;
Whither I am going.
Hel. I do beseech you, sir,
Since you are like to see the king before me,
Commend the paper to his gracious hand,

6. Enter a Gentleman.] Rowe. Enter a gentle Astringer. F_1. Enter a gentle Astranger. F_2. Enter a Gentleman a stranger. F_3F_4.
16. *virtues*] *virtue* S. Walker conj.
29. *I do*] *I* Hanmer.

Which I presume shall render you no blame
But rather make you thank your pains for it.
I will come after you with what good speed
Our means will make us means.

Gent. This I'll do for you.

Hel. And you shall find yourself to be well thank'd,
Whate'er falls more. We must to horse again.
Go, go, provide. [*Exeunt.*

SCENE II. *Rousillon. Before the* COUNT'S *palace.*

Enter Clown, *and* PAROLLES, *following.*

Par. Good Monsieur Lavache, give my Lord Lafeu this letter: I have ere now, sir, been better known to you, when I have held familiarity with fresher clothes; but I am now, sir, muddied in fortune's mood, and smell somewhat strong of her strong displeasure.

Clo. Truly, fortune's displeasure is but sluttish, if it smell so strongly as thou speakest of: I will henceforth eat no fish of fortune's buttering. Prithee, allow the wind.

Par. Nay, you need not to stop your nose, sir; I spake but by a metaphor.

Clo. Indeed, sir, if your metaphor stink, I will stop my nose; or against any man's metaphor. Prithee, get thee further.

Par. Pray you, sir, deliver me this paper.

Clo. Foh! prithee, stand away: a paper from fortune's close-stool to give to a nobleman! Look, here he comes himself.

35. *make us means.*] *make us.* Anon. conj.

36—38. Printed as prose in Ff. First as verse by Pope.

SCENE II. Before...palace.] Edd. Inner-court of the palace. Capell.

following.] Capell. ill-favoured. Collier MS.

1. *Monsieur*] *Mr* Ff.

Lavache] Edd. (Tollet conj.). *Lavatch* Ff. *Lapatch* Jervis conj.

4. *mood*] *moat* Theobald. See note (XVII).

10. *spake*] F_1. *speake* F_2. *speak* F_3F_4.

12. *or against*] *against* Theobald.

Enter LAFEU.

Here is a purr of fortune's, sir, or of fortune's cat,—but not a musk-cat,—that has fallen into the unclean fishpond of her displeasure, and, as he says, is muddied withal: pray you, sir, use the carp as you may; for he looks like a poor, decayed, ingenious, foolish, rascally knave. I do pity his distress in my similes of comfort and leave him to your lordship. [*Exit.*

Par. My lord, I am a man whom fortune hath cruelly scratched.

Laf. And what would you have me to do? 'Tis too late to pare her nails now. Wherein have you played the knave with fortune, that she should scratch you, who of herself is a good lady and would not have knaves thrive long under her? There's a quart d'écu for you: let the justices make you and fortune friends: I am for other business.

Par. I beseech your honour to hear me one single word.

Laf. You beg a single penny more: come, you shall ha't; save your word.

Par. My name, my good lord, is Parolles.

Laf. You beg more than 'word,' then. Cox my passion! give me your hand. How does your drum?

Par. O my good lord, you were the first that found me!

Laf. Was I, in sooth? and I was the first that lost thee.

Par. It lies in you, my lord, to bring me in some grace, for you did bring me out.

18. *Here*] Clo. *Here* Ff.
purr] *purre* $F_1F_2F_3$. *pur* F_4. *puss* Mason conj.
or of] *or* Warburton.

19. *musk-cat*] Theobald. *Muscat* Ff. *mouse-cat* Anon. conj.
has] *hath* Pope.

22. *ingenious*] *ingenuous* Anon. conj.

23. *similes*] Theobald (Warburton). *smiles* Ff.

31. *under her?*] $F_2F_3F_4$. *under?* F_1.
quart'd'écu] Pope. *cardecue* Ff.

36. *You*] *If you* Anon. conj.

39. '*word*'] *word* F_1F_2. *one word* F_3F_4. *a word* Collier (Egerton MS.).

45. *lies in you*] *lies on you* Capell.

Laf. Out upon thee, knave! dost thou put upon me at once both the office of God and the devil? One brings thee in grace and the other brings thee out. [*Trumpets sound.*] The king's coming; I know by his trumpets. Sirrah, inquire further after me; I had talk of you last night: though you are a fool and a knave, you shall eat; go to, follow.

Par. I praise God for you. [*Exeunt.*

SCENE III. *Rousillon. The* COUNT'S *palace.*

Flourish. Enter KING, COUNTESS, LAFEU, *the two* French Lords, *with* Attendants.

King. We lost a jewel of her; and our esteem
Was made much poorer by it: but your son,
As mad in folly, lack'd the sense to know
Her estimation home.

Count. 'Tis past, my liege;
And I beseech your majesty to make it
Natural rebellion, done i' the blaze of youth;
When oil and fire, too strong for reason's force,
O'erbears it and burns on.

King. My honour'd lady,
I have forgiven and forgotten all;
Though my revenges were high bent upon him,
And watch'd the time to shoot.

Laf. This I must say,
But first I beg my pardon, the young lord
Did to his majesty, his mother and his lady
Offence of mighty note; but to himself
The greatest wrong of all. He lost a wife
Whose beauty did astonish the survey
Of richest eyes, whose words all ears took captive,
Whose dear perfection hearts that scorn'd to serve

49. [Trumpets sound.] Sound trumpets. Theobald. om. Ff.

SCENE III. The Count's palace.] A Room of State in the Palace. Capell.

COUNTESS] old Lady Ff.

1. *of her*] F_1F_2. om. F_3F_4. *esteem*] *estate* Warburton conj. (withdrawn).

6. *blaze*] Warburton. *blade* Ff.

8. *O'erbears ... burns*] *O'er-bear ... burn* Hanmer.

12, 13. *But...lady*] Hanmer ends these lines at *did...lady*.

Humbly call'd mistress.
King. Praising what is lost
Makes the remembrance dear. Well, call him hither;
We are reconciled, and the first view shall kill
All repetition: let him not ask our pardon;
The nature of his great offence is dead,
And deeper than oblivion we do bury
The incensing relics of it: let him approach,
A stranger, no offender; and inform him
So 'tis our will he should.
Gent. I shall, my liege. [*Exit.*
King. What says he to your daughter? have you spoke?
Laf. All that he is hath reference to your highness.
King. Then shall we have a match. I have letters sent me
That set him high in fame.

Enter BERTRAM.

Laf. He looks well on't.
King. I am not a day of season,
For thou mayst see a sunshine and a hail
In me at once: but to the brightest beams
Distracted clouds give way; so stand thou forth;
The time is fair again.
Ber. My high-repented blames,
Dear sovereign, pardon to me.
King. All is whole;
Not one word more of the consumed time.
Let's take the instant by the forward top;
For we are old, and on our quick'st decrees
The inaudible and noiseless foot of Time
Steals ere we can effect them. You remember
The daughter of this lord?

21. *We are*] *We're* Pope.
23. *nature*] *matter* Hanmer.
24. *we do*] *do we* Reed.
28. *What...spoke?*] As two lines in Ff, ending *daughter...spoke?*
30, 31. Printed as prose in Ff. First as verse by Pope.
31. *set*] Rowe. *sets* Ff.
32. *I am*] *I'm* Pope.
SCENE IV. Pope.
Enter Bertram.] Enter Count Bertram. Ff.
39. *forward*] *forehead* Anon. conj.

Ber. Admiringly, my liege, at first
I stuck my choice upon her, ere my heart
Durst make too bold a herald of my tongue:
Where the impression of mine eye infixing,
Contempt his scornful perspective did lend me,
Which warp'd the line of every other favour;
Scorn'd a fair colour, or express'd it stolen;
Extended or contracted all proportions
To a most hideous object: thence it came
That she whom all men praised and whom myself,
Since I have lost, have loved, was in mine eye
The dust that did offend it.

King. Well excused:
That thou didst love her, strikes some scores away
From the great compt: but love that comes too late,
Like a remorseful pardon slowly carried,
To the great sender turns a sour offence,
Crying 'That's good that's gone.' Our rash faults
Make trivial price of serious things we have,
Not knowing them until we know their grave:
Oft our displeasures, to ourselves unjust,
Destroy our friends and after weep their dust:
Our own love waking cries to see what's done,
While shameful hate sleeps out the afternoon.
Be this sweet Helen's knell, and now forget her.
Send forth your amorous token for fair Maudlin:

44. *Admiringly, my liege, at first*] F_3F_4. *Admiringly my liege, at first* F_1F_2. *Admiringly, my liege. At first* Rowe. *Admiringly, my liege. Even at first* Hanmer. *Admiringly, my liege; at the first sight* Capell. *Admiringly. My liege, at first* Collier.

49. *warp'd*] *warpt* F_1F_2. *wrapt* F_3F_4.

50. *Scorn'd*] *Scorch'd* Hanmer (Warburton). *Scors'd* Becket conj.

58, 59. *Like...offence,*] (*Like...To an offender*) *turns to sour repentance* Hanmer.

carried,...sender] Theobald. *carried...sender,* Ff. *carried,...sender;* Rowe.

59. *sour*] *sore* Collier MS.

60. *that's gone*] *that is gone* Rowe (ed. 2).

Our] *Our own* Capell.

faults] *thoughts* Long MS.

61. *trivial*] *triviall* F_1F_2. *triall* F_3. *trial* F_4.

65, 66. *Our...afternoon*] omitted in Collier MS.

65. *own*] *old* Collier (Mason conj.).

66. *shameful hate*] *shapeful hate* F_4. *shame full late* W. G. C. (Fras. Mag.) conj.

sleeps] *slept* Johnson conj.

67, 68. *forget her...fair Maudlin*] *forget...Margaret* Anon. conj.

The main consents are had; and here we'll stay
To see our widower's second marriage-day.
Count. Which better than the first, O dear heaven, bless!
Or, ere they meet, in me, O nature, cesse!
Laf. Come on, my son, in whom my house's name
Must be digested, give a favour from you
To sparkle in the spirits of my daughter,
That she may quickly come. [*Bertram gives a ring.*] By my old beard,
And every hair that's on't, Helen, that's dead,
Was a sweet creature: such a ring as this,
The last that e'er I took her leave at court,
I saw upon her finger.
Ber. Hers it was not.
King. Now, pray you, let me see it; for mine eye,
While I was speaking, oft was fasten'd to't.
This ring was mine; and, when I gave it Helen,
I bade her, if her fortunes ever stood
Necessitied to help, that by this token
I would relieve her. Had you that craft, to reave her
Of what should stead her most?
Ber. My gracious sovereign,
Howe'er it pleases you to take it so,
The ring was never hers.
Count. Son, on my life,
I have seen her wear it; and she reckon'd it
At her life's rate.
Laf. I am sure I saw her wear it.
Ber. You are deceived, my lord; she never saw it:
In Florence was it from a casement thrown me,

71. Count.] Theobald. Continued to King in Ff.
O dear] *dear* Lloyd conj.
72. *meet,*] Rowe. *meete* F_1F_2. *meet* F_3F_4.
in me] *in one* Long MS.
cesse] F_1. *ceasse* F_2. *ceass* F_3. *cease* F_4.
74. *digested*] F_1F_4. *disgested* F_2F_3.
76. [B. gives a ring.] Hanmer.
79. *that e'er I*] *that ere I* Ff. *that e'er she* Rowe. *time e'er she* Hanmer. *time, ere she* Collier (Collier MS.).
that...leave] *leave that I took of her* Jervis conj.
85. *Necessitied*] $F_1F_2F_3$. *Necessited* F_4.
90. *I have*] *I've* Pope.
91. *life's*] Rowe. *lives* Ff.
I am] *I'm* Pope.

Wrapp'd in a paper, which contain'd the name
Of her that threw it: noble she was, and thought
I stood engaged: but when I had subscribed
To mine own fortune and inform'd her fully
I could not answer in that course of honour
As she had made the overture, she ceased
In heavy satisfaction and would never
Receive the ring again.

King. Plutus himself,
That knows the tinct and multiplying medicine,
Hath not in nature's mystery more science
Than I have in this ring: 'twas mine, 'twas Helen's,
Whoever gave it you. Then, if you know
That you are well acquainted with yourself,
Confess 'twas hers, and by what rough enforcement
You got it from her: she call'd the saints to surety
That she would never put it from her finger,
Unless she gave it to yourself in bed,
Where you have never come, or sent it us
Upon her great disaster.

Ber. She never saw it.

King. Thou speak'st it falsely, as I love mine honour;
And makest conjectural fears to come into me,
Which I would fain shut out. If it should prove
That thou art so inhuman,—'twill not prove so;—
And yet I know not: thou didst hate her deadly,
And she is dead; which nothing, but to close
Her eyes myself, could win me to believe,
More than to see this ring. Take him away.
[*Guards seize Bertram.*
My fore-past proofs, howe'er the matter fall,
Shall tax my fears of little vanity,
Having vainly fear'd too little. Away with him!

96. *engaged*] Rowe. *ingag'd* Ff. *ungag'd* Theobald. *in gage* Jackson conj.

101. *Plutus*] Rowe (ed. 2). *Platus* Ff.

110. *yourself*] *you selfe* F_2.

114. *conjectural*] *connecturall* F_1.

115. *would fain*] *should fain* Capell (corrected in MS.).

out.] *out,* $F_1F_2F_3$. *out;* F_4.

120. [Guards seize B.] Rowe.

122. *tax*] F_3F_4. *taxe* F_2. *taze* F_1.

We'll sift this matter further.

Ber. If you shall prove
This ring was ever hers, you shall as easy
Prove that I husbanded her bed in Florence,
Where yet she never was. [*Exit, guarded.*

King. I am wrapp'd in dismal thinkings.

Enter a Gentleman.

Gent. Gracious sovereign,
Whether I have been to blame or no, I know not:
Here's a petition from a Florentine,
Who hath for four or five removes come short
To tender it herself. I undertook it,
Vanquish'd thereto by the fair grace and speech
Of the poor suppliant, who by this I know
Is here attending: her business looks in her
With an importing visage; and she told me,
In a sweet verbal brief, it did concern
Your highness with herself.

King. [*reads*] Upon his many protestations to marry me when his wife was dead, I blush to say it, he won me. Now is the Count Rousillon a widower: his vows are forfeited to me, and my honour's paid to him. He stole from Florence, taking no leave, and I follow him to his country for justice: grant it me, O king! in you it best lies; otherwise a seducer flourishes, and a poor maid is undone. DIANA CAPILET.

Laf. I will buy me a son-in-law in a fair, and toll for this: I'll none of him.

127. [Exit, guarded.] Rowe.

128. SCENE V. Pope.
I am] *I'm* Pope.
thinkings] *thinking* Rowe.
Enter...] Ff (after line 127). Enter the Astringer. Grant White.

129. *I have*] *I've* Pope.
to blame] *too blame* Ff.

131. *hath*] *had* Heath conj.
for four] *some four* Warburton.

136. *importing*] *important* Boswell (1821).

139. King. [reads] A letter. Ff. The King reads a letter. Rowe.

143. *his*] F_1F_2. *this* F_3F_4.

144. *you it best*] *your breast it* Hanmer.

145, 157. *Capilet*] Ff. *Capulet* Rowe.

146. *fair*] *faire* F_1. *feare* F_2. *fear* F_3F_4.
and toll] *a toule* Becket conj.

146, 147. *toll for this: I'll*] *toule for this. Ile* F_1. *toule him for this. Ile* $F_2F_3F_4$. *toll for him. For this, I'll* Theobald. *toll him: for this, I'll* Steevens. *toll: for this, I'll* Collier (Mason conj.). *towl him: for this, I'll* Grant White.

147. *this...him*] *him...this* Anon. conj.

King. The heavens have thought well on thee, Lafeu,
To bring forth this discovery. Seek these suitors:
Go speedily and bring again the count.
I am afeard the life of Helen, lady,
Was foully snatch'd.

Count. Now, justice on the doers!

Re-enter BERTRAM, *guarded.*

King. I wonder, sir, sith wives are monsters to you,
And that you fly them as you swear them lordship,
Yet you desire to marry.

Enter Widow *and* DIANA.

What woman's that?

Dia. I am, my lord, a wretched Florentine,
Derived from the ancient Capilet:
My suit, as I do understand, you know,
And therefore know how far I may be pitied.

Wid. I am her mother, sir, whose age and honour
Both suffer under this complaint we bring,
And both shall cease, without your remedy.

King. Come hither, count; do you know these women?

Ber. My lord, I neither can nor will deny
But that I know them: do they charge me further?

Dia. Why do you look so strange upon your wife?

150. [Exeunt some Attendants. Capell. Exeunt Gentleman and some Attendants. Malone.

151. *afeard*] *afraid* Rowe.

152. Re-enter B., guarded.] Capell. Enter Bertram. Ff (after line 150).

153. *sir, sith wives are monsters*] Dyce. *sir, sir, wives are monsters* F_1. *sir, wives are such monsters* F_2. *sir, wives are so monstrous* F_3F_4. *sir, since wives are monsters* Steevens (Tyrwhitt conj.). *sir, sin wives are monsters* Becket conj. *sir, for wives are monsters* Collier (Egerton MS.).

154. *them lordship*] *to them* Rowe (ed. 2). *them worship* Anon. conj.

155. *marry*] *wed* Pope.

Enter Widow and Diana.] Enter Widdow, Diana, and Parolles. Ff. Re-enter Gentleman with Widow and Diana. Malone. Enter the Astringer with... Grant White.

157. *Capilet*] *Capulets* Heath conj.

163. *hither*] $F_2F_3F_4$. *hether* F_1.

count; do you] *count; do you not* Hanmer. *count; say, do you* Capell. *county, do you* S. Walker conj.

Ber. She's none of mine, my lord.

Dia. If you shall marry,
You give away this hand, and that is mine;
You give away heaven's vows, and those are mine;
You give away myself, which is known mine;
For I by vow am so embodied yours,
That she which marries you must marry me,
Either both or none.

Laf. Your reputation comes too short for my daughter; you are no husband for her.

Ber. My lord, this a fond and desperate creature,
Whom sometime I have laugh'd with: let your highness
Lay a more noble thought upon mine honour
Than for to think that I would sink it here.

King. Sir, for my thoughts, you have them ill to friend
Till your deeds gain them: fairer prove your honour
Than in my thought it lies.

Dia. Good my lord,
Ask him upon his oath, if he does think
He had not my virginity.

King. What say'st thou to her?

Ber. She's impudent, my lord,
And was a common gamester to the camp.

Dia. He does me wrong, my lord; if I were so,
He might have bought me at a common price:
Do not believe him. O, behold this ring,
Whose high respect and rich validity
Did lack a parallel; yet for all that
He gave it to a commoner o' the camp,
If I be one.

Count. He blushes, and 'tis it:

168. *that is*] *this is* or *that were* Seymour conj.

170. *myself*] *my flesh* Hanmer.

174. *too*] om. Hanmer, who reads lines 174, 175 as verse, ending *comes* ...*her*.

[To Bertram. Rowe.

179. *Than for*] *Than e'er* Pope. *Than so* Collier MS.

181. *them: fairer*] Hanmer (Theobald conj.). *them fairer:* Ff.

182. *Good*] *Now, good* Hanmer.

192, 204. *o'*] Rowe. *a'* Ff.

193. Count.] Coun. F_1. Boun. F_2. Old La. F_3F_4.

'tis it] Capell. *'tis hit* Ff. *'tis his* Pope. *is hit* Malone conj. *'tis fit* Henley conj.

Of six preceding ancestors, that gem,
Conferr'd by testament to the sequent issue,
Hath it been owed and worn. This is his wife;
That ring's a thousand proofs.

King. Methought you said
You saw one here in court could witness it.

Dia. I did, my lord, but loath am to produce
So bad an instrument: his name's Parolles.

Laf. I saw the man to-day, if man he be.

King. Find him, and bring him hither.
[*Exit an Attendant.*

Ber. What of him?
He's quoted for a most perfidious slave,
With all the spots o' the world tax'd and debosh'd;
Whose nature sickens but to speak a truth.
Am I or that or this for what he'll utter,
That will speak any thing?

King. She hath that ring of yours.

Ber. I think she has: certain it is I liked her,
And boarded her i' the wanton way of youth:
She knew her distance, and did angle for me,
Madding my eagerness with her restraint,
As all impediments in fancy's course
Are motives of more fancy; and, in fine,
Her infinite cunning, with her modern grace,
Subdued me to her rate: she got the ring;
And I had that which any inferior might
At market-price have bought.

Dia. I must be patient:

195. *to the sequent*] *to 'th sequent* F_1F_2. *to th' sequent* F_3F_4. *to th' subsequent* Pope.

196. *it*] *so* Hanmer.

202. [Exit an Attendant. Dyce.
him?] $F_2F_3F_4$. *him:* F_1.

205. *Whose nature sickens but... truth.*] Hanmer. *Whose nature sickens: but...truth,* Ff. *Which nature sickens with: but to speak truth,* Rowe.

210. *for me*] F_1. *of me* $F_2F_3F_4$.

214. *infinite cunning*] Singer (S. Walker conj.). *insuite comming* F_1. *insuit comming* F_2F_3. *insuit coming* F_4. *in suit coming* Hanmer. *insuit cunning* Easy conj. *instant comity* Bubier conj.

infinite...grace] *own suit joining with her mother's, scarce* Heath conj.

modern] *modest* Long MS.

216. *any*] *an* or *my* S. Walker conj.

You, that have turn'd off a first so noble wife,
May justly diet me. I pray you yet,
Since you lack virtue I will lose a husband,
Send for your ring, I will return it home,
And give me mine again.

Ber. I have it not.

King. What ring was yours, I pray you?

Dia. Sir, much like
The same upon your finger.

King. Know you this ring? this ring was his of late.

Dia. And this was it I gave him, being abed.

King. The story then goes false, you threw it him
Out of a casement.

Dia. I have spoke the truth.

Enter PAROLLES.

Ber. My lord, I do confess the ring was hers.

King. You boggle shrewdly, every feather starts you.
Is this the man you speak of?

Dia. Ay, my lord.

King. Tell me, sirrah, but tell me true, I charge you,
Not fearing the displeasure of your master,
Which on your just proceeding I'll keep off,
By him and by this woman here what know you?

Par. So please your majesty, my master hath been an honourable gentleman: tricks he hath had in him, which gentlemen have.

King. Come, come, to the purpose: did he love this woman?

218. *have turn'd off*] Ff. *turn'd off* Rowe (ed. 2).

219. *diet*] *edict* Jackson conj.

221. *it*] *this* Hanmer.

223, 224. *Sir,...finger*] Metre as in Capell. As one line in Ff. *Much like that same upon your finger, sir.* Hanmer.

228. Dia. *I have...truth*] omitted by Rowe.

[Enter P.] Ff. Re-enter Attendant, with P. Dyce (after line 230).

229. SCENE VI. Pope.

231. *Ay*] *It is* Theobald.

232. *Tell me, sirrah*] *Now tell me, sirrah* Capell.

sirrah, but tell me true] *but tell me true, sirrah* Hanmer.

237. *gentleman*] *gentlemen* F_2.

Par. Faith, sir, he did love her; but how?

King. How, I pray you?

Par. He did love her, sir, as a gentleman loves a woman.

King. How is that?

Par. He loved her, sir, and loved her not.

King. As thou art a knave, and no knave. What an equivocal companion is this!

Par. I am a poor man, and at your majesty's command.

Laf. He's a good drum, my lord, but a naughty orator.

Dia. Do you know he promised me marriage?

Par. Faith, I know more than I'll speak.

King. But wilt thou not speak all thou knowest?

Par. Yes, so please your majesty. I did go between them, as I said; but more than that, he loved her: for indeed he was mad for her, and talked of Satan, and of Limbo, and of Furies, and I know not what: yet I was in that credit with them at that time, that I knew of their going to bed, and of other motions, as promising her marriage, and things which would derive me ill will to speak of; therefore I will not speak what I know.

King. Thou hast spoken all already, unless thou canst say they are married: but thou art too fine in thy evidence; therefore stand aside.
This ring, you say, was yours?

Dia. Ay, my good lord.

King. Where did you buy it? or who gave it you?

Dia. It was not given me, nor I did not buy it.

King. Who lent it you?

Dia. It was not lent me neither.

King. Where did you find it, then?

Dia. I found it not.

King. If it were yours by none of all these ways,

241, 242. *but how?* King. *How,*] King. *But how, how,* Malone conj.

243. *gentleman*] Rowe. *Gent.* Ff.

246. *knave.*] *knave,* Ff. *knave;* Rowe.

252. *But*] *What!* Capell conj.

254. *than that, he*] F_4. *then that he* F_1F_2. *then that, he* F_3. *loved her:*] *lov'd her,*—Capell.

259. *which*] F_1F_2. *that* F_3F_4.

261—263. Collier prints as three lines ending *canst...fine...aside.*

266. *nor I did not*] F_1F_2. *nor did not* F_3F_4. *nor did I* Theobald.

How could you give it him?
Dia. I never gave it him.
Laf. This woman's an easy glove, my lord; she goes off and on at pleasure.
King. This ring was mine; I gave it his first wife.
Dia. It might be yours or hers, for aught I know.
King. Take her away; I do not like her now;
To prison with her: and away with him.
Unless thou tell'st me where thou hadst this ring,
Thou diest within this hour.
Dia. I'll never tell you.
King. Take her away.
Dia. I'll put in bail, my liege.
King. I think thee now some common customer.
Dia. By Jove, if ever I knew man, 'twas you.
King. Wherefore hast thou accused him all this while?
Dia. Because he's guilty, and he is not guilty:
He knows I am no maid, and he'll swear to't;
I'll swear I am a maid, and he knows not.
Great king, I am no strumpet, by my life;
I am either maid, or else this old man's wife.
King. She does abuse our ears: to prison with her.
Dia. Good mother, fetch my bail. Stay, royal sir:
[*Exit Widow.*
The jeweller that owes the ring is sent for,
And he shall surety me. But for this lord,
Who hath abused me, as he knows himself,
Though yet he never harm'd me, here I quit him:
He knows himself my bed he hath defiled;
And at that time he got his wife with child:
Dead though she be, she feels her young one kick:
So there's my riddle,—One that's dead is quick:
And now behold the meaning.

270. *gave it*] *gave 't* S. Walker conj.
281. *Jove*] *God* Nicholson conj.
[To Lafeu. Hanmer.
287. *I am*] *I'm* Pope.
old] om. Long MS.
[Pointing to Laf. Rowe.
289. [Exit Widow.] Pope.

Re-enter Widow, *with* HELENA.

King. Is there no exorcist
Beguiles the truer office of mine eyes?
Is't real that I see?
Hel. No, my good lord;
'Tis but the shadow of a wife you see,
The name and not the thing.
Ber. Both, both. O, pardon!
Hel. O my good lord, when I was like this maid,
I found you wondrous kind. There is your ring;
And, look you, here's your letter; this it says:
'When from my finger you can get this ring
And are by me with child,' &c. This is done:
Will you be mine, now you are doubly won?
Ber. If she, my liege, can make me know this clearly,
I'll love her dearly, ever, ever dearly.
Hel. If it appear not plain and prove untrue,
Deadly divorce step between me and you!
O my dear mother, do I see you living?
Laf. Mine eyes smell onions; I shall weep anon:
[*To Parolles*] Good Tom Drum, lend me a handkercher: so,
I thank thee: wait on me home, I'll make sport with thee:
Let thy courtesies alone, they are scurvy ones.
King. Let us from point to point this story know,
To make the even truth in pleasure flow.
[*To Diana*] If thou be'st yet a fresh uncropped flower,
Choose thou thy husband, and I'll pay thy dower;
For I can guess that by thy honest aid
Thou kept'st a wife herself, thyself a maid.

298. Re-enter...] Capell. Enter Hellen and Widow. Ff.
307. *And are*] Rowe. *And is* Ff.
This is done] *This now is done* Hanmer.
315—317. Hanmer prints as three lines ending *handkerchief,...with thee:...ones.*
315. [To Parolles] Rowe.
Good...handkercher] as a verse in Ff. *Now good...* Hanmer.
handkercher] *handkerchief* Rowe.
316. *I thank*] *'thank* Hanmer.
320. [To Diana] Rowe.
323. *Thou kept'st*] *Thou'st kept* Anon. conj.
kept'st] *keptst* F_1. *keepist* F_2. *keepest* F_3F_4. *keep'st* Rowe (ed. 1). *kep'st* Rowe (ed. 2).

Of that and all the progress, more or less,
Resolvedly more leisure shall express:
All yet seems well; and if it end so meet,
The bitter past, more welcome is the sweet. [*Flourish.*

EPILOGUE.

King. The king's a beggar, now the play is done:
All is well ended, if this suit be won,
That you express content; which we will pay,
With strife to please you, day exceeding day:
Ours be your patience then, and yours our parts;
Your gentle hands lend us, and take our hearts. [*Exeunt.*

324. *or*] *and* Theobald.

325. *Resolvedly*] F_4. *Resoldvedly* F_1. *Resoldv'dly* F_2F_3.

327. [Flourish.] Ff. Exeunt. Rowe.

EPILOGUE.] Rowe. EPILOGUE spoken by the King. Pope. Advancing. Capell.

4. *strife*] *strift* F_1.

exceeding] *succeeding.* See note (XVIII).

NOTES.

Note I.

Dramatis Personæ. In the Folios Rousillon is spelt, almost without exception, 'Rossillion,' and Helena in the stage directions 'Hellen.' As the Clown's name occurs in the play we have introduced it among the 'Dramatis Personæ,' changing however the spelling from 'Lavatch' to 'Lavache.'

Violenta, whose name occurs in the stage direction at the beginning of Act III. Sc. 5, is a mute personage, but as it is possible that Diana's first speech in that scene should be given to her, we have retained the name in the list.

Note II.

I. 1. 153. It cannot be doubted that there is some omission here. The editors, except Steevens, who is satisfied with the text as it stands, substantially agree either with Hanmer's emendation or Malone's. Mr Grant White, however, thinks that in either case the transition would be too abrupt and that the passage omitted was longer and more important.

If it were not for the

> 'Pretty fond adoptious christendoms
> That blinking Cupid gossips,'

we should be inclined to suppose that the whole passage was by another hand. Indeed all the foregoing dialogue between Helena and Parolles is a blot on the play. Mr Badham (*Cambridge Essays*, 1856, p. 256) would strike out the whole passage (105—152) from 'Ay, you have &c.' to 'Will you any thing with it?' as an interpolation.

Note III.

I. 3. 50. No one has been able to discover the origin of the names 'Charbon' and 'Poysam,' or to guess at any probable meaning for them. Yet it is not likely that they should have been given at random. Is it possible that Shakespeare may have written 'Chairbonne' and 'Poisson,' alluding to the respective lenten fare of the Puritan and the Papist?

The same suggestion was made independently by Mr Easy (*Notes and Queries*, 3rd S. IV. 106) after the present note was in the printers' hands (Ibid. p. 203).

NOTE IV.

I. 3. 106. We have not inserted Theobald's admirable emendation in the text, because it is probable that something more has been omitted, perhaps a whole line of the MS.

Becket would transpose the sentences and read thus:

'......level. This she delivered......exclaim in.—Queen of Virgins! that......afterward. This I held......'

We take this opportunity of saying that many of Becket's proposed changes are so sweeping that we found it impossible to record them in the compass of a foot-note, and at the same time so improbable, that we did not think it worth while to record them separately at the end.

NOTE V.

I. 3. 118. We have followed the Folios in placing Helena's entry after line 118, rather than after 126, as most recent editors have done. The Countess may be supposed to be observing Helena earnestly as she enters with slow step and downcast eyes. Her words have thus more force and point.

NOTE VI.

II. 1. 1, 2. The editors have for the most part followed Hanmer's correction 'lord......lord' for 'lords......lords,' the reading of the Folios, on the ground that there is no reason why the lords who are taking leave should be divided into two sections. But from the stage direction 'divers young Lords,' it is clear that there are more than two. Mr Staunton thinks that the king first addresses himself to the young lords in general, and then turns to the two who are spokesmen in the scene and bids them share in the advice just given to their companions.

We rather incline to think that the young lords are divided into two sections according as they intended to take service with the 'Florentines' or the 'Senoys.' The king had said, I. 2. 13—15:

> Yet, for our gentlemen that mean to see
> The Tuscan service, freely have they leave
> To stand on either part.

Throughout this scene the two speakers whom Rowe and all subsequent editors have called 'First' and 'Second Lord' are called in the Folios 'Lord G.' and 'Lord E.' In all likelihood, as Capell has suggested, the parts were originally played by two actors whose names began respectively with G and E; and, in fact, in the list of 'Principall Actors' prefixed to the first Folio we find the names 'Gilburne,' 'Goughe' and 'Ecclestone.' The same actors doubtless took the parts of the two gentlemen who bring the letter to Helena in the 2nd scene of Act III., and who in the stage directions of the Folio are termed '*Fren. G.*' and '*Fren. E.*' Mr Collier indeed interprets these words to mean 'French Envoy' and 'French Gentleman,' but they are spoken of as 'two gentlemen' in the stage direction at line 41, and one was as much an 'envoy' as the other. This interpretation moreover leaves the 'G.' and 'E.' of the former scene and of subsequent scenes quite unexplained. Some have supposed the 'two gentlemen' of III. 1, to be the same as the 'two lords' of II. 1, and as far as the action of the Drama is concerned, there is no reason why they should not be, but when the two lords reappear in III. 6 they are introduced thus; 'Enter Count Rossillion and the Frenchmen, as at first:' which seems to prove that the two gentlemen were different persons though played by the same actors. In this latter scene the two lords are called Cap. G. and Cap. E. according to their rank in the Florentine service. The confusion of speakers in the dialogue at the close of this scene will be remedied if we suppose the Folio to have printed *Cap. G.* by mistake for *Cap. E.* in line 97 and *Cap. E.* for *Cap. G.* in lines 99, 105. 'Lord E.' appears again in IV. 1, and 'Cap. G.' and 'Cap. E.' in IV. 3.

NOTE VII.

II. I. 3. Johnson in his note to this passage says that all the latter copies have '...if both again,' and that Sir T. Hanmer reads 'if both gain all.' The statement as to Hanmer's reading was corrected in the 'Steevens and Johnson' of 1793, but that as to all the latter copies, though equally erroneous, was allowed to remain.

NOTE VIII.

II. I. 23. In the absence of any guidance from the Folios we have thought it better to follow Pope, who makes the king leave the stage, than Capell, who supposes that he retires to a couch. Bertram and Parolles could hardly, consistently with the etiquette of a court, or indeed the rules of good manners (of which Shakespeare had an instinctive knowledge), carry on a whispered conversation in the royal presence. The king we may suppose is carried out on a couch. When Bertram says, 'Stay: the king,' the ushers in attendance throw open the folding doors at the back of the stage, Bertram and Parolles retire close to one of the side doors, and while they are speaking together then the king is borne in upon his couch to the front of the stage. To say that the king retires to a couch, as Capell does, would imply that he was able to walk, but from what Lafeu says, lines 61, 62, it is clear that he could not even stand. We must therefore suppose that he is reclining on a couch throughout the whole scene. Thus, at his first appearance, his illness would be made evident to the spectators. After they have set the couch down, the attendants retire to the back of the stage so as to be out of ear-shot.

NOTE IX.

II. 1. 46. As printed in the Folios, the words 'what will ye do?' seem to be a taunt addressed, after the speaker's manner, to the young lords when their backs were turned and they were out of hearing.

NOTE X.

II. 1. 142. The correction made by Theobald is found also in a MS. note on the margin of the copy of the first Folio, which belongs to Lord Ellesmere, i.e. 'ffits' for 'shifts.' Theobald's emendation 'loneliness' for 'loveliness,' I. 3. 162, is also found there.

NOTE XI.

II. 3. 282. In the margin of the third Folio belonging to the Capell collection an unknown hand has made the correction 'detested' for 'detected.'

NOTE XII.

II. 5. 36. Another reading proposed by an anonymous correspondent of Theobald's will be found in his Letters to Warburton, Nichols' *Illustrations*, II. 346.

NOTE XIII.

III. 3. 3. Mr Grant White says that the Folio has merely '*Sir it*' —'*is*' having dropped out. He appears to have quoted from the reprint of the first Folio, published in 1808. The copies to which we have access read '*Sir it is.*'

NOTE XIV.

III. 7. 22. In this, as in so many other cases, Capell was the first to restore the true reading from F_1. Steevens follows him, but as usual without acknowledgement. Sometimes as at V. 3. 193, he passes his authority over in silence, sometimes as at I. 2. 35, he sedulously attributes to some one else that which was undoubtedly Capell's by priority of publication. At IV. 3. 152 he assigns to an anonymous correspondent a reading which Hanmer had introduced. Steevens probably derived his knowledge of it from Capell, who had adopted it. Such unworthy practices go far to explain and justify the enmities of which Steevens was the object during his life-time.

NOTE XV.

IV. 2. 25. The word *Jove's* has here probably been substituted for the original *God's* in obedience to the statute against profanity. Read '*God's*' and all is plain. 'How,' asks Diana, 'can you believe me if I swear by the purity and holiness of God to do an impure and unholy deed?'

Johnson said in his note that he could hardly distinguish whether the reading of the first Folio were *Iove's* or *Love's*. Ritson, who was not ashamed lusco dicere 'lusce,' taunted him bitterly.

NOTE XVI.

IV. 3. 55. Mr Singer says that the old copy (meaning the first Folio) misprints *selfe* for *itselfe*. Mr Collier tells us that some copies of F_1 have *itselfe*. All the copies we know of read *it selfe*.

NOTE XVII.

V. 2. 4. Warburton adopts Theobald's reading and copies in substance his note, but he has not claimed it in his copy of Theobald's edition. The conjecture was originally made in one of Theobald's letters to Warburton. Capell adopted the emendation, but afterwards repented.

NOTE XVIII.

EPILOGUE, 4. Mr Collier, in his second edition, quotes this substitution of 'succeeding' for 'exceeding,' but does not say by whom it was proposed.

TWELFTH NIGHT;

OR,

WHAT YOU WILL.

DRAMATIS PERSONÆ[1].

ORSINO, Duke of Illyria.
SEBASTIAN, brother to Viola.
ANTONIO, a sea captain, friend to Sebastian.
A Sea Captain, friend to Viola.
VALENTINE, CURIO, } gentlemen attending on the Duke.
SIR TOBY BELCH, uncle to Olivia.
SIR ANDREW AGUECHEEK.
MALVOLIO, steward to Olivia.
FABIAN, FESTE, a Clown, } servants to Olivia.

OLIVIA.
VIOLA.
MARIA, Olivia's woman.

Lords, Priests, Sailors, Officers, Musicians, and other Attendants.

SCENE: *A city in Illyria, and the sea-coast near it.*

[1] First given by Rowe. See note (I).

TWELFTH NIGHT;

OR,

WHAT YOU WILL.

ACT I.

SCENE I. *An apartment in the* DUKE'S *palace.*

Enter DUKE, CURIO, *and other* Lords; Musicians *attending.*

Duke. If music be the food of love, play on;
Give me excess of it, that, surfeiting,
The appetite may sicken, and so die.
That strain again! it had a dying fall:
O, it came o'er my ear like the sweet sound,
That breathes upon a bank of violets,
Stealing and giving odour! Enough; no more:
'Tis not so sweet now as it was before.
O spirit of love, how quick and fresh art thou!
That, notwithstanding thy capacity
Receiveth as the sea, nought enters there,
Of what validity and pitch soe'er,
But falls into abatement and low price,

TWELFTH NIGHT] TWELFE NIGHT F_1.

Musicians...] Musick...Capell. om. Ff.

2, 3. *surfeiting, The appetite may*] *surfeiting The app'tite, Love may* Warburton.

5. *sound*] Ff. *wind* Rowe (ed. 1). *south* Pope. *sou' wind* Anon. conj. *scent* Dent MS. apud Halliwell. *sough* Anon. conj.

11. *sea,*] Rowe (ed. 2). *sea.* Ff. *sea;* Rowe (ed. 1).

Even in a minute! so full of shapes is fancy,
That it alone is high fantastical.
Cur. Will you go hunt, my lord?
Duke. What, Curio?
Cur. The hart.
Duke. Why, so I do, the noblest that I have:
O, when mine eyes did see Olivia first,
Methought she purged the air of pestilence!
That instant was I turn'd into a hart;
And my desires, like fell and cruel hounds,
E'er since pursue me.

Enter VALENTINE.

How now! what news from her?
Val. So please my lord, I might not be admitted;
But from her handmaid do return this answer:
The element itself, till seven years' heat,
Shall not behold her face at ample view;
But, like a cloistress, she will veiled walk
And water once a day her chamber round
With eye-offending brine: all this to season
A brother's dead love, which she would keep fresh
And lasting in her sad remembrance.
Duke. O, she that hath a heart of that fine frame
To pay this debt of love but to a brother,
How will she love, when the rich golden shaft
Hath kill'd the flock of all affections else
That live in her; when liver, brain and heart,
These sovereign thrones, are all supplied, and fill'd

14. *is fancy*] *in fancy* Theobald (Warburton).

15. *That it alone is*] *And thou all o'er art* Hanmer.

high] *hight* Warburton.

16. *Curio*] *Curia* F_4.

19. *mine*] *my* Pope (ed. 2).

20. *Methought ... pestilence!*] (*Methought...pestilence*) Capell.

23. *E'er*] Rowe. *Ere* $F_1F_2F_4$. *E're* F_3.

Enter V.] Ff (after *her*).

26. *years' heat*] Harness. *yeares heate* F_1F_2. *yeares heat* F_3. *years heat* F_4. *years hence* Rowe (ed. 2). See note (II).

29. *chamber*] F_1. *chambers* F_2F_3 F_4. *chamber's* Capell.

32. *remembrance*] *remembrance still* Pope. *rememberance* Capell conj. MS.

38. *These*] *Three* Hanmer (Warburton).

38, 39. *are ... fill'd Her ... perfections*] *are...fill'd,* (*O sweet perfection!*)

Her sweet perfections with one self king!
Away before me to sweet beds of flowers:
Love-thoughts lie rich when canopied with bowers. [*Exeunt.*

SCENE II. *The sea-coast.*

Enter VIOLA, *a* Captain, *and* Sailors.

Vio. What country, friends, is this?

Cap. This is Illyria, lady.

Vio. And what should I do in Illyria?
My brother he is in Elysium.
Perchance he is not drown'd: what think you, sailors?

Cap. It is perchance that you yourself were saved.

Vio. O my poor brother! and so perchance may he be.

Cap. True, madam: and, to comfort you with chance,
Assure yourself, after our ship did split,
When you and those poor number saved with you
Hung on our driving boat, I saw your brother,
Most provident in peril, bind himself,
Courage and hope both teaching him the practice,
To a strong mast that lived upon the sea;
Where, like Arion on the dolphin's back,
I saw him hold acquaintance with the waves
So long as I could see.

Vio. For saying so, there's gold:
Mine own escape unfoldeth to my hope,
Whereto thy speech serves for authority,
The like of him. Know'st thou this country?

Warburton conj. *are...filled, Her...perfections,* Pope. *are...fill'd, (Her sweet perfection)* Capell. *her...perfections Are...fill'd* Collier conj.

39. *self*] *selfe* F_1. *selfe same* F_2. *self same* F_3. *self-same* F_4.

41. *Love-thoughts*] $F_1F_2F_3$. *Love thoughts* F_4.

SCENE II. The sea-coast] Capell. The street. Rowe.

2. *This is*] om. Pope.

7. *and so*] *so* Pope.

10. *those*] *that* Rowe (ed. 2). *this* Capell. *the* Anon. conj.

11. *our*] *your* Rowe.
driving] *droving* F_3F_4.

15. *Arion*] Pope. *Orion* Ff.

18. *For...gold*] *There's gold for saying so* Pope.

21. *Know'st*] *And knowest* Hanmer.

Cap. Ay, madam, well; for I was bred and born
Not three hours' travel from this very place.

Vio. Who governs here?

Cap. A noble Duke, in nature as in name.

Vio. What is his name?

Cap. Orsino.

Vio. Orsino! I have heard my father name him:
He was a bachelor then.

Cap. And so is now, or was so very late;
For but a month ago I went from hence,
And then 'twas fresh in murmur,—as, you know,
What great ones do the less will prattle of,—
That he did seek the love of fair Olivia.

Vio. What's she?

Cap. A virtuous maid, the daughter of a count
That died some twelvemonth since; then leaving her
In the protection of his son, her brother,
Who shortly also died: for whose dear love,
They say, she hath abjured the company
And sight of men.

Vio. O that I served that lady,
And might not be delivered to the world,
Till I had made mine own occasion mellow,
What my estate is!

Cap. That were hard to compass;
Because she will admit no kind of suit,
No, not the Duke's.

Vio. There is a fair behaviour in thee, captain;
And though that nature with a beauteous wall
Doth oft close in pollution, yet of thee
I will believe thou hast a mind that suits
With this thy fair and outward character.

24—27. *Who......Orsino*] As two lines in Hanmer, ending *nature...Orsino.*

25. *in name*] *in his name* Hanmer.

29—35. *He was ... she?*] As six lines in Steevens (1793), ending, *now, ...month...fresh...do,...seek...she?*

37. *twelvemonth*] *twelve months* Rowe.

39. *love*] *loss* S. Walker conj.

40. *hath*] F_1. *had* $F_2F_3F_4$.

40, 41. *company And sight*] Hanmer. *sight And company* Ff.

42. *And*] *And't* Hanmer. *delivered*] *deliver'd* Rowe.

43. *mellow,*] Hanmer. *mellow* Ff. *fellow* Anon. conj.

50. *will*] *well* S. Walker conj.

I prithee, and I'll pay thee bounteously,
Conceal me what I am, and be my aid
For such disguise as haply shall become
The form of my intent. I'll serve this Duke:
Thou shalt present me as an eunuch to him:
It may be worth thy pains; for I can sing,
And speak to him in many sorts of music,
That will allow me very worth his service.
What else may hap to time I will commit;
Only shape thou thy silence to my wit.

Cap. Be you his eunuch, and your mute I'll be:
When my tongue blabs, then let mine eyes not see.

Vio. I thank thee: lead me on. [*Exeunt.*

SCENE III. OLIVIA'S *house.*

Enter Sir TOBY BELCH *and* MARIA.

Sir To. What a plague means my niece, to take the death of her brother thus? I am sure care's an enemy to life.

Mar. By my troth, Sir Toby, you must come in earlier o' nights: your cousin, my lady, takes great exceptions to your ill hours.

Sir Toby. Why, let her except, before excepted.

Mar. Ay, but you must confine yourself within the modest limits of order.

Sir To. Confine! I'll confine myself no finer than I am: these clothes are good enough to drink in; and so be these boots too: an they be not, let them hang themselves in their own straps.

Mar. That quaffing and drinking will undo you: I heard my lady talk of it yesterday; and of a foolish knight that you brought in one night here to be her wooer.

Sir To. Who, Sir Andrew Aguecheek?

Mar. Ay, he.

SCENE III. OLIVIA's house.] Rowe.
4. *o'*] Capell. *a* Ff.
cousin] *neice* Rowe (ed. 2).
6. *except,*] Ff. *except* Hanmer.
before] *as before* Rann (Farmer conj.).
11. *an*] Theobald. *and* Ff. *if* Pope.

Sir To. He's as tall a man as any's in Illyria.

Mar. What's that to the purpose?

Sir To. Why, he has three thousand ducats a year.

Mar. Ay, but he'll have but a year in all these ducats: he's a very fool and a prodigal.

Sir To. Fie, that you'll say so! he plays o' the viol-de-gamboys, and speaks three or four languages word for word without book, and hath all the good gifts of nature.

Mar. He hath indeed, almost natural: for besides that he's a fool, he's a great quarreller; and but that he hath the gift of a coward to allay the gust he hath in quarrelling, 'tis thought among the prudent he would quickly have the gift of a grave.

Sir To. By this hand, they are scoundrels and substractors that say so of him. Who are they?

Mar. They that add, moreover, he's drunk nightly in your company.

Sir To. With drinking healths to my niece: I'll drink to her as long as there is a passage in my throat and drink in Illyria: he's a coward and a coystrill that will not drink to my niece till his brains turn o' the toe like a parish-top. What, wench! Castiliano vulgo; for here comes Sir Andrew Agueface.

Enter Sir ANDREW AGUECHEEK.

Sir And. Sir Toby Belch! how now, Sir Toby Belch!

Sir To. Sweet Sir Andrew!

Sir And. Bless you, fair shrew.

Mar. And you too, sir.

Sir To. Accost, Sir Andrew, accost.

18. *any's*] *any* Pope.

20. *has*] F_3F_4. *ha's* F_1F_2.

23, 24. *viol-de-gamboys*] *viol-de-gambo* Rowe.

26. *indeed, almost*] *indeed all, most* Collier (Upton conj.).

28. *gust*] *gift* Meredith conj.

31. *substractors*] *subtractors* Warburton.

33. *that add, moreover,*] *add, moreover, that* Anon. conj.

36. *there is*] *there's* Pope (ed. 2).

37. *coystrill*] *coystril* F_4. *kestrel* Hanmer.

39. *vulgo*] *volto* Hanmer (Warburton). *volgo* Johnson.

40. *Agueface*] *Ague-cheek* Theobald.

41. SCENE IV. Pope.
Enter...] Enter Sir Andrew. Ff.

Sir And. What's that?

Sir To. My niece's chambermaid.

Sir And. Good Mistress Accost, I desire better acquaintance.

Mar. My name is Mary, sir.

Sir And. Good Mistress Mary Accost,—

Sir To. You mistake, knight: 'accost' is front her, board her, woo her, assail her.

Sir And. By my troth, I would not undertake her in this company. Is that the meaning of 'accost'?

Mar. Fare you well, gentlemen.

Sir To. An thou let part so, Sir Andrew, would thou mightst never draw sword again.

Sir And. An you part so, mistress, I would I might never draw sword again. Fair lady, do you think you have fools in hand?

Mar. Sir, I have not you by the hand.

Sir And. Marry, but you shall have; and here's my hand.

Mar. Now, sir, 'thought is free': I pray you, bring your hand to the buttery-bar and let it drink.

Sir And. Wherefore, sweet-heart? what's your metaphor?

Mar. It's dry, sir.

Sir And. Why, I think so: I am not such an ass but I can keep my hand dry. But what's your jest?

Mar. A dry jest, sir.

Sir And. Are you full of them?

Mar. Ay, sir, I have them at my fingers' ends: marry, now I let go your hand, I am barren. [*Exit.*

Sir To. O knight, thou lackest a cup of canary: when did I see thee so put down?

48. Sir And.] Ma. F_1. *acquaintance*] *acquaintance*— S. Walker conj. See note (III).

51. *Mary Accost*] Rowe. *Mary, accost* Ff.

52, 53. *board her*] *bourd her* Whalley conj. *bourd with her* Steevens conj.

57. *An thou let part*] Capell. *And thou let part* F_1F_2. *And thou let her part* F_3F_4. *If thou let her part* Pope. *An thou let her part* Theobald.

59. *An*] Theobald. *And* Ff. *If* Pope.

65. *Now*] *Nay* S. Walker conj.

74. *fingers'*] *fingers* F_1F_2. *finger* F_3F_4. *finger's* Steevens.

75. [Exit.] Exit Maria. Ff.

Sir And. Never in your life, I think; unless you see canary put me down. Methinks sometimes I have no more wit than a Christian or an ordinary man has: but I am a great eater of beef and I believe that does harm to my wit.

Sir To. No question.

Sir And. An I thought that, I'ld forswear it. I'll ride home to-morrow, Sir Toby.

Sir To. Pourquoi, my dear knight?

Sir And. What is 'pourquoi'? do or not do? I would I had bestowed that time in the tongues that I have in fencing, dancing and bear-baiting: O, had I but followed the arts!

Sir To. Then hadst thou had an excellent head of hair.

Sir And. Why, would that have mended my hair?

Sir To. Past question; for thou seest it will not curl by nature.

Sir And. But it becomes me well enough, does't not?

Sir To. Excellent; it hangs like flax on a distaff; and I hope to see a housewife take thee between her legs and spin it off.

Sir And. Faith, I'll home to-morrow, Sir Toby: your niece will not be seen; or if she be, it's four to one she'll none of me: the count himself here hard by woos her.

Sir To. She'll none o' the count: she'll not match above her degree, neither in estate, years, nor wit; I have heard her swear't. Tut, there's life in't, man.

Sir And. I'll stay a month longer. I am a fellow o' the strangest mind i' the world; I delight in masques and revels sometimes altogether.

Sir To. Art thou good at these kickshawses, knight?

Sir And. As any man in Illyria, whatsoever he be, under the degree of my betters; and yet I will not compare with an old man.

79. *put me*] F_1. *put* $F_2F_3F_4$.

80. *has*] F_4. *ha's* $F_1F_2F_3$.

83. *An*] Theobald. *And* Ff. *If* Pope.

85. *Pourquoi*] *Pur-quoy* Ff.

93, 94. *curl by*] Theobald. *cool my* Ff.

95. *me*] *we* F_1.

101, 102. *count*] Ff. *Duke* Rowe.

104. *swear't*] *sweare t* F_1. *sweare* F_2. *swear* F_3F_4. *swear it* Theobald.

108. *kickshawses*] F_3. *kicke-chawses* F_1F_2. *kick-shaws* F_4.

111. *an old man*] *a nobleman* Theobald conj.

Sir To. What is thy excellence in a galliard, knight?

Sir And. Faith, I can cut a caper.

Sir To. And I can cut the mutton to't.

Sir And. And I think I have the back-trick simply as strong as any man in Illyria.

Sir To. Wherefore are these things hid? wherefore have these gifts a curtain before 'em? are they like to take dust, like Mistress Mall's picture? why dost thou not go to church in a galliard and come home in a coranto? My very walk should be a jig; I would not so much as make water but in a sink-a-pace. What dost thou mean? Is it a world to hide virtues in? I did think, by the excellent constitution of thy leg, it was formed under the star of a galliard.

Sir And. Ay, 'tis strong, and it does indifferent well in a flame-coloured stock. Shall we set about some revels?

Sir To. What shall we do else? were we not born under Taurus?

Sir And. Taurus! That's sides and heart.

Sir To. No, sir; it is legs and thighs. Let me see thee caper: ha! higher: ha, ha! excellent! [*Exeunt.*

SCENE IV. *The* DUKE'S *palace.*

Enter VALENTINE, *and* VIOLA *in man's attire.*

Val. If the Duke continue these favours towards you, Cesario, you are like to be much advanced: he hath known you but three days, and already you are no stranger.

Vio. You either fear his humour or my negligence,

112. *excellence*] *excellence?* Mason conj.

115. [Dances fantastically. Collier (Collier MS.).

120. *coranto*] Rowe (ed. 2). *carranto* Ff.

122. *sink-a-pace*] *cinque-pace* Hanmer.

123. *think*] *not think* Rowe.

127. *in a*] *in* Warburton.

flame-coloured] Rowe (ed. 2). *dam'd colour'd* Ff. *damask-coloured* Knight. *dun-colour'd* Collier MS. *damson-coloured* Phelps conj. *dove-coloured* Anon. conj.

stock] *stocke* F_1F_2. *stocken* F_3F_4. *stocking* Pope.

set] Rowe (ed. 2). *sit* Ff.

130. *That's*] F_3F_4. *That* F_1F_2.

132. [Sir A. dances again. Collier (Collier MS.).

SCENE IV.] SCENE V. Pope.

The DUKE'S palace.] The Palace. Rowe.

that you call in question the continuance of his love: is he inconstant, sir, in his favours?

Val. No, believe me.

Vio. I thank you. Here comes the count.

Enter DUKE, CURIO, *and* Attendants.

Duke. Who saw Cesario, ho?

Vio. On your attendance, my lord; here.

Duke. Stand you a while aloof. Cesario,
Thou know'st no less but all; I have unclasp'd
To thee the book even of my secret soul:
Therefore, good youth, address thy gait unto her;
Be not denied access, stand at her doors,
And tell them, there thy fixed foot shall grow
Till thou have audience.

Vio. Sure, my noble lord,
If she be so abandon'd to her sorrow
As it is spoke, she never will admit me.

Duke. Be clamorous and leap all civil bounds
Rather than make unprofited return.

Vio. Say I do speak with her, my lord, what then?

Duke. O, then unfold the passion of my love,
Surprise her with discourse of my dear faith:
It shall become thee well to act my woes;
She will attend it better in thy youth
Than in a nuncio's of more grave aspect.

Vio. I think not so, my lord.

Duke. Dear lad, believe it;
For they shall yet belie thy happy years,
That say thou art a man: Diana's lip
Is not more smooth and rubious; thy small pipe
Is as the maiden's organ, shrill and sound;
And all is semblative a woman's part.
I know thy constellation is right apt
For this affair. Some four or five attend him;
All, if you will; for I myself am best

8. *count*] Ff. *Duke* Rowe.

9. Enter...] Ff (after line 7).

CURIO, and Attendants.] attended. Capell.

27. *nuncio's*] Ff. *nuncio* Theobald.

32. *and sound*] *in sound* Anon. conj.

When least in company. Prosper well in this,
And thou shalt live as freely as thy lord,
To call his fortunes thine.

Vio. I'll do my best
To woo your lady: [*Aside*] yet, a barful strife!
Whoe'er I woo, myself would be his wife. [*Exeunt.*

SCENE V. OLIVIA'S *house.*

Enter MARIA *and* CLOWN.

Mar. Nay, either tell me where thou hast been, or I will not open my lips so wide as a bristle may enter in way of thy excuse: my lady will hang thee for thy absence.

Clo. Let her hang me: he that is well hanged in this world needs to fear no colours.

Mar. Make that good.

Clo. He shall see none to fear.

Mar. A good lenten answer: I can tell thee where that saying was born, of 'I fear no colours.'

Clo. Where, good Mistress Mary?

Mar. In the wars; and that may you be bold to say in your foolery.

Clo. Well, God give them wisdom that have it; and those that are fools, let them use their talents.

Mar. Yet you will be hanged for being so long absent; or, to be turned away, is not that as good as a hanging to you?

Clo. Many a good hanging prevents a bad marriage; and, for turning away, let summer bear it out.

Mar. You are resolute, then?

Clo. Not so, neither; but I am resolved on two points.

40. *lady*] *lady* [Exit Duke] Johnson.
[Aside] Capell.
a barful] F_4. *a barrefull* F_1 F_2 F_3. *O baneful* Pope. *O barful* Collier (Thirlby conj. MS.). *a woeful* Daniel conj.
SCENE V.] SCENE VI. Pope.
OLIVIA'S house.] Rowe.

5. *to fear*] *fear* F_3 F_4.
colours] *collars* Anon. conj.
8. *lenten*] Rowe. *lenton* Ff.
16. *to be*] F_1. *be* F_2 F_3 F_4.
18. *Many*] *Marry*, Theobald.
19. *turning away*] *turning o' hay* Smith conj. *turning of whey* Letherland conj.
20, 28. *You*] *Your* F_2.

Mar. That if one break, the other will hold; or, if both break, your gaskins fall.

Clo. Apt, in good faith; very apt. Well, go thy way; if Sir Toby would leave drinking, thou wert as witty a piece of Eve's flesh as any in Illyria.

Mar. Peace, you rogue, no more o' that. Here comes my lady: make your excuse wisely, you were best. [*Exit.*

Clo. Wit, an't be thy will, put me into good fooling! Those wits, that think they have thee, do very oft prove fools; and I, that am sure I lack thee, may pass for a wise man: for what says Quinapalus? 'Better a witty fool than a foolish wit.'

Enter Lady OLIVIA *with* MALVOLIO.

God bless thee, lady!

Oli. Take the fool away.

Clo. Do you not hear, fellows? Take away the lady.

Oli. Go to, you're a dry fool; I'll no more of you: besides, you grow dishonest.

Clo. Two faults, madonna, that drink and good counsel will amend: for give the dry fool drink, then is the fool not dry: bid the dishonest man mend himself; if he mend, he is no longer dishonest; if he cannot, let the botcher mend him. Any thing that's mended is but patched: virtue that transgresses is but patched with sin; and sin that amends is but patched with virtue. If that this simple syllogism will serve, so; if it will not, what remedy? As there is no true cuckold but calamity, so beauty's a flower. The lady bade take away the fool; therefore, I say again, take her away.

Oli. Sir, I bade them take away you.

Clo. Misprision in the highest degree! Lady, cucullus non facit monachum; that's as much to say as I wear not motley in my brain. Good madonna, give me leave to prove you a fool.

23. *gaskins*] *gaskings* F4.
28. [Exit.] Pope. om. Ff.
29. SCENE VII. Pope.
an't] Hanmer. *and 't* Ff.
good] *a good* Warburton.
34. Enter...] Ff (after line 28). Enter O. attended. Capell.
37. *you're*] *y'are* Ff.
39. *madonna*] *Madona* Ff., and passim.
46. *cuckold*] *counsellor* Hanmer.
51. *to say as I wear*] *to say, as I were* F4. *as to say, as I were* Rowe (ed. 1). *as to say, I wear* Id. (ed. 2).

Oli. Can you do it?

Clo. Dexteriously, good madonna.

Oli. Make your proof.

Clo. I must catechize you for it, madonna: good my mouse of virtue, answer me.

Oli. Well, sir, for want of other idleness, I'll bide your proof.

Clo. Good madonna, why mournest thou?

Oli. Good fool, for my brother's death.

Clo. I think his soul is in hell, madonna.

Oli. I know his soul is in heaven, fool.

Clo. The more fool, madonna, to mourn for your brother's soul being in heaven. Take away the fool, gentlemen.

Oli. What think you of this fool, Malvolio? doth he not mend?

Mal. Yes, and shall do till the pangs of death shake him: infirmity, that decays the wise, doth ever make the better fool.

Clo. God send you, sir, a speedy infirmity, for the better increasing your folly! Sir Toby will be sworn that I am no fox; but he will not pass his word for two pence that you are no fool.

Oli. How say you to that, Malvolio?

Mal. I marvel your ladyship takes delight in such a barren rascal: I saw him put down the other day with an ordinary fool that has no more brain than a stone. Look you now, he's out of his guard already; unless you laugh and minister occasion to him, he is gagged. I protest, I take these wise men, that crow so at these set kind of fools, no better than the fools' zanies.

Oli. O, you are sick of self-love, Malvolio, and taste with a distempered appetite. To be generous, guiltless and

55. *Dexteriously*] *Dexterously* F_4.
58. *mouse*] *muse* Anon. conj.
answer me] *answer* F_3F_4.
59. *bide*] *abide* Steevens (1785).
65. *fool*] F_1F_2. *fool you* F_3F_4.
71, 72. *the better*] Ff. *better the* Rowe (ed. 2).
80. *brain*] *brains* F_3F_4.
83. *these*] *those* Hanmer.
wise men] F_3F_4. *wisemen* F_1F_2.
84. *no better*] *to be no better* Capell.
86. *guiltless*] F_3F_4. *guiltlesse* F_1F_2. *guileless* Anon. conj.

of free disposition, is to take those things for bird-bolts that you deem cannon-bullets: there is no slander in an allowed fool, though he do nothing but rail; nor no railing in a known discreet man, though he do nothing but reprove.

Clo. Now Mercury endue thee with leasing, for thou speakest well of fools!

Re-enter MARIA.

Mar. Madam, there is at the gate a young gentleman much desires to speak with you.

Oli. From the Count Orsino, is it?

Mar. I know not, madam: 'tis a fair young man, and well attended.

Oli. Who of my people hold him in delay?

Mar. Sir Toby, madam, your kinsman.

Oli. Fetch him off, I pray you; he speaks nothing but madman: fie on him! [*Exit Maria.*] Go you, Malvolio: if it be a suit from the count, I am sick, or not at home; what you will, to dismiss it. [*Exit Malvolio.*] Now you see, sir, how your fooling grows old, and people dislike it.

Clo. Thou hast spoke for us, madonna, as if thy eldest son should be a fool; whose skull Jove cram with brains! for,—here he comes,—one of thy kin has a most weak pia mater.

Enter Sir TOBY.

Oli. By mine honour, half drunk. What is he at the gate, cousin?

Sir To. A gentleman.

Oli. A gentleman! what gentleman?

Sir To. 'Tis a gentleman here—a plague o' these pickle-herring! How now, sot!

91. *leasing*] *learning* Rowe. *pleasing* Warburton.

93. Re-enter M.] Enter M. Ff.

95, 102. *Count*] *Duke* Hanmer.

99. *kinsman*] *uncle* Rowe (ed. 2).

101. Exit Maria] Capell.

103. Exit Malvolio] Ff.

Now you] *Now* Rowe.

106, 107. *for,—here he comes,—*] Edd. *for here he comes* Ff. *for here comes* Rowe (ed. 2).

107. *has*] *that has* Collier MS.

108. SCENE VIII. Pope.

Enter...] Ff (after *comes*, line 107).

109. *cousin*] *uncle* Rowe (ed. 2).

112. *gentleman here—*] Steevens. *gentleman heere.* F_1. *gentleman here.* $F_2F_3F_4$. *gentleman. Here,*—[belches.] Theobald. *gentleman-heir* Warburton. *gentleman*:—[hiccups.] Capell.

113. *herring*] *herrings* Malone.

Clo. Good Sir Toby!

Oli. Cousin, cousin, how have you come so early by this lethargy?

Sir To. Lechery! I defy lechery. There's one at the gate.

Oli. Ay, marry, what is he?

Sir To. Let him be the devil, an he will, I care not: give me faith, say I. Well, it's all one. [*Exit.*

Oli. What's a drunken man like, fool?

Clo. Like a drowned man, a fool and a mad man: one draught above heat makes him a fool; the second mads him; and a third drowns him.

Oli. Go thou and seek the crowner, and let him sit o' my coz; for he's in the third degree of drink, he's drowned: go, look after him.

Clo. He is but mad yet, madonna; and the fool shall look to the madman. [*Exit.*

Re-enter MALVOLIO.

Mal. Madam, yond young fellow swears he will speak with you. I told him you were sick; he takes on him to understand so much, and therefore comes to speak with you. I told him you were asleep; he seems to have a foreknowledge of that too, and therefore comes to speak with you. What is to be said to him, lady? he's fortified against any denial.

Oli. Tell him he shall not speak with me.

Mal. Has been told so; and he says, he'll stand at your door like a sheriff's post, and be the supporter to a bench, but he'll speak with you.

Oli. What kind o' man is he?

Mal. Why, of mankind.

Oli. What manner of man?

Mal. Of very ill manner; he'll speak with you, will you or no.

115. *Cousin, cousin*] *Uncle, uncle* Rowe.

119. *an*] Hanmer. *and* Ff.

125. *crowner*] *coroner* Rowe.

126. *coz*] *uncle* Rowe (ed. 2). *cousin* Capell conj.

129. Exit.] Exit Clown. Rowe. Re-enter M.] Enter M. Ff.

130. *yond*] Ff. *yon'* Capell.

138. *Has*] *Ha's* Ff. *He has* Pope.

139. *and be*] *or be* Hanmer. *to*] *of* Reed (1803).

141. *o'*] *of* Steevens.

144. *manner*] F_1F_2. *manners* F_3F_4.

Oli. Of what personage and years is he?

Mal. Not yet old enough for a man, nor young enough for a boy; as a squash is before 'tis a peascod, or a codling when 'tis almost an apple: 'tis with him in standing water, between boy and man. He is very well-favoured and he speaks very shrewishly; one would think his mother's milk were scarce out of him.

Oli. Let him approach: call in my gentlewoman.

Mal. Gentlewoman, my lady calls. [*Exit.*

Re-enter MARIA.

Oli. Give me my veil: come, throw it o'er my face. We'll once more hear Orsino's embassy.

Enter VIOLA, *and* Attendants.

Vio. The honourable lady of the house, which is she?

Oli. Speak to me; I shall answer for her. Your will?

Vio. Most radiant, exquisite and unmatchable beauty,—I pray you, tell me if this be the lady of the house, for I never saw her: I would be loath to cast away my speech, for besides that it is excellently well penned, I have taken great pains to con it. Good beauties, let me sustain no scorn; I am very comptible, even to the least sinister usage.

Oli. Whence came you, sir?

Vio. I can say little more than I have studied, and that question's out of my part. Good gentle one, give me modest assurance if you be the lady of the house, that I may proceed in my speech.

Oli. Are you a comedian?

Vio. No, my profound heart: and yet, by the very fangs of malice I swear, I am not that I play. Are you the lady of the house?

Oli. If I do not usurp myself, I am.

Vio. Most certain, if you are she, you do usurp your-

149. *in*] *e'en* Capell.
155. SCENE IX. Pope.
Re-enter M.] Enter M. Ff.
157. VIOLA] VIOLENTA. F_1.
...and Attendants.] Edd. om. Ff.
164. *comptible*] *prompt* Hanmer. *domptable* Mason conj.
169. *my*] om. $F_3 F_4$.
172. *fangs*] *phangs* Ff. *pangs* Rowe (ed. 1).

self; for what is yours to bestow is not yours to reserve. But this is from my commission: I will on with my speech in your praise, and then show you the heart of my message.

Oli. Come to what is important in't: I forgive you the praise.

Vio. Alas, I took great pains to study it, and 'tis poetical.

Oli. It is the more like to be feigned: I pray you, keep it in. I heard you were saucy at my gates, and allowed your approach rather to wonder at you than to hear you. If you be not mad, be gone; if you have reason, be brief: 'tis not that time of moon with me to make one in so skipping a dialogue.

Mar. Will you hoist sail, sir? here lies your way.

Vio. No, good swabber; I am to hull here a little longer. Some mollification for your giant, sweet lady. Tell me your mind: I am a messenger.

Oli. Sure, you have some hideous matter to deliver, when the courtesy of it is so fearful. Speak your office.

Vio. It alone concerns your ear. I bring no overture of war, no taxation of homage: I hold the olive in my hand; my words are as full of peace as matter.

Oli. Yet you began rudely. What are you? what would you?

Vio. The rudeness that hath appeared in me have I learned from my entertainment. What I am, and what I would, are as secret as maidenhead; to your ears, divinity, to any other's, profanation.

Oli. Give us the place alone: we will hear this divinity. [*Exeunt Maria and Attendants.*] Now, sir, what is your text?

184. *and*] *and I* Pope.

186. *not mad*] *mad* Rann (Mason conj.). *but mad* Collier (ed. 2, Staunton conj.).

187. *that time of moon*] Ff. *the time of the moon* Rowe. *that time of the moon* Pope.

192. *Tell...messenger*] Oli. *Tell... mind.* Vio. *I......messenger* Hanmer (Warburton). See note (IV).

196. *taxation*] $F_1F_2F_3$. *taxations* F_4.

olive] Rowe. *Olyffe* $F_1F_2F_3$. *Oliff* F_4.

202. *secret as maidenhead*] *sacred as maidhood* Theobald conj.

maidenhead] F_1. *a maiden-heard* F_2. *a maiden-head* F_3 F_4. *maidenhood* Collier MS.

203. *other's*] Pope (ed. 2). *others* Ff.

205. Exeunt M. and Attendants.] Capell. Exit M. Rowe.

Vio. Most sweet lady,—

Oli. A comfortable doctrine, and much may be said of it. Where lies your text?

Vio. In Orsino's bosom.

Oli. In his bosom! In what chapter of his bosom?

Vio. To answer by the method, in the first of his heart.

Oli. O, I have read it: it is heresy. Have you no more to say?

Vio. Good madam, let me see your face.

Oli. Have you any commission from your lord to negotiate with my face? You are now out of your text: but we will draw the curtain and show you the picture. Look you, sir, such a one I was this present: is't not well done? [*Unveiling.*

Vio. Excellently done, if God did all.

Oli. 'Tis in grain, sir; 'twill endure wind and weather.

Vio. 'Tis beauty truly blent, whose red and white
Nature's own sweet and cunning hand laid on:
Lady, you are the cruell'st she alive,
If you will lead these graces to the grave
And leave the world no copy.

Oli. O, sir, I will not be so hard-hearted; I will give out divers schedules of my beauty: it shall be inventoried, and every particle and utensil labelled to my will: as, item, two lips, indifferent red; item, two grey eyes, with lids to them; item, one neck, one chin, and so forth. Were you sent hither to praise me?

Vio. I see you what you are, you are too proud;
But, if you were the devil, you are fair.
My lord and master loves you: O, such love
Could be but recompensed, though you were crown'd

208. *your text*] *the text* Rowe.

218. *such...is't*] *such a one I wear this present: is't* Theobald (Warburton). *such a one I was. This presence, is't* Steevens conj. *such as once I was, this presents: is't* Rann (Mason conj). *such a one I was, this presents* Becket conj. *such a one as I was this presents, is't* Jackson conj. *such a one as I was this present: is't* Boswell. *such a one I was as this presents: is't* Singer conj. *such a one I am at this present: is't* Collier MS.

[Unveiling.] Rowe.

231. *praise*] *'praise* Steevens (Malone).

235. *Could*] *Should* Collier MS.

The nonpareil of beauty!
Oli. How does he love me?
Vio. With adorations, fertile tears,
With groans that thunder love, with sighs of fire.
Oli. Your lord does know my mind; I cannot love him:
Yet I suppose him virtuous, know him noble,
Of great estate, of fresh and stainless youth;
In voices well divulged, free, learn'd and valiant;
And in dimension and the shape of nature
A gracious person: but yet I cannot love him;
He might have took his answer long ago.
Vio. If I did love you in my master's flame,
With such a suffering, such a deadly life,
In your denial I would find no sense;
I would not understand it.
Oli. Why, what would you?
Vio. Make me a willow cabin at your gate,
And call upon my soul within the house;
Write loyal cantons of contemned love
And sing them loud even in the dead of night;
Halloo your name to the reverberate hills
And make the babbling gossip of the air
Cry out 'Olivia!' O, you should not rest
Between the elements of air and earth,
But you should pity me!
Oli. You might do much.
What is your parentage?
Vio. Above my fortunes, yet my state is well:
I am a gentleman.
Oli. Get you to your lord;
I cannot love him: let him send no more;
Unless, perchance, you come to me again,
To tell me how he takes it. Fare you well:

237. *adorations, fertile*] *adorations, fertill* Ff. *adorations, with fertile* Pope. *adoration's fertile* Rann. See note (V).
244. *but*] om. Pope.
249. *would you?*] *would you do?* Rowe.
252. *cantons*] *cantos* Rowe (ed. 2). *canzons* Capell.
254. *Halloo*] *Hallow* F_1. *Hollaw* F_2. *Hollow* F_3 F_4.
reverberate] *reverberant* Theobald.
258, 259. *You...parentage.*] As one line in Capell.

I thank you for your pains: spend this for me.
Vio. I am no fee'd post, lady; keep your purse:
My master, not myself, lacks recompense.
Love make his heart of flint that you shall love;
And let your fervour, like my master's, be
Placed in contempt! Farewell, fair cruelty. [*Exit.*
Oli. 'What is your parentage?'
'Above my fortunes, yet my state is well:
I am a gentleman.' I'll be sworn thou art;
Thy tongue, thy face, thy limbs, actions, and spirit,
Do give thee five-fold blazon: not too fast: soft, soft!
Unless the master were the man. How now!
Even so quickly may one catch the plague?
Methinks I feel this youth's perfections
With an invisible and subtle stealth
To creep in at mine eyes. Well, let it be.
What ho, Malvolio!

Re-enter MALVOLIO.

Mal. Here, madam, at your service.
Oli. Run after that same peevish messenger,
The county's man: he left this ring behind him,
Would I or not: tell him I'll none of it.
Desire him not to flatter with his lord,
Nor hold him up with hopes; I am not for him:
If that the youth will come this way to-morrow,
I'll give him reasons for't: hie thee, Malvolio.
Mal. Madam, I will. [*Exit.*
Oli. I do I know not what, and fear to find
Mine eye too great a flatterer for my mind.
Fate, show thy force: ourselves we do not owe;
What is decreed must be, and be this so. [*Exit.*

275. *soft, soft!*] *soft;* Capell.

276. *master were the man*] *man the master were* Hanmer, who ends lines 275—278 at *fast...were...catch...perfections.*

281. Re-enter M.] Enter M. Ff.

283. *county's*] Capell. *Countes* F_1. *Counts* F_2 F_3 F_4. *Duke's* Rowe.

left] *left here* Hanmer.

288. *reasons for't: hie thee*] F_1. *reasons for 't: hye thee* F_2. *reasons for 't by thee* F_3. *reason for 't by thee* F_4. *reason for 't. Hye thee* Hanmer.

292. *owe*] *know* Long MS.

293. [Exit] Rowe. Finis, Actus primus. F_1. Finis, Actus primi. F_2 F_3 F_4.

ACT II.

SCENE I. *The sea-coast.*

Enter ANTONIO *and* SEBASTIAN.

Ant. Will you stay no longer? nor will you not that I go with you?

Seb. By your patience, no. My stars shine darkly over me: the malignancy of my fate might perhaps distemper yours; therefore I shall crave of you your leave that I may bear my evils alone: it were a bad recompense for your love, to lay any of them on you.

Ant. Let me yet know of you whither you are bound.

Seb. No, sooth, sir: my determinate voyage is mere extravagancy. But I perceive in you so excellent a touch of modesty, that you will not extort from me what I am willing to keep in; therefore it charges me in manners the rather to express myself. You must know of me then, Antonio, my name is Sebastian, which I called Roderigo. My father was that Sebastian of Messaline, whom I know you have heard of. He left behind him myself and a sister, both born in an hour: if the heavens had been pleased, would we had so ended! but you, sir, altered that; for some hour before you took me from the breach of the sea was my sister drowned.

Ant. Alas the day!

Seb. A lady, sir, though it was said she much resembled me, was yet of many accounted beautiful: but, though I could not with such estimable wonder overfar believe

SCENE I. The sea-coast.] Capell. The street. Rowe.

1, 2. *longer?...with you?*] *longer:... with you.* F.

5. *I shall crave*] *I crave* Rowe.

9. *sooth*] *in sooth* Johnson. *'sooth* Capell.

14. *Roderigo*] Collier. *Rodorigo* Ff.

15. *Messaline*] *Metelin* Hanmer. *Mitylene* Capell conj.

17. *an*] F_1F_2. *one* F_3F_4.

19. *hour*] *houre* F_1F_2. *houres* F_3. *hours* F_4.

19. *breach*] *beach* Grey conj.

22. *though*] *who, tho'* Hanmer.

24. *not...overfar*] *not overfar* Warburton conj. *not with self-estimation wander so far* Collier (Collier MS.).

that, yet thus far I will boldly publish her; she bore a mind that envy could not but call fair. She is drowned already, sir, with salt water, though I seem to drown her remembrance again with more.

Ant. Pardon me, sir, your bad entertainment.

Seb. O good Antonio, forgive me your trouble.

Ant. If you will not murder me for my love, let me be your servant.

Seb. If you will not undo what you have done, that is, kill him whom you have recovered, desire it not. Fare ye well at once: my bosom is full of kindness, and I am yet so near the manners of my mother, that upon the least occasion more mine eyes will tell tales of me. I am bound to the Count Orsino's court: farewell. [*Exit.*

Ant. The gentleness of all the gods go with thee!
I have many enemies in Orsino's court,
Else would I very shortly see thee there.
But, come what may, I do adore thee so,
That danger shall seem sport, and I will go. [*Exit.*

SCENE II. *A street.*

Enter VIOLA, MALVOLIO *following.*

Mal. Were not you even now with the Countess Olivia?

Vio. Even now, sir; on a moderate pace I have since arrived but hither.

Mal. She returns this ring to you, sir: you might have saved me my pains, to have taken it away yourself. She adds, moreover, that you should put your lord into a desperate assurance she will none of him: and one thing more, that you be never so hardy to come again in his affairs,

not with such estimators wander over-far to Singer MS. *not with such estimate wander overfar to* Bailey conj.

with...wonder] Omit as spurious. Warburton conj.

26. *envy could not but*] *envy itself would* Capell conj.

38. *Count*] *Duke* Rowe.

40. *many*] F_1F_2. *made* F_3F_4.

SCENE II. Enter...] Enter V. and M. at severall doores. Ff.

1. *even ev'n* Ff. *e'en* Rowe.

4. *sir:*] *sir; for being your Lord's she'll none of it.* Hanmer.

unless it be to report your lord's taking of this. Receive it so.

Vio. She took the ring of me: I'll none of it.

Mal. Come, sir, you peevishly threw it to her; and her will is, it should be so returned: if it be worth stooping for, there it lies in your eye; if not, be it his that finds it. [*Exit.*

Vio. I left no ring with her: what means this lady?
Fortune forbid my outside have not charm'd her!
She made good view of me; indeed, so much,
That methought her eyes had lost her tongue,
For she did speak in starts distractedly.
She loves me, sure; the cunning of her passion
Invites me in this churlish messenger.
None of my lord's ring! why, he sent her none.
I am the man: if it be so, as 'tis,
Poor lady, she were better love a dream.
Disguise, I see, thou art a wickedness,
Wherein the pregnant enemy does much.
How easy is it for the proper-false
In women's waxen hearts to set their forms!
Alas, our frailty is the cause, not we!
For such as we are made of, such we be.
How will this fadge? my master loves her dearly;

9, 10. *Receive it so*] *Receive it, sir* Capell.

11. *the ring of me: I'll*] *the ring of me, Ile* Ff (*I'le* F_3F_4). *the ring of me! I'll* Malone (Anon. conj.). *no ring of me; I'll* Malone conj. *this ring of me! She'll* Id. conj.

16. *have not*] *should have* Hanmer.

18. *That*] F_1. *That sure* $F_2F_3F_4$. *That oft*] Jackson conj. *That, as* Anon. conj.

That...her] *Methought her eager* Seymour conj.

had lost] *did let* Hanmer. *had crost* Warburton. *had los'd* Becket conj.

22. *None...none.*] This line is transposed by Hanmer to the beginning of the speech.

23. *I am the*] *I should be* Hanmer.

man: if it be so, as 'tis,] *man, if...so, as tis,* F_1. *man, if...so as tis,* F_2 (*'tis,* F_3F_4). *man, if...so: as 'tis,* Hanmer. *if it be so,* (*as, 'tis;*) Theobald.

27, 28. *the proper-false......their forms*] *thy purpose false...thy forms* Jackson conj.

27. *proper-false*] Malone. *proper false* Ff.

29. *our*] $F_2F_3F_4$. *O* F_1.

30. *made of, such*] Rann (Tyrwhitt conj.). *made, if such* Ff. *made, ev'n such* Hanmer. See note (VI).

And I, poor monster, fond as much on him;
And she, mistaken, seems to dote on me.
What will become of this? As I am man,
My state is desperate for my master's love;
As I am woman,—now alas the day!—
What thriftless sighs shall poor Olivia breathe!
O time! thou must untangle this, not I;
It is too hard a knot for me to untie! [*Exit.*

SCENE III. OLIVIA'S *house.*

Enter SIR TOBY *and* SIR ANDREW.

Sir To. Approach, Sir Andrew: not to be a-bed after midnight is to be up betimes; and 'diluculo surgere,' thou know'st,—

Sir An. Nay, by my troth, I know not: but I know, to be up late is to be up late.

Sir To. A false conclusion: I hate it as an unfilled can. To be up after midnight and to go to bed then, is early: so that to go to bed after midnight is to go to bed betimes. Does not our life consist of the four elements?

Sir And. Faith, so they say; but I think it rather consists of eating and drinking.

Sir To. Thou'rt a scholar; let us therefore eat and drink. Marian, I say! a stoup of wine!

Enter Clown.

Sir And. Here comes the fool, i' faith.

Clo. How now, my hearts! did you never see the picture of 'we three'?

32. *monster*] *minister* Hanmer.

32, 33. *as much on him; And*] *as much on him As* Dyce conj.

34. *man*] *a man* F_3F_4.

39. *to untie*] *t'unty* Ff.

SCENE III. OLIVIA'S house.] Rowe.

2. *diluculo*] Rowe. *Deliculo* F_1. *Diliculo* $F_2F_3F_4$.

3. *know'st,—*] Theobald. *know'st.* Ff.

9. *Does...life*] Rowe (ed. 2). *Does ...lives* Ff. *Do...lives* Malone.

12. *Thou'rt* Capell. *Th'art* Ff. *Thou art* Steevens.

13. *Marian*] *Maria* Pope.

stoup] *stoope* $F_1F_2F_3$. *stoop* F_4.

Sir To. Welcome, ass. Now let's have a catch.

Sir And. By my troth, the fool has an excellent breast. I had rather than forty shillings I had such a leg, and so sweet a breath to sing, as the fool has. In sooth, thou wast in very gracious fooling last night, when thou spokest of Pigrogromitus, of the Vapians passing the equinoctial of Queubus: 'twas very good, i' faith. I sent thee sixpence for thy leman: hadst it?

Clo. I did impeticos thy gratillity; for Malvolio's nose is no whipstock: my lady has a white hand, and the Myrmidons are no bottle-ale houses.

Sir And. Excellent! why, this is the best fooling, when all is done. Now, a song.

Sir To. Come on; there is sixpence for you: let's have a song.

Sir And. There's a testril of me too: if one knight give a—

Clo. Would you have a love-song, or a song of good life?

Sir To. A love-song, a love-song.

Sir And. Ay, ay: I care not for good life.

Clo. [*Sings*]

O mistress mine, where are you roaming?
O, stay and hear; your true love's coming,
  That can sing both high and low:
Trip no further, pretty sweeting;
Journeys end in lovers meeting,
  Every wise man's son doth know.

Sir And. Excellent good, i' faith.

Sir To. Good, good.

Clo. [*Sings*]

What is love? 'tis not hereafter;
Present mirth hath present laughter;
  What's to come is still unsure:

18. *breast*] *breath* L. H. apud Theobald conj.

22. *Pigrogromitus*] *Pigrogomitus* Boswell.

24. *leman*] Theobald. *Lemon* Ff.

25. *impeticos thy gratillity*] *impeticoat thy gratuity* Rann (Johnson conj.).

27. *Myrmidons*] Theobald. *Mermidons* Ff. *Mirmidons* Pope.

33. *give a—*] See note (VII).

39. *and hear;*] *and heare,* F_1F_2. *and hear,* F_3F_4. *for here* Collier MS.

42. *lovers*] *lovers'* Warburton.

46. *love?*] Pope. *love,* Ff.

In delay there lies no plenty;
Then come kiss me, sweet and twenty,
Youth's a stuff will not endure.

Sir And. A mellifluous voice, as I am true knight.

Sir To. A contagious breath.

Sir And. Very sweet and contagious, i'faith.

Sir To. To hear by the nose, it is dulcet in contagion. But shall we make the welkin dance indeed? shall we rouse the night-owl in a catch that will draw three souls out of one weaver? shall we do that?

Sir And. An you love me, let's do't: I am dog at a catch.

Clo. By'r lady, sir, and some dogs will catch well.

Sir And. Most certain. Let our catch be, 'Thou knave.'

Clo. 'Hold thy peace, thou knave,' knight? I shall be constrained in't to call thee knave, knight.

Sir And. 'Tis not the first time I have constrained one to call me knave. Begin, fool: it begins 'Hold thy peace.'

Clo. I shall never begin if I hold my peace.

Sir And. Good, i'faith. Come, begin. [*Catch sung.*

Enter MARIA.

Mar. What a caterwauling do you keep here! If my lady have not called up her steward Malvolio and bid him turn you out of doors, never trust me.

Sir To. My lady's a Cataian, we are politicians, Malvolio's a Peg-a-Ramsey, and 'Three merry men be we.' Am not I consanguineous? am I not of her blood? Tillyvally. Lady! [*Sings*] 'There dwelt a man in Babylon, lady, lady!'

Clo. Beshrew me, the knight's in admirable fooling.

Sir And. Ay, he does well enough if he be disposed,

49. *delay*] *decay* Warburton.

50. *Then come kiss me*] *Come, a kiss then* Johnson conj.

52. *true*] *a true* Rowe.

57. *souls*] *sols* (i.e. *sous*) Jackson conj.

59. *An*] Pope. *And* Ff.
dog] *dogge* F_1F_2. *a dog* F_3F_4.

64. *knight?*] Capell. *knight.* Ff.

70. SCENE IV. Pope.

75. *am I not*] *am not I* F_3F_4.

76, 81. [Sings] Singing. Rowe.

and so do I too: he does it with a better grace, but I do it more natural.

Sir To. [*Sings*] 'O, the twelfth day of December',—

Mar. For the love o' God, peace!

Enter MALVOLIO.

Mal. My masters, are you mad? or what are you? Have you no wit, manners, nor honesty, but to gabble like tinkers at this time of night? Do ye make an alehouse of my lady's house, that ye squeak out your coziers' catches without any mitigation or remorse of voice? Is there no respect of place, persons, nor time in you?

Sir To. We did keep time, sir, in our catches. Sneck up!

Mal. Sir Toby, I must be round with you. My lady bade me tell you, that, though she harbours you as her kinsman, she's nothing allied to your disorders. If you can separate yourself and your misdemeanours, you are welcome to the house; if not, an it would please you to take leave of her, she is very willing to bid you farewell.

Sir To. 'Farewell, dear heart, since I must needs be gone.'

Mar. Nay, good Sir Toby.

Clo. 'His eyes do show his days are almost done.'

Mal. Is't even so?

Sir To. 'But I will never die.'

Clo. Sir Toby, there you lie.

Mal. This is much credit to you.

Sir To. 'Shall I bid him go?'

Clo. 'What an if you do?'

Sir To. 'Shall I bid him go, and spare not?'

Clo. 'O no, no, no, no, you dare not.'

81. *O*] *O'* S. Walker conj. *the twelfth*] *the twelfe* F_1F_2. *twelf* F_3F_4.
85. *ye*] *you* Hanmer.
86. *coziers'*] *cottiers* Warburton.
89, 90. *Sneck up*] F_3F_4. *Snecke up* F_1F_2. *Strike up* Rowe (ed. 2). *Sneak-cup* Rann (Steevens and Capell conj.). *Sneb up* Becket conj. *Snack up* Jackson conj. *Snick up* Collier (Dyce).
90. [Hiccoughs. Theobald.
92. *though*] F_1F_2. om. F_3F_4.
93. *kinsman*] *uncle* Rowe (ed. 2).
95. *an*] Rowe (ed. 2). *and* Ff.
97. See note (VIII).
98. Mar.] Mal. Steevens.
101. *never*] *nevery* F_2.
105. *an*] Theobald. *and* Ff.
107. *no, no, no, no*] *no, no, no* Theobald.

Sir To. Out o' tune, sir: ye lie. Art any more than a steward? Dost thou think, because thou art virtuous, there shall be no more cakes and ale?

Clo. Yes, by Saint Anne, and ginger shall be hot i' the mouth too.

Sir To. Thou'rt i' the right. Go, sir, rub your chain with crums. A stoup of wine, Maria!

Mal. Mistress Mary, if you prized my lady's favour at any thing more than contempt, you would not give means for this uncivil rule: she shall know of it, by this hand. [*Exit.*

Mar. Go shake your ears.

Sir And. 'Twere as good a deed as to drink when a man's a-hungry, to challenge him the field, and then to break promise with him and make a fool of him.

Sir To. Do't, knight: I'll write thee a challenge; or I'll deliver thy indignation to him by word of mouth.

Mar. Sweet Sir Toby, be patient for to-night: since the youth of the count's was to-day with my lady, she is much out of quiet. For Monsieur Malvolio, let me alone with him: if I do not gull him into a nayword, and make him a common recreation, do not think I have wit enough to lie straight in my bed: I know I can do it.

Sir To. Possess us, possess us; tell us something of him.

Mar. Marry, sir, sometimes he is a kind of puritan.

Sir And. O, if I thought that, I'ld beat him like a dog!

Sir To. What, for being a puritan? thy exquisite reason, dear knight?

Sir And. I have no exquisite reason for't, but I have reason good enough.

108. *tune, sir:*] *tune sir,* Ff. *time, sir?* Theobald. *tune!—sir,* Collier. *tune, sir?* Staunton.

Art] *Art thou* Rowe.

113. *Thou'rt*] Rowe. *Th'art* Ff.

chain] *chin* Johnson conj.

114. *stoup*] *stope* Ff. *stoop* Rowe.

120. *the field*] *to the field* Rowe (ed. 2).

125. *the youth*] *that youth* Collier MS.

count's] *Duke's* Rowe.

127. *a nayword*] Rowe. *an ayword* Ff. *a byeword* L. H. apud Theobald conj.

130. Sir To.] Sir And. S. Walker conj.

132. *puritan*] *a puritan* Hanmer.

Mar. The devil a puritan that he is, or any thing constantly, but a time-pleaser; an affectioned ass, that cons state without book and utters it by great swarths: the best persuaded of himself, so crammed, as he thinks, with excellencies, that it is his grounds of faith that all that look on him love him; and on that vice in him will my revenge find notable cause to work.

Sir To. What wilt thou do?

Mar. I will drop in his way some obscure epistles of love; wherein, by the colour of his beard, the shape of his leg, the manner of his gait, the expressure of his eye, forehead, and complexion, he shall find himself most feelingly personated. I can write very like my lady your niece: on a forgotten matter we can hardly make distinction of our hands.

Sir To. Excellent! I smell a device.

Sir And. I have 't in my nose too.

Sir To. He shall think, by the letters that thou wilt drop, that they come from my niece, and that she 's in love with him.

Mar. My purpose is, indeed, a horse of that colour.

Sir And. And your horse now would make him an ass.

Mar. Ass, I doubt not.

Sir And. O, 'twill be admirable!

Mar. Sport royal, I warrant you: I know my physic will work with him. I will plant you two, and let the fool make a third, where he shall find the letter: observe his construction of it. For this night, to bed, and dream on the event. Farewell. [*Exit.*

Sir To. Good night, Penthesilea.

Sir And. Before me, she's a good wench.

Sir To. She's a beagle, true-bred, and one that adores me: what o' that?

139. *affectioned*] *affected* Hanmer.
140. *state without book*] *stale wit out of books* Anon. conj.
swarths] *swaths* Collier.
142. *grounds*] F_1. *ground* $F_2F_3F_4$.
155. *letters*] *letter* Collier MS.
156. *they come*] *it comes* Collier MS.
she's] *she is* F_4.
159. Sir And.] Sir To. Harness (Tyrwhitt conj.).
160. *Ass, I*] *As I* S. Walker conj.
163. *with him*] *him him* Rowe (ed. 2).
164. *his*] F_1. *this* $F_2F_3F_4$.

Sir And. I was adored once too.

Sir To. Let's to bed, knight. Thou hadst need send for more money.

Sir And. If I cannot recover your niece, I am a foul way out.

Sir To. Send for money, knight: if thou hast her not i' the end, call me cut.

Sir And. If I do not, never trust me, take it how you will.

Sir To. Come, come, I'll go burn some sack; 'tis too late to go to bed now: come, knight; come, knight.

[*Exeunt.*

SCENE IV. *The* DUKE'S *palace.*

Enter DUKE, VIOLA, CURIO, *and others.*

Duke. Give me some music. Now, good morrow, friends.
Now, good Cesario, but that piece of song,
That old and antique song we heard last night:
Methought it did relieve my passion much,
More than light airs and recollected terms
Of these most brisk and giddy-paced times:
Come, but one verse.

Cur. He is not here, so please your lordship, that should sing it.

Duke. Who was it?

Cur. Feste, the jester, my lord; a fool that the lady Olivia's father took much delight in. He is about the house.

Duke. Seek him out, and play the tune the while.

[*Exit Curio. Music plays.*

Come hither, boy: if ever thou shalt love,
In the sweet pangs of it remember me;
For such as I am all true lovers are,

SCENE IV.] SCENE V. Pope.
The DUKE'S palace.] The Palace. Rowe.

5. *terms*] *tunes* Knight conj.
13. *Seek*] *Go, seek* Capell.
[Exit Curio.] Pope.

Unstaid and skittish in all motions else,
Save in the constant image of the creature
That is beloved. How dost thou like this tune?

Vio. It gives a very echo to the seat
Where Love is throned.

Duke. Thou dost speak masterly:
My life upon't, young though thou art, thine eye
Hath stay'd upon some favour that it loves:
Hath it not, boy?

Vio. A little, by your favour.

Duke. What kind of woman is't?

Vio. Of your complexion.

Duke. She is not worth thee, then. What years, i' faith?

Vio. About your years, my lord.

Duke. Too old, by heaven: let still the woman take
An elder than herself; so wears she to him,
So sways she level in her husband's heart:
For, boy, however we do praise ourselves,
Our fancies are more giddy and unfirm,
More longing, wavering, sooner lost and worn,
Than women's are.

Vio. I think it well, my lord.

Duke. Then let thy love be younger than thyself,
Or thy affection cannot hold the bent;
For women are as roses, whose fair flower
Being once display'd, doth fall that very hour.

Vio. And so they are: alas, that they are so;
To die, even when they to perfection grow!

Re-enter CURIO *and* Clown.

Duke. O, fellow, come, the song we had last night.
Mark it, Cesario, it is old and plain;
The spinsters and the knitters in the sun

17. *motions*] *notions* Warburton (Theobald conj.). See note (IX).

20. *to the seat*] *from the seat* Warburton.

34. *worn*] F_4. *worne* $F_1F_2F_3$. *won* Hanmer.

41. Re-enter...] Enter... Ff.

And the free maids that weave their thread with bones
Do use to chant it: it is silly sooth,
And dallies with the innocence of love,
Like the old age.

Clo. Are you ready, sir?

Duke. Ay; prithee, sing. [*Music.*

SONG.

Clo. Come away, come away, death,
And in sad cypress let me be laid;
Fly away, fly away, breath;
I am slain by a fair cruel maid.
My shroud of white, stuck all with yew,
O, prepare it!
My part of death, no one so true
Did share it.

Not a flower, not a flower sweet,
On my black coffin let there be strown;
Not a friend, not a friend greet
My poor corpse, where my bones shall be thrown:
A thousand thousand sighs to save,
Lay me, O, where
Sad true lover never find my grave,
To weep there!

Duke. There 's for thy pains.

Clo. No pains, sir; I take pleasure in singing, sir.

Duke. I'll pay thy pleasure then.

Clo. Truly, sir, and pleasure will be paid, one time or another.

Duke. Give me now leave to leave thee.

Clo. Now, the melancholy god protect thee; and the tailor make thy doublet of changeable taffeta, for thy mind is a very opal. I would have men of such constancy put

45. *free*] *fair* Grey conj.
47. *dallies*] *tallies* Warburton.
50. *Ay; prithee*] *Ay; pr'ythee* Capell. *I prethee* Ff.
53. *Fly...fly*] Rowe. *Fye...fie* F_1 F_2. *Fie...fie* F_3 F_4.
56. *O, prepare*] *Prepare* Pope.
64. *O, where*] *where* Pope.
65. *Sad*] om. Pope.
true lover] *true-love* Capell.
never] *ne'er* Rann.
71. *another*] *other* Rowe.
72. *Give me...thee*] *I give thee...me* Harness.
73. Clo.] Duk. F_2.

to sea, that their business might be every thing and their intent every where; for that's it that always makes a good voyage of nothing. Farewell. [*Exit.*

Duke. Let all the rest give place.
[*Curio and Attendants retire.*
Once more, Cesario,
Get thee to yond same sovereign cruelty:
Tell her, my love, more noble than the world,
Prizes not quantity of dirty lands;
The parts that fortune hath bestow'd upon her,
Tell her, I hold as giddily as fortune;
But 'tis that miracle and queen of gems
That nature pranks her in attracts my soul.

Vio. But if she cannot love you, sir?

Duke. I cannot be so answer'd.

Vio. Sooth, but you must.
Say that some lady, as perhaps there is,
Hath for your love as great a pang of heart
As you have for Olivia: you cannot love her;
You tell her so; must she not then be answer'd?

Duke. There is no woman's sides
Can bide the beating of so strong a passion
As love doth give my heart; no woman's heart
So big, to hold so much; they lack retention.
Alas, their love may be call'd appetite,—
No motion of the liver, but the palate,—
That suffer surfeit, cloyment and revolt;
But mine is all as hungry as the sea,
And can digest as much: make no compare
Between that love a woman can bear me
And that I owe Olivia.

Vio. Ay, but I know,—

77. *every where*] *no where* Warburton.
79. SCENE VI. Pope.
[C. and A. retire.] Edd. Exeunt C. and A. Capell. om. Ff.
86. *pranks her in*] *pranks, her mind,* Warburton. *pranks in her* Jackson conj.
88. *I*] Hanmer. *It* Ff.
97, 98. *appetite,—...palate,—*] Capell. *appetite,...pallat* F_1F_2. *appetite: ...pallat,* F_3F_4.
99. *suffer*] *suffers* Rowe.
101. *digest*] *disgest* F_2.

Duke. What dost thou know?
Vio. Too well what love women to men may owe:
In faith, they are as true of heart as we.
My father had a daughter loved a man,
As it might be, perhaps, were I a woman,
I should your lordship.
Duke. And what's her history?
Vio. A blank, my lord. She never told her love,
But let concealment, like a worm i' the bud,
Feed on her damask cheek: she pined in thought;
And with a green and yellow melancholy
She sat like patience on a monument,
Smiling at grief. Was not this love indeed?
We men may say more, swear more: but indeed
Our shows are more than will; for still we prove
Much in our vows, but little in our love.
Duke. But died thy sister of her love, my boy?
Vio. I am all the daughters of my father's house,
And all the brothers too: and yet I know not.
Sir, shall I to this lady?
Duke. Ay, that's the theme.
To her in haste; give her this jewel; say,
My love can give no place, bide no denay. [*Exeunt.*

SCENE V. OLIVIA'S *garden.*

Enter SIR TOBY, SIR ANDREW, *and* FABIAN.

Sir To. Come thy ways, Signior Fabian.

Fab. Nay, I'll come: if I lose a scruple of this sport, let me be boiled to death with melancholy.

109. *And what's*] *What's* Pope.
113. *a green and yellow*] *agrein and hallow* Becket conj.
114. *sat like...monument,*] *sat, like ...monument* Hunter conj.
120, 121. *I am all the daughters... And all the brothers too;—and yet*] *She's all the daughters....And I am all the sons, but yet* Hanmer.
124. *My*] $F_1 F_3 F_4$. *Thy* F_2.
SCENE V.] SCENE VII. Pope.
OLIVIA'S garden.] Pope.
3. *boiled*] *broiled* Grey conj.

Sir To. Wouldst thou not be glad to have the niggardly rascally sheep-biter come by some notable shame?

Fab. I would exult, man: you know, he brought me out o' favour with my lady about a bear-baiting here.

Sir To. To anger him we'll have the bear again; and we will fool him black and blue: shall we not, Sir Andrew?

Sir And. An we do not, it is pity of our lives.

Sir To. Here comes the little villain.

Enter MARIA.

How now, my metal of India!

Mar. Get ye all three into the box-tree: Malvolio's coming down this walk: he has been yonder i' the sun practising behaviour to his own shadow this half hour: observe him, for the love of mockery; for I know this letter will make a contemplative idiot of him. Close, in the name of jesting! Lie thou there [*throws down a letter*]; for here comes the trout that must be caught with tickling. [*Exit.*

Enter MALVOLIO.

Mal. 'Tis but fortune; all is fortune. Maria once told me she did affect me: and I have heard herself come thus near, that, should she fancy, it should be one of my complexion. Besides, she uses me with a more exalted respect than any one else that follows her. What should I think on't?

Sir To. Here's an overweening rogue!

Fab. O, peace! Contemplation makes a rare turkey-cock of him: how he jets under his advanced plumes!

Sir And. 'Slight, I could so beat the rogue!

Sir To. Peace, I say.

7. *o'*] *of* Rowe.
10. *An*] Pope. *And* Ff.
it is] *'tis* Rowe (ed. 1). *it's* Id. (ed. 2).
11. Enter M.] Ff (after line 10).
12. *metal*] Malone. *Mettle* F_1. *Nettle* $F_2F_3F_4$.
18. [Men hide themselves. Capell. [throws down a letter] Theobald.
21. SCENE VIII. Pope.
30. *'Slight*] $F_3 F_4$. *Slight* $F_1 F_2$. *'Slife* Rowe.
31, 35. Sir To.] Fab. Edd. conj.

Mal. To be Count Malvolio!

Sir To. Ah, rogue!

Sir And. Pistol him, pistol him.

Sir To. Peace, peace!

Mal. There is example for't; the lady of the Strachy married the yeoman of the wardrobe.

Sir And. Fie on him, Jezebel!

Fab. O, peace! now he's deeply in: look how imagination blows him.

Mal. Having been three months married to her, sitting in my state,—

Sir To. O, for a stone-bow, to hit him in the eye!

Mal. Calling my officers about me, in my branched velvet gown; having come from a day-bed, where I have left Olivia sleeping,—

Sir To. Fire and brimstone!

Fab. O, peace, peace!

Mal. And then to have the humour of state; and after a demure travel of regard, telling them I know my place as I would they should do theirs, to ask for my kinsman Toby,—

Sir To. Bolts and shackles!

Fab. O, peace, peace, peace! now, now.

Mal. Seven of my people, with an obedient start, make out for him: I frown the while; and perchance wind up my watch, or play with my—some rich jewel. Toby approaches; courtesies there to me,—

Sir To. Shall this fellow live?

Fab. Though our silence be drawn from us with cars, yet peace.

36. *Strachy*] *Stratarch* Hanmer. *Trachy* Warburton. *Trachyne* Capell conj. *Straccio* Smith conj. *Starchy* Steevens conj. *Stitchery* Becket conj. *Stratico* R. P. Knight conj. *Astrakhan* C. Knight conj. *Strozzi* Collier conj. *Stracci* Lloyd conj. *Sophy* or *Saucery* or *Satrape* Anon. apud Halliwell conj.

37. *the wardrobe*] *her wardrobe* Capell conj.

38. *him*] *her* Lloyd conj.

49. *humour*] *honour* Collier MS.

51. *kinsman*] *uncle* Rowe (ed. 2).

56. *my—some*] Collier. *my some* $F_1 F_2$. *some* $F_3 F_4$.

59. *Though...cars*] *Silence! though our ears be withdrawn from us* Becket conj.

with cars] F_1. *with cares* $F_2 F_3 F_4$. *by th' ears* Hanmer. *with carts* Johnson conj. *with cables* Tyrwhitt conj. *with cats* Jackson conj. *with tears* Singer conj. *with racks* S. Walker conj. *with cords* Grant White. *with*

Mal. I extend my hand to him thus, quenching my familiar smile with an austere regard of control,—

Sir To. And does not Toby take you a blow o' the lips then?

Mal. Saying, 'Cousin Toby, my fortunes having cast me on your niece give me this prerogative of speech,'—

Sir To. What, what?

Mal. 'You must amend your drunkenness.'

Sir To. Out, scab!

Fab. Nay, patience, or we break the sinews of our plot.

Mal. 'Besides, you waste the treasure of your time with a foolish knight,'—

Sir And. That's me, I warrant you.

Mal. 'One Sir Andrew,'—

Sir And. I knew 'twas I; for many do call me fool.

Mal. What employment have we here?

[*Taking up the letter.*

Fab. Now is the woodcock near the gin.

Sir To. O, peace! and the spirit of humours intimate reading aloud to him!

Mal. By my life, this is my lady's hand: these be her very C's, her U's and her T's; and thus makes she her great P's. It is, in contempt of question, her hand.

Sir And. Her C's, her U's and her T's: why that?

Mal. [*reads*] To the unknown beloved, this, and my good wishes:—her very phrases! By your leave, wax. Soft! and the impressure her Lucrece, with which she uses to seal: 'tis my lady. To whom should this be?

Fab. This wins him, liver and all.

Mal. [*reads*] Jove knows I love:
But who?
Lips, do not move;
No man must know.

screws Bailey conj. *with cart-ropes* Hunter conj. *with curs* Anon. conj.

65. *Cousin*] Ff. *Uncle* Rowe (ed. 2).

76. *employment*] *implement* Hanmer (Theobald conj.).

[Taking...] Taking up a letter. Rowe.

78. *and*] *now* Rowe.

84, 89, 96. [reads] Capell.

85. *Soft!*] Rowe. *Soft,* Ff.

89—92. *Jove...know*] As prose in Ff.

90. *But who?*] *Alas! but who?* Hanmer.

91. *Lips,*] Edd. (Capell MS.). *Lips* Ff.

'No man must know.' What follows? the numbers altered! 'No man must know:' if this should be thee, Malvolio?

Sir To. Marry, hang thee, brock!

Mal. [*reads*] I may command where I adore;
But silence, like a Lucrece knife,
With bloodless stroke my heart doth gore:
M, O, A, I, doth sway my life.

Fab. A fustian riddle!

Sir To. Excellent wench, say I.

Mal. 'M, O, A, I, doth sway my life.' Nay, but first, let me see, let me see, let me see.

Fab. What dish o' poison has she dressed him!

Sir To. And with what wing the staniel checks at it!

Mal. 'I may command where I adore.' Why, she may command me: I serve her; she is my lady. Why, this is evident to any formal capacity; there is no obstruction in this: and the end,—what should that alphabetical position portend? If I could make that resemble something in me,—Softly! M, O, A, I,—

Sir To. O, ay, make up that: he is now at a cold scent.

Fab. Sowter will cry upon't for all this, though it be as rank as a fox.

Mal. M,—Malvolio; M,—why, that begins my name.

Fab. Did not I say he would work it out? the cur is excellent at faults.

Mal. M,—but then there is no consonancy in the sequel; that suffers under probation: A should follow, but O does.

93. *numbers altered!*] Capell. *numbers alter'd:* Ff. *number's alter'd* Rowe (ed. 2). *numbers alter* Hanmer.

97. *Lucrece knife*] Rowe (ed. 2). *Lucresse knife* F_1F_2. *Lucress wife* F_3F_4. *Lucrece' knife* Dyce (S. Walker conj.).

96—99. *I may...my life*] As in Hanmer. Printed as two lines in Ff.

103. *let me see, let me see, let me see*] *let me see, let me see* F_3F_4.

104. *o'*] Dyce. *a* F_1F_2. *of* F_3F_4.

105. *staniel*] Hanmer. *stallion* Ff. *falcon* Collier MS.

110. *portend?......me,—*] Capell. *portend, ... me?* Ff. *portend. ... me?* Rowe (ed. 1). *portend?...me?* Id. (ed. 2). *portend?...me.* Hanmer.

112. *make up*] *make out* Hanmer. *take up* Anon. conj.

113. *be*] *ben't* Hanmer.

115. *M, Malvolio...name*] *M,—why...name. M,—Malvolio!* or *M,—M,—M,—why...name* Edd. conj.

118. *sequel;*] Rowe. *sequel* Ff.

119. *suffers*] *suffices* Anon. conj.

Fab. And O shall end, I hope.

Sir To. Ay, or I'll cudgel him, and make him cry O!

Mal. And then I comes behind.

Fab. Ay, an you had any eye behind you, you might see more detraction at your heels than fortunes before you.

Mal. M, O, A, I; this simulation is not as the former: and yet, to crush this a little, it would bow to me, for every one of these letters are in my name. Soft! here follows prose. [*Reads*] If this fall into thy hand, revolve. In my stars I am above thee; but be not afraid of greatness: some are born great, some achieve greatness, and some have greatness thrust upon 'em. Thy Fates open their hands; let thy blood and spirit embrace them; and, to inure thyself to what thou art like to be, cast thy humble slough and appear fresh. Be opposite with a kinsman, surly with servants; let thy tongue tang arguments of state; put thyself into the trick of singularity: she thus advises thee that sighs for thee. Remember who commended thy yellow stockings, and wished to see thee ever cross-gartered: I say, remember. Go to, thou art made, if thou desirest to be so; if not, let me see thee a steward still, the fellow of servants, and not worthy to touch Fortune's fingers. Farewell. She that would alter services with thee,

THE FORTUNATE-UNHAPPY.

Daylight and champain discovers not more: this is open. I will be proud, I will read politic authors, I will baffle Sir Toby, I will wash off gross acquaintance, I will be point-devise the very man. I do not now fool myself, to let imagination jade me; for every reason excites to this, that my lady

123. *an*] Hanmer. *and* Ff. *and if* Capell conj.

125. *simulation*] *similation* Capell conj. MS.

126. *bow to me*] $F_1 F_2$. *bow me* $F_3 F_4$.

127. *are*] *is* Rowe (ed. 2).

128. [Reads] Capell.

129. *born*] Rowe. *become* Ff.

achieve] *atcheeues* F_1. See note (x).

130. *thrust upon 'em*] *thrust vppon em* F_1. *thrust upon em* F_2. *put upon em* F_3. *put upon them* F_4. *thrust upon them* Rowe (ed. 2).

131, 132. *them;...be,*] *them,...be:* $F_1 F_2 F_3$. *them,...be;* F_4.

134. *tang*] Ff. *tang with* Hanmer.

141, 142. *thee*, THE FORTUNATE-UNHAPPY. *Daylight*] Capell. *thee, the fortunate unhappy daylight* Ff (*tht* F_1). *thee. The fortunate and happy daylight* Rowe. *thee the fortunate and happy. Daylight* Hanmer.

142. *champain*] Dyce. *champian* $F_1 F_2$. *champion* $F_3 F_4$. *champaign* Collier (ed. 1).

discovers not] Ff. *discovers no* Pope. *discover no* Hanmer.

143. *politic*] *pollticke* F_1.

144, 145. *point-devise*] *point devise* Ff. *point-de-vice* Steevens.

145. *not now*] F_1. *now* $F_2 F_3 F_4$. *not* Hanmer.

146. *every*] *very* Capell conj.

loves me. She did commend my yellow stockings of late, she did praise my leg being cross-gartered; and in this she manifests herself to my love, and with a kind of injunction drives me to these habits of her liking. I thank my stars I am happy. I will be strange, stout, in yellow stockings, and cross-gartered, even with the swiftness of putting on. Jove and my stars be praised! Here is yet a postscript.
[*Reads*] Thou canst not choose but know who I am. If thou entertainest my love, let it appear in thy smiling; thy smiles become thee well; therefore in my presence still smile, dear my sweet, I prithee.
Jove, I thank thee: I will smile; I will do every thing that thou wilt have me. [*Exit.*

Fab. I will not give my part of this sport for a pension of thousands to be paid from the Sophy.

Sir To. I could marry this wench for this device.

Sir And. So could I too.

Sir To. And ask no other dowry with her but such another jest.

Sir And. Nor I neither.

Fab. Here comes my noble gull-catcher.

Re-enter MARIA.

Sir To. Wilt thou set thy foot o' my neck?

Sir And. Or o' mine either?

Sir To. Shall I play my freedom at tray-trip, and become thy bond-slave?

Sir And. I' faith, or I either?

Sir To. Why, thou hast put him in such a dream, that when the image of it leaves him he must run mad.

Mar. Nay, but say true; does it work upon him?

Sir To. Like aqua-vitæ with a midwife.

Mar. If you will then see the fruits of the sport, mark his first approach before my lady: he will come to her in yellow stockings, and 'tis a colour she abhors, and cross-gartered, a fashion she detests; and he will smile upon her,

149. *kind of*] *kind* Capell conj.

151. *be strange, stout*] *bestir me, strut* Anon. conj.

stockings] *stocking* F_2.

154. [Reads] Collier.

156. *dear*] *deero* F_1.

162. *So*] *And so* Hanmer.

165. SCENE IX. Pope.

167. Re-enter M.] Enter M. Ff (after line 164).

169. *at*] *at a* F_3 F_4.

which will now be so unsuitable to her disposition, being addicted to a melancholy as she is, that it cannot but turn him into a notable contempt. If you will see it, follow me.

Sir To. To the gates of Tartar, thou most excellent devil of wit!

Sir And. I'll make one too. [*Exeunt.*

ACT III.

SCENE I. OLIVIA'S *garden.*

Enter VIOLA, *and* Clown *with a tabor.*

Vio. Save thee, friend, and thy music: dost thou live by thy tabor?

Clo. No, sir, I live by the church.

Vio. Art thou a churchman?

Clo. No such matter, sir: I do live by the church; for I do live at my house, and my house doth stand by the church.

Vio. So thou mayst say, the king lies by a beggar, if a beggar dwell near him; or, the church stands by thy tabor, if thy tabor stand by the church.

Clo. You have said, sir. To see this age! A sentence is but a cheveril glove to a good wit: how quickly the wrong side may be turned outward!

Vio. Nay, that's certain; they that dally nicely with words may quickly make them wanton.

Clo. I would, therefore, my sister had had no name, sir.

Vio.. Why, man?

Clo. Why, sir, her name's a word; and to dally with

181. *a melancholy*] *melancholy* F_3 F_4.

183. *gates of Tartar*] *gates Tartar* F_4. *gates, Tartar* Rowe. *gates of Tartarus* Collier MS.

185. [Exeunt.] Exeunt. Finis Actus secundus. F_1. Exeunt. Finis Actus secundi. $F_2F_3F_4$.

OLIVIA'S garden] Pope. A garden. Rowe.

with a tabor.] Malone. meeting. Capell.

2. *thy*] F_1. *the* $F_2F_3F_4$.

5. *sir: I do*] *sir: and yet I do* Capell conj.

7. *king*] *kings* F_1.

lies] *lives* Collier (Capell conj.).

15. *had had*] *had* Hanmer.

that word might make my sister wanton. But indeed words are very rascals since bonds disgraced them.

Vio. Thy reason, man?

Clo. Troth, sir, I can yield you none without words; and words are grown so false, I am loath to prove reason with them.

Vio. I warrant thou art a merry fellow and carest for nothing.

Clo. Not so, sir, I do care for something; but in my conscience, sir, I do not care for you: if that be to care for nothing, sir, I would it would make you invisible.

Vio. Art not thou the Lady Olivia's fool?

Clo. No, indeed, sir; the Lady Olivia has no folly: she will keep no fool, sir, till she be married; and fools are as like husbands as pilchards are to herrings; the husband's the bigger: I am indeed not her fool, but her corrupter of words.

Vio. I saw thee late at the Count Orsino's.

Clo. Foolery, sir, does walk about the orb like the sun, it shines every where. I would be sorry, sir, but the fool should be as oft with your master as with my mistress: I think I saw your wisdom there.

Vio. Nay, an thou pass upon me, I'll no more with thee. Hold, there's expenses for thee.

Clo. Now Jove, in his next commodity of hair, send thee a beard!

Vio. By my troth, I'll tell thee, I am almost sick for one; [*Aside*] though I would not have it grow on my chin. Is thy lady within?

Clo. Would not a pair of these have bred, sir?

Vio. Yes, being kept together and put to use.

Clo. I would play Lord Pandarus of Phrygia, sir, to bring a Cressida to this Troilus.

Vio. I understand you, sir; 'tis well begged.

29. *not thou*] *thou not* Steevens (1793), corrected in MS.

32. *pilchards*] Capell. *pilchers* Ff.

35, 97. *Count*] *Duke* Rowe.

36. *orb...sun*] Ff. *orb; like the sun* Dyce.

40. *an*] Pope. *and* Ff.

41. *expenses*] *sixpence* Badham conj. [Gives him a piece of money. Hanmer.

45. [Aside] Edd.

47. *bred*] *breed* Malone conj.

Clo. The matter, I hope, is not great, sir, begging but a beggar: Cressida was a beggar. My lady is within, sir. I will construe to them whence you come; who you are and what you would are out of my welkin, I might say 'element,' but the word is over-worn. [*Exit.*

Vio. This fellow is wise enough to play the fool;
And to do that well craves a kind of wit:
He must observe their mood on whom he jests,
The quality of persons, and the time,
And, like the haggard, check at every feather
That comes before his eye. This is a practice
As full of labour as a wise man's art:
For folly that he wisely shows is fit;
But wise men, folly-fall'n, quite taint their wit.

Enter SIR TOBY, *and* SIR ANDREW.

Sir To. Save you, gentleman.

Vio. And you, sir.

Sir And. Dieu vous garde, monsieur.

Vio. Et vous aussi; votre serviteur.

Sir And. I hope, sir, you are; and I am yours.

Sir To. Will you encounter the house? my niece is desirous you should enter, if your trade be to her.

Vio. I am bound to your niece, sir; I mean, she is the list of my voyage.

52. *begging*] Pope. *begging*, Ff.
54. *construe*] *conster* Ff.
them] *her Hanmer*.
55. *are*] F_1. *is* $F_2F_3F_4$.
61. *And*] Ff. *Not* Rann (Johnson conj.). *Nor* Harness.
63. *wise man's*] *wise-mans* Ff.
64. *folly that he*] *he that folly* Badham conj.
65. *wise men, folly-fall'n, quite taint*] Capell (Theobald and Tyrwhitt conj.). *wisemens folly falne, quite taint* F_1. *wise mens folly falne, quite taint* $F_2F_3F_4$ (*faln* F_3F_4). *wise mens olly fall'n, quite taints* Rowe (ed. 2). *wise men's, folly fall'n, quite taints* Theobald. *wise men's folly shewn, quite taints* Hanmer. *wise men's folly, fall'n, quite taints* Heath conj. *wise men, folly-blown, quite taint their wit* Anon. conj.
65. SIR ANDREW] Andrew Ff.
66. SCENE II. Pope.
Sir To.] Sir And. Theobald.
68, 70. Sir And.] Sir To. Theobald.
68. *vous garde*] *vou guard* Ff.
69. *vous aussi*] *vouz ousie* F_1. *vouz ausie* $F_2F_3F_4$.
votre serviteur] *vostre serviture* Ff.
71. Sir To.] om. Theobald.

Sir To. Taste your legs, sir; put them to motion.

Vio. My legs do better understand me, sir, than I understand what you mean by bidding me taste my legs.

Sir To. I mean, to go, sir, to enter.

Vio. I will answer you with gait and entrance. But we are prevented.

Enter OLIVIA *and* MARIA.

Most excellent accomplished lady, the heavens rain odours on you!

Sir And. That youth's a rare courtier: 'Rain odours;' well.

Vio. My matter hath no voice, lady, but to your own most pregnant and vouchsafed ear.

Sir And. 'Odours,' 'pregnant,' and 'vouchsafed:' I'll get 'em all three all ready.

Oli. Let the garden door be shut, and leave me to my hearing. [*Exeunt Sir Toby, Sir Andrew, and Maria.*] Give me your hand, sir.

Vio. My duty, madam, and most humble service.

Oli. What is your name?

Vio. Cesario is your servant's name, fair princess.

Oli. My servant, sir! 'Twas never merry world
Since lowly feigning was call'd compliment:
You're servant to the Count Orsino, youth.

Vio. And he is yours, and his must needs be yours:
Your servant's servant is your servant, madam.

Oli. For him, I think not on him: for his thoughts,
Would they were blanks, rather than fill'd with me!

Vio. Madam, I come to whet your gentle thoughts
On his behalf.

Oli. O, by your leave, I pray you,
I bade you never speak again of him:
But, would you undertake another suit,

80. MARIA] Gentlewoman Ff.

88. *all ready*] Malone. *already* F_1F_2. *ready* F_3F_4.
[writing in his table-book. Collier (Collier MS.).

89. *Let*] *Maria, let* Capell conj. reading as verse.

90. [Exeunt...] Rowe.
SCENE III. Pope.

97. *You're*] *Y'are* Ff.

I had rather hear you to solicit that
Than music from the spheres.

Vio. Dear lady,—

Oli. Give me leave, beseech you. I did send,
After the last enchantment you did here,
A ring in chase of you: so did I abuse
Myself, my servant and, I fear me, you:
Under your hard construction must I sit,
To force that on you, in a shameful cunning,
Which you knew none of yours: what might you think?
Have you not set mine honour at the stake
And baited it with all the unmuzzled thoughts
That tyrannous heart can think? To one of your receiving
Enough is shown: a cypress, not a bosom,
Hides my heart. So, let me hear you speak.

Vio. I pity you.

Oli. That's a degree to love.

Vio. No, not a grize; for 'tis a vulgar proof,
That very oft we pity enemies.

Oli. Why, then, methinks 'tis time to smile again.
O world, how apt the poor are to be proud!
If one should be a prey, how much the better
To fall before the lion than the wolf! [*Clock strikes.*
The clock upbraids me with the waste of time.
Be not afraid, good youth, I will not have you:
And yet, when wit and youth is come to harvest,
Your wife is like to reap a proper man:

106. *I had*] *I'd* Pope.
107. *Dear*] *O dearest* Hanmer. *lady,—*] Theobald. *lady.* Ff.
108. *Give*] *Nay, give* Capell. *beseech*] *I beseech* F_3F_4.
109. *enchantment you did here*] Warburton (Thirlby conj.). *enchantment you did heare* F_1 F_2. *enchantment you did hear* F_3F_4. *enchantment, you did hear* Theobald.
113. *shameful*] *shame-fac'd* Collier MS.
117. *one of*] om. Hanmer. *receiving*] *conceiving* Mason conj.
118—120. S. Walker arranges as three lines ending *shown...heart...you.*
118. *cypress*] *Cipresse* F_1 F_2 F_3. *Cipress* F_4. *Cyprus* Theobald.
119. *Hides*] *Hideth* Delius conj. *heart* F_1. *poor heart* $F_2F_3F_4$. *me*] *us* Rowe (ed. 2).
121. *grize*] F_1. *grice* $F_2F_3F_4$.
125. *the better*] *better* F_3F_4.
129. *is come*] *are come* Pope (ed. 2).

There lies your way, due west.
Vio. Then westward-ho!
Grace and good disposition attend your ladyship!
You'll nothing, madam, to my lord by me?
Oli. Stay:
I prithee, tell me what thou think'st of me.
Vio. That you do think you are not what you are.
Oli. If I think so, I think the same of you.
Vio. Then think you right: I am not what I am.
Oli. I would you were as I would have you be!
Vio. Would it be better, madam, than I am?
I wish it might, for now I am your fool.
Oli. O, what a deal of scorn looks beautiful
In the contempt and anger of his lip!
A murderous guilt shows not itself more soon
Than love that would seem hid: love's night is noon.
Cesario, by the roses of the spring,
By maidhood, honour, truth and every thing,
I love thee so, that, maugre all thy pride,
Nor wit nor reason can my passion hide.
Do not extort thy reasons from this clause,
For that I woo, thou therefore hast no cause;
But rather reason thus with reason fetter,
Love sought is good, but given unsought is better.
Vio. By innocence I swear, and by my youth,
I have one heart, one bosom and one truth,
And that no woman has; nor never none
Shall mistress be of it, save I alone.
And so adieu, good madam: never more
Will I my master's tears to you deplore.
Oli. Yet come again; for thou perhaps mayst move
That heart, which now abhors, to like his love. [*Exeunt.*

131, 132. S. Walker would end the lines *west...disposition...ladyship.*

132. *attend*] *'tend* Steevens. *your ladyship*] *you* Hanmer.

133. *me?*] Rowe. *me:* Ff.

135. *I*] om. Pope.

140. *am?*] Ff. *am,* Rowe (ed. 2).

142, 143. *beautiful... lip!*] Rowe. *beautiful?...lip,* Ff.

148. *thy*] *my* Collier MS.

150. *thy*] *'wry* Hanmer.

157, 158. *it, save I alone. And*] *it.* Oli. *Save I alone!* Vio. *And* Hanmer.

SCENE II. OLIVIA'S *house.*

Enter SIR TOBY, SIR ANDREW, *and* FABIAN.

Sir And. No, faith, I'll not stay a jot longer.

Sir To. Thy reason, dear venom, give thy reason.

Fab. You must needs yield your reason, Sir Andrew.

Sir And. Marry, I saw your niece do more favours to the count's serving-man than ever she bestowed upon me; I saw 't i' the orchard.

Sir To. Did she see thee the while, old boy? tell me that.

Sir And. As plain as I see you now.

Fab. This was a great argument of love in her toward you.

Sir And. 'Slight, will you make an ass o' me?

Fab. I will prove it legitimate, sir, upon the oaths of judgement and reason.

Sir To. And they have been grand-jurymen since before Noah was a sailor.

Fab. She did show favour to the youth in your sight only to exasperate you, to awake your dormouse valour, to put fire in your heart, and brimstone in your liver. You should then have accosted her; and with some excellent jests, fire-new from the mint, you should have banged the youth into dumbness. This was looked for at your hand, and this was balked: the double gilt of this opportunity you let time wash off, and you are now sailed into the north of my lady's opinion; where you will hang like an icicle on a Dutchman's beard, unless you do redeem it by some laudable attempt either of valour or policy.

SCENE II.] SCENE IV. Pope. OLIVIA'S house.] Rowe.
5, 31. *count's*] *Duke's* Rowe.
5. *upon*] *on* Rowe (ed. 2).
7. *thee the*] F_3F_4. *the* F_1F_2. *you the* Long MS.
12. *'Slight*] F_3F_4. *S'light* F_1F_2.
13. *I will*] F_1. *I* $F_2F_3F_4$.
27. *laudable*] om. Rowe.

Sir And. An't be any way, it must be with valour; for policy I hate: I had as lief be a Brownist as a politician.

Sir To. Why, then, build me thy fortunes upon the basis of valour. Challenge me the count's youth to fight with him; hurt him in eleven places: my niece shall take note of it; and assure thyself, there is no love-broker in the world can more prevail in man's commendation with woman than report of valour.

Fab. There is no way but this, Sir Andrew.

Sir And. Will either of you bear me a challenge to him?

Sir To. Go, write it in a martial hand; be curst and brief; it is no matter how witty, so it be eloquent and full of invention: taunt him with the license of ink: if thou thou'st him some thrice, it shall not be amiss; and as many lies as will lie in thy sheet of paper, although the sheet were big enough for the bed of Ware in England, set 'em down: go, about it. Let there be gall enough in thy ink, though thou write with a goose-pen, no matter: about it.

Sir And. Where shall I find you?

Sir To. We'll call thee at the cubiculo: go.

[*Exit Sir Andrew.*

Fab. This is a dear manakin to you, Sir Toby.

Sir To. I have been dear to him, lad, some two thousand strong, or so.

Fab. We shall have a rare letter from him: but you'll not deliver't?

Sir To. Never trust me, then; and by all means stir on the youth to an answer. I think oxen and wainropes cannot hale them together. For Andrew, if he were opened, and you find so much blood in his liver as will clog the foot of a flea, I'll eat the rest of the anatomy.

28. *An't*] Hanmer. *And 't* Ff.
youth to fight] *youth; go, fight* Tyrwhitt conj.
32. *with him*] *with you* Ritson conj.
35. *woman*] *women* Hanmer.
39. *curst*] *curt* Grey conj.
45. *go, about*] Capell. *go about* Ff. *and go about* Rowe.
46. *write*] *write it* Rowe.
49. *the*] *thy* Hanmer.
50. SCENE V. Pope.
57. *Andrew*] *Sir Andrew* Collier (Collier MS.).
58. *and*] *an* S. Walker conj.

Fab. And his opposite, the youth, bears in his visage no grêat presage of cruelty.

Enter MARIA.

Sir To. Look, where the youngest wren of nine comes.

Mar. If you desire the spleen, and will laugh yourselves into stitches, follow me. Yond gull Malvolio is turned heathen, a very renegado; for there is no Christian, that means to be saved by believing rightly, can ever believe such impossible passages of grossness. He's in yellow stockings.

Sir To. And cross-gartered?

Mar. Most villanously; like a pedant that keeps a school i' the church. I have dogged him, like his murderer. He does obey every point of the letter that I dropped to betray him: he does smile his face into more lines than is in the new map with the augmentation of the Indies: you have not seen such a thing as 'tis. I can hardly forbear hurling things at him. I know my lady will strike him: if she do, he'll smile and take 't for a great favour.

Sir To. Come, bring us, bring us where he is. [*Exeunt.*

SCENE III. *A street.*

Enter SEBASTIAN *and* ANTONIO.

Seb. I would not by my will have troubled you;
But, since you make your pleasure of your pains,
I will no further chide you.

Ant. I could not stay behind you: my desire,
More sharp than filed steel, did spur me forth;
And not all love to see you, though so much
As might have drawn one to a longer voyage,

62. *nine*] Theobald. *mine* Ff.

64. *yond*] *yon'* Capell.

65. *heathen*] *a heathen* S. Walker conj.

renegado] Rowe. *Renegatho* Ff.

73. *is*] Ff. *are* Steevens.

78. [Exeunt.] Exeunt Omnes Ff.

SCENE III.] SCENE VI. Pope.

A street.] Capell. The street. Rowe.

7. *one*] *me* Heath conj.

But jealousy what might befall your travel,
Being skilless in these parts; which to a stranger,
Unguided and unfriended, often prove
Rough and unhospitable: my willing love,
The rather by these arguments of fear,
Set forth in your pursuit.

Seb. My kind Antonio,
I can no other answer make but thanks,
And thanks; and ever......oft good turns
Are shuffled off with such uncurrent pay:
But, were my worth as is my conscience firm,
You should find better dealing. What's to do?
Shall we go see the reliques of this town?

Ant. To-morrow, sir: best first go see your lodging.

Seb. I am not weary, and 'tis long to night:
I pray you, let us satisfy our eyes
With the memorials and the things of fame
That do renown this city.

Ant. Would you'ld pardon me;
I do not without danger walk these streets:
Once, in a sea-fight, 'gainst the count his galleys
I did some service; of such note indeed,
That were I ta'en here it would scarce be answer'd.

Seb. Belike you slew great number of his people.

Ant. The offence is not of such a bloody nature;

15, 16. *And thanks...pay*] Omitted in F_2 F_3 F_4.

15. *And thanks; and ever......oft good turns*] *And thankes: and ever oft good turnes* F_1. *And thanks: and ever oft-good turns* Pope (ed. 1). *And thanks: and ever-oft good turns* Id. (ed. 2). *And thanks, and ever thanks; and oft good turns* Theobald. *And thanks, and ever; oft good turns* Steevens (1778). *And thanks again and ever; oft good turns* Rann (Tollet conj.). *And thanks, and ever thanks: oft good turns* Malone. *And thanks, and ever thanks: often good turns* Steevens (1794). *And thanks, and ever thanks; too oft good turns* Seymour conj. *And thanks, still thanks; and very oft good turns* Collier (Collier MS.). *And thanks, and ever thanks; though oft good turns* Lettsom conj. *And thanks: and very oft good turns* Grant White. *And thanks, and thanks; and very oft good turns* Id. conj.

17. *worth*] *wealth* Collier MS.

20. *lodging.*] *lodging?* F_1.

26. *count his*] *Duke his* Rowe. *County's* Malone conj.

29. *people.*] *people?* Dyce.

Albeit the quality of the time and quarrel
Might well have given us bloody argument.
It might have since been answer'd in repaying
What we took from them; which, for traffic's sake,
Most of our city did: only myself stood out;
For which, if I be lapsed in this place,
I shall pay dear.

Seb. Do not then walk too open.

Ant. It doth not fit me. Hold, sir, here's my purse.
In the south suburbs, at the Elephant,
Is best to lodge: I will bespeak our diet,
Whiles you beguile the time and feed your knowledge
With viewing of the town: there shall you have me.

Seb. Why I your purse?

Ant. Haply your eye shall light upon some toy
You have desire to purchase; and your store,
I think, is not for idle markets, sir.

Seb. I'll be your purse-bearer and leave you
For an hour.

Ant. To the Elephant.

Seb. I do remember. [*Exeunt.*

SCENE IV. OLIVIA'S *garden.*

Enter OLIVIA *and* MARIA.

Oli. I have sent after him: he says he'll come;
How shall I feast him? what bestow of him?
For youth is bought more oft than begg'd or borrow'd.

36. *lapsed*] *latched* Hunter conj.

47, 48. *you For an*] Ff. *you for An* Theobald. As prose in Boswell.

48. Exeunt.] Ff. Exeunt severally. Capell.

SCENE IV.] SCENE VII. Pope.

OLIVIA'S garden.] Capell. Olivia's house. Rowe.

1. *he says he'll*] *say, he will* Theobald.

2, 3. *bestow of him? For youth is ...borrow'd*] *bestow? for youth Is... borrow'd of* Badham conj.

2. *of*] *on* Pope.

I speak too loud.
Where is Malvolio? he is sad and civil,
And suits well for a servant with my fortunes:
Where is Malvolio?

Mar. He's coming, madam; but in very strange manner. He is, sure, possessed, madam.

Oli. Why, what's the matter? does he rave?

Mar. No, madam, he does nothing but smile: your ladyship were best to have some guard about you, if he come; for, sure, the man is tainted in's wits.

Oli. Go call him hither. [*Exit Maria.*] I am as mad as he,
If sad and merry madness equal be.

Re-enter MARIA, *with* MALVOLIO.

How now, Malvolio!

Mal. Sweet lady, ho, ho.

Oli. Smilest thou?
I sent for thee upon a sad occasion.

Mal. Sad, lady! I could be sad: this does make some obstruction in the blood, this cross-gartering; but what of that? if it please the eye of one, it is with me as the very true sonnet is, 'Please one, and please all.'

Oli. Why, how dost thou, man? what is the matter with thee?

4, 5. *I speak...civil*] Printed as in Pope; as one line in Ff.

5. *Where is*] Pope. *Where's* Ff.

7—10. *Where is...rave?*] As prose in Pope; as three lines in Ff, ending *madam ... madam ... rave?* As three lines in Hanmer, ending *madam... possest...rave?*

8. *He's*] *He is* Hanmer.
very] om. Hanmer.

11. *nothing*] *nothing else* Hanmer, who reads lines 11—14 as four verses, ending *smile;...guard...man...hither.*

13. *in's*] *in his* Hanmer.

14. [Exit M.] Dyce.
I am] *I'm* Pope.

15. *merry*] *mercy* F_2.

Re-enter M. with Malvolio.] Dyce. Enter Malvolio. Ff (after *hither*, line 14).

16. *How*] Ol. *How* F_2.

17. *ho, ho*] F_1. *ha, ha* F_2 F_3 F_4. om. Capell, reading *How now...thou?* as one line.
[Smiles fantastically. Rowe (smile. ed. 1).

18, 19. *Smilest...occasion*] As one line in Ff.

20—25. *Sad...thee?*] Printed as seven lines in Ff, ending *sad...blood...that? ...true...all...man...thee?*

23. *is*] *it* F_2. *has it* Capell.

24. Oli.] Mal. F_1.

Mal. Not black in my mind, though yellow in my legs. It did come to his hands, and commands shall be executed: I think we do know the sweet Roman hand.

Oli. Wilt thou go to bed, Malvolio?

Mal. To bed! ay, sweet-heart, and I'll come to thee.

Oli. God comfort thee! Why dost thou smile so and kiss thy hand so oft?

Mar. How do you, Malvolio?

Mal. At your request! yes; nightingales answer daws.

Mar. Why appear you with this ridiculous boldness before my lady?

Mal. 'Be not afraid of greatness:' 'twas well writ.

Oli. What meanest thou by that, Malvolio?

Mal. 'Some are born great,'—

Oli. Ha!

Mal. 'Some achieve greatness,'—

Oli. What sayest thou?

Mal. 'And some have greatness thrust upon them.'

Oli. Heaven restore thee!

Mal. 'Remember who commended thy yellow stockings,'—

Oli. Thy yellow stockings!

Mal. 'And wished to see thee cross-gartered.'

Oli. Cross-gartered!

Mal. 'Go to, thou art made, if thou desirest to be so;'—

Oli. Am I made?

Mal. 'If not, let me see thee a servant still.'

Oli. Why, this is very midsummer madness.

Enter Servant.

Ser. Madam, the young gentleman of the Count Orsino's is returned: I could hardly entreat him back: he attends your ladyship's pleasure.

Oli. I'll come to him. [*Exit Servant.*] Good Maria, let this fellow be looked to. Where's my cousin Toby?

28. *the sweet*] *that sweet* Rowe (ed. 2).

38. *meanest*] *meanst* F_1.

47. *Thy*] *My* Lettsom conj.

53. *very*] *a very* Rann.

54. *Count*] *Duke* Rowe.

57. [Exit Servant.] Capell.

58. *cousin*] *uncle* Rowe (ed. 2).

Let some of my people have a special care of him: I would not have him miscarry for the half of my dowry.

[*Exeunt Olivia and Maria.*

Mal. O, ho! do you come near me now? no worse man than Sir Toby to look to me! This concurs directly with the letter: she sends him on purpose, that I may appear stubborn to him; for she incites me to that in the letter. 'Cast thy humble slough,' says she; 'be opposite with a kinsman, surly with servants; let thy tongue tang with arguments of state; put thyself into the trick of singularity;' and consequently sets down the manner how; as, a sad face, a reverend carriage, a slow tongue, in the habit of some sir of note, and so forth. I have limed her; but it is Jove's doing, and Jove make me thankful! And when she went away now, 'Let this fellow be looked to:' fellow! not Malvolio, nor after my degree, but fellow. Why, every thing adheres together, that no dram of a scruple, no scruple of a scruple, no obstacle, no incredulous or unsafe circumstance —What can be said? Nothing that can be can come between me and the full prospect of my hopes. Well, Jove, not I, is the doer of this, and he is to be thanked.

Re-enter MARIA, *with* SIR TOBY *and* FABIAN.

Sir To. Which way is he, in the name of sanctity? If all the devils of hell be drawn in little, and Legion himself possessed him, yet I'll speak to him.

Fab. Here he is, here he is. How is't with you, sir? how is't with you, man?

Mal. Go off; I discard you: let me enjoy my private: go off.

Mar. Lo, how hollow the fiend speaks within him! did not I tell you? Sir Toby, my lady prays you to have a care of him.

60. [Exeunt O. and M.] Capell. Exit. Ff.

61. SCENE VIII. Pope.

66. *tang with*] *langer with* F_1. *tang* Capell.

70. *Jove's*] *God's* Halliwell. *Love's* Grant White conj.

71. *Jove*] *God* Halliwell. *Love* Grant White conj.

78. Re-enter......] Capell. Enter T., F., and M. Ff.

79. SCENE IX. Pope.

sanctity] *sanity* S. Walker conj.

82. *How is't*] Sir To. *How is't* Anon. conj.

84. *private*] *privacy* Rowe.

Mal. Ah, ha! does she so?

Sir To. Go to, go to; peace, peace; we must deal gently with him: let me alone. How do you, Malvolio? how is't with you? What, man! defy the devil: consider, he's an enemy to mankind.

Mal. Do you know what you say?

Mar. La you, an you speak ill of the devil, how he takes it at heart! Pray God, he be not bewitched!

Fab. Carry his water to the wise woman.

Mar. Marry, and it shall be done to-morrow morning, if I live. My lady would not lose him for more than I'll say.

Mal. How now, mistress!

Mar. O Lord!

Sir To. Prithee, hold thy peace; this is not the way: do you not see you move him? let me alone with him.

Fab. No way but gentleness; gently, gently: the fiend is rough, and will not be roughly used.

Sir To. Why, how now, my bawcock! how dost thou, chuck?

Mal. Sir!

Sir To. Ay, Biddy, come with me. What, man! 'tis not for gravity to play at cherry-pit with Satan: hang him, foul collier!

Mar. Get him to say his prayers, good Sir Toby, get him to pray.

Mal. My prayers, minx!

Mar. No, I warrant you, he will not hear of godliness.

Mal. Go, hang yourselves all! you are idle shallow things: I am not of your element: you shall know more hereafter. [*Exit.*

Sir To. Is't possible?

Fab. If this were played upon a stage now, I could condemn it as an improbable fiction.

91. *me*] *him* Rowe.
do you] *do you do* F_4.
95. *an*] Capell. *and* Ff. *if* Pope.
103. *this*] *that* F_4.
104. *let me alone with him*] Omitted in F_3F_4.
107. *bawcock*] F_1F_2. *havock* F_3F_4.
110. *Ay, Biddy, come with me.*] See note (XI).
116. Mar.] Fab. Anon. conj.

Sir To. His very genius hath taken the infection of the device, man.

Mar. Nay, pursue him now, lest the device take air and taint.

Fab. Why, we shall make him mad indeed.

Mar. The house will be the quieter.

Sir To. Come, we'll have him in a dark room and bound. My niece is already in the belief that he's mad: we may carry it thus, for our pleasure and his penance, till our very pastime, tired out of breath, prompt us to have mercy on him: at which time we will bring the device to the bar and crown thee for a finder of madmen. But see, but see.

Enter SIR ANDREW.

Fab. More matter for a May morning.

Sir And. Here's the challenge, read it: I warrant there's vinegar and pepper in't.

Fab. Is't so saucy?

Sir And. Ay, is't, I warrant him: do but read.

Sir To. Give me. [*Reads*] Youth, whatsoever thou art, thou art but a scurvy fellow.

Fab. Good, and valiant.

Sir To. [*reads*] Wonder not, nor admire not in thy mind, why I do call thee so, for I will show thee no reason for't.

Fab. A good note; that keeps you from the blow of the law.

Sir To. [*reads*] Thou comest to the lady Olivia, and in my sight she uses thee kindly: but thou liest in thy throat; that is not the matter I challenge thee for.

Fab. Very brief, and to exceeding good sense—less.

Sir To. [*reads*] I will waylay thee going home; where if it be thy chance to kill me,—

125. *lest*] F_4. *least* $F_1F_2F_3$.
128. *will*] *well* F_2.
136. SCENE X. Pope.
140. *Ay, is't*] Collier. *I, ist?* F_1 F_2. *I, is't?* F_3F_4. *Ay, is it,* Boswell.
141. [Reads.] Rowe.
146. *good*] *very good* Rowe (ed. 1).
151. *to*] om. Rowe.
sense—less] *sence-lesse* F_1 F_2. *sense-lesse* F_3. *sense-less* F_4. *senseless* Capell.

Fab. Good.

Sir To. [*reads*] Thou killest me like a rogue and a villain.

Fab. Still you keep o' the windy side of the law: good.

Sir To. [*reads*] Fare thee well; and God have mercy upon one of our souls! He may have mercy upon mine; but my hope is better, and so look to thyself. Thy friend, as thou usest him, and thy sworn enemy, ANDREW AGUECHEEK.

If this letter move him not, his legs cannot: I'll give 't him.

Mar. You may have very fit occasion for 't: he is now in some commerce with my lady, and will by and by depart.

Sir To. Go, Sir Andrew; scout me for him at the corner of the orchard like a bum-baily: so soon as ever thou seest him, draw; and, as thou drawest, swear horrible; for it comes to pass oft that a terrible oath, with a swaggering accent sharply twanged off, gives manhood more approbation than ever proof itself would have earned him. Away!

Sir And. Nay, let me alone for swearing. [*Exit.*

Sir To. Now will not I deliver his letter: for the behaviour of the young gentleman gives him out to be of good capacity and breeding; his employment between his lord and my niece confirms no less: therefore this letter, being so excellently ignorant, will breed no terror in the youth: he will find it comes from a clodpole. But, sir, I will deliver his challenge by word of mouth; set upon Aguecheek a notable report of valour; and drive the gentleman, as I know his youth will aptly receive it, into a most hideous opinion of his rage, skill, fury and impetuosity. This will so fright them both, that they will kill one another by the look, like cockatrices.

159. *mine*] *thine* Johnson conj.

162. *If*] To. *If* Ff.

168. *bum-baily*] *bum-bailiff* Theobald.

169. *horrible*] F_1. *horribly* F_2 F_3 F_4.

180. *it comes*] $F_1 F_2$. *that it comes* F_3 F_4.

Re-enter OLIVIA, *with* VIOLA.

Fab. Here he comes with your niece: give them way till he take leave, and presently after him.

Sir To. I will meditate the while upon some horrid message for a challenge.

[*Exeunt Sir Toby, Fabian, and Maria.*

Oli. I have said too much unto a heart of stone
And laid mine honour too unchary out:
There's something in me that reproves my fault;
But such a headstrong potent fault it is,
That it but mocks reproof.

Vio. With the same 'haviour that your passion bears
Goes on my master's grief.

Oli. Here, wear this jewel for me, 'tis my picture;
Refuse it not; it hath no tongue to vex you;
And I beseech you come again to-morrow.
What shall you ask of me that I'll deny,
That honour saved may upon asking give?

Vio. Nothing but this;—your true love for my master.

Oli. How with mine honour may I give him that
Which I have given to you?

Vio. I will acquit you.

Oli. Well, come again to-morrow: fare thee well:
A fiend like thee might bear my soul to hell. [*Exit.*

Re-enter SIR TOBY *and* FABIAN.

Sir To. Gentleman, God save thee.

Vio. And you, sir.

Sir To. That defence thou hast, betake thee to't: of what nature the wrongs are thou hast done him, I know

186. Re-enter O. and V.] Collier (after line 184). Enter O. and V. Ff.
187. SCENE XI. Pope.
190. [Exeunt Sir T., F. and M.] Capell. Exeunt. $F_2F_3F_4$. om. F_1.
191. *I have*] *I've* Pope.
192. *out*] Theobald. *on't* Ff.
196, 197. *'haviour that your...Goes ...grief*] *'haviour Your...goes...grief* Capell conj.
197. *Goes...grief*] Rowe. *Goes... greefes* F_1F_2. *Goes...griefs* F_3F_4. *Go ...griefs* Malone.
202. *That honour saved*] *That honour (sav'd)* $F_1 F_2$. *That (honour sav'd)* $F_3 F_4$.
208. SCENE XII. Pope.

not; but thy intercepter, full of despite, bloody as the hunter, attends thee at the orchard-end: dismount thy tuck, be yare in thy preparation, for thy assailant is quick, skilful and deadly.

Vio. You mistake, sir; I am sure no man hath any quarrel to me: my remembrance is very free and clear from any image of offence done to any man.

Sir To. You'll find it otherwise, I assure you: therefore, if you hold your life at any price, betake you to your guard; for your opposite hath in him what youth, strength, skill and wrath can furnish man withal.

Vio. I pray you, sir, what is he?

Sir To. He is knight, dubbed with unhatched rapier and on carpet consideration; but he is a devil in private brawl: souls and bodies hath he divorced three; and his incensement at this moment is so implacable, that satisfaction can be none but by pangs of death and sepulchre. Hob, nob, is his word; give 't or take 't.

Vio. I will return again into the house and desire some conduct of the lady. I am no fighter. I have heard of some kind of men that put quarrels purposely on others, to taste their valour: belike this is a man of that quirk.

Sir To. Sir, no; his indignation derives itself out of a very competent injury: therefore, get you on and give him his desire. Back you shall not to the house, unless you undertake that with me which with as much safety you might answer him: therefore, on, or strip your sword stark naked; for meddle you must, that's certain, or forswear to wear iron about you.

Vio. This is as uncivil as strange. I beseech you, do

212. *intercepter*] *interpreter* Warburton.

216. *sir; I am sure*] Theobald. *sir I am sure,* F_1F_2. *sir, I am sure,* F_3F_4. *sir, I am sure* Rowe.

222. *man*] *a man* F_3F_4.

224. *knight*] *a knight* Collier MS.

unhatched] *unhack'd* Pope. *an hatcht* Malone conj.

229. *nob*] *nod* Rowe (ed. 2).

234. *Sir, no*] *No, sir, no* Hanmer.

derives] *drives* F_4.

235. *competent*] F_4. *computent* $F_1F_2F_3$.

238. *him:*] $F_1F_3F_4$. *him?* F_2. *to him;* Hanmer.

or] *and* Hanmer.

your sword] *you of sword* Anon. conj.

241. *as uncivil*] *an uncivil* Capell (corrected in MS.).

me this courteous office, as to know of the knight what my offence to him is: it is something of my negligence, nothing of my purpose.

Sir To. I will do so. Signior Fabian, stay you by this gentleman till my return. [*Exit.*

Vio. Pray you, sir, do you know of this matter?

Fab. I know the knight is incensed against you, even to a mortal arbitrement; but nothing of the circumstance more.

Vio. I beseech you, what manner of man is he?

Fab. Nothing of that wonderful promise, to read him by his form, as you are like to find him in the proof of his valour. He is, indeed, sir, the most skilful, bloody and fatal opposite that you could possibly have found in any part of Illyria. Will you walk towards him? I will make your peace with him if I can.

Vio. I shall be much bound to you for't: I am one that had rather go with sir priest than sir knight: I care not who knows so much of my mettle. [*Exeunt.*

Re-enter SIR TOBY, *with* SIR ANDREW.

Sir To. Why, man, he's a very devil; I have not seen such a firago. I had a pass with him, rapier, scabbard and all, and he gives me the stuck in with such a mortal motion, that it is inevitable; and on the answer, he pays you as surely as your feet hit the ground they step on. They say he has been fencer to the Sophy.

Sir And. Pox on't, I'll not meddle with him.

Sir To. Ay, but he will not now be pacified: Fabian can scarce hold him yonder.

Sir And. Plague on't, an I thought he had been va-

242. *as to know*] *to know* Capell.
260. [Exeunt.] om. Capell. See note (XII).
Re-enter...] Capell. Enter Toby and Andrew. Ff. Re-enter Sir T. with Sir A. hanging back. Collier (Collier MS).
261. SCENE XIII. Pope. SCENE V. Dyce and Staunton.
262. *firago*] *virago* Rowe.
263. *stuck in*] *stuck—in* Johnson. *stuck-in*, Capell. *stuckin* Singer.
264. *you*] *your* F_2.
265. *hit*] Rowe. *hits* Ff.
269. *yonder*] om. Rowe.
270. *an*] Theobald. *and* Ff. *if* Pope.

liant and so cunning in fence, I'ld have seen him damned ere I'ld have challenged him. Let him let the matter slip, and I'll give him my horse, grey Capilet.

Sir To. I'll make the motion: stand here, make a good show on't: this shall end without the perdition of souls. [*Aside*] Marry, I'll ride your horse as well as I ride you.

Re-enter FABIAN *and* VIOLA.

[*To Fab.*] I have his horse to take up the quarrel: I have persuaded him the youth's a devil.

Fab. He is as horribly conceited of him; and pants and looks pale, as if a bear were at his heels.

Sir To. [*To Vio.*] There's no remedy, sir; he will fight with you for's oath sake: marry, he hath better bethought him of his quarrel, and he finds that now scarce to be worth talking of: therefore draw, for the supportance of his vow; he protests he will not hurt you.

Vio. [*Aside*] Pray God defend me! A little thing would make me tell them how much I lack of a man.

Fab. Give ground, if you see him furious.

Sir To. Come, Sir Andrew, there's no remedy; the gentleman will, for his honour's sake, have one bout with you; he cannot by the duello avoid it: but he has promised me, as he is a gentleman and a soldier, he will not hurt you. Come on; to't.

Sir And. Pray God, he keep his oath!

Vio. I do assure you, 'tis against my will. [*They draw.*

Enter ANTONIO.

Ant. Put up your sword. If this young gentleman
Have done offence, I take the fault on me:

273. *Capilet*] *Capulet* Dyce.
276. [Aside] Theobald.
Re-enter F. and V.] Enter F. and V. Ff. om. Capell. Enter F. and V. unwillingly. Collier MS.
277. [To Fab.] Rowe.
take up] *make up* Anon. conj.
281. [To Vio.] Capell.
282. *oath sake*] *oath's sake* Capell.
283. *scarce to be*] *to be scarce* Capell conj.
286. [Aside] Capell.
295. SCENE XIV. Pope.
[They draw.] Rowe. They go back from each other. Collier (Collier MS.).
Enter A.] Ff (after line 294). Enter A.; draws, and runs between. Capell.

If you offend him, I for him defy you.

Sir To. You, sir! why, what are you?

Ant. One, sir, that for his love dares yet do more
Than you have heard him brag to you he will.

Sir To. Nay, if you be an undertaker, I am for you. [*They draw.*

Enter Officers.

Fab. O good Sir Toby, hold! here come the officers.

Sir To. I'll be with you anon.

Vio. Pray, sir, put your sword up, if you please.

Sir And. Marry, will I, sir; and, for that I promised you, I'll be as good as my word: he will bear you easily and reins well.

First Off. This is the man; do thy office.

Sec. Off. Antonio, I arrest thee at the suit of Count Orsino.

Ant. You do mistake me, sir.

First Off. No, sir, no jot; I know your favour well,
Though now you have no sea-cap on your head.
Take him away: he knows I know him well.

Ant. I must obey. [*To Vio.*] This comes with seeking you:
But there's no remedy; I shall answer it.
What will you do, now my necessity
Makes me to ask you for my purse? It grieves me
Much more for what I cannot do for you
Than what befalls myself. You stand amazed;
But be of comfort.

Sec. Off. Come, sir, away.

Ant. I must entreat of you some of that money.

298. [Drawing. Rowe.

302. [They draw.] Edd. Draws. Rowe.

Enter Officers.] Enter two Officers. Capell. Enter Officers. Dyce and Staunton (after line 308).

304. [To Antonio. Capell.

305. [To Sir Andrew. Rowe.

310—312. As two lines in Capell, ending *suit...sir.*

310. *Count*] *Duke* Rowe.

316. [To Vio.] Collier.

318, 319. *do, now...purse?*] Dyce and Staunton. *do: now...purse.* F_1. *doe? now...purse.* $F_2 F_3 F_4$.

324. *money*] *money back* Capell, reading 323—325 as two lines, ending *you...sir?*

Vio. What money, sir?
For the fair kindness you have show'd me here,
And, part, being prompted by your present trouble,
Out of my lean and low ability
I'll lend you something: my having is not much;
I'll make division of my present with you:
Hold, there's half my coffer.
Ant. Will you deny me now?
Is't possible that my deserts to you
Can lack persuasion? Do not tempt my misery,
Lest that it make me so unsound a man
As to upbraid you with those kindnesses
That I have done for you.
Vio. I know of none;
Nor know I you by voice or any feature:
I hate ingratitude more in a man
Than lying, vainness, babbling, drunkenness,
Or any taint of vice whose strong corruption
Inhabits our frail blood.
Ant. O heavens themselves!
Sec. Off. Come, sir, I pray you, go.
Ant. Let me speak a little. This youth that you see here
I snatch'd one half out of the jaws of death;
Relieved him with such sanctity of love;
And to his image, which methought did promise
Most venerable worth, did I devotion.
First Off. What's that to us? The time goes by: away!
Ant. But O how vile an idol proves this god!
Thou hast, Sebastian, done good feature shame.

331. *Hold, there's*] *Hold, There's* S. Walker conj.
there's] *there is* Hanmer.
now?] $F_3 F_4$. *now*, $F_1 F_2$.

334. *Lest*] F_4. *Least* $F_1 F_2 F_3$.

339. *lying, vainness, babbling, drunkenness*] Steevens (1793). *lying, vainnesse, babling drunkennesse* Ff. *lying vainness, babbling drunkenness* Rowe (ed. 2).

342. *pray you, go*] *pray, go* S. Walker conj., ending the line at *little*. *pray you* Lloyd conj.

343. *speak*] *but speak* Hanmer.
This youth] *Why, this youth* Hanmer, ending lines 342, 343 at *speak ..here*.

345. *love;*] Ff. *love*,— Capell. After this S. Walker supposes a line to be lost.

346. *his*] *this* S. Walker conj.

347. *venerable*] *veritable* Collier (Collier MS.).

349. *vile*] Pope. *vilde* $F_1 F_2 F_3$. *vild* F_4.

In nature there's no blemish but the mind;
None can be call'd deform'd but the unkind:
Virtue is beauty; but the beauteous evil
Are empty trunks, o'erflourish'd by the devil.

First Off. The man grows mad: away with him! Come, come, sir.

Ant. Lead me on. [*Exit with Officers.*

Vio. Methinks his words do from such passion fly,
That he believes himself: so do not I.
Prove true, imagination, O, prove true,
That I, dear brother, be now ta'en for you!

Sir To. Come hither, knight; come hither, Fabian: we'll whisper o'er a couplet or two of most sage saws.

Vio. He named Sebastian: I my brother know
Yet living in my glass; even such and so
In favour was my brother, and he went
Still in this fashion, colour, ornament,
For him I imitate: O, if it prove,
Tempests are kind and salt waves fresh in love! [*Exit.*

Sir To. A very dishonest paltry boy, and more a coward than a hare: his dishonesty appears in leaving his friend here in necessity and denying him; and for his cowardship, ask Fabian.

Fab. A coward, a most devout coward, religious in it.

Sir And. 'Slid, I'll after him again and beat him.

Sir To. Do; cuff him soundly, but never draw thy sword.

Sir And. An I do not,— [*Exit.*

Fab. Come, let's see the event.

Sir To. I dare lay any money 'twill be nothing yet. [*Exeunt.*

353. *beauteous evil*] *beauteous-evil* Malone.

355. *The man*] *Surely the man* Hanmer.

Come] 2. Off. *Come* Capell. This word begins a line in Ff.

356. with Officers.] Theobald. om. Ff.

362. *we'll*] *Weel* F_1. *Well* $F_2F_3F_4$.

367. *O, if*] *so if* Becket conj.

368. [Exit.] $F_2F_3F_4$. om. F_1.

373. *a most*] om. Hanmer.

374. *'Slid*] *Od's lid* Hanmer.

375. *never*] *ne'er* Hanmer.

377. *An*] Theobald. *And* Ff. *If* Pope.

not,—] Theobald. *not.* Ff.

378. *let's*] *let us* Hanmer.

379. *any*] om. Hanmer.

[Exeunt.] Rowe. [Exit. Ff.

ACT IV.

SCENE I. *Before* OLIVIA'S *house.*

Enter SEBASTIAN *and* Clown.

Clo. Will you make me believe that I am not sent for you?

Seb. Go to, go to, thou art a foolish fellow:
Let me be clear of thee.

Clo. Well held out, i' faith! No, I do not know you; nor I am not sent to you by my lady, to bid you come speak with her; nor your name is not Master Cesario; nor this is not my nose neither. Nothing that is so is so.

Seb. I prithee, vent thy folly somewhere else:
Thou know'st not me.

Clo. Vent my folly! he has heard that word of some great man and now applies it to a fool. Vent my folly! I am afraid this great lubber, the world, will prove a cockney. I prithee now, ungird thy strangeness and tell me what I shall vent to my lady: shall I vent to her that thou art coming?

Seb. I prithee, foolish Greek, depart from me:
There's money for thee: if you tarry longer,
I shall give worse payment.

Clo. By my troth, thou hast an open hand. These wise men that give fools money get themselves a good report—after fourteen years' purchase.

SCENE I. Before...] The street before... Capell. The street. Rowe. om. Ff.

9, 10. Arranged as in Capell; as prose in Ff.

13. *great lubber, the world*] *great lubberly World* Collier MS. *great lubberly word* Grant White (Douce conj.). *lubberly word* Staunton conj. See note (XIII).

15. *that thou*] *that that* F_2.

17. *Greek*] $F_3 F_4$. *greeke* $F_1 F_2$. *geck* Hanmer (Theobald conj.). *grig* or *glecker* Anon. conj.

17—19. Arranged as in Capell; as prose in Ff.

19. *worse*] *worser* Anon. conj.

21. *report—*] Staunton. *report,* Ff.

Enter SIR ANDREW, SIR TOBY, *and* FABIAN.

Sir And. Now, sir, have I met you again? there's for you.

Seb. Why, there's for thee, and there, and there. Are all the people mad?

Sir To. Hold, sir, or I'll throw your dagger o'er the house.

Clo. This will I tell my lady straight: I would not be in some of your coats for two pence. [*Exit.*

Sir To. Come on, sir; hold.

Sir And. Nay, let him alone: I'll go another way to work with him; I'll have an action of battery against him, if there be any law in Illyria: though I stroke him first, yet it's no matter for that.

Seb. Let go thy hand.

Sir To. Come, sir, I will not let you go. Come, my young soldier, put up your iron: you are well fleshed; come on.

Seb. I will be free from thee. What wouldst thou now? If thou darest tempt me further, draw thy sword.

Sir To. What, what? Nay, then I must have an ounce or two of this malapert blood from you.

Enter OLIVIA.

Oli. Hold, Toby; on thy life, I charge thee, hold!

Sir To. Madam!

Oli. Will it be ever thus? Ungracious wretch,
Fit for the mountains and the barbarous caves,
Where manners ne'er were preach'd! out of my sight!
Be not offended, dear Cesario.

24. [Striking Sebastian. Rowe.
25. *and there, and there*] *and there, and there, and there* Capell.
[Beating Sir Andrew. Rowe.
30. [Exit.] Rowe. om. Ff.
31. *Come on, sir*] *Come, sir* Rann. *Come off, sir* Anon. conj.
[Holding Sebastian. Rowe.
34. *be*] *he* F_2.
stroke] F_1F_2. *strook* F_3. *struck* F_4.
38. *put up...fleshed*] [To Sir And.] *put up...fleshed* Badham conj.
40. [Wrenches from him and draws. Capell.
43. [They draw and fight. Rowe.
44. SCENE II. Pope.

Rudesby, be gone!
[*Exeunt Sir Toby, Sir Andrew, and Fabian.*
I prithee, gentle friend,
Let thy fair wisdom, not thy passion, sway
In this uncivil and unjust extent
Against thy peace. Go with me to my house;
And hear thou there how many fruitless pranks
This ruffian hath botch'd up, that thou thereby
Mayst smile at this: thou shalt not choose but go:
Do not deny. Beshrew his soul for me,
He started one poor heart of mine in thee.

Seb. What relish is in this? how runs the stream?
Or I am mad, or else this is a dream:
Let fancy still my sense in Lethe steep;
If it be thus to dream, still let me sleep!

Oli. Nay, come, I prithee: would thou'ldst be ruled by me!

Seb. Madam, I will.

Oli. O, say so, and so be! [*Exeunt.*

SCENE II. OLIVIA'S *house.*

Enter MARIA *and* Clown.

Mar. Nay, I prithee, put on this gown and this beard; make him believe thou art Sir Topas the curate: do it quickly; I'll call Sir Toby the whilst. [*Exit.*

Clo. Well, I'll put it on, and I will dissemble myself in 't; and I would I were the first that ever dissembled in such a gown. I am not tall enough to become the function well, nor lean enough to be thought a good student; but to be said an honest man and a good housekeeper goes as

50. [Exeunt...] Capell. Exeunt Sir T. and Sir A. Rowe.
55. *botch'd*] *bouck'd* Becket conj.
63. *prithee*] *pray* Pope.
SCENE II.] SCENE III. Pope.
OLIVIA'S house.] Rowe.

3. [Exit.] Exit M. Theobald.
6. *tall*] *fat* Reed (1803) (Farmer conj.). *pale* Tyrwhitt conj. *of taille* Becket conj.
7. *student*] *studient* F_1.

fairly as to say a careful man and a great scholar. The competitors enter.

Enter SIR TOBY *and* MARIA.

Sir To. Jove bless thee, master Parson.

Clo. Bonos dies, Sir Toby: for, as the old hermit of Prague, that never saw pen and ink, very wittily said to a niece of King Gorboduc, 'That that is is;' so I, being master Parson, am master Parson; for, what is 'that' but 'that,' and 'is' but 'is'?

Sir To. To him, Sir Topas.

Clo. What, ho, I say! peace in this prison!

Sir To. The knave counterfeits well; a good knave.

Mal. [*within*] Who calls there?

Clo. Sir Topas the curate, who comes to visit Malvolio the lunatic.

Mal. Sir Topas, Sir Topas, good Sir Topas, go to my lady.

Clo. Out, hyperbolical fiend! how vexest thou this man! talkest thou nothing but of ladies?

Sir To. Well said, master Parson.

Mal. Sir Topas, never was man thus wronged: good Sir Topas, do not think I am mad: they have laid me here in hideous darkness.

Clo. Fie, thou dishonest Satan! I call thee by the most modest terms; for I am one of those gentle ones that will use the devil himself with courtesy: sayest thou that house is dark?

Mal. As hell, Sir Topas.

9. *careful*] *graceful* Hanmer (Warburton).

10. Enter Sir T. and M.] Theobald. Enter Toby. Ff.

11. *Jove*] *God* Edd. conj.

11, 14, 15, 27. *master*] *M.* Ff and passim.

13. *Prague*] Rowe. *Prage* F_1F_2 F_3. *Prauge* F_4.

14. *Gorboduc*] *Gorboduck* Pope. *Gorbodacke* $F_1F_2F_4$. *Gorbodack* F_3.

18. [rapping at an inner door. Capell.

20. Mal. [within] Malvolio within (as a stage direction) Mal. Ff.

26. *nothing but of*] *of nothing but* Anon. conj.

33. *that*] *this* Rann. *the* or *that the* Anon. conj.

Clo. Why, it hath bay windows transparent as barricadoes, and the clearstores toward the south north are as lustrous as ebony; and yet complainest thou of obstruction?

Mal. I am not mad, Sir Topas: I say to you, this house is dark.

Clo. Madman, thou errest: I say, there is no darkness but ignorance; in which thou art more puzzled than the Egyptians in their fog.

Mal. I say, this house is as dark as ignorance, though ignorance were as dark as hell; and I say, there was never man thus abused. I am no more mad than you are: make the trial of it in any constant question.

Clo. What is the opinion of Pythagoras concerning wild fowl?

Mal. That the soul of our grandam might haply inhabit a bird.

Clo. What thinkest thou of his opinion?

Mal. I think nobly of the soul, and no way approve his opinion.

Clo. Fare thee well. Remain thou still in darkness: thou shalt hold the opinion of Pythagoras ere I will allow of thy wits; and fear to kill a woodcock, lest thou dispossess the soul of thy grandam. Fare thee well.

Mal. Sir Topas, Sir Topas!

Sir To. My most exquisite Sir Topas!

Clo. Nay, I am for all waters.

Mar. Thou mightst have done this without thy beard and gown: he sees thee not.

Sir To. To him in thine own voice, and bring me word how thou findest him: I would we were well rid of this knavery. If he may be conveniently delivered, I would he were; for I am now so far in offence with my niece, that I

37. *clearstores*] *cleere stores* F_1. *cleare stones* F_2. *clear stones* F_3F_4. *clear stories* Boswell (Blakeway conj.).

49. *wild fowl*] *the soul* Theobald conj.

50. *haply*] Capell. *happily* Ff.

58. *soul*] *soule* F_1. *house* $F_2F_3F_4$.

61. *waters*] *wanters* or *ventures* Anon. conj.

65. *well*] F_1. *all* $F_2F_3F_4$. *all well* Collier MS.

cannot pursue with any safety this sport to the upshot. Come by and by to my chamber. [*Exeunt Sir Toby and Maria.*

Clo. [*Singing*] Hey, Robin, jolly Robin,
Tell me how thy lady does.

Mal. Fool,—

Clo. My lady is unkind, perdy.

Mal. Fool,—

Clo. Alas, why is she so?

Mal. Fool, I say,—

Clo. She loves another—Who calls, ha?

Mal. Good fool, as ever thou wilt deserve well at my hand, help me to a candle, and pen, ink and paper: as I am a gentleman, I will live to be thankful to thee for't.

Clo. Master Malvolio?

Mal. Ay, good fool.

Clo. Alas, sir, how fell you besides your five wits?

Mal. Fool, there was never man so notoriously abused: I am as well in my wits, fool, as thou art.

Clo. But as well? then you are mad indeed, if you be no better in your wits than a fool.

Mal. They have here propertied me; keep me in darkness, send ministers to me, asses, and do all they can to face me out of my wits.

Clo. Advise you what you say; the minister is here. Malvolio, Malvolio, thy wits the heavens restore! endeavour thyself to sleep, and leave thy vain bibble babble.

Mal. Sir Topas,—

Clo. Maintain no words with him, good fellow. Who, I, sir? not I, sir. God be wi' you, good Sir Topas. Marry, amen. I will, sir, I will.

Mal. Fool, fool, fool, I say,—

68. *to the upshot*] Rowe. *the upshot* Ff.

69. *chamber*] *champer* F_2.
[Exeunt...] Exit with Maria. Theobald. Exit Ff.

70. SCENE IV. Pope.
[Singing] Rowe.

70, 71. *Hey...does.*] *Hey, jolly Robin, tell to me, How does thy lady do?* Farmer conj.

71. *thy*] *my* Rowe (ed. 2).

83. *besides*] *beside* Capell conj.

86. *you are*] *thou art* Rowe (ed. 2).

88. *have here*] *have* Pope.

96. *be wi' you*] *buy you* Ff. *b' w' you* Pope.

97. *sir, I will*] F_1. *sir, I will sir* $F_2F_3F_4$.

Clo. Alas, sir, be patient. What say you, sir? I am shent for speaking to you.

Mal. Good fool, help me to some light and some paper: I tell thee, I am as well in my wits as any man in Illyria.

Clo. Well-a-day that you were, sir!

Mal. By this hand, I am. Good fool, some ink, paper and light; and convey what I will set down to my lady: it shall advantage thee more than ever the bearing of letter did.

Clo. I will help you to't. But tell me true, are you not mad indeed? or do you but counterfeit?

Mal. Believe me, I am not; I tell thee true.

Clo. Nay, I'll ne'er believe a madman till I see his brains. I will fetch you light and paper and ink.

Mal. Fool, I'll requite it in the highest degree: I prithee, be gone.

Clo. [*Singing*] I am gone, sir,
And anon, sir,
I'll be with you again,
In a trice,
Like to the old vice,
Your need to sustain;

Who, with dagger of lath,
In his rage and his wrath,
Cries, ah, ha! to the devil:
Like a mad lad,
Pare thy nails, dad;
Adieu, goodman Drivel. [*Exit.*

109, 110. *are you not*] *are you* Johnson conj.

110. *or*] *and* Malone conj.

116—127. Arranged as in Capell. As eight lines in Ff.

116. [Singing] Rowe. om. Ff.

119, 120. *In a trice, Like to the*] *With a trice, Like the* Collier MS. *With a trice, Like to the* Collier (ed. 2).

126. *dad;*] *dad,* Ff. *dad?* Farmer conj.

127. *goodman Drivel*] Rowe (ed. 2). *good man diuell* F_1. *good man Divell* F_2. *good man Devil* F_3F_4. *goodman Mean-evil* Johnson conj. *good Mean-evil* Mason conj. *goodman Civil*, or *good man, be civil* Anon. conj.

SCENE III. OLIVIA'S *garden.*

Enter SEBASTIAN.

Seb. This is the air; that is the glorious sun;
This pearl she gave me, I do feel't and see't;
And though 'tis wonder that enwraps me thus,
Yet 'tis not madness. Where's Antonio, then?
I could not find him at the Elephant:
Yet there he was; and there I found this credit,
That he did range the town to seek me out.
His counsel now might do me golden service;
For though my soul disputes well with my sense,
That this may be some error, but no madness,
Yet doth this accident and flood of fortune
So far exceed all instance, all discourse,
That I am ready to distrust mine eyes
And wrangle with my reason, that persuades me
To any other trust but that I am mad,
Or else the lady's mad; yet, if 'twere so,
She could not sway her house, command her followers,
Take and give back affairs and their dispatch
With such a smooth, discreet, and stable bearing
As I perceive she does: there's something in't
That is deceivable. But here the lady comes.

Enter OLIVIA *and* Priest.

Oli. Blame not this haste of mine. If you mean well,
Now go with me and with this holy man
Into the chantry by: there, before him,
And underneath that consecrated roof,

SCENE III.] SCENE V. Pope.

OLIVIA'S garden.] Capell. Another apartment in O.'s house. Theobald.

6. *this credit*] *in credit* Becket conj. *this credit* [He takes a letter from his pocket] Jackson conj.

credit] F_3F_4. *credite* F_1 F_2. *credent* Theobald conj. *current* Hanmer. *credited* Mason conj.

15. *I am*] *I'm* Pope.

18. *affairs and their dispatch*] *and thus dispatch affairs* Collier (Collier MS.).

21. *the lady comes*] *she comes* Pope. *comes the lady* Steevens.

Plight me the full assurance of your faith;
That my most jealous and too doubtful soul
May live at peace. He shall conceal it
Whiles you are willing it shall come to note,
What time we will our celebration keep
According to my birth. What do you say?

Seb. I'll follow this good man, and go with you;
And, having sworn truth, ever will be true.

Oliv. Then lead the way, good father; and heavens so shine,
That they may fairly note this act of mine! [*Exeunt.*

ACT V.

SCENE I. *Before* OLIVIA'S *house.*

Enter Clown *and* FABIAN.

Fab. Now, as thou lovest me, let me see his letter.

Clo. Good Master Fabian, grant me another request.

Fab. Any thing.

Clo. Do not desire to see this letter.

Fab. This is, to give a dog, and in recompense desire my dog again.

Enter DUKE, VIOLA, CURIO, *and* Lords.

Duke. Belong you to the Lady Olivia, friends?

Clo. Ay, sir; we are some of her trappings.

Duke. I know thee well: how dost thou, my good fellow?

Clo. Truly, sir, the better for my foes and the worse for my friends.

27. *jealous*] *iealious* F_1.
28. *live*] *henceforth live* Hanmer.
29. *Whiles*] *While* Grant White.
34. *and heavens*] F_1F_2. *and heaven* F_3F_4. *heav'ns* Pope.
35. [Exeunt.] Exeunt. Finis Actus Quartus. F_1. Finis actus Quarti. $F_2F_3F_4$.

Before OLIVIA'S house] Capell. The street. Pope.

1. *his*] F_1. *this* $F_2F_3F_4$.
6. Lords.] Attendants. Capell.

Duke. Just the contrary; the better for thy friends.

Clo. No, sir, the worse.

Duke. How can that be?

Clo. Marry, sir, they praise me and make an ass of me; now my foes tell me plainly I am an ass: so that by my foes, sir, I profit in the knowledge of myself; and by my friends I am abused: so that, conclusions to be as kisses, if your four negatives make your two affirmatives, why then, the worse for my friends, and the better for my foes.

Duke. Why, this is excellent.

Clo. By my troth, sir, no; though it please you to be one of my friends.

Duke. Thou shalt not be the worse for me: there's gold.

Clo. But that it would be double-dealing, sir, I would you could make it another.

Duke. O, you give me ill counsel.

Clo. Put your grace in your pocket, sir, for this once, and let your flesh and blood obey it.

Duke. Well, I will be so much a sinner, to be a double-dealer: there's another.

Clo. Primo, secundo, tertio, is a good play; and the old saying is, the third pays for all: the triplex, sir, is a good tripping measure; or the bells of Saint Bennet, sir, may put you in mind; one, two, three.

Duke. You can fool no more money out of me at this throw: if you will let your lady know I am here to speak with her, and bring her along with you, it may awake my bounty further.

Clo. Marry, sir, lullaby to your bounty till I come again. I go, sir; but I would not have you to think that my desire of having is the sin of covetousness: but, as you say, sir, let your bounty take a nap, I will awake it anon. [*Exit.*

Vio. Here comes the man, sir, that did rescue me.

18. *that, conclusions...kisses*] *that, conclusion to be asked, is* Theobald (Warburton). *the conclusion to be asked is* Hanmer. *that conclusions follow as kisses* Heath conj. See note (XIV).

20. *for my friends*] *of my friends* F_3F_4.

33. *triplex*] *triplet* Collier (Collier MS.).

34. *or*] *as* Mason conj.

Bennet] *Bennet's* Anon. conj.

44. SCENE II. Pope.

Enter ANTONIO *and* Officers.

Duke. That face of his I do remember well;
Yet, when I saw it last, it was besmear'd
As black as Vulcan in the smoke of war:
A bawbling vessel was he captain of,
For shallow draught and bulk unprizable;
With which such scathful grapple did he make
With the most noble bottom of our fleet,
That very envy and the tongue of loss
Cried fame and honour on him. What's the matter?

First Off. Orsino, this is that Antonio
That took the Phœnix and her fraught from Candy;
And this is he that did the Tiger board,
When your young nephew Titus lost his leg:
Here in the streets, desperate of shame and state,
In private brabble did we apprehend him.

Vio. He did me kindness, sir, drew on my side;
But in conclusion put strange speech upon me:
I know not what 'twas but distraction.

Duke. Notable pirate! thou salt-water thief!
What foolish boldness brought thee to their mercies,
Whom thou, in terms so bloody and so dear,
Hast made thine enemies?

Ant. Orsino, noble sir,
Be pleased that I shake off these names you give me:
Antonio never yet was thief or pirate,
Though I confess, on base and ground enough,
Orsino's enemy. A witchcraft drew me hither:
That most ingrateful boy there by your side,
From the rude sea's enraged and foamy mouth
Did I redeem; a wreck past hope he was:
His life I gave him and did thereto add
My love, without retention or restraint,

Enter A...] Ff (after line 43).

60. *did*] *shew'd* Capell (corrected in MS.).

66. *Orsino, noble sir*] *Noble sir, Orsino* Hanmer.

71. *ingrateful*] *ungrateful* F_4.

73. *wreck*] Pope. *wracke* F_1F_2. *wrack* F_3F_4.

All his in dedication; for his sake
Did I expose myself, pure for his love,
Into the danger of this adverse town;
Drew to defend him when he was beset:
Where being apprehended, his false cunning,
Not meaning to partake with me in danger,
Taught him to face me out of his acquaintance,
And grew a twenty years removed thing
While one would wink; denied me mine own purse,
Which I had recommended to his use
Not half an hour before.

Vio. How can this be?

Duke. When came he to this town?

Ant. To-day, my lord; and for three months before,
No interim, not a minute's vacancy,
Both day and night did we keep company.

Enter OLIVIA *and* Attendants.

Duke. Here comes the countess: now heaven walks on earth.
But for thee, fellow; fellow, thy words are madness:
Three months this youth hath tended upon me;
But more of that anon. Take him aside.

Oli. What would my lord, but that he may not have,
Wherein Olivia may seem serviceable?
Cesario, you do not keep promise with me.

Vio. Madam!

Duke. Gracious Olivia,—

Oli. What do you say, Cesario? Good my lord,—

Vio. My lord would speak; my duty hushes me.

Oli. If it be aught to the old tune, my lord,
It is as fat and fulsome to mine ear
As howling after music.

Duke. Still so cruel?

76. *his*] F_1. *this* $F_2F_3F_4$.
in] *is* F_3F_4.
77. *for*] *of* F_3F_4.
84. *me*] *be* F_3F_4.
87. *he*] *you* Hanmer.
89. *interim*] *intrim* F_1.
91. SCENE III. Pope.
Enter O...] Ff. Dyce, after line 94.
97. *do not*] *don't* Hanmer.
99. *Olivia,—*] Theobald. *Olivia.* Ff.
100. *lord,—*] Pope. *lord.* Ff.
103. *fat*] *flat* Hanmer (Warburton).
104. *Still*] *Still, still* Capell.

Oli. Still so constant, lord.
Duke. What, to perverseness? you uncivil lady,
To whose ingrate and unauspicious altars
My soul the faithfull'st offerings hath breathed out
That e'er devotion tender'd! What shall I do?
Oli. Even what it please my lord, that shall become him.
Duke. Why should I not, had I the heart to do it,
Like to the Egyptian thief at point of death,
Kill what I love?—a savage jealousy
That sometime savours nobly. But hear me this:
Since you to non-regardance cast my faith,
And that I partly know the instrument
That screws me from my true place in your favour,
Live you the marble-breasted tyrant still;
But this your minion, whom I know you love,
And whom, by heaven I swear, I tender dearly,
Him will I tear out of that cruel eye,
Where he sits crowned in his master's spite.
Come, boy, with me; my thoughts are ripe in mischief:
I'll sacrifice the lamb that I do love,
To spite a raven's heart within a dove.
Vio. And I, most jocund, apt and willingly,
To do you rest, a thousand deaths would die.
Oli. Where goes Cesario?
Vio. After him I love
More than I love these eyes, more than my life,
More, by all mores, than e'er I shall love wife.
If I do feign, you witnesses above
Punish my life for tainting of my love!
Oli. Ay me, detested! how am I beguiled!
Vio. Who does beguile you? who does do you wrong?
Oli. Hast thou forgot thyself? is it so long?

105. *so constant, lord*] *lord, so constant* Hanmer.
108. *hath*] Capell. *have* Ff. *has* Pope.
111. *do it*] *do't* Pope.
114. *me*] om. Pope.
125. [Going. Theobald.
127. [Following. Theobald.
133. *Ay*] F_4. *Aye* $F_1F_2F_3$. *Ah* Hanmer.

Call forth the holy father.

Duke. Come, away!

Oli. Whither, my lord? Cesario, husband, stay.

Duke. Husband!

Oli. Ay, husband: can he that deny?

Duke. Her husband, sirrah!

Vio. No, my lord, not I.

Oli. Alas, it is the baseness of thy fear
That makes thee strangle thy propriety:
Fear not, Cesario; take thy fortunes up;
Be that thou know'st thou art, and then thou art
As great as that thou fear'st.

Enter Priest.

O, welcome, father!
Father, I charge thee, by thy reverence,
Here to unfold, though lately we intended
To keep in darkness what occasion now
Reveals before 'tis ripe, what thou dost know
Hath newly pass'd between this youth and me.

Priest. A contract of eternal bond of love,
Confirm'd by mutual joinder of your hands,
Attested by the holy close of lips,
Strengthen'd by interchangement of your rings;
And all the ceremony of this compact
Seal'd in my function, by my testimony:
Since when, my watch hath told me, toward my grave
I have travell'd but two hours.

Duke. O thou dissembling cub! what wilt thou be
When time hath sow'd a grizzle on thy case?
Or will not else thy craft so quickly grow,
That thine own trip shall be thine overthrow?
Farewell, and take her; but direct thy feet

136. [Exit an Attendant. Capell. [To Viola. Theobald.

144. *that thou*] *thou* F_3F_4.

Enter Priest.] Ff. Re-enter Attendant, with Priest. Capell.

150. *of eternal*] *and eternal* Collier (Malone conj. withdrawn).

159. *on thy case*] *on thy face* Madden conj. *upon thee* Keightley conj. See note (XV).

Where thou and I henceforth may never meet.

Vio. My lord, I do protest—

Oli. O, do not swear!
Hold little faith, though thou hast too much fear.

Enter SIR ANDREW.

Sir And. For the love of God, a surgeon! Send one presently to Sir Toby.

Oli. What's the matter?

Sir And. He has broke my head across and has given Sir Toby a bloody coxcomb too: for the love of God, your help! I had rather than forty pound I were at home.

Oli. Who has done this, Sir Andrew?

Sir And. The count's gentleman, one Cesario: we took him for a coward, but he's the very devil incardinate.

Duke. My gentleman, Cesario?

Sir And. 'Od's lifelings, here he is! You broke my head for nothing; and that that I did, I was set on to do't by Sir Toby.

Vio. Why do you speak to me? I never hurt you:
You drew your sword upon me without cause;
But I bespake you fair, and hurt you not.

Sir And. If a bloody coxcomb be a hurt, you have hurt me: I think you set nothing by a bloody coxcomb.

Enter SIR TOBY *and* Clown.

Here comes Sir Toby halting; you shall hear more: but if he had not been in drink, he would have tickled you othergates than he did.

Duke. How now, gentleman! how is't with you?

164. *protest—*] Rowe. *protest* Ff.
165. *Hold*] F_1. *How* $F_2F_3F_4$.
Enter Sir A.] Ff. Enter Sir A. with his head broke. Rowe.
166. SCENE IV. Pope.
Send] F_1F_2. *and* F_3F_4. *and send* Rowe (ed. 2).
169. *He has*] *H'as* Ff. *has given*] F_1F_2. *given* F_3F_4. *h'as given* Capell.
174. *incardinate*] *incarnate* Rowe.
183. Enter Sir Toby...] Enter Toby... Ff (after line 181). Enter Sir T. drunk, led by the Clown. Capell.
185, 186. *othergates*] *other gates* Ff.

Sir To. That's all one: has hurt me, and there's the end on't. Sot, didst see Dick surgeon, sot?

Clo. O, he's drunk, Sir Toby, an hour agone; his eyes were set at eight i' the morning.

Sir To. Then he's a rogue, and a passy measures panyn: I hate a drunken rogue.

Oli. Away with him! Who hath made this havoc with them?

Sir And. I'll help you, Sir Toby, because we'll be dressed together.

Sir To. Will you help? an ass-head and a coxcomb and a knave, a thin-faced knave, a gull!

Oli. Get him to bed, and let his hurt be look'd to.

[*Exeunt Clown, Fabian, Sir Toby, and Sir Andrew.*

Enter SEBASTIAN.

Seb. I am sorry, madam, I have hurt your kinsman;
But, had it been the brother of my blood,
I must have done no less with wit and safety.
You throw a strange regard upon me, and by that
I do perceive it hath offended you:
Pardon me, sweet one, even for the vows
We made each other but so late ago.

Duke. One face, one voice, one habit, and two persons,

188. *has*] Ff. *h'as* Rowe (ed. 1). *ha's* Id. (ed. 2). *he has* Pope.

188, 189. *the end*] *th'end* F_1F_2. *an end* F_3F_4.

189. *didst*] *didst thou* F_3F_4.

190. *Sir Toby*] F_1. *sir above* $F_2F_3F_4$. *Sir Toby, above* Theobald.

191. *set at*] F_1F_2. *at* F_3F_4.

192. *rogue, and a passy measures panyn:*] F_1. *Rogue after a passy measures Pavin:* $F_2F_3F_4$. *rogue, and a past-measure painim.* Pope. *rogue, and a passy-measure pavin:* Steevens. *rogue:—and after a passy-measure or a pavin,* Rann. *rogue. After a passy-measure, or a pavin,* Reed (Tyrwhitt conj.). *rogue and a pazzomezzo paynim* Becket conj. *rogue and a passy measures paynim:* Grant White. *rogue. After a passing measure and a pavin* Anon. conj. (Gent. Mag.).

198, 199. *help? an ass-head...gull!*] Malone. *help an ass-head...gull?* Ff.

200. [Exeunt...] Dyce and Staunton. Exe. Clo. To. & And. Rowe. Exeunt Clown and some Attendants, with Sir T. and Sir A. Capell.

201. SCENE V. Pope.

kinsman] *uncle* Rowe (ed. 2).

203. [All stand in amaze. Theobald.

204. *You throw a strange*] *You throw A strange* S. Walker conj.

upon] *on* Pope.

upon me, and by that] *on me, by that* Lettsom conj.

and by that] *by which* Pope. *and By that* Capell.

A natural perspective, that is and is not!
Seb. Antonio, O my dear Antonio!
How have the hours rack'd and tortured me,
Since I have lost thee!
Ant. Sebastian are you?
Seb. Fear'st thou that, Antonio?
Ant. How have you made division of yourself?
An apple, cleft in two, is not more twin
Than these two creatures. Which is Sebastian?
Oli. Most wonderful!
Seb. Do I stand there? I never had a brother;
Nor can there be that deity in my nature,
Of here and every where. I had a sister,
Whom the blind waves and surges have devour'd.
Of charity, what kin are you to me?
What countryman? what name? what parentage?
Vio. Of Messaline: Sebastian was my father;
Such a Sebastian was my brother too,
So went he suited to his watery tomb:
If spirits can assume both form and suit
You come to fright us.
Seb. A spirit I am indeed;
But am in that dimension grossly clad
Which from the womb I did participate.
Were you a woman, as the rest goes even,
I should my tears let fall upon your cheek,
And say 'Thrice-welcome, drowned Viola!'
Vio. My father had a mole upon his brow.
Seb. And so had mine.
Vio. And died that day when Viola from her birth
Had number'd thirteen years.
Seb. O, that record is lively in my soul!
He finished indeed his mortal act
That day that made my sister thirteen years.

209. *natural*] *nat'ral* Pope.
213. *Fear'st thou*] Ff. *Fear'd thou* Rowe (ed. 2). *Fear'd you* Pope.
219. *that*] F_1. *a* $F_2F_3F_4$.
222. [To Viola. Rowe.
224. *Messaline*] *Metelin* Hanmer.
231. *goes*] F_1. *goe* F_2. *go* F_3F_4.
233. *And*] *As* Capell (corrected in MS.).

Vio. If nothing lets to make us happy both
But this my masculine usurp'd attire,
Do not embrace me till each circumstance
Of place, time, fortune, do cohere and jump
That I am Viola: which to confirm,
I'll bring you to a captain in this town,
Where lie my maiden weeds; by whose gentle help
I was preserved to serve this noble count.
All the occurrence of my fortune since
Hath been between this lady and this lord.

Seb. [*To Olivia*] So comes it, lady, you have been mistook:
But nature to her bias drew in that.
You would have been contracted to a maid;
Nor are you therein, by my life, deceived,
You are betroth'd both to a maid and man.

Duke. Be not amazed; right noble is his blood.
If this be so, as yet the glass seems true,
I shall have share in this most happy wreck.
[*To Viola*] Boy, thou hast said to me a thousand times
Thou never shouldst love woman like to me.

Vio. And all those sayings will I over-swear;
And all those swearings keep as true in soul
As doth that orbed continent the fire
That severs day from night.

Duke. Give me thy hand;
And let me see thee in thy woman's weeds.

Vio. The captain that did bring me first on shore
Hath my maid's garments: he upon some action
Is now in durance, at Malvolio's suit,
A gentleman, and follower of my lady's.

Oli. He shall enlarge him: fetch Malvolio hither:
And yet, alas, now I remember me,

246. *captain*] *captain's* Grant White (Collier MS.).

247. *maiden*] *maids* Theobald.
by whose] *he, by whose* Staunton conj.

248. *preserved*] *preferr'd* Theobald.
count] *Duke* Rowe.

249. *occurrence*] *occurrents* Hanmer.

250. *Hath*] *Have* Hanmer.

251. [To Olivia.] Rowe.

252. *drew*] *true* Collier MS.

258. *wreck*] Rowe. *wracke* F_1F_2 *wrack* F_3F_4.

260. *shouldst*] *shoulst* F_2.

263, 264. *fire...severs*] *fires...sever* Singer.

They say, poor gentleman, he's much distract.

Re-enter Clown *with a letter, and* FABIAN.

A most extracting frenzy of mine own
From my remembrance clearly banish'd his.
How does he, sirrah?

Clo. Truly, madam, he holds Belzebub at the stave's end as well as a man in his case may do: has here writ a letter to you; I should have given 't you to-day morning, but as a madman's epistles are no gospels, so it skills not much when they are delivered.

Oli. Open 't, and read it.

Clo. Look then to be well edified when the fool delivers the madman. [*Reads*] By the Lord, madam,—

Oli. How now! art thou mad?

Clo. No, madam, I do but read madness: an your ladyship will have it as it ought to be, you must allow Vox.

Oli. Prithee, read i' thy right wits.

Clo. So I do, madonna; but to read his right wits is to read thus: therefore perpend, my princess, and give ear.

Oli. Read it you, sirrah. [*To Fabian.*

Fab. [*Reads*] By the Lord, madam, you wrong me, and the world shall know it: though you have put me into darkness and given your drunken cousin rule over me, yet have I the benefit of my senses as well as your ladyship. I have your own letter that induced me to the semblance I put on; with the which I doubt not but to do myself much right, or you much shame. Think of me as you please. I leave my duty a little unthought of and speak out of my injury.

THE MADLY-USED MALVOLIO.

Oli. Did he write this?

Clo. Ay, madam.

272. Re-enter...] Enter... Ff. and FABIAN.] om. Capell.
273. SCENE VI. Pope. *extracting*] F_1. *exacting* $F_2F_3F_4$. *distracting* Hanmer.
274. *banish'd*] *banisht* F_1. *banish* $F_2F_3F_4$.
277. *has*] *h'as* Rowe. *he has* Malone.
281. *Open 't*] *Open it* Malone.
283. [Reads] Rowe.
284. *art thou*] *art* Pope.
285. *an*] Pope. *and* Ff.
286. *Vox*] *for't* Heath conj. *oaths* Mason conj.
287. *read*] *read it* F_3F_4. *right wits*] *wits right* Johnson conj.
290. [To Fabian.] Rowe.
291. [Reads] Ff.
293. *cousin*] *uncle* Rowe (ed. 2). *the benefit*] *benefit* Rowe, F_3F_4.

Duke. This savours not much of distraction.

Oli. See him deliver'd, Fabian; bring him hither.

[*Exit Fabian.*

My lord, so please you, these things further thought on,
To think me as well a sister as a wife,
One day shall crown the alliance on't, so please you,
Here at my house and at my proper cost.

Duke. Madam, I am most apt to embrace your offer.
[*To Viola*] Your master quits you; and for your service done him,
So much against the mettle of your sex,
So far beneath your soft and tender breeding,
And since you call'd me master for so long,
Here is my hand: you shall from this time be
Your master's mistress.

Oli. A sister! you are she.

Re-enter FABIAN, *with* MALVOLIO.

Duke. Is this the madman?

Oli. Ay, my lord, this same.
How now, Malvolio!

Mal. Madam, you have done me wrong,
Notorious wrong.

Oli. Have I, Malvolio? no.

Mal. Lady, you have. Pray you, peruse that letter.
You must not now deny it is your hand:
Write from it, if you can, in hand or phrase;
Or say 'tis not your seal, not your invention:
You can say none of this: well, grant it then
And tell me, in the modesty of honour,
Why you have given me such clear lights of favour,
Bade me come smiling and cross-garter'd to you,
To put on yellow stockings and to frown

302. [Exit Fabian.] Capell.

305. *on't, so*] *an't so* Heath conj. *and, so* Collier (Collier MS.).

308. [To Viola] Rowe.

309. *mettle*] Ff. *metal* Rowe.

313. *mistress.* Oli. *A...she*] *mistress, and his sister she* Hanmer.

Re-enter F. with M.] Capell. Enter M. Ff. Enter M. with straw about him, as from prison. Collier MS.

314. SCENE VII. Pope.

315. *you have*] *you've* S. Walker conj.

320. *seal, not*] *seal, nor* F_4.

Upon Sir Toby and the lighter people;
And, acting this in an obedient hope,
Why have you suffer'd me to be imprison'd,
Kept in a dark house, visited by the priest,
And made the most notorious geck and gull
That e'er invention play'd on? tell me why.

Oli. Alas, Malvolio, this is not my writing,
Though, I confess, much like the character:
But out of question 'tis Maria's hand.
And now I do bethink me, it was she
First told me thou wast mad; then camest in smiling,
And in such forms which here were presupposed
Upon thee in the letter. Prithee, be content:
This practice hath most shrewdly pass'd upon thee;
But when we know the grounds and authors of it,
Thou shalt be both the plaintiff and the judge
Of thine own cause.

Fab. Good madam, hear me speak,
And let no quarrel nor no brawl to come
Taint the condition of this present hour,
Which I have wonder'd at. In hope it shall not,
Most freely I confess, myself and Toby
Set this device against Malvolio here,
Upon some stubborn and uncourteous parts
We had conceived against him: Maria writ
The letter at Sir Toby's great importance;
In recompense whereof he hath married her.
How with a sportful malice it was follow'd,
May rather pluck on laughter than revenge;
If that the injuries be justly weigh'd
That have on both sides pass'd.

330. *and gull*] F_1. *or gull* $F_2F_3F_4$.
336. *then*] *thou* Rann.
camest in] *cam'st thou* Theobald.
337. *presupposed*] *preimpos'd* Collier (Collier MS.).
342. *hear*] *here* F_2.
346. *confess, myself*] Theobald. *confess myself*, Ff.
Toby] *Sir Toby* Theobald.
349. *against*] *in* Rann (Tyrwhitt conj.).
355, 356. S. Walker would end line 355 at *fool*.

Oli. Alas, poor fool, how have they baffled thee!

Clo. Why, 'some are born great, some achieve greatness, and some have greatness thrown upon them.' I was one, sir, in this interlude; one Sir Topas, sir; but that's all one. 'By the Lord, fool, I am not mad.' But do you remember? 'Madam, why laugh you at such a barren rascal? an you smile not, he's gagged:' and thus the whirligig of time brings in his revenges.

Mal. I'll be revenged on the whole pack of you. [*Exit.*

Oli. He hath been most notoriously abused.

Duke. Pursue him, and entreat him to a peace:
He hath not told us of the captain yet:
When that is known, and golden time convents,
A solemn combination shall be made
Of our dear souls. Meantime, sweet sister,
We will not part from hence. Cesario, come;
For so you shall be, while you are a man;
But when in other habits you are seen,
Orsino's mistress and his fancy's queen.

[*Exeunt all, except Clown.*

Clo. [*Sings*]

When that I was and a little tiny boy,
With hey, ho, the wind and the rain,
A foolish thing was but a toy,
For the rain it raineth every day.

But when I came to man's estate,
With hey, ho, &c.
'Gainst knaves and thieves men shut their gate,
For the rain, &c.

356. *fool*] *Foole* $F_1F_2F_3$. *Fool* F_4. *soul* Collier (Collier MS.). *tool* Anon. conj.

thee!] Capell. *thee?* Ff.

358. *thrown*] *thrust* Theobald.

360, 361. *remember? 'Madam, why*] Malone (Tyrwhitt conj.). *remember, Madam, why* Ff. *remember, Madam,—'why* Theobald.

362. *an*] Pope. *and* Ff.

whirligig] Capell. *whirlegigge* F_1. *whirle-gigge* F_2F_3. *whirl-gigg* F_4.

364. [Exit.] Rowe.

368. *convents*] *consents* Steevens conj. *convenes* Anon. MS. apud Halliwell.

370. *Meantime*] *In the mean time* Hanmer.

374. [Exeunt...] Dyce and Staunton. Exeunt. Ff.

375—394. Farmer would omit as spurious.

375. *and*] *an* Theobald.

tiny] Rowe (ed. 2). *tine* Ff.

381. *knaves and thieves*] *knave and thief* Steevens (Farmer conj.).

But when I came, alas! to wive,
  With hey, ho, &c.
By swaggering could I never thrive,
  For the rain, &c.

But when I came unto my beds,
  With hey, ho, &c.
With toss-pots still had drunken heads,
  For the rain, &c.

A great while ago the world begun,
  With hey, ho, &c.
But that's all one, our play is done,
  And we'll strive to please you every day.
[*Exit.*

387—389. *beds...heads*] Ff. *bed ...head* Hanmer.

389. *toss-pots*] *tospottes* F_1.

still had] *I had* Hanmer. *still I had* Collier.

drunken] *broken* Anon. conj.

391. *begun*] Rowe. *begon* F_1F_2. *be gon* F_3. *be gone* F_4.

392. *With hey, ho*] $F_2F_3F_4$. *hey, ho* F_1.

394. [Exit.] Rowe. om. Ff.

NOTES.

NOTE I.

IN our enumeration of the Dramatis Personæ we have omitted what Johnson calls 'the cant of the modern stage,' i.e. the unnecessary descriptions given by Rowe.

NOTE II.

I. 1. 26. Mr Knight reads 'years' heat,' but follows Malone in interpreting 'heat' as a participle. It is more probably a substantive.

NOTE III.

I. 3. 48. Sidney Walker supposed that as the first Folio has no stop after 'acquaintance' it was intended that the sentence should be regarded as incomplete, and he therefore would read 'acquaintance—'. The real reason of the omission of the stop in F_1 is that the word occurs so near the end of the line that there was no room for its insertion. It is found in all the other Folios.

NOTE IV.

I. 5. 192. Mr Dyce conjectures that something more than the speaker's name has been omitted in the Folios before 'Tell me your mind.' Capell proposed to omit these words, on the ground that, in addition to other objections against them, they cause the speech to end metrically. We leave the text undisturbed, because we think that there is some corruption which Hanmer's plausible emendation does not remove.

NOTE V.

I. 5. 237. Sidney Walker conjectures that 'a word or words are lost before *adorations*, involving the same metaphor as the rest of the two lines.' Perhaps the lost word may have been 'earthward' or 'earthly,' so that all the four elements 'of which our life consists' (II. 3. 9) would be represented in the symptoms of Orsino's passion.

Note VI.

II. 2. 30. Johnson would transpose lines 28 and 29, and retain the reading of the Folios 'if':

'For such as we are made, if such we be,
Alas, our frailty is the cause, not we.'

Note VII.

II. 3. 33. The first Folio reads simply 'give a' without any stop at all, perhaps as before, because there was no room to insert it. More probably however a line has been omitted. The other Folios have 'give a—'. Mr Singer suggests that the hiatus may either have been intentional, or may have been filled up with the words 'another should.' Mr Collier's MS. corrector inserts a whole clause; reading, 'if one knight give a-way sixpence, so will I give another: go to.'

Note VIII.

II. 3. 97, 99, 101, 102. These lines are printed in the Folios in Roman type, while all the other songs and snatches of songs in the scene are in italics. It is evident, however, that they are intended to be sung.

Note IX.

II. 4. 17. Warburton says, 'The Folio reads *notions*, which is right.' This is incorrect: all the Folios have 'motions.'

Note X.

II. 5. 129. The first Folio here reads 'atcheeues,' but as it has 'atcheeue' in III. 4. 41, and 'atchieue' in V. 1. 357, it is plain that the first is a mere misprint. In many other passages, doubtless, the incorrect grammar found in the oldest editions is due to the printer, not to the author.

Note XI.

III. 4. 110. Mr Ritson suggested that 'Ay, Biddy, come with me,' is a fragment of an old song, and should be printed as such.

NOTE XII.

III. 4. 260. Mr Dyce and Mr Staunton make Scene V. to commence here in 'The street adjoining Olivia's garden.' The fourth scene is continued in the Folios, and, as in all other instances throughout the play, the beginning of each scene is accurately marked, we have thought it better to follow them in this. According to the Folios, Fabian and Viola leave the stage just as Sir Toby and Sir Andrew enter, and, not meeting them, may be supposed to return to the place appointed in lines 239, 240. Capell, contrary to the directions in the Folios, keeps Fabian and Viola on the stage. They are indeed all the while within sight of Sir Toby, as appears from lines 268, 269, but not necessarily visible to the audience. The comic effect would, no doubt, be heightened if Fabian were seen using all his efforts to prevent Viola from running away, but this is scarcely a sufficient reason for deserting our only authority.

NOTE XIII.

IV. I. 13. Mr Knight suggests that this may be intended to be spoken aside, as if the meaning were, 'I am afraid the world will prove this great lubber (Sebastian) a cockney.'

NOTE XIV.

V. I. 18. The meaning seems to be nothing more recondite than this: as in the syllogism it takes two premisses to make one conclusion, so it takes two people to make one kiss.

NOTE XV.

V. I. 159. In Mr Foss's copy of the first Folio, Sir Frederic Madden says the reading is 'cafe' instead of 'case,' and this leads him to conjecture that 'face' is the true reading. But in Capell's copy the reading is plainly 'case,' and as there is abundant authority to prove that 'case' was a sportsman's term for the skin of an animal, we retain it.

THE WINTER'S TALE.

DRAMATIS PERSONÆ[1].

LEONTES, king of Sicilia.
MAMILLIUS[2], young prince of Sicilia.
CAMILLO, ANTIGONUS, CLEOMENES, DION, — Four Lords of Sicilia.
POLIXENES, king of Bohemia[3].
FLORIZEL, prince of Bohemia[3].
ARCHIDAMUS, a Lord of Bohemia[3].
Old Shepherd, reputed father of Perdita.
Clown, his son.
AUTOLYCUS, a rogue.
A Mariner[4].
A Gaoler[4].

HERMIONE, queen to Leontes.
PERDITA, daughter to Leontes and Hermione.
PAULINA, wife to Antigonus.
EMILIA, a lady attending on Hermione[5].
MOPSA[4], DORCAS[4], — Shepherdesses.

Other Lords and Gentlemen, Ladies[4], Officers[4], and Servants, Shepherds, and Shepherdesses.

Time[4], as Chorus[4].

SCENE: *Partly in Sicilia, and partly in Bohemia*[6].

[1] DRAMATIS PERSONÆ. Given imperfectly as 'The Names of the Actors' in Ff.

[2] MAMILLIUS] Mamillus. Rowe (ed. 2).

[3] Bohemia] Bithynia. Hanmer.

[4] Words and clauses omitted in Ff.

[5] a lady......Hermione.] Rowe. a Lady. Ff.

[6] SCENE...] Rowe. om. Ff.

THE WINTER'S TALE.

ACT I.

SCENE I. *Antechamber in* LEONTES' *palace.*

Enter CAMILLO *and* ARCHIDAMUS.

Arch. If you shall chance, Camillo, to visit Bohemia, on the like occasion whereon my services are now on foot, you shall see, as I have said, great difference betwixt our Bohemia and your Sicilia.

Cam. I think, this coming summer, the King of Sicilia means to pay Bohemia the visitation which he justly owes him.

Arch. Wherein our entertainment shall shame us we will be justified in our loves; for indeed—

Cam. Beseech you,—

Arch. Verily, I speak it in the freedom of my knowledge: we cannot with such magnificence—in so rare—I know not what to say. We will give you sleepy drinks, that your senses, unintelligent of our insufficience, may, though they cannot praise us, as little accuse us.

SCENE I. Antechamber...] Theobald. A Palace. Rowe.

1. *Bohemia*] *Bithynia* Hanmer (and throughout).

5. *coming*] *comming* F_1. *common* $F_2F_3F_4$.

8. *us*] *us*, Theobald. *us:* Ff.

11. *Verily*] F_3F_4. *Verely* F_1F_2.

Cam. You pay a great deal too dear for what's given freely.

Arch. Believe me, I speak as my understanding instructs me and as mine honesty puts it to utterance.

Cam. Sicilia cannot show himself over-kind to Bohemia. They were trained together in their childhoods; and there rooted betwixt them then such an affection, which cannot choose but branch now. Since their more mature dignities and royal necessities made separation of their society, their encounters, though not personal, have been royally attorneyed with interchange of gifts, letters, loving embassies; that they have seemed to be together, though absent; shook hands, as over a vast; and embraced, as it were, from the ends of opposed winds. The heavens continue their loves!

Arch. I think there is not in the world either malice or matter to alter it. You have an unspeakable comfort of your young prince Mamillius: it is a gentleman of the greatest promise that ever came into my note.

Cam. I very well agree with you in the hopes of him: it is a gallant child; one that indeed physics the subject, makes old hearts fresh: they that went on crutches ere he was born desire yet their life to see him a man.

Arch. Would they else be content to die?

Cam. Yes; if there were no other excuse why they should desire to live.

Arch. If the king had no son, they would desire to live on crutches till he had one. [*Exeunt.*

25. *have*] $F_2F_3F_4$. *hath* F_1.
royally] *so royally* Collier (Collier MS.).

26. *gifts*] $F_1F_3F_4$. *gift* F_2.

28. *vast*] F_1. *vast sea* $F_2F_3F_4$.

30. *loves*] *love* Hanmer.

33. *Mamillius*] *Mamillus* Rowe (ed. 2).

SCENE II. *A room of state in the same.*

Enter LEONTES, HERMIONE, MAMILLIUS, POLIXENES, CAMILLO, *and* Attendants.

Pol. Nine changes of the watery star hath been
The shepherd's note since we have left our throne
Without a burthen: time as long again
Would be fill'd up, my brother, with our thanks;
And yet we should, for perpetuity,
Go hence in debt: and therefore, like a cipher,
Yet standing in rich place, I multiply
With one 'We thank you,' many thousands moe
That go before it.

Leon. Stay your thanks a while;
And pay them when you part.

Pol. Sir, that's to-morrow.
I am question'd by my fears, of what may chance
Or breed upon our absence; that may blow
No sneaping winds at home, to make us say
'This is put forth too truly:' besides, I have stay'd
To tire your royalty.

Leon. We are tougher, brother,
Than you can put us to't.

Pol. No longer stay.

Leon. One seven-night longer.

Pol. Very sooth, to-morrow.

SCENE II. A room......] Capell. Scene opens to the Presence. Theobald.

CAMILLO] om. Theobald.

and Attendants] Theobald. om. Ff.

1. *hath*] *have* Capell.

1, 2. *been...note*] *been* (*The shepherd's note,*) Warburton.

8. *moe*] *more* Rowe.

9. *a while*] *awhile* Reed.

11. *I am*] *I'm* Pope.

12. *absence;*] *absence,* Ff.

12, 13. *that may blow No*] *there may blow Some* Hanmer. *may there blow No* Warburton.

12—14. *that...truly:*] *that...truly!* Steevens (Farmer conj.).

14. *truly*] *early* Hanmer. *tardily* Capell.

17. *seven-night*] *seve'night* F_1F_2 F_3. *sev'night* F_4.

Leon. We'll part the time between's, then: and in that
I'll no gainsaying.
Pol. Press me not, beseech you, so.
There is no tongue that moves, none, none i' the world,
So soon as yours could win me: so it should now,
Were there necessity in your request, although
'Twere needful I denied it. My affairs
Do even drag me homeward: which to hinder
Were in your love a whip to me; my stay
To you a charge and trouble: to save both,
Farewell, our brother.
Leon. Tongue-tied our queen? speak you.
Her. I had thought, sir, to have held my peace until
You had drawn oaths from him not to stay. You, sir,
Charge him too coldly. Tell him, you are sure
All in Bohemia's well; this satisfaction
The by-gone day proclaim'd: say this to him,
He's beat from his best ward.
Leon. Well said, Hermione.
Her. To tell, he longs to see his son, were strong:
But let him say so then, and let him go;
But let him swear so, and he shall not stay,
We'll thwack him hence with distaffs.
Yet of your royal presence I'll adventure
The borrow of a week. When at Bohemia
You take my lord, I'll give him my commission
To let him there a month behind the gest
Prefix'd for's parting: yet, good deed, Leontes,
I love thee not a jar o' the clock behind
What lady she her lord. You'll stay?
Pol. No, madam.

19. *beseech you, so.*] *'beseech you!* Hanmer. *so, beseech you:* Capell.

20. *world*] $F_1F_3F_4$. *would* F_2.

28. *to have*] *to've* Pope.

29. *You had*] *You 'ad* Theobald.

33. [He walks apart. Collier (Collier MS.).

38. [To Polixenes. Rowe.

40. *give him*] *give you* Hanmer (Warburton).

41. *behind*] *beyond* Heath conj. *gest*] F_1F_2. *guest* F_3F_4. *just* Theobald conj. *geste* Hanmer. *list* Heath conj.

42. *good deed,*] (*good-deed*) F_1. (*good-heed*) F_2. (*good heed*) F_3F_4. See note (I).

44. *lady she*] *lady should* Collier (Egerton and Collier MSS.). *lady-she* Staunton.

Her. Nay, but you will?
Pol. I may not, verily.
Her. Verily!
You put me off with limber vows; but I,
Though you would seek to unsphere the stars with oaths,
Should yet say 'Sir, no going.' Verily,
You shall not go: a lady's 'Verily' 's
As potent as a lord's. Will you go yet?
Force me to keep you as a prisoner,
Not like a guest; so you shall pay your fees
When you depart, and save your thanks. How say you?
My prisoner? or my guest? by your dread 'Verily,'
One of them you shall be.
Pol. Your guest, then, madam:
To be your prisoner should import offending;
Which is for me less easy to commit
Than you to punish.
Her. Not your gaoler, then,
But your kind hostess. Come, I'll question you
Of my lord's tricks and yours when you were boys:
You were pretty lordings then?
Pol. We were, fair queen,
Two lads that thought there was no more behind
But such a day to-morrow as to-day,
And to be boy eternal.
Her. Was not my lord
The verier wag o' the two?
Pol. We were as twinn'd lambs that did frisk i' the sun,
And bleat the one at the other: what we changed
Was innocence for innocence; we knew not
The doctrine of ill-doing, nor dream'd
That any did. Had we pursued that life,
And our weak spirits ne'er been higher rear'd
With stronger blood, we should have answer'd heaven
Boldly 'not guilty;' the imposition clear'd

50. '*Verily*' '*s*] Staunton and Grant White. *Verely 'is* F_1F_2. *verily is* F_3F_4.

65, 66. *Was...two?*] As in Ff. In one line. Hanmer.

70. *nor dream'd*] F_1. *no nor dream'd* $F_2F_3F_4$. *neither dream'd* Spedding conj.

Hereditary ours.
Her. By this we gather
You have tripp'd since.
Pol. O my most sacred lady!
Temptations have since then been born to's: for
In those unfledged days was my wife a girl;
Your precious self had then not cross'd the eyes
Of my young play-fellow.
Her. Grace to boot!
Of this make no conclusion, lest you say
Your queen and I are devils: yet go on;
The offences we have made you do we'll answer,
If you first sinn'd with us and that with us
You did continue fault and that you slipp'd not
With any but with us.
Leon. Is he won yet?
Her. He'll stay, my lord.
Leon. At my request he would not.
Hermione, my dearest, thou never spokest
To better purpose.
Her. Never?
Leon. Never, but once.
Her. What! have I twice said well? when was't before?
I prithee tell me; cram's with praise, and make's
As fat as tame things: one good deed dying tongueless
Slaughters a thousand waiting upon that.
Our praises are our wages: you may ride's
With one soft kiss a thousand furlongs ere
With spur we heat an acre. But to the goal:

77. *to 's*] *to us* Capell.
80. *Grace*] *Oh! Grace* Hanmer. *God's grace* S. Walker conj.
boot] *both* Heath conj.
81. *lest*] F_4. *least* $F_1F_2F_3$.
88. *dearest*] *dear'st* S. Walker conj.
never] *ne'er* Pope.
90. *was't*] *'twas* Steevens (1778). *was it* Mason conj.
91. *cram's ... make's*] *cram us ... make us* Capell.
96. *heat an acre. But to the goal:—*] *heat an Acre. But to th' Goale:* Ff. (*Goal* F_3F_4). *heat an acre, but to th' goal.* Warburton. *clear an acre. But to the good:* Collier (Collier MS.).

My last good deed was to entreat his stay:
What was my first? it has an elder sister,
Or I mistake you: O, would her name were Grace!
But once before I spoke to the purpose: when?
Nay, let me have't; I long.

Leon. Why, that was when
Three crabbed months had sour'd themselves to death,
Ere I could make thee open thy white hand,
And clap thyself my love: then didst thou utter
'I am yours for ever.'

Her. 'Tis Grace indeed.
Why, lo you now, I have spoke to the purpose twice:
The one for ever earn'd a royal husband;
The other for some while a friend.

Leon. [*Aside*] Too hot, too hot!
To mingle friendship far is mingling bloods.
I have tremor cordis on me: my heart dances;
But not for joy; not joy. This entertainment
May a free face put on, derive a liberty
From heartiness, from bounty, fertile bosom,
And well become the agent; 't may, I grant;
But to be paddling palms and pinching fingers,
As now they are, and making practised smiles,
As in a looking-glass, and then to sigh, as 'twere
The mort o' the deer; O, that is entertainment
My bosom likes not, nor my brows! Mamillius,
Art thou my boy?

Mam. Ay, my good lord.

Leon. I' fecks!

100. *spoke*] F_1F_2. *spake* F_3F_4.
purpose:] Capell. *purpose?* Ff.
104. *And clap*] $F_2F_3F_4$. *A clap* F_1. *And clepe* Rowe (ed. 2).
105. *'Tis*] Ff. *This is* Hanmer. *It is* Capell.
106. *I have*] *I've* Pope.
108. [Giving her hand to Pol. Capell.
[Aside.] Rowe.
112. *derive*] F_1. *derives* $F_2F_3F_4$.
113. *bounty, fertile bosom*] *bounty's fertile bosom* Hanmer. *bounty:—fertile become* Jackson conj.
114. *well*] F_1. *we'l* F_2F_4. *wee'l* F_3.
become] *becomes* Rowe (ed. 2).
't may] *it may* Steevens.
117. *looking-glass*] *glass* S. Walker conj.
119. *Mamillius*] *Mamillus* Rowe (ed. 2).

Why, that's my bawcock. What, hast smutch'd thy nose?
They say it is a copy out of mine. Come, captain,
We must be neat; not neat, but cleanly, captain:
And yet the steer, the heifer and the calf
Are all call'd neat.—Still virginalling
Upon his palm!—How now, you wanton calf!
Art thou my calf?

Mam. Yes, if you will, my lord.

Leon. Thou want'st a rough pash and the shoots that I have,
To be full like me: yet they say we are
Almost as like as eggs; women say so,
That will say any thing: but were they false
As o'er-dyed blacks, as wind, as waters, false
As dice are to be wish'd by one that fixes
No bourn 'twixt his and mine, yet were it true
To say this boy were like me. Come, sir page,
Look on me with your welkin eye: sweet villain!
Most dear'st! my collop! Can thy dam?—may't be?—
Affection! thy intention stabs the centre:
Thou dost make possible things not so held,
Communicatest with dreams;—how can this be?—

121. *hast*] Capell. *has't* Ff.

122. *They...captain,*] As two lines in Capell, ending *mine...captain.*

it is] *it's* Warburton. *'t 's* Anon. conj.

[Wipes the boy's face. Hanmer. [Pulling the boy to him and wiping him. Capell.

123. *but*] F_1. om. $F_2 F_3 F_4$.

124. *heifer*] *heycfer* $F_1 F_2$.

125. [Observing Polixenes and Hermione. Rowe.

128. *pash*] *bush* Becket conj.

129. *full like*] *full, like* Ff.

132. *o'er-dyed*] *o're-dy'd* $F_1 F_2 F_3$. *o're di'd* F_4. *our dead* Collier (Collier MS.). *oft dyed* Staunton conj.

wind] *winds* Rowe (ed. 2).

134. *bourn*] Capell. *bourne* Rowe. *borne* $F_1 F_2$. *born* $F_3 F_4$.

135. *were*] *is* Hanmer.

136. *welkin eye*] *welking eye* Rowe (ed. 2). *welkin-eye* Theobald.

137. *dam?—*] *dam?* Rowe. *dam,* Ff.

137, 138. *may't be?—Affection,...centre*] Steevens. *may't be? Affection, thy intention stabs to the center* Capell. *may't be Affection?...centre* Ff. *may't be—Imagination! thou dost stab to th' center* Rowe.

138—146. *Affection ...... brows.*] Erased in Collier MS.

139. *not so*] F_1. *not be so* $F_2 F_3 F_4$. *not to be so* Hanmer.

held,] *held?* Staunton.

140, 141. *dreams;—how... be?—With...unreal*] Rann (Theobald conj.). *dreames (how...be?) With...unreall:* $F_1 F_2$. *dreams (how...be?) With...unreal,* $F_3 F_4$. *dreams—how...be With ...unreal?* Pope. *dreams?—how! can this be?—With...unreal* Staunton.

With what's unreal thou coactive art,
And fellow'st nothing: then 'tis very credent
Thou mayst co-join with something; and thou dost,
And that beyond commission, and I find it,
And that to the infection of my brains
And hardening of my brows.

Pol. What means Sicilia?

Her. He something seems unsettled.

Pol. How, my lord!
What cheer? how is't with you, best brother?

Her. You look
As if you held a brow of much distraction:
Are you moved, my lord?

Leon. No, in good earnest.
How sometimes nature will betray its folly,
Its tenderness, and make itself a pastime
To harder bosoms! Looking on the lines
Of my boy's face, methoughts I did recoil
Twenty-three years, and saw myself unbreech'd,
In my green velvet coat, my dagger muzzled,
Lest it should bite its master, and so prove,
As ornaments oft do, too dangerous:
How like, methought, I then was to this kernel,

142. *fellow'st*] *follow'st* Rowe (ed. 2).
nothing] *nothings* Hanmer.

147, 148. *How, my lord! What... brother?*] Rann (Steevens). *How? my lord?* Leo. *What...brother?* Ff. *How? my lord?* Leo. *What...my best brother?* Rowe. *How? my lord? What ...my best brother?* Hanmer. *Now, my lord? What...brother?* Capell. *How is't, my lord? What...brother?* Long MS. *How now, my lord?* Leo. *What...brother?* Singer MS. *Ho, my lord! What...brother?* Dyce conj.

148—150. *What...lord?*] S. Walker arranges as three lines, ending *with you,...brow...lord?*

148. *is't*] *is it* Rowe (ed. 2).
best] *my best* Rowe (ed. 2).

150. *Are you*] *Are not you* Theobald. *Are you not* Hanmer.
earnest.] *earnest, no.*— Capell.

151. [Aside. Capell.

151, 152. *its...Its*] *it's...It's* F_1F_2. *its...It's* F_3F_4.

154. *methoughts*] F_4. *me thoughts* $F_1F_2F_3$. *my thoughts* Collier (Egerton MS.). *methought* Staunton. See note (II).
recoil] F_4. *requoyle* F_1F_2. *recoyl* F_3. *recall* Grey conj.

157. *its*] *it's* Ff.

158. *ornaments...do*] Rowe. *ornaments...do's* Ff (*does* F_4). *ornament... does* Capell.
do] Rowe. *do's* $F_1F_2F_3$. *does* F_4.

This squash, this gentleman. Mine honest friend,
Will you take eggs for money?

Mam. No, my lord, I'll fight.

Leon. You will! why, happy man be's dole! My brother,
Are you so fond of your young prince, as we
Do seem to be of ours?

Pol. If at home, sir,
He's all my exercise, my mirth, my matter:
Now my sworn friend, and then mine enemy;
My parasite, my soldier, statesman, all:
He makes a July's day short as December;
And with his varying childness cures in me
Thoughts that would thick my blood.

Leon. So stands this squire
Officed with me: we two will walk, my lord,
And leave you to your graver steps. Hermione,
How thou lovest us, show in our brother's welcome;
Let what is dear in Sicily be cheap:
Next to thyself and my young rover, he's
Apparent to my heart.

Her. If you would seek us,
We are yours i' the garden: shall's attend you there?

Leon. To your own bents dispose you: you'll be found,
Be you beneath the sky. [*Aside*] I am angling now,
Though you perceive me not how I give line.
Go to, go to!
How she holds up the neb, the bill to him!
And arms her with the boldness of a wife
To her allowing husband!

[*Exeunt Polixenes, Hermione, and Attendants.*

Gone already!
Inch-thick, knee-deep, o'er head and ears a fork'd one!
Go, play, boy, play: thy mother plays, and I

161. *eggs*] *ayes* Becket conj.
162. *my lord*] om. Hanmer.
163. *will!*] Rowe. *will:* Ff. *be's*] *be his* Capell.
170. *childness*] *childishness* Pope.
171. *would*] F_1. *should* $F_2F_3F_4$. *thick*] *think* F_4.
177. *would*] *will* Theobald.
180. [Aside] Aside, observing Her. Rowe (after line 182).
183. *neb*] *nib* Rowe (ed. 2).
185. [Exeunt...] Rowe.

Play too; but so disgraced a part, whose issue
Will hiss me to my grave: contempt and clamour
Will be my knell. Go, play, boy, play. There have been,
Or I am much deceived, cuckolds ere now;
And many a man there is, even at this present,
Now while I speak this, holds his wife by the arm,
That little thinks she has been sluiced in 's absence
And his pond fish'd by his next neighbour, by
Sir Smile, his neighbour: nay, there's comfort in't
Whiles other men have gates and those gates open'd,
As mine, against their will. Should all despair
That have revolted wives, the tenth of mankind
Would hang themselves. Physic for't there is none;
It is a bawdy planet, that will strike
Where 'tis predominant; and 'tis powerful, think it,
From east, west, north and south: be it concluded,
No barricado for a belly; know't;
It will let in and out the enemy
With bag and baggage: many thousand on's
Have the disease, and feel't not. How now, boy!

Mam. I am like you, they say.

Leon. Why, that's some comfort.
What, Camillo there?

Cam. Ay, my good lord.

Leon. Go play, Mamillius; thou'rt an honest man.
[*Exit Mamillius.*
Camillo, this great sir will yet stay longer.

Cam. You had much ado to make his anchor hold:
When you cast out, it still came home.

194. *in's*] *in his* Capell.

202—206. *and 'tis...baggage.*] Put in the margin as spurious by Hanmer.

202, 203. *powerful, think it, From ...south:*] Capell. *powrefull: thinke it: From...south*, Ff.

203—206. *From east......baggage.*] Omitted by Warburton.

204. *know't*] *know it* Capell (corrected in MS.).

206. *many...on's*] $F_1F_2F_3$. *many a...one's* F_4. *many a...of's* Rowe.

208, 209. *Why...there?*] S. Walker arranges as one line.

208. *they*] $F_2F_3F_4$. om. F_1.

209. *What,*] *What? is* Hanmer.

211. *Mamillius*] *Mamillus* Rowe (ed. 2).

[Exit M.] Rowe.

212. SCENE III. Pope.

213. *his anchor*] *the anchor* Hanmer.

Leon. Didst note it?
Cam. He would not stay at your petitions; made
His business more material.
Leon. Didst perceive it?
[*Aside*] They're here with me already; whispering, rounding
'Sicilia is a so-forth:' 'tis far gone,
When I shall gust it last. How came't, Camillo,
That he did stay?
Cam. At the good queen's entreaty.
Leon. At the queen's be't: 'good' should be pertinent;
But, so it is, it is not. Was this taken
By any understanding pate but thine?
For thy conceit is soaking, will draw in
More than the common blocks: not noted, is't,
But of the finer natures? by some severals
Of head-piece extraordinary? lower messes
Perchance are to this business purblind? say.
Cam. Business, my lord! I think most understand
Bohemia stays here longer.
Leon. Ha!
Cam. Stays here longer.
Leon. Ay, but why?
Cam. To satisfy your highness, and the entreaties
Of our most gracious mistress.
Leon. Satisfy!
The entreaties of your mistress! satisfy!
Let that suffice. I have trusted thee, Camillo,
With all the nearest things to my heart, as well

215. *petitions; made*] *petitions made;* Pope.

217. [Aside] Hanmer.

whispering, rounding] *whisp'ring round* Hanmer.

218. *is a so-forth*] *is a—so forth* Rann (Mason conj.). *is—and so forth* Malone conj. *is a sea-froth* Jackson conj.

224. *is soaking*] *in soaking* Grey conj.

230, 231. Leon. *Ha!* Cam. *Stays here longer.* Leon. *Ay*] Leo. *Ha? stays here longer. Ay* Hanmer. Leo. *Ha?* Cam. *Bohemia stays here longer.* Leo. *Ay* Capell.

233. *Satisfy!*] *Satisfie?* Ff. *Satisfie* Theobald.

235. *I have*] *I've* Pope.

236. *nearest things to*] Ff. *things nearest* Pope. *near'st things to* S. Walker conj.

as well] *with all* Hanmer. *as well as* Capell conj.

My chamber-councils; wherein, priest-like, thou
Hast cleansed my bosom, I from thee departed
Thy penitent reform'd: but we have been
Deceived in thy integrity, deceived
In that which seems so.

Cam. Be it forbid, my lord!

Leon. To bide upon't, thou art not honest; or,
If thou inclinest that way, thou art a coward,
Which hoxes honesty behind, restraining
From course required; or else thou must be counted
A servant grafted in my serious trust
And therein negligent; or else a fool
That seest a game play'd home, the rich stake drawn,
And takest it all for jest.

Cam. My gracious lord,
I may be negligent, foolish and fearful;
In every one of these no man is free,
But that his negligence, his folly, fear,
Among the infinite doings of the world,
Sometime puts forth. In your affairs, my lord,
If ever I were wilful-negligent,
It was my folly; if industriously
I play'd the fool, it was my negligence,
Not weighing well the end; if ever fearful
To do a thing, where I the issue doubted,
Whereof the execution did cry out
Against the non-performance, 'twas a fear
Which oft infects the wisest: these, my lord,
Are such allow'd infirmities that honesty
Is never free of. But, beseech your Grace,
Be plainer with me; let me know my trespass
By its own visage: if I then deny it,

241. *my lord!*] Hanmer. (*my Lord.*) Ff. *my lord.* Pope. *my lord—* Theobald.

244. *hoxes*] Ff. *hockles* Hanmer.

253. *Among*] F_1. *Amongst* $F_2F_3F_4$. *doings*] F_1. *doing* $F_2F_3F_4$.

254. *forth. In*] Theobald. *forth in* Ff. *my lord,*] Theobald. (*my Lord.*) Ff. *my Lord.* Rowe.

256. *industriously*] *injuriously* Hanmer.

261. *non-performance*] Ff. *now-performance* Heath conj.

266. *its*] *it's* Ff.

'Tis none of mine.
Leon. Ha' not you seen, Camillo,—
But that's past doubt, you have, or your eye-glass
Is thicker than a cuckold's horn,—or heard,—
For to a vision so apparent rumour
Cannot be mute,—or thought,—for cogitation
Resides not in that man that does not think,—
My wife is slippery? If thou wilt confess,
Or else be impudently negative,
To have nor eyes nor ears nor thought, then say
My wife's a hobby-horse; deserves a name
As rank as any flax-wench that puts to
Before her troth-plight: say't and justify't.
Cam. I would not be a stander-by to hear
My sovereign mistress clouded so, without
My present vengeance taken: 'shrew my heart,
You never spoke what did become you less
Than this; which to reiterate were sin
As deep as that, though true.
Leon. Is whispering nothing?
Is leaning cheek to cheek? is meeting noses?
Kissing with inside lip? stopping the career
Of laughter with a sigh?—a note infallible
Of breaking honesty;—horsing foot on foot?
Skulking in corners? wishing clocks more swift?
Hours, minutes? noon, midnight? and all eyes
Blind with the pin and web but theirs, theirs only,
That would unseen be wicked? is this nothing?
Why, then the world and all that's in't is nothing;
The covering sky is nothing; Bohemia nothing;
My wife is nothing; nor nothing have these nothings,
If this be nothing.
Cam. Good my lord, be cured

267. *Ha'*] Ff. *Have* Capell.
272. *think*] *think it* Theobald. *think't* Hanmer. See note (III).
273. *wilt*] Ff. *wilt,* Rowe.
276. *hobby-horse*] Rowe (ed. 2). *holy-horse* Ff. *hoby-horse* Capell.
277. *puts to*] *buts tow* Jackson conj.
285. *meeting*] F_4. *meating* F_1 F_2 F_3. *meting* Thirlby conj.
290. *noon*] F_1. *the noon* $F_2F_3F_4$. *noon-day* or *high noon* Anon. conj.
eyes] *eyes else* S. Walker conj.

Of this diseased opinion, and betimes;
For 'tis most dangerous.
Leon. Say it be, 'tis true.
Cam. No, no, my lord.
Leon. It is; you lie, you lie:
I say thou liest, Camillo, and I hate thee,
Pronounce thee a gross lout, a mindless slave,
Or else a hovering temporizer, that
Canst with thine eyes at once see good and evil,
Inclining to them both: were my wife's liver
Infected as her life, she would not live
The running of one glass.
Cam. Who does infect her?
Leon. Why, he that wears her like her medal, hanging
About his neck, Bohemia: who, if I
Had servants true about me, that bare eyes
To see alike mine honour as their profits,
Their own particular thrifts, they would do that
Which should undo more doing: ay, and thou,
His cup-bearer,—whom I from meaner form
Have bench'd and rear'd to worship, who mayst see
Plainly as heaven sees earth and earth sees heaven,
How I am gall'd,—mightst bespice a cup,
To give mine enemy a lasting wink;
Which draught to me were cordial.
Cam. Sir, my lord,
I could do this, and that with no rash potion,
But with a lingering dram, that should not work
Maliciously like poison: but I cannot
Believe this crack to be in my dread mistress,
So sovereignly being honourable.

304. *wife's*] Rowe. *wives* Ff.

307. *her medal*] Rowe. *her medull* F_1 F_2 F_3. *her medul* F_4. *his medal* Theobald. *a medal* Collier MS.

309. *bare*] Theobald. *bear* Ff.

312. *ay*] Capell. *I* Ff.

316. *gall'd*] Ff. *galled* Steevens. *gull'd* Rann.

mightst] F_1. *thou mightst* F_2 F_3 F_4.

318. *Sir*] *Sure* Collier (Collier MS.).

321. *Maliciously like*] *Maliciously, like* F_4. *Maliciously, like a* Rowe. *Like a malicious* Hanmer.

323. *So...honourable.*] *So sovereignly (being honourable)* Malone conj.

323—325. *So...unsettled*] S. Walker arranges as three lines, ending *lov'd thee...think...unsettled.* End 323 *I have* Spedding conj.

I have loved thee,—
Leon. Make that thy question, and go rot!
Dost think I am so muddy, so unsettled,
To appoint myself in this vexation; sully
The purity and whiteness of my sheets,
Which to preserve is sleep, which being spotted
Is goads, thorns, nettles, tails of wasps;
Give scandal to the blood o' the prince my son,
Who I do think is mine and love as mine,
Without ripe moving to't? Would I do this?
Could man so blench?
Cam. I must believe you, sir:
I do; and will fetch off Bohemia for't;
Provided that, when he's removed, your highness
Will take again your queen as yours at first,
Even for your son's sake; and thereby for sealing
The injury of tongues in courts and kingdoms
Known and allied to yours.
Leon. Thou dost advise me
Even so as I mine own course have set down:
I'll give no blemish to her honour, none.
Cam. My lord,
Go then; and with a countenance as clear
As friendship wears at feasts, keep with Bohemia
And with your queen. I am his cupbearer:
If from me he have wholesome beverage,
Account me not your servant.

324. *I have loved thee,—* Leon. *Make that...rot!*] *I haue lou'd thee,* Leo. *Make that...rot:* F_1. *I have lov'd thee.* Leo. *Make that...rot:* $F_2F_3F_4$. Leo. *I've lov'd thee.—Make 't...rot:* Theobald. *So lov'd.* Leo. *Make that ...rot:* Hanmer. Leo. *I've lov'd thee. Mark this question, and go do 't* Heath conj. Leo. *Make that thy question, and go rot! I have lov'd thee.* Capell (Tyrwhitt conj.). Leo. *Have I lov'd thee? Make that...rot.* Long MS.

326, 327. *vexation; sully The*] *vexation? sully The* Theobald. *vexation? Sully the* Ff.

329. *thorns...tails*] *and thorns... and tails* Hanmer.

nettles] *nettles, pismires* Anon. conj.

wasps;] *wasps? or would I* Capell.

332. *to't?...this?*] *to't...this?* Hanmer.

333. *man*] *any man* Long MS.

337. *for sealing*] *forsealing* Anon. conj.

341. *blemish to her*] *blemish t' her* S. Walker conj. reading lines 341, 342 as one line.

Leon. This is all:
Do't and thou hast the one half of my heart;
Do't not, thou splitt'st thine own.
Cam. I'll do't, my lord.
Leon. I will seem friendly, as thou hast advised me.
[*Exit.*

Cam. O miserable lady! But, for me,
What case stand I in? I must be the poisoner
Of good Polixenes: and my ground to do't
Is the obedience to a master, one
Who, in rebellion with himself, will have
All that are his so too. To do this deed,
Promotion follows. If I could find example
Of thousands that had struck anointed kings
And flourish'd after, I'ld not do't; but since
Nor brass nor stone nor parchment bears not one,
Let villany itself forswear't. I must
Forsake the court: to do't, or no, is certain
To me a break-neck. Happy star reign now!
Here comes Bohemia.

Re-enter POLIXENES.

Pol. This is strange: methinks
My favour here begins to warp. Not speak?
Good day, Camillo.
Cam. Hail, most royal sir!
Pol. What is the news i' the court?
Cam. None rare, my lord.
Pol. The king hath on him such a countenance
As he had lost some province and a region
Loved as he loves himself: even now I met him
With customary compliment; when he,
Wafting his eyes to the contrary and falling
A lip of much contempt, speeds from me and
So leaves me, to consider what is breeding

364. Re-enter P.] Enter P. Ff. SCENE IV. Pope.
365. *My*] *Me* F_2.
366. *Hail*] *Hoyle* F_2.

That changes thus his manners.
Cam. I dare not know, my lord.
Pol. How! dare not! do not. Do you know, and dare not?
Be intelligent to me: 'tis thereabouts;
For, to yourself, what you do know, you must,
And cannot say, you dare not. Good Camillo,
Your changed complexions are to me a mirror
Which shows me mine changed too; for I must be
A party in this alteration, finding
Myself thus alter'd with't.
Cam. There is a sickness
Which puts some of us in distemper; but
I cannot name the disease; and it is caught
Of you that yet are well.
Pol. How! caught of me!
Make me not sighted like the basilisk:
I have look'd on thousands, who have sped the better
By my regard, but kill'd none so. Camillo,—
As you are certainly a gentleman; thereto
Clerk-like experienced, which no less adorns
Our gentry than our parents' noble names,
In whose success we are gentle,—I beseech you,
If you know aught which does behove my knowledge
Thereof to be inform'd, imprison't not
In ignorant concealment.
Cam. I may not answer.
Pol. A sickness caught of me, and yet I well!
I must be answer'd. Dost thou hear, Camillo,
I conjure thee, by all the parts of man

376. *my lord*] om. Hanmer.

377. *do not*] *dare not* Hanmer. om. Long MS.

Do you...dare not?...me:] *do you...dare not?...me,* Ff. *You do... dare not...me:* Hanmer. *Do you... dare not...me?* Capell.

379. *you do*] F_1F_2. *do you* F_3F_4.

384. *with't*] *with it* Rowe (ed. 2).

389. *I have*] F_1F_4. *I* F_2F_3. *I've* Pope.

391. *are certainly a*] Ff. *are, certain,* Capell.

thereto] om. Pope.

392. *Clerk-like*] Ff. *Clerk-like,* Capell.

experienced] *experienc'd* F_1. *expedienc'd* $F_2F_3F_4$.

Which honour does acknowledge, whereof the least
Is not this suit of mine, that thou declare
What incidency thou dost guess of harm
Is creeping toward me; how far off, how near;
Which way to be prevented, if to be;
If not, how best to bear it.

Cam. Sir, I will tell you;
Since I am charged in honour and by him
That I think honourable: therefore mark my counsel,
Which must be ev'n as swiftly follow'd as
I mean to utter it, or both yourself and me
Cry lost, and so good night!

Pol. On, good Camillo.

Cam. I am appointed him to murder you.

Pol. By whom, Camillo?

Cam. By the king.

Pol. For what?

Cam. He thinks, nay, with all confidence he swears,
As he had seen't, or been an instrument
To vice you to't, that you have touch'd his queen
Forbiddenly.

Pol. O, then my best blood turn
To an infected jelly and my name
Be yoked with his that did betray the Best!
Turn then my freshest reputation to
A savour that may strike the dullest nostril
Where I arrive, and my approach be shunn'd,
Nay, hated too, worse than the great'st infection
That e'er was heard or read!

Cam. Swear his thought over
By each particular star in heaven and

404. *toward*] *towards* Rowe (ed. 2).
405. *to be*] Ff. *it be* Theobald.
406. *I will*] *I'll* Pope.
410. *utter it*] *utter't* S. Walker conj.
me] *I* Collier MS.
412. *I am appointed him*] F_1. *I appointed him* $F_2F_3F_4$. *I am appointed* Rowe. *I am appointed, sir* Hanmer. *I am appointed by him* Long MS. *I appointed am* Anon. MS. apud Halliwell.
416. *To vice*] *To 'ntice* Heath conj.
422, 424. *shunn'd...read*] *fear'd ...read of* Anon. MS. apud Halliwell.
424. *his thought*] *this though* Theobald. *this thought* Id. conj.
over] *over!* Jackson conj.

By all their influences, you may as well
Forbid the sea for to obey the moon,
As or by oath remove or counsel shake
The fabric of his folly, whose foundation
Is piled upon his faith and will continue
The standing of his body.

Pol. How should this grow?

Cam. I know not: but I am sure 'tis safer to
Avoid what's grown than question how 'tis born.
If therefore you dare trust my honesty,
That lies enclosed in this trunk which you
Shall bear along impawn'd, away to-night!
Your followers I will whisper to the business;
And will by twos and threes at several posterns,
Clear them o' the city. For myself, I'll put
My fortunes to your service, which are here
By this discovery lost. Be not uncertain;
For, by the honour of my parents, I
Have utter'd truth: which if you seek to prove,
I dare not stand by; nor shall you be safer
Than one condemn'd by the king's own mouth, thereon
His execution sworn.

Pol. I do believe thee:
I saw his heart in's face. Give me thy hand:
Be pilot to me and thy places shall
Still neighbour mine. My ships are ready and
My people did expect my hence departure
Two days ago. This jealousy
Is for a precious creature: as she's rare,
Must it be great; and, as his person's mighty,
Must it be violent; and as he does conceive
He is dishonour'd by a man which ever
Profess'd to him, why, his revenges must

432. *I am*] *I'm* Pope.

433. *'tis*] *it is* S. Walker conj., reading lines 431—433 as four lines, ending *body...sure...question...born.*

444. *by*] *by't* Hanmer.

445, 446. *mouth, thereon His*] Capell. *mouth: Thereon his* Ff. *mouth, His* Hanmer. *mouth, and thereon His* S. Walker conj.

448. *places*] *paces* Malone conj.

451. *jealousy*] *jealousy of his* S. Walker conj.

In that be made more bitter. Fear o'ershades me:
Good expedition be my friend, and comfort
The gracious queen, part of his theme, but nothing
Of his ill-ta'en suspicion! Come, Camillo;
I will respect thee as a father if
Thou bear'st my life off hence: let us avoid.

Cam. It is in mine authority to command
The keys of all the posterns: please your highness
To take the urgent hour. Come, sir, away. [*Exeunt.*

ACT II.

SCENE I. *A room in* LEONTES' *palace.*

Enter HERMIONE, MAMILLIUS, *and* Ladies.

Her. Take the boy to you: he so troubles me,
'Tis past enduring.

First Lady. Come, my gracious lord,
Shall I be your playfellow?

Mam. No, I'll none of you.

First Lady. Why, my sweet lord?

Mam. You'll kiss me hard, and speak to me as if
I were a baby still. I love you better.

Sec. Lady. And why so, my lord?

Mam. Not for because
Your brows are blacker; yet black brows, they say,
Become some women best, so that there be not

458. *and*] *Heav'n* Hanmer. *God* Singer conj.

458, 459. *comfort...theme*] *consort ...throne* Jackson conj. See note (IV).

459. *queen,*] *queen's;* Warburton. *theme*] *theame* F_1F_2. *theam* F_3F_4. *dream* Collier (Collier MS.).

465. *hour. Come*] *hour.* Pol. *Come* Long MS.

SCENE I. A room...] The Palace. Theobald. The Scene continues. Pope.

Enter...] Enter HERMIONE, MAMILLIUS, Ladies: LEONTES, ANTIGONUS, Lords. Ff. (Lord. $F_2F_3F_4$).

6, 7. *I love...lord?*] As one line by S. Walker.

7. *my lord*] *pray, my lord* Hanmer. *my good lord* Steevens.

Too much hair there, but in a semicircle,
Or a half-moon made with a pen.
Sec. Lady. Who taught you this?
Mam. I learn d it out of women's faces. Pray now
What colour are your eyebrows?
First Lady. Blue, my lord.
Mam. Nay, that's a mock: I have seen a lady's nose
That has been blue, but not her eyebrows.
First Lady. Hark ye;
The queen your mother rounds apace: we shall
Present our services to a fine new prince
One of these days; and then you'ld wanton with us,
If we would have you.
Sec. Lady. She is spread of late
Into a goodly bulk: good time encounter her!
Her. What wisdom stirs amongst you? Come, sir, now
I am for you again: pray you, sit by us,
And tell's a tale.
Mam. Merry or sad shall't be?
Her. As merry as you will.
Mam. A sad tale's best for winter: I have one
Of sprites and goblins.
Her. Let's have that, good sir.
Come on, sit down: come on, and do your best
To fright me with your sprites; you're powerful at it.
Mam. There was a man—
Her. Nay, come, sit down; then on.
Mam. Dwelt by a churchyard: I will tell it softly;
Yond crickets shall not hear it.
Her. Come on, then,
And give't me in mine ear.

10. *semicircle*] *cemicircle* F_1.
11. *Or*] *Like* Hanmer.
taught you this] Rowe. *taught 'this* F_1. *taught this* $F_2F_3F_4$.
13. *are*] F_1. *be* $F_2F_3F_4$.
18. *you'ld*] F_3. *youl'd* F_1 F_2. *you'l* F_4. *you'll* Rowe.
23. *shall't*] *shall it* Steevens.
25, 26. *for winter...goblins*] As one line in Hanmer.
I have...goblins] Arranged as by Dyce; as one line in Ff.
26. *good sir*] *sir* Steevens.
26, 28. *sprites*] Capell. *sprights* Ff.
31. *Yond*] Ff. *Yon'* Capell.
31, 32. *Come...ear*] Arranged as in Capell; as one line in Ff.
32. *give't*] *give it* Hanmer.

Enter LEONTES, *with* ANTIGONUS, Lords, *and* others.

Leon. Was he met there? his train? Camillo with him?
First Lord. Behind the tuft of pines I met them; never
Saw I men scour so on their way: I eyed them
Even to their ships.
Leon. How blest am I
In my just censure, in my true opinion!
Alack, for lesser knowledge! how accursed
In being so blest! There may be in the cup
A spider steep'd, and one may drink, depart,
And yet partake no venom; for his knowledge
Is not infected: but if one present
The abhorr'd ingredient to his eye, make known
How he hath drunk, he cracks his gorge, his sides,
With violent hefts. I have drunk, and seen the spider.
Camillo was his help in this, his pander:
There is a plot against my life, my crown;
All's true that is mistrusted: that false villain
Whom I employ'd was pre-employ'd by him:
He has discover'd my design, and I
Remain a pinch'd thing; yea, a very trick
For them to play at will. How came the posterns
So easily open?
First Lord. By his great authority;
Which often hath no less prevail'd than so
On your command.
Leon. I know't too well.
Give me the boy: I am glad you did not nurse him:
Though he does bear some signs of me, yet you

32. Enter...] Capell. Enter L., A., and Lords. Rowe. om. F_1. Enter L. $F_2F_3F_4$.

33. SCENE II. Pope.

34. First Lord] Capell (and throughout the Scene). Lord. Ff.

36. *Even*] *On even* Hanmer.

blest] *blessed then* Steevens conj.

40. *drink, depart*] *drink; depart* Ff. *drink a part* Collier MS. *deep o't* Staunton conj. *drain it deep* Jervis conj.

50. *has*] *hath* Rowe.

51. *pinch'd*] *perch'd* Jackson conj.

54. *often hath no less prevail'd than so*] *hath prevailed oftentimes no less Than so* Hanmer.

55. *command*] *commandement* S. Walker conj.

too well.] *too well, too well.* Anon. conj.

56. *I am*] *I'm* Pope.

Have too much blood in him.

Her. What is this? sport?

Leon. Bear the boy hence; he shall not come about her;
Away with him! and let her sport herself
With that she's big with; for 'tis Polixenes
Has made thee swell thus.

Her. But I'ld say he had not,
And I'll be sworn you would believe my saying,
Howe'er you lean to the nayward.

Leon. You, my lords,
Look on her, mark her well; be but about
To say 'she is a goodly lady,' and
The justice of your hearts will thereto add
''Tis pity she's not honest, honourable:'
Praise her but for this her without-door form,
Which on my faith deserves high speech, and straight
The shrug, the hum or ha, these petty brands
That calumny doth use; O, I am out,
That mercy does, for calumny will sear
Virtue itself: these shrugs, these hums and ha's,
When you have said 'she's goodly,' come between
Ere you can say 'she's honest:' but be't known,
From him that has most cause to grieve it should be,
She's an adulteress.

Her. Should a villain say so,
The most replenish'd villain in the world,
He were as much more villain: you, my lord,
Do but mistake.

Leon. You have mistook, my lady,
Polixenes for Leontes: O thou thing!
Which I'll not call a creature of thy place,
Lest barbarism, making me the precedent,

61. [Some bear off Mamillius. Capell.

62. *But I'ld*] F_4. *But Il'd* F_1F_2 F_3. *I'd but* Hanmer.

68. *honest, honourable*] *honest: honourable* Ff. *honest-honourable* S. Walker conj.

73. *does*] *do's* Ff. *doth* Hanmer. *sear*] *fear* Rowe (ed. 2).

76. *be't*] Ff. *be it* Steevens. *it be* Id. (1793), corrected in MS.

84. *Lest*] *Least* Ff.

Should a like language use to all degrees
And mannerly distinguishment leave out
Betwixt the prince and beggar: I have said
She's an adulteress; I have said with whom:
More, she's a traitor and Camillo is
A federary with her; and one that knows,
What she should shame to know herself
But with her most vile principal, that she's
A bed-swerver, even as bad as those
That vulgars give bold'st titles; ay, and privy
To this their late escape.

Her. No, by my life,
Privy to none of this. How will this grieve you,
When you shall come to clearer knowledge, that
You thus have publish'd me! Gentle my lord,
You scarce can right me throughly then to say
You did mistake.

Leon. No; if I mistake
In those foundations which I build upon,
The centre is not big enough to bear
A school-boy's top. Away with her, to prison!
He who shall speak for her is afar off guilty
But that he speaks.

Her. There's some ill planet reigns:
I must be patient till the heavens look
With an aspect more favourable. Good my lords,
I am not prone to weeping, as our sex

90. *federary*] *feodary* Collier (ed. 2. Malone conj.).
and one] *one* Hanmer. *ay, and one* S. Walker conj.

91. *shame*] *be asham'd* Hanmer.
herself] *herself with none* Anon. conj.

92. *But......principal*] omitted by Capell.
vile] Pope. *vild* Ff.

92, 93. *she's A bed-swerver*] *she Is a bed-swerver* S. Walker conj. ending lines 90—93 at *one...herself...she.*

93. *bed-swerver*] *bed-swarver* Ff.
even] *e'en* S. Walker conj.

94. *That vulgars*] *That vulgar* Rowe. *The vulgar* Hanmer.
bold'st] *bold* Steevens (1793).

99. *then to*] *than to* Rowe (ed. 1).

100. *No*] *No, no* Steevens (1793).
I mistake] *I do mistake* Hanmer.

103. *her, to*] Ff. *her to* Pope.

104. *her is*] *her's* S. Walker conj.
afar off] F_4. *a farre-off* F_1 F_2. *afar-off* F_3. *far off* Pope. *far of* Theobald.

105. *But*] *In* Hanmer.

107. *an aspect more favourable*] *aspect of more favour* Hanmer.

Commonly are; the want of which vain dew
Perchance shall dry your pities: but I have
That honourable grief lodged here which burns
Worse than tears drown: beseech you all, my lords,
With thoughts so qualified as your charities
Shall best instruct you, measure me; and so
The king's will be perform'd!

Leon. Shall I be heard?

Her. Who is't that goes with me? Beseech your highness,
My women may be with me; for you see
My plight requires it. Do not weep, good fools;
There is no cause: when you shall know your mistress
Has deserved prison, then abound in tears
As I come out: this action I now go on
Is for my better grace. Adieu, my lord:
I never wish'd to see you sorry; now
I trust I shall. My women, come; you have leave.

Leon. Go, do our bidding; hence!

[*Exit Queen, guarded; with Ladies.*

First Lord. Beseech your highness, call the queen again.

Ant. Be certain what you do, sir, lest your justice
Prove violence; in the which three great ones suffer,
Yourself, your queen, your son.

First Lord. For her, my lord,
I dare my life lay down and will do't, sir,
Please you to accept it, that the queen is spotless
I' the eyes of heaven and to you; I mean,
In this which you accuse her.

Ant. If it prove
She's otherwise, I'll keep my stables where
I lodge my wife; I'll go in couples with her;
Than when I feel and see her no farther trust her;

115. [To the Guard. Capell.

124. *you have*] *you've* Pope.

125. Exit...] Theobald. om. Ff.

127. *lest*] F_3F_4. *least* F_1F_2.

134. *my stables*] *my stable-stand* Hanmer. *my stable* Rann. *me stables* Collier (Collier MS.). *my stabler* or *my stablers* Edd. conj.

136. *Than*] Pope (ed. 2). *Then* Ff. See note (V).

farther] F_1. *further* $F_2F_3F_4$.

For every inch of woman in the world,
Ay, every dram of woman's flesh is false,
If she be.

Leon. Hold your peaces.

First Lord. Good my lord,—

Ant. It is for you we speak, not for ourselves:
You are abused and by some putter-on
That will be damn'd for't; would I knew the villain,
I would land-damn him. Be she honour-flaw'd,
I have three daughters; the eldest is eleven;
The second and the third, nine, and some five;
If this prove true, they'll pay for't: by mine honour,
I'll geld 'em all; fourteen they shall not see,
To bring false generations: they are co-heirs;
And I had rather glib myself than they
Should not produce fair issue.

Leon. Cease; no more.
You smell this business with a sense as cold
As is a dead man's nose: but I do see't and feel't,
As you feel doing thus; and see withal
The instruments that feel.

Ant. If it be so,
We need no grave to bury honesty:
There's not a grain of it the face to sweeten
Of the whole dungy earth.

Leon. What! lack I credit?

First Lord. I had rather you did lack than I, my lord,

141. *abused and by*] *abus'd and by* F_1. *abus'd by* $F_2F_3F_4$. *abused by* Rowe.

143. *I would...him.*] *And I would —damn him;—* Mitford conj.

143. *land-damn*] *Land-damne* F_1. *land-damm* Hanmer. *laudanum* Farmer conj. *lamback* Collier (ed. 2) (Collier MS.). *half-damn* Heath conj. *live-damn* S. Walker conj. *landan* or *lantam* or *rantan* Halliwell conj. See note (VI).

145. *nine, and some five*] Theobald. *nine: and some fiue* F_1. *nine: and sonnes five* F_2F_3. *nine: and sons five* F_4.

147. *'em*] F_3F_4. *em* F_1F_2. *them* Capell.

149. *glib*] *lib* Grey conj. *unsib* Heath conj.

152. *but I do*] *I* Pope.

153. [Laying hold of his arm. Hanmer. Sinking his brows. Johnson. Striking his brows. Steevens.

154. *The...so*] *The instruments of that you feel.* Ant. *If so* Heath conj. *that*] *I* Hanmer.

Upon this ground; and more it would content me
To have her honour true than your suspicion,
Be blamed for't how you might.

Leon. Why, what need we
Commune with you of this, but rather follow
Our forceful instigation? Our prerogative
Calls not your counsels, but our natural goodness
Imparts this; which if you, or stupified
Or seeming so in skill, cannot or will not
Relish a truth like us, inform yourselves
We need no more of your advice: the matter,
The loss, the gain, the ordering on't, is all
Properly ours.

Ant. And I wish, my liege,
You had only in your silent judgement tried it,
Without more overture.

Leon. How could that be?
Either thou art most ignorant by age,
Or thou wert born a fool. Camillo's flight,
Added to their familiarity,
Which was as gross as ever touch'd conjecture,
That lack'd sight only, nought for approbation
But only seeing, all other circumstances
Made up to the deed,—doth push on this proceeding:
Yet, for a greater confirmation,
For in an act of this importance 'twere
Most piteous to be wild, I have dispatch'd in post
To sacred Delphos, to Apollo's temple,
Cleomenes and Dion, whom you know
Of stuff'd sufficiency: now from the oracle
They will bring all; whose spiritual counsel had,
Shall stop or spur me. Have I done well?

160. *her*] *your* Rowe (ed. 2).

162. *of*] F_1. *for* $F_2F_3F_4$.
but] *not* Hanmer.

167. *a truth*] *as truth* Rowe (ed. 1).

169, 170. *on't, is all Properly*] Theobald. *on't, Is all properly* Ff. *on't, Is properly all* Pope. *on't are all Properly* Hanmer.

177. *lack'd*] *lack'd,* Staunton.

182. *I have*] *I hane* F_1. *I've* Hanmer.

184. *Cleomenes*] Capell. *Cleomines* Ff (and throughout).
Dion] F_1. *Deon* $F_2F_3F_4$.

187. *me*] *me on* Hanmer.

First Lord. Well done, my lord.
Leon. Though I am satisfied and need no more
Than what I know, yet shall the oracle
Give rest to the minds of others, such as he
Whose ignorant credulity will not
Come up to the truth. So have we thought it good
From our free person she should be confined,
Lest that the treachery of the two fled hence
Be left her to perform. Come, follow us;
We are to speak in public; for this business
Will raise us all.
Ant. [*Aside*] To laughter, as I take it,
If the good truth were known. [*Exeunt.*

SCENE II. *A prison.*

Enter PAULINA, *a* Gentleman, *and* Attendants.

Paul. The keeper of the prison, call to him;
Let him have knowledge who I am. [*Exit Gent.*
Good lady,
No court in Europe is too good for thee;
What dost thou then in prison?

Re-enter Gentleman, *with the* Gaoler.

Now, good sir,
You know me, do you not?
Gaol. For a worthy lady
And one who much I honour.
Paul. Pray you, then,

193. *have we*] F_1F_2. *we have* F_3F_4.
195. *Lest*] F_4. *Least* $F_1F_2F_3$.
198. [Aside] Hanmer.
SCENE II.] SCENE III. Pope.
A prison.] Pope. Outer room of a prison. Capell.
Enter PAULINA...] Hanmer. Enter Paulina, a Gentleman, Gaoler, Emilia. Ff.
2. *knowledge*] *the knowledge* Rowe.
2, 6. *who*] F_1. *whom* $F_2F_3F_4$.
[Exit Gent.] Rowe (after line 1). om. Ff.
4. Re-enter...] Rowe (after *do you not?*). om. Ff.

Conduct me to the queen.
Gaol. I may not, madam:
To the contrary I have express commandment.
Paul. Here's ado,
To lock up honesty and honour from
The access of gentle visitors! Is't lawful, pray you,
To see her women? any of them? Emilia?
Gaol. So please you, madam,
To put apart these your attendants, I
Shall bring Emilia forth.
Paul. I pray now, call her.
Withdraw yourselves. [*Exeunt Gentleman and Attendants.*
Gaol. And, madam,
I must be present at your conference.
Paul. Well, be't so, prithee. [*Exit Gaoler.*
Here's such ado to make no stain a stain
As passes colouring.

Re-enter Gaoler, *with* EMILIA.

Dear gentlewoman,
How fares our gracious lady?
Emil. As well as one so great and so forlorn
May hold together: on her frights and griefs,
Which never tender lady hath borne greater,
She is something before her time deliver'd.
Paul. A boy?
Emil. A daughter; and a goodly babe,

7—10. Arranged as in Hanmer. *Here's...from*, as one line in Ff. Capell ends the lines *queen...contrary... ado,...from.*

11—13. Hanmer ends the lines *lawful...them?...madam.*

13. *So please*] *If it so please* Hanmer.

14. *apart*] *a-part* $F_1F_2F_3$. *a part* F_4.

15. *pray now*] F_1. *pray you now* $F_2F_3F_4$.

16. [Exeunt Gent. and Attendants.] Exeunt Gent. &c. Theobald. om. Ff.

17. *your*] *all your* Hanmer, ending the lines *be ..well, well...prithee.*

18. *Well, be't*] *Well; be it* Rowe. *Well, well; Be it* Hanmer.

[Exit G.] Exit Kee. Capell. om. Ff.

19. *Here's*] *Here is* Capell, reading lines 18—21 as three, ending *ado... colouring...lady?*

20. Re-enter...] Re-enter Keeper with E. Capell. Enter Emilia. F_2F_3 F_4. om. F_1.

21. *our*] *one* F_2.

Lusty and like to live: the queen receives
Much comfort in't; says 'My poor prisoner,
I am innocent as you.'

Paul. I dare be sworn:
These dangerous unsafe lunes i' the king, beshrew them!
He must be told on't, and he shall: the office
Becomes a woman best; I'll take't upon me:
If I prove honey-mouth'd, let my tongue blister,
And never to my red-look'd anger be
The trumpet any more. Pray you, Emilia,
Commend my best obedience to the queen:
If she dares trust me with her little babe,
I'll show't the king and undertake to be
Her advocate to the loud'st. We do not know
How he may soften at the sight o' the child:
The silence often of pure innocence
Persuades when speaking fails.

Emil. Most worthy madam,
Your honour and your goodness is so evident,
That your free undertaking cannot miss
A thriving issue: there is no lady living
So meet for this great errand. Please your ladyship
To visit the next room, I'll presently
Acquaint the queen of your most noble offer;
Who but to-day hammer'd of this design,
But durst not tempt a minister of honour,
Lest she should be denied.

Paul. Tell her, Emilia,
I'll use that tongue I have: if wit flow from't
As boldness from my bosom, let't not be doubted
I shall do good.

Emil. Now be you blest for it!
I'll to the queen: please you, come something nearer.

29. *I am*] *I'm* Pope.
30. *unsafe*] *unsane* Collier (Collier MS.).
lunes] *lures* Becket conj.
i' the] *i' th'* Ff. *o' the* Steevens.
31. *on't*] *of it* Pope.
he shall] *shall* Rowe.
33. *honey-mouth'd*] *honey-mouth* Warburton.
45. *there is*] *there's* Hanmer.
49. *hammer'd of*] *hammered of* Ff. *hammer'd on* Hanmer.
51. *Lest*] Rowe. *Least* Ff.
53. *let't*] F_3F_4. *le't* F_1F_2. *let it* Steevens.

Gaol. Madam, if't please the queen to send the babe,
I know not what I shall incur to pass it,
Having no warrant.
Paul. You need not fear it, sir:
This child was prisoner to the womb and is
By law and process of great nature thence
Freed and enfranchised; not a party to
The anger of the king nor guilty of,
If any be, the trespass of the queen.
Gaol. I do believe it.
Paul. Do not you fear: upon mine honour, I
Will stand betwixt you and danger. [*Exeunt.*

SCENE III. *A room in* LEONTES' *palace.*

Enter LEONTES, ANTIGONUS, Lords, *and* Servants.

Leon. Nor night nor day no rest: it is but weakness
To bear the matter thus; mere weakness. If
The cause were not in being,—part o' the cause,
She the adulteress; for the harlot king
Is quite beyond mine arm, out of the blank
And level of my brain, plot-proof; but she
I can hook to me: say that she were gone,
Given to the fire, a moiety of my rest
Might come to me again. Who's there?
First Serv. My lord?
Leon. How does the boy?
First Serv. He took good rest to-night;
'Tis hoped his sickness is discharged.
Leon. To see his nobleness!

59. *This child*] *The child* Rowe.
64—66. As two lines in Capell, ending *upon...danger.*
66. *betwixt*] *'twixt* Pope.
SCENE III.] SCENE IV. Pope.
A room...] Scene changes to the Palace. Theobald.
Enter...and Servants] Enter Leontes, Servants, Paulina, Antigonus and Lords. Ff.

2. *weakness. If*] Collier. *weaknesse, if* Ff.
3. *being,—*] *being:* Ff.
5. *arm*] *aim* Field conj.
9. First Atten. [advancing] Capell. Ser. Ff. Enrer. F_2. Enter. F_3F_4. om. F_1.
10, 11. *rest to-night; 'Tis hoped his*] *rest to night: 'tis hop'd His* Ff. *rest To-night tis hop'd his* Hanmer.

Conceiving the dishonour of his mother,
He straight declined, droop'd, took it deeply,
Fasten'd and fix'd the shame on't in himself,
Threw off his spirit, his appetite, his sleep,
And downright languish'd. Leave me solely: go,
See how he fares. [*Exit Serv.*] Fie, fie! no thought of him:
The very thought of my revenges that way
Recoil upon me: in himself too mighty,
And in his parties, his alliance; let him be
Until a time may serve: for present vengeance,
Take it on her. Camillo and Polixenes
Laugh at me, make their pastime at my sorrow:
They should not laugh if I could reach them, nor
Shall she within my power.

Enter PAULINA, *with a child.*

First Lord. You must not enter.

Paul. Nay, rather, good my lords, be second to me:
Fear you his tyrannous passion more, alas,
Than the queen's life? a gracious innocent soul,
More free than he is jealous.

Ant. That's enough.

Sec. Serv. Madam, he hath not slept to-night; commanded
None should come at him.

Paul. Not so hot, good sir:
I come to bring him sleep. 'Tis such as you,
That creep like shadows by him and do sigh

14. *declined*] *declin'd upon't* Capell.
deeply] *most deeply* Hanmer.
18. [Exit...] Theobald.
20. *Recoil*] *Recoyle* F_1F_2. *Recoyl* F_3F_4. *Recoils* Hanmer.
21. *And in...be*] F_1. omitted in $F_2F_3F_4$.
And] om. Capell.
alliance;] *Alliance;* F_1. *alliances,—* Capell conj.
21, 22. *let him be Until*] *let him Be 'till* Hanmer.
26. SCENE V. Pope.
Enter P....child.] Rowe. Enter P. Ff.
First Lord.] Malone. Lord. Ff.
30. *That's enough.*] Marked as aside by Capell.
31. Sec. Serv.] Ser. Ff. Atten. [within. Theobald. 2 A. Capell.

At each his needless heavings, such as you
Nourish the cause of his awaking: I
Do come with words as medicinal as true,
Honest as either, to purge him of that humour
That presses him from sleep.

Leon. What noise there, ho?

Paul. No noise, my lord; but needful conference
About some gossips for your highness.

Leon. How!
Away with that audacious lady! Antigonus,
I charged thee that she should not come about me:
I knew she would.

Ant. I told her so, my lord,
On your displeasure's peril and on mine,
She should not visit you.

Leon. What, canst not rule her?

Paul. From all dishonesty he can: in this,
Unless he take the course that you have done,
Commit me for committing honour, trust it,
He shall not rule me.

Ant. La you now, you hear:
When she will take the rein I let her run;
But she'll not stumble.

Paul. Good my liege, I come;
And, I beseech you, hear me, who professes
Myself your loyal servant, your physician,
Your most obedient counsellor, yet that dares
Less appear so in comforting your evils,
Than such as most seem yours: I say, I come
From your good queen.

Leon. Good queen!

Paul. Good queen, my lord,
Good queen; I say good queen;

37. *medicinal*] *med'cinal* Capell.

39. *What*] $F_2F_3F_4$. *Who* F_1.

49. *trust it*] *trust me* Hanmer.

50. *La you*] *La-you* Ff. *Lo-you* Pope.

51. *rein*] Rowe. *raine* F_1F_2. *rain* F_3F_4.

53. *professes*] *profess* Rowe (ed. 2).

57. *seem*] *seems* Pope (ed. 2).

58, 59. Paul. *Good...say good queen*] As one line in Capell.

59. *I say good queen*] As one line in Ff.

And would by combat make her good, so were I
A man, the worst about you.
Leon. Force her hence.
Paul. Let him that makes but trifles of his eyes
First hand me: on mine own accord I'll off;
But first I'll do my errand. The good queen,
For she is good, hath brought you forth a daughter;
Here 'tis; commends it to your blessing.
[*Laying down the child.*
Leon. Out!
A mankind witch! Hence with her, out o' door:
A most intelligencing bawd!
Paul. Not so:
I am as ignorant in that as you
In so entitling me, and no less honest
Than you are mad; which is enough, I'll warrant,
As this world goes, to pass for honest.
Leon. Traitors!
Will you not push her out? Give her the bastard.
Thou dotard! thou art woman-tired, unroosted
By thy dame Partlet here. Take up the bastard;
Take't up, I say; give't to thy crone.
Paul. For ever
Unvenerable be thy hands, if thou
Takest up the princess by that forced baseness
Which he has put upon't!
Leon. He dreads his wife.
Paul. So I would you did; then 'twere past all doubt
You'ld call your children yours.
Leon. A nest of traitors!
Ant. I am none, by this good light.
Paul. Nor I; nor any

60. *her*] *it* Heath conj.
good, so] Theobald. *good so*, Ff. *good*, Rowe (ed. 2).
61. *the worst*] *on th' worst* Hanmer (Warburton).
66. [Laying...] Rowe. om. Ff.
73. [To Ant. Rowe.
74. *thou art*] *that art* Capell.
woman-tired] *woman-tyr'd* F_1 F_2F_3. *woman-tir'd* F_4.
75. *thy dame*] *the dame* Rowe (ed. 2).
76. *thy crone*] *thy croane* F_1. *the croane* F_2F_3. *the croan* F_4.
78. *forced*] *falsed* Collier conj.

But one that's here, and that's himself; for he
The sacred honour of himself, his queen's,
His hopeful son's, his babe's, betrays to slander,
Whose sting is sharper than the sword's; and will not,—
For, as the case now stands, it is a curse
He cannot be compell'd to't,—once remove
The root of his opinion, which is rotten
As ever oak or stone was sound.

Leon. A callat
Of boundless tongue, who late hath beat her husband
And now baits me! This brat is none of mine;
It is the issue of Polixenes:
Hence with it, and together with the dam
Commit them to the fire!

Paul. It is yours;
And, might we lay the old proverb to your charge,
So like you, 'tis the worse. Behold, my lords,
Although the print be little, the whole matter
And copy of the father, eye, nose, lip;
The trick of's frown; his forehead; nay, the valley,
The pretty dimples of his chin and cheek; his smiles;
The very mould and frame of hand, nail, finger:
And thou, good goddess Nature, which hast made it
So like to him that got it, if thou hast
The ordering of the mind too, 'mongst all colours
No yellow in't, lest she suspect, as he does,
Her children not her husband's!

Leon. A gross hag!
And, lozel, thou art worthy to be hang'd,
That wilt not stay her tongue.

Ant. Hang all the husbands
That cannot do that feat, you'll leave yourself
Hardly one subject.

Leon. Once more, take her hence.

85. *his babe's*] *this babe's* Capell.
90. *sound*] F_1. *found* $F_2F_3F_4$.
95. *them*] *it* Capell conj.
100. *valley*] *valleys* Hanmer.
101. *pretty*] om. Hanmer.
of his chin] *of's chin* Dyce.
his smiles] omitted by Capell.
109. *That*] *Thou* Rowe (ed. 2).
[Aside. Anon. conj.

Paul. A most unworthy and unnatural lord
Can do no more.
Leon. I'll ha' thee burnt.
Paul. I care not:
It is an heretic that makes the fire,
Not she which burns in't. I'll not call you tyrant;
But this most cruel usage of your queen—
Not able to produce more accusation
Than your own weak-hinged fancy—something savours
Of tyranny and will ignoble make you,
Yea, scandalous to the world.
Leon. On your allegiance,
Out of the chamber with her! Were I a tyrant,
Where were her life? she durst not call me so,
If she did know me one. Away with her!
Paul. I pray you, do not push me; I'll be gone.
Look to your babe, my lord; 'tis yours: Jove send her
A better guiding spirit! What needs these hands?
You, that are thus so tender o'er his follies,
Will never do him good, not one of you.
So, so: farewell; we are gone. [*Exit.*
Leon. Thou, traitor, hast set on thy wife to this.
My child? away with't! Even thou, that hast
A heart so tender o'er it, take it hence
And see it instantly consumed with fire;
Even thou and none but thou. Take it up straight:
Within this hour bring me word 'tis done,
And by good testimony, or I'll seize thy life,
With what thou else call'st thine. If thou refuse
And wilt encounter with my wrath, say so;
The bastard brains with these my proper hands
Shall I dash out. Go, take it to the fire;

113. *ha' thee*] *have thee* Steevens.
118. *something*] *sometimes* Rowe.
120. *the world*] *all the world* Pope.
125. *Jove*] *God* Anon. conj.
her] *him* Heath conj.
126. *better guiding*] *better-guiding* S. Walker conj.
needs] F_1. *neede* F_2. *need* F_3 F_4.
130. SCENE VI. Pope.
131. *with't!*] *with't?* Ff.
thou,] *thou, thou* Theobald.
137. *what thou else call'st*] *all that's* Hanmer, ending line 136 at *seize.*

For thou set'st on thy wife.
Ant. I did not, sir:
These lords, my noble fellows, if they please,
Can clear me in't.
Lords. We can: my royal liege,
He is not guilty of her coming hither.
Leon. You're liars all.
First Lord. Beseech your highness, give us better credit:
We have always truly served you; and beseech you
So to esteem of us: and on our knees we beg,
As recompense of our dear services
Past and to come, that you do change this purpose,
Which being so horrible, so bloody, must
Lead on to some foul issue: we all kneel.
Leon. I am a feather for each wind that blows:
Shall I live on to see this bastard kneel
And call me father? better burn it now
Than curse it then. But be it; let it live.
It shall not neither. You, sir, come you hither;
You that have been so tenderly officious
With Lady Margery, your midwife there,
To save this bastard's life,—for 'tis a bastard,
So sure as this beard's grey,—what will you adventure
To save this brat's life?
Ant. Any thing, my lord,
That my ability may undergo,
And nobleness impose: at least thus much:

141. *set'st*] *sett'd'st* Hanmer.

142. *These lords*] *The Lords* Hanmer.

143. Lords.] Ff. Lord. Rowe. 1. L. Capell.

143, 144. Lords. *We can...hither*] Lords. *We can.* First Lord. *My... hither* Anon. conj.

146. First Lord.] 1. L. Capell. Lord. Ff. Lords. Rowe.

147. *We have*] *We've* Pope.

beseech you] Rowe. *beseech'* F_1. *beseech* $F_2F_3F_4$.

149. *services*] *service* Hanmer, ending line 148 at *knees*.

152. *we all kneel*] Lords. *We all kneel* Anon. conj.

153. *feather*] $F_1F_2F_3$. *father* F_4.

157. [To Ant. Rowe.

159. *midwife*] *Mid-wife* Ff. *mild wife* Rann (Capell conj.).

161. *this*] *his* Theobald conj. *thy* Collier (Egerton MS.).

164. *at least*] F_1. *at last* $F_2F_3F_4$.

I'll pawn the little blood which I have left
To save the innocent: any thing possible.
Leon. It shall be possible. Swear by this sword
Thou wilt perform my bidding.
Ant. I will, my lord.
Leon. Mark and perform it: seest thou? for the fail
Of any point in't shall not only be
Death to thyself but to thy lewd-tongued wife,
Whom for this time we pardon. We enjoin thee,
As thou art liege-man to us, that thou carry
This female bastard hence and that thou bear it
To some remote and desert place quite out
Of our dominions, and that there thou leave it,
Without more mercy, to its own protection
And favour of the climate. As by strange fortune
It came to us, I do in justice charge thee,
On thy soul's peril and thy body's torture,
That thou commend it strangely to some place
Where chance may nurse or end it. Take it up.
Ant. I swear to do this, though a present death
Had been more merciful. Come on, poor babe:
Some powerful spirit instruct the kites and ravens
To be thy nurses! Wolves and bears, they say,
Casting their savageness aside have done
Like offices of pity. Sir, be prosperous
In more than this deed does require! And blessing
Against this cruelty fight on thy side,
Poor thing, condemn'd to loss! [*Exit with the child.*
Leon. No, I'll not rear
Another's issue.

166. *any thing possible*] *what's possible* Hanmer.

171. *lewd-tongued*] *loud-tongued* Anon. conj.

177. *more*] F$_1$. *much* F$_2$F$_3$F$_4$.
its] F$_3$F$_4$. *it* F$_1$F$_2$. See note (VII).

181. *strangely to some*] *to some stranger* Hanmer.

182. *chance*] F$_1$F$_2$. *change* F$_3$F$_4$.

189—191. *require!...loss!*] *require; and...side* (*Poor...losse.*) Ff. *require; and...side! Poor...loss.*— Theobald.

190. *this*] *his* Roderick conj.

191. [Exit...child.] Rowe. Exit. Ff.
rear] F$_3$F$_4$. *reare* F$_1$. *rare* F$_2$.

Enter a Servant.

Serv. Please your highness, posts
From those you sent to the oracle are come
An hour since: Cleomenes and Dion,
Being well arrived from Delphos, are both landed,
Hasting to the court.

First Lord. So please you, sir, their speed
Hath been beyond account.

Leon. Twenty three days
They have been absent: 'tis good speed; foretells
The great Apollo suddenly will have
The truth of this appear. Prepare you, lords;
Summon a session, that we may arraign
Our most disloyal lady; for, as she hath
Been publicly accused, so shall she have
A just and open trial. While she lives
My heart will be a burthen to me. Leave me,
And think upon my bidding. [*Exeunt.*

ACT III.

SCENE I. *A sea-port in Sicilia.*

Enter CLEOMENES *and* DION.

Cleo. The climate's delicate, the air most sweet,
Fertile the isle, the temple much surpassing
The common praise it bears.

Dion. I shall report,

192. [Enter a Servant.] Ff. Enter a Messenger. Rowe. om. Capell.
Serv.] Ff. Mes. Rowe. 2. A. Capell.
196. First Lord.] 1. L. Capell. Lord. Ff.
197. *account*] F_4. *accompt* $F_1F_2F_3$.
198. *'tis good speed; foretells*] *this good speed foretels* Pope.
foretells] *and foretells* or *it foretells* Keightley conj.
ACT III. SCENE I.] ACT II. SCENE IV. Theobald conj.
A sea-port...] Edd. A part of Sicily near the seaside. Theobald. The same. A street in some town. Capell.
Enter C. and D.] Enter C., D., and an Attendant. S. Walker conj.
2. *isle*] *soil* Hanmer (Warburton conj.).
3. *I shall report,*] *It shames report.* Warburton.

For most it caught me, the celestial habits,
Methinks I so should term them, and the reverence
Of the grave wearers. O, the sacrifice!
How ceremonious, solemn and unearthly
It was i' the offering!
Cleo. But of all, the burst
And the ear-deafening voice o' the oracle,
Kin to Jove's thunder, so surprised my sense,
That I was nothing.
Dion. If the event o' the journey
Prove as successful to the queen,—O be't so!—
As it hath been to us rare, pleasant, speedy,
The time is worth the use on't.
Cleo. Great Apollo
Turn all to the best! These proclamations,
So forcing faults upon Hermione,
I little like.
Dion. The violent carriage of it
Will clear or end the business: when the oracle,
Thus by Apollo's great divine seal'd up,
Shall the contents discover, something rare
Even then will rush to knowledge. Go: fresh horses!
And gracious be the issue! [*Exeunt.*

SCENE II. *A court of Justice.*

Enter LEONTES, Lords, *and* Officers.

Leon. This sessions, to our great grief we pronounce,
Even pushes 'gainst our heart: the party tried
The daughter of a king, our wife, and one

4. *For most*] *Foremost* Warburton. *it*] *they* Hanmer.

14. *time...use*] *use...time* Hanmer (Warburton).

SCENE II. A court...] Scene represents a Court of Justice. Theobald.

Enter...] Enter Leontes, Lords, Officers: Hermione (as to her Triall), Ladies: Cleomines, Dion. Ff. At the upper End, a Throne; Lords, on either Hand, Judges, and other Officers, seated; People attending. Enter Leontes, and train of Lords, to his Throne. Capell.

1. *sessions*] *session* Theobald. *pronounce*] *pronounce it* Keightley conj.

2. *Even*] *Ever* Anon. conj.

Of us too much beloved. Let us be clear'd
Of being tyrannous, since we so openly
Proceed in justice, which shall have due course,
Even to the guilt or the purgation.
Produce the prisoner.

Off. It is his highness' pleasure that the queen
Appear in person here in court. Silence!

Enter HERMIONE *guarded;* PAULINA *and* Ladies *attending.*

Leon. Read the indictment.

Off. [*reads*] Hermione, queen to the worthy Leontes, king of Sicilia, thou art here accused and arraigned of high treason, in committing adultery with Polixenes, king of Bohemia, and conspiring with Camillo to take away the life of our sovereign lord the king, thy royal husband: the pretence whereof being by circumstances partly laid open, thou, Hermione, contrary to the faith and allegiance of a true subject, didst counsel and aid them, for their better safety, to fly away by night.

Her. Since what I am to say must be but that
Which contradicts my accusation and
The testimony on my part no other
But what comes from myself, it shall scarce boot me
To say 'not guilty:' mine integrity
Being counted falsehood, shall, as I express it,
Be so received. But thus, if powers divine
Behold our human actions, as they do,
I doubt not then but innocence shall make
False accusation blush, and tyranny
Tremble at patience. You, my lord, best know,
Who least will seem to do so, my past life
Hath been as continent, as chaste, as true,
As I am now unhappy; which is more
Than history can pattern, though devised
And play'd to take spectators. For behold me

10. *Silence!*] See note (VIII).
Enter...] Hermione is brought in, guarded; Pauline, and Ladies, attending. Theobald. om. Ff.

12. Off. [reads]. Capell. Officer. Ff.

16. *circum stances*] F_1. *circumstance* F_2 F_3 F_4.

29. *accusation*] F_1. *accusations* F_2 F_3 F_4.

31. *Who*] Rowe. *Whom* Ff.

A fellow of the royal bed, which owe
A moiety of the throne, a great king's daughter,
The mother to a hopeful prince, here standing
To prate and talk for life and honour 'fore
Who please to come and hear. For life, I prize it
As I weigh grief, which I would spare: for honour,
'Tis a derivative from me to mine,
And only that I stand for. I appeal
To your own conscience, sir, before Polixenes
Came to your court, how I was in your grace,
How merited to be so; since he came,
With what encounter so uncurrent I
Have strain'd, to appear thus: if one jot beyond
The bound of honour, or in act or will
That way inclining, harden'd be the hearts
Of all that hear me, and my near'st of kin
Cry fie upon my grave!

Leon. I ne'er heard yet
That any of these bolder vices wanted
Less impudence to gainsay what they did
Than to perform it first.

Her. That's true enough;
Though 'tis a saying, sir, not due to me.

Leon. You will not own it.

Her. More than mistress of
Which comes to me in name of fault, I must not
At all acknowledge. For Polixenes,
With whom I am accused, I do confess
I loved him as in honour he required,
With such a kind of love as might become
A lady like me, with a love even such,
So and no other, as yourself commanded:

36. *owe*] *owes* Steevens (1785).
39. *prate*] *plead* Keightley conj.
41. *grief*] See note (IX).
which...spare:] (*which...spare*) Ff.
47, 48. *I Have*] *have I* Hanmer.
I Have strain'd] *have I Been stain'd* Johnson conj. *I Have stray'd* Collier (Mason conj.).
49. *bound*] *bounds* Rowe.
53. *these*] *those* F_4.
55. *That's*] *That is* Rowe.
57. *mistress of*] *I'm mistress of* Hanmer. *misreport* or *misprision* Anon. conj. A line omitted. Anon. conj.
58. *Which*] *What* Rowe. *That* Seymour conj.

Which not to have done I think had been in me
Both disobedience and ingratitude
To you and toward your friend; whose love had spoke,
Even since it could speak, from an infant, freely
That it was yours. Now, for conspiracy,
I know not how it tastes; though it be dish'd
For me to try how: all I know of it
Is that Camillo was an honest man;
And why he left your court, the gods themselves,
Wotting no more than I, are ignorant.
Leon. You knew of his departure, as you know
What you have underta'en to do in's absence.
Her. Sir,
You speak a language that I understand not:
My life stands in the level of your dreams,
Which I'll lay down.
Leon. Your actions are my dreams;
You had a bastard by Polixenes,
And I but dream'd it. As you were past all shame,—
Those of your fact are so,—so past all truth:
Which to deny concerns more than avails; for as
Thy brat hath been cast out, like to itself,
No father owning it,—which is, indeed,
More criminal in thee than it,—so thou
Shalt feel our justice, in whose easiest passage
Look for no less than death.
Her. Sir, spare your threats:
The bug which you would fright me with I seek.
To me can life be no commodity:
The crown and comfort of my life, your favour,
I do give lost; for I do feel it gone,

67. *toward*] F_1F_2. *towards* F_3F_4. *friend*] F_1. *friends* $F_2F_3F_4$.
68. *Even*] *Ever* Long MS.
75, 76. *know What you*] *know what You* S. Walker conj., reading lines 75—77 as two lines, ending *know what...Sir.*
83. *fact*] *pack* Johnson conj. *sect* Farmer conj. *pact* Anon. conj. *fact are so,—so past*] *fact are) so you're past* Hanmer.
84. *Which to deny*] *To deny* Capell.
84, 85. *for as...itself*] As two lines in Steevens (1793), ending *as... itself.*
85. *brat hath been*] *brat's* Hanmer, reading *for as...itself* as one line. *like*] *left* Keightley conj.
90. *me*] *we* Capell (corrected in MS.).

But know not how it went. My second joy
And first-fruits of my body, from his presence
I am barr'd, like one infectious. My third comfort,
Starr'd most unluckily, is from my breast,
The innocent milk in it most innocent mouth,
Haled out to murder: myself on every post
Proclaimed a strumpet: with immodest hatred
The child-bed privilege denied, which 'longs
To women of all fashion; lastly, hurried
Here to this place, i' the open air, before
I have got strength of limit. Now, my liege,
Tell me what blessings I have here alive,
That I should fear to die? Therefore proceed.
But yet hear this; mistake me not; no life,
I prize it not a straw, but for mine honour,
Which I would free, if I shall be condemn'd
Upon surmises, all proofs sleeping else
But what your jealousies awake, I tell you
'Tis rigour and not law. Your honours all,
I do refer me to the oracle:
Apollo be my judge!

First Lord. This your request
Is altogether just: therefore bring forth,
And in Apollo's name, his oracle. [*Exeunt certain Officers.*

Her. The Emperor of Russia was my father:
O that he were alive, and here beholding
His daughter's trial! that he did but see
The flatness of my misery, yet with eyes
Of pity, not revenge!

Re-enter Officers, *with* CLEOMENES *and* DION.

Off. You here shall swear upon this sword of justice,
That you, Cleomenes and Dion, have

95. *And*] *The* Rowe (ed. 2).
96. *I am*] *I'm* Pope.
98. *it*] Ff. *its* Rowe. See note (VII).
100. *strumpet:...hatred*] *strumpet ...hatred;* Hanmer.
104. *limit*] $F_1 F_2$. *limbs* $F_3 F_4$. *limbs. And* Hanmer. *limb. And* Johnson conj.
107. *no life,*] *no! life,* Hanmer. *my life,* Grant White. *for life,* Keightley conj.
114. SCENE III. Pope.
116. [Exeunt...] Capell. om. Ff.
121. Re-enter...] Re-enter Officers, with C. and D., bringing in the Oracle. Capell. Enter Dion and Cleomenes. $F_2F_3F_4$ (at line 114). om. F_1.
122. *this*] F_1. *the* $F_2F_3F_4$.

Been both at Delphos, and from thence have brought
This seal'd-up oracle, by the hand deliver'd
Of great Apollo's priest and that since then
You have not dared to break the holy seal
Nor read the secrets in't.

Cleo. Dion. All this we swear.

Leon. Break up the seals and read.

Off. [*reads*] Hermione is chaste; Polixenes blameless; Camillo a true subject; Leontes a jealous tyrant; his innocent babe truly begotten; and the king shall live without an heir, if that which is lost be not found.

Lords. Now blessed be the great Apollo!

Her. Praised!

Leon. Hast thou read truth?

Off. Ay, my lord; even so
As it is here set down.

Leon. There is no truth at all i' the oracle:
The sessions shall proceed: this is mere falsehood.

Enter Servant.

Serv. My lord the king, the king!

Leon. What is the business?

Serv. O sir, I shall be hated to report it!
The prince your son, with mere conceit and fear
Of the queen's speed, is gone.

Leon. How! gone!

Serv. Is dead.

Leon. Apollo's angry; and the heavens themselves
Do strike at my injustice. [*Hermione faints.*] How now there!

Paul. This news is mortal to the queen: look down
And see what death is doing.

Leon. Take her hence:
Her heart is but o'ercharged; she will recover:

130. [reads] Capell.
chaste] *cast* F_2.
135, 136. *Ay...down*] Arranged as in Capell; as one line in Ff.
136. *it is*] om. Hanmer.
137. *truth*] *the truth* Hanmer. *true* Jervis conj.
138. *sessions*] *session* Theobald.
Enter Servant.] Rowe. om. Ff. Enter a Gentleman, hastily. Capell.
144. H. faints.] Rowe.
How now there!] *How now there?* Ff. *How now? there!* Johnson.

I have too much believed mine own suspicion:
Beseech you, tenderly apply to her
Some remedies for life.

[*Exeunt Paulina and Ladies, with Hermione.*

Apollo, pardon
My great profaneness 'gainst thine oracle!
I'll reconcile me to Polixenes;
New woo my queen; recall the good Camillo,
Whom I proclaim a man of truth, of mercy;
For, being transported by my jealousies
To bloody thoughts and to revenge, I chose
Camillo for the minister to poison
My friend Polixenes: which had been done,
But that the good mind of Camillo tardied
My swift command, though I with death and with
Reward did threaten and encourage him,
Not doing it and being done: he, most humane
And fill'd with honour, to my kingly guest
Unclasp'd my practice, quit his fortunes here,
Which you knew great, and to the hazard
Of all incertainties himself commended,
No richer than his honour: how he glisters
Thorough my rust! and how his piety
Does my deeds make the blacker!

Re-enter PAULINA.

Paul. Woe the while!
O, cut my lace, lest my heart, cracking it,
Break too!

First Lord. What fit is this, good lady?

Paul. What studied torments, tyrant, hast for me?
What wheels? racks? fires? what flaying? boiling?

148. SCENE IV. Pope.

150. [Exeunt...] Malone. Exeunt ... Rowe (after line 148). om. Ff.

165. *great*] *to be great* Anon. conj. *hazard*] F_1. *certain hazard* $F_2F_3F_4$. *fearful hazard* Rann conj. *doubtful hazard* Malone conj. *hazarding* Anon. conj.

168. *Thorough my*] Malone. *Through my* F_1. *Through my dark* $F_2F_3F_4$.

169. SCENE V. Pope. Re-enter P.] Re-enter P., hastily. Capell. Enter P. Rowe. om. Ff.

170. *lest*] F_3F_4. *least* F_1F_2.

171, 193, 213. First Lord.] 1. L. Capell. Lord. Ff.

173. *racks? fires?*] *what racks? what fires?* Keightley conj. *flaying? boiling?*] F_1. *flay-*

In leads or oils? what old or newer torture
Must I receive, whose every word deserves
To taste of thy most worst? Thy tyranny
Together working with thy jealousies,
Fancies too weak for boys, too green and idle
For girls of nine, O, think what they have done
And then run mad indeed, stark mad! for all
Thy by-gone fooleries were but spices of it.
That thou betray'dst Polixenes, 'twas nothing;
That did but show thee, of a fool, inconstant
And damnable ingrateful: nor was't much,
Thou wouldst have poison'd good Camillo's honour,
To have him kill a king; poor trespasses,
More monstrous standing by: whereof I reckon
The casting forth to crows thy baby-daughter
To be or none or little; though a devil
Would have shed water out of fire ere done't:
Nor is't directly laid to thee, the death
Of the young prince, whose honourable thoughts,
Thoughts high for one so tender, cleft the heart
That could conceive a gross and foolish sire
Blemish'd his gracious dam: this is not, no,
Laid to thy answer: but the last,—O lords,
When I have said, cry 'woe!'—the queen, the queen,
The sweet'st, dear'st creature's dead, and vengeance for't
Not dropp'd down yet.

First Lord. The higher powers forbid!

Paul. I say she's dead, I'll swear't. If word nor oath
Prevail not, go and see: if you can bring
Tincture or lustre in her lip, her eye,
Heat outwardly or breath within, I'll serve you

ing? boyling? burning, $F_2F_3F_4$. *flaying, rather! boiling* Capell. *flaying, burning, boiling* Collier MS.

174. *leads or oils*] *lead or oil* S. Walker conj.

newer] F_1. *new* $F_2F_3F_4$.

175. *every*] F_1. *very* $F_2F_3F_4$.

181. *but*] om. Theobald.

of] F_1. *for* $F_2F_3F_4$.

183. *thee, of a fool,*] Ff. *thee of a soul* Theobald. *thee off, a fool,* Warburton.

184. *damnable*] *damnably* Long MS.

ingrateful] *ungrateful* Rann.

188. *to crows*] *of crows* F_4.

thy] F_1. *the* $F_2F_3F_4$.

198. *sweet'st, dear'st*] *sweetest* Hanmer.

As I would do the gods. But, O thou tyrant!
Do not repent these things, for they are heavier
Than all thy woes can stir: therefore betake thee
To nothing but despair. A thousand knees
Ten thousand years together, naked, fasting,
Upon a barren mountain, and still winter
In storm perpetual, could not move the gods
To look that way thou wert.

Leon. Go on, go on:
Thou canst not speak too much; I have deserved
All tongues to talk their bitterest.

First Lord. Say no more:
Howe'er the business goes, you have made fault
I' the boldness of your speech.

Paul. I am sorry for't:
All faults I make, when I shall come to know them,
I do repent. Alas! I have show'd too much
The rashness of a woman: he is touch'd
To the noble heart. What's gone and what's past help
Should be past grief: do not receive affliction
At my petition; I beseech you, rather
Let me be punish'd, that have minded you
Of what you should forget. Now, good my liege,
Sir, royal sir, forgive a foolish woman:
The love I bore your queen, lo, fool again!
I'll speak of her no more, nor of your children;
I'll not remember you of my own lord,
Who is lost too: take your patience to you,
And I'll say nothing.

Leon. Thou didst speak but well
When most the truth; which I receive much better

205. *Do*] F_1. *Dot* F_2. *Dost* $F_3 F_4$.

205, 206. *Do...stir:*] *Dost...stir?* Pope.

206. *woes*] *vows* Hanmer.

217. *I have*] *I've* Pope.

220. *receive*] *revive* Staunton conj.

221. *my petition*] *my relation* Singer conj. *repetition* Collier (Collier MS.). *petition;...you,*] F_1. *petition, ...you,* F_2 F_3 F_4. *petition,......you;* Rowe.

228. *Who is*] *Who's* S. Walker conj. *take your*] *take you your* Rowe (ed. 2).

228, 229. *to you, And I'll*] *to you, and I will* S. Walker conj. *to you, sir, And I'll* Keightley conj.

Than to be pitied of thee. Prithee, bring me
To the dead bodies of my queen and son:
One grave shall be for both; upon them shall
The causes of their death appear, unto
Our shame perpetual. Once a day I'll visit
The chapel where they lie, and tears shed there
Shall be my recreation: so long as nature
Will bear up with this exercise, so long
I daily vow to use it. Come and lead me
To these sorrows. [*Exeunt.*

SCENE III. *Bohemia. A desert country near the sea.*

Enter ANTIGONUS *with a Child, and a* Mariner.

Ant. Thou art perfect, then, our ship hath touch'd upon
The deserts of Bohemia?
Mar. Ay, my lord; and fear
We have landed in ill time: the skies look grimly
And threaten present blusters. In my conscience,
The heavens with that we have in hand are angry
And frown upon 's.
Ant. Their sacred wills be done! Go, get aboard;
Look to thy bark: I'll not be long before
I call upon thee.
Mar. Make your best haste, and go not
Too far i' the land: 'tis like to be loud weather;
Besides, this place is famous for the creatures
Of prey that keep upon't.
Ant. Go thou away:

238—240. *Will...sorrows*] Johnson ends these lines at *exercise...come,...sorrows.*

240. *To*] *Unto* S. Walker conj.
sorrows] *my sorrows* Hanmer.

SCENE III.] SCENE VI. Pope.
Bohemia. A desert...] Malone. om. Ff. A desert Country; the Sea at a little distance. Rowe.

Enter A...] Rowe. Enter Antigonus, a Mariner, Babe, Shepherd, and Clown. Ff.

2. *my lord*] om. Hanmer.

3. *We have*] *We've* Pope.

6. *upon's*] *upon us* Capell.
Go, get] *go get* F_1. *get* $F_2F_3F_4$. *get thee* Rowe.

9. *upon*] *on* Hanmer.

I'll follow instantly.
Mar. I am glad at heart
To be so rid o' the business. [*Exit.*
Ant. Come, poor babe:
I have heard, but not believed, the spirits o' the dead
May walk again: if such thing be, thy mother
Appear'd to me last night, for ne'er was dream
So like a waking. To me comes a creature,
Sometimes her head on one side, some another;
I never saw a vessel of like sorrow,
So fill'd and so becoming: in pure white robes,
Like very sanctity, she did approach
My cabin where I lay; thrice bow'd before me,
And gasping to begin some speech, her eyes
Became two spouts: the fury spent, anon
Did this break from her: 'Good Antigonus,
Since fate, against thy better disposition,
Hath made thy person for the thrower-out
Of my poor babe, according to thine oath,
Places remote enough are in Bohemia,
There weep and leave it crying; and, for the babe
Is counted lost for ever, Perdita,
I prithee, call't. For this ungentle business,
Put on thee by my lord, thou ne'er shalt see
Thy wife Paulina more.' And so, with shrieks,
She melted into air. Affrighted much,
I did in time collect myself, and thought
This was so and no slumber. Dreams are toys:
Yet for this once, yea, superstitiously,
I will be squared by this. I do believe
Hermione hath suffer'd death; and that
Apollo would, this being indeed the issue
Of King Polixenes, it should here be laid,

14. *I am*] *I'm* Pope.
19. *a waking*] *awaking* Anon. conj.
20. *on*] F_1. *is on* $F_2F_3F_4$.
some] *some'* Capell.
another] *on other* Anon. conj.
22. *becoming*] *becomming* F_1. *o'er-running* Collier (Collier MS.).
29. *thrower-out*] *thower-out* F_1.
32. *weep*] *wend* Collier (Collier MS.).
39. *so*] *sooth* Warburton conj.
44. *Polixenes*] *Polexenus* F_2.

Either for life or death, upon the earth
Of its right father. Blossom, speed thee well!
There lie, and there thy character: there these;
Which may, if fortune please, both breed thee, pretty,
And still rest thine. The storm begins: poor wretch,
That for thy mother's fault art thus exposed
To loss and what may follow! Weep I cannot,
But my heart bleeds; and most accursed am I
To be by oath enjoin'd to this. Farewell!
The day frowns more and more: thou'rt like to have
A lullaby too rough: I never saw
The heavens so dim by day. A savage clamour!
Well may I get aboard! This is the chase:
I am gone for ever. [*Exit, pursued by a bear.*

Enter a Shepherd.

Shep. I would there were no age between ten and three-and-twenty, or that youth would sleep out the rest; for there is nothing in the between but getting wenches with child, wronging the ancientry, stealing, fighting—Hark you now! Would any but these boiled brains of nineteen and two-and-twenty hunt this weather? They have scared away two of my best sheep, which I fear the wolf will sooner find than the master: if any where I have them, 'tis by the sea-side, browzing of ivy. Good luck, an't be thy will! what have we here? Mercy on's, a barne; a very pretty barne! A boy or a child, I wonder? A pretty one; a very pretty one: sure, some scape: though I am not bookish, yet I can read waiting-gentlewoman in the scape. This has been some stair-work, some trunk-work, some behind-door-

46. *its*] *it's* Ff.
[Laying down the child. Rowe.
47. [Laying down a bundle. Johnson.
48. *please...pretty*] *please, both breed thee (pretty)* Ff. *please, both breed thee pretty*, Reed (1813). *please both breed thee, (pretty!)* Staunton.
pretty] *pretty one* Rowe.
54. *thou'rt*] *thou art* F_4.
58. Enter...] Ff. Enter an old Shepherd. Rowe. Enter a Shepherd. Crooke. Collier MS.
59. SCENE VII. Pope.
ten] *thirteen* Hanmer. *sixteen* Edd. conj. See note (X).
64. *scared*] *scarr'd* Ff.
67. *an't*] Pope (ed. 2). *and 't* Ff.
thy will] F_1. *the will* $F_2F_3F_4$.
68. *here?*] *here?* [taking up the child. Rowe.
69. *boy*] *god* Grant White.
child] *maid-child* Keightley conj.

work: they were warmer that got this than the poor thing is here. I'll take it up for pity: yet I'll tarry till my son come; he hallooed but even now. Whoa, ho, hoa!

Enter Clown.

Clo. Hilloa, loa!

Shep. What, art so near? If thou'lt see a thing to talk on when thou art dead and rotten, come hither. What ailest thou, man?

Clo. I have seen two such sights, by sea and by land! but I am not to say it is a sea, for it is now the sky: betwixt the firmament and it you cannot thrust a bodkin's point.

Shep. Why, boy, how is it?

Clo. I would you did but see how it chafes, how it rages, how it takes up the shore! but that's not to the point. O, the most piteous cry of the poor souls! sometimes to see 'em, and not to see 'em; now the ship boring the moon with her main-mast, and anon swallowed with yest and froth, as you'ld thrust a cork into a hogshead. And then for the land-service, to see how the bear tore out his shoulder-bone; how he cried to me for help and said his name was Antigonus, a nobleman. But to make an end of the ship, to see how the sea flap-dragoned it: but, first, how the poor souls roared, and the sea mocked them; and how the poor gentleman roared and the bear mocked him, both roaring louder than the sea or weather.

Shep. Name of mercy, when was this, boy?

Clo. Now, now: I have not winked since I saw these sights: the men are not yet cold under water, nor the bear half dined on the gentleman: he's at it now.

Shep. Would I had been by, to have helped the old man!

75. *hallooed*] *hallow'd* F_1 F_2 F_3. *hollow'd* F_4.

76. Enter Clown.] Ff. Dyce puts it after *hither*, line 78.

Clo.] Clo. [within. Dyce. Clo. [without. Staunton.

85. *takes*] *rakes* Hanmer.

87. *and not*] *and then not* Capell.

89. *for*] om. Rowe (ed. 2).

89, 90. *for the land-service*] *the land-service* Rowe (ed. 2). *the land-sight* Hanmer.

100. *gentleman*] *old gentleman* Malone conj.

101. *the old man*] *the nobleman* Theobald. *tho' old man* Jackson conj.

Clo. I would you had been by the ship side, to have helped her: there your charity would have lacked footing.

Shep. Heavy matters! heavy matters! but look thee here, boy. Now bless thyself: thou mettest with things dying, I with things new-born. Here's a sight for thee; look thee, a bearing-cloth for a squire's child! look thee here; take up, take up, boy; open't. So, let's see: it was told me I should be rich by the fairies. This is some changeling: open't. What's within, boy?

Clo. You're a made old man: if the sins of your youth are forgiven you, you're well to live. Gold! all gold!

Shep. This is fairy gold, boy, and 'twill prove so: up with't, keep it close: home, home, the next way. We are lucky, boy; and to be so still requires nothing but secrecy. Let my sheep go: come, good boy, the next way home.

Clo. Go you the next way with your findings. I'll go see if the bear be gone from the gentleman and how much he hath eaten: they are never curst but when they are hungry: if there be any of him left, I'll bury it.

Shep. That's a good deed. If thou mayest discern by that which is left of him what he is, fetch me to the sight of him.

Clo. Marry, will I; and you shall help to put him i'the ground.

Shep. 'Tis a lucky day, boy, and we'll do good deeds on't. [*Exeunt.*

102. *would*] *would not* Theobald conj.

ship] *ship's* Collier.

103. [Aside. Theobald.

105. *mettest*] *met'st* $F_1F_2F_3$. *meet'st* F_4.

111. *made*] Theobald (L. H. conj.). *mad* Ff.

112. *you're*] *you are* F_4.

113. *'twill*] *will* Theobald.

114. *with't*] *with it* Rowe (ed. 2).

122. *sight*] *fight* F_1. See note (XI).

ACT IV. SCENE I.

Enter TIME, *the* Chorus.

Time. I, that please some, try all, both joy and terror
Of good and bad, that makes and unfolds error,
Now take upon me, in the name of Time,
To use my wings. Impute it not a crime
To me or my swift passage, that I slide
O'er sixteen years and leave the growth untried
Of that wide gap, since it is in my power
To o'erthrow law and in one self-born hour
To plant and o'erwhelm custom. Let me pass
The same I am, ere ancient'st order was
Or what is now received: I witness to
The times that brought them in; so shall I do
To the freshest things now reigning and make stale
The glistering of this present, as my tale
Now seems to it. Your patience this allowing,
I turn my glass and give my scene such growing
As you had slept between: Leontes leaving,
The effects of his fond jealousies so grieving
That he shuts up himself, imagine me,
Gentle spectators, that I now may be
In fair Bohemia; and remember well,
I mentioned a son o' the king's, which Florizel
I now name to you; and with speed so pace
To speak of Perdita, now grown in grace
Equal with wondering: what of her ensues

ACT IV. SCENE I.] Actus Quartus, Scena Prima. Ff. om. Warburton. ACT IV. Capell. See note (XII).

1—32. Spurious. Heath conj.

2. *makes and unfolds*] Ff. *make and unfold* Rowe. *mask and unfold* Theobald.

6. *growth*] *gulf* Warburton.

7—9. *gap, since......custom. Let*] *gap. Since...custom, let* Lloyd conj.

11. *witness*] *witness'd* Capell.

17, 18, 19. *leaving,...jealousies...himself, imagine*] *leaving,—jealousies ...himself;—imagine* Staunton. *leaving ...jealousies,...himself. Imagine* F_1. *leaving...jealousies,...himself, imagine* $F_2F_3F_4$.

18. *The*] *To the* Keightley conj.

19, 20. *imagine me,...that I*] *imagine we.. that you* Johnson conj.

22. *I mentioned*] F_1. *I mention here* $F_2F_3F_4$. *There is* Hanmer. *I mention'd* Capell.

which] *whom* Pope.

I list not prophesy; but let Time's news
Be known when 'tis brought forth. A shepherd's daughter,
And what to her adheres, which follows after,
Is the argument of Time. Of this allow,
If ever you have spent time worse ere now;
If never, yet that Time himself doth say
He wishes earnestly you never may. [*Exit.*

SCENE II. *Bohemia. The palace of* POLIXENES.

Enter POLIXENES *and* CAMILLO.

Pol. I pray thee, good Camillo, be no more importunate: 'tis a sickness denying thee any thing; a death to grant this.

Cam. It is fifteen years since I saw my country: though I have for the most part been aired abroad, I desire to lay my bones there. Besides, the penitent king, my master, hath sent for me; to whose feeling sorrows I might be some allay, or I o'erween to think so, which is another spur to my departure.

Pol. As thou lovest me, Camillo, wipe not out the rest of thy services by leaving me now: the need I have of thee, thine own goodness hath made; better not to have had thee than thus to want thee: thou, having made me businesses, which none without thee can sufficiently manage, must either stay to execute them thyself, or take away with thee the very services thou hast done; which if I have not enough considered, as too much I cannot, to be more thankful to thee shall be my study; and my profit therein, the heaping friendships. Of that fatal country, Sicilia, prithee speak no more; whose very naming punishes me with the remembrance of that penitent, as thou callest him, and reconciled

SCENE II.] Scena Secunda. Ff.
The palace of Polixenes.] ? Court of Bohemia. Pope. A room in Polixenes' Palace. Capell.
3. *fifteen*] *sixteen* Hanmer.
12. *businesses*] *business* Rowe (ed. 2).
17. *my*] *thy* Long MS.
17, 18. *heaping friendships*] *heaping friendship* Hanmer. *reaping friendships* Warburton.

king, my brother; whose loss of his most precious queen and children are even now to be afresh lamented. Say to me, when sawest thou the Prince Florizel, my son? Kings are no less unhappy, their issue not being gracious, than they are in losing them when they have approved their virtues.

Cam. Sir, it is three days since I saw the prince. What his happier affairs may be, are to me unknown: but I have missingly noted, he is of late much retired from court and is less frequent to his princely exercises than formerly he hath appeared.

Pol. I have considered so much, Camillo, and with some care; so far, that I have eyes under my service which look upon his removedness; from whom I have this intelligence, that he is seldom from the house of a most homely shepherd; a man, they say, that from very nothing, and beyond the imagination of his neighbours, is grown into an unspeakable estate.

Cam. I have heard, sir, of such a man, who hath a daughter of most rare note: the report of her is extended more than can be thought to begin from such a cottage.

Pol. That's likewise part of my intelligence; but, I fear, the angle that plucks our son thither. Thou shalt accompany us to the place; where we will, not appearing what we are, have some question with the shepherd; from whose simplicity I think it not uneasy to get the cause of my son's resort thither. Prithee, be my present partner in this business, and lay aside the thoughts of Sicilia.

Cam. I willingly obey your command.

Pol. My best Camillo! We must disguise ourselves.
[*Exeunt.*

28. *missingly*] (*missingly*) Ff. *musingly* Hanmer. *missing him* Warburton.

32. *care; so far,*] Capell. *care, so farre,* $F_1F_1F_3$. *care so far,* F_4.

41. *part*] *a part* Theobald.

41, 42. *but, I fear, the angle*] *but* (*I fear*) *the Angle* Ff. *and, I fear, the Engle* Theobald. *and, I fear, the angle* Hanmer. *but, I fear the angle* Steevens.

46. *thither*] *thether* F_1.

49. Exeunt.] Rowe. Exit. Ff.

SCENE III. *A road near the* Shepherd's *cottage.*

Enter AUTOLYCUS, *singing.*

When daffodils begin to peer,
With heigh! the doxy over the dale,
Why, then comes in the sweet o' the year;
For the red blood reigns in the winter's pale.

The white sheet bleaching on the hedge,
With heigh! the sweet birds, O, how they sing!
Doth set my pugging tooth on edge;
For a quart of ale is a dish for a king.

The lark, that tirra-lyra chants,
With heigh! with heigh! the thrush and the jay,
Are summer songs for me and my aunts,
While we lie tumbling in the hay.

I have served Prince Florizel and in my time wore three-pile; but now I am out of service:

But shall I go mourn for that, my dear?
The pale moon shines by night:
And when I wander here and there,
I then do most go right.

If tinkers may have leave to live,
And bear the sow-skin budget,
Then my account I well may give,
And in the stocks avouch it.

SCENE III.] Scena Tertia. Ff. SCENE II. Warburton.

A road...] Malone. om. Ff. The country. Pope. Fields near the Shepherd's. Capell.

1. *daffodils*] Johnson. *daffadils* Ff.

3, 4. *comes...For...reigns in the winter's*] *comes...For...reigns o'er the winter's* Hanmer. *come...'Fore...reins in the winter* Warburton. *comes...For ...runs in the winter* Thirlby conj. *comes......For......runs in the winters* Mason conj.

6. *heigh*] *hey* Ff.

7. *pugging*] *progging* Hanmer. *prigging* Collier MS.

on] Theobald. *an* Ff.

9. *that*] *with* Rowe (ed. 2).

tirra-lyra] *tirra-Lyra* $F_1 F_2$. *tirra Lyra* F_3. *tirra Lycra* F_4.

10. *With heigh! with heigh!*] *With heigh, with heigh* $F_2F_3F_4$. *With heigh,* F_1. *With heigh ho!* S. Walker conj.

18. *most go*] *go most* Pope.

20. *sow-skin*] *show-skin?* F_4.

budget] Rowe. *bowget* Ff.

My traffic is sheets; when the kite builds, look to lesser linen. My father named me Autolycus; who being, as I am, littered under Mercury, was likewise a snapper-up of unconsidered trifles. With die and drab I purchased this caparison, and my revenue is the silly cheat. Gallows and knock are too powerful on the highway: beating and hanging are terrors to me: for the life to come, I sleep out the thought of it. A prize! a prize!

Enter Clown.

Clo. Let me see: every 'leven wether tods; every tod yields pound and odd shilling; fifteen hundred shorn, what comes the wool to?

Aut. [*Aside*] If the springe hold, the cock's mine.

Clo. I cannot do't without counters. Let me see; what am I to buy for our sheep-shearing feast? Three pound of sugar; five pound of currants; rice—what will this sister of mine do with rice? But my father hath made her mistress of the feast, and she lays it on. She hath made me four and twenty nosegays for the shearers, three-man songmen all, and very good ones; but they are most of them means and bases; but one puritan amongst them, and he sings psalms to hornpipes. I must have saffron to colour the warden pies; mace; dates, none, that's out of my note; nutmegs, seven; a race or two of ginger, but that I may beg; four pound of prunes, and as many of raisins o' the sun.

Aut. O that ever I was born! [*Grovelling on the ground.*

24, 25. *Autolycus; who...was likewise*] *Autolicus, being littered under Mercury, who, as I am, was likewise* Theobald.

26. *this*] F_1. om. $F_2F_3F_4$.

27. *silly*] *sly* Hanmer.

28. *knock*] *knocks* Hanmer.

28, 29. *beating and hanging*] *hanging and beating* Collier conj.

31. SCENE III. Warburton.

'leven wether] *'leven weather* Capell. *Leaven-weather* Ff. *eleven weather* Rowe. *eleventh weather* Hanmer. *living wether* Malone conj.

tod] F_1. *told* $F_2F_3F_4$.

32. *pound and odd*] *a pound and one odd* Hanmer.

34. [Aside] Rowe.

35. *counters*] Capell. *compters* Ff.

37. *sugar*] *sugar* [reading out of a Note. Capell.

currants] Rowe. *currence* Ff.

40. *three-man*] *they're men* or *they're main* or *thrum-men* Theobald conj.

42. *amongst*] *among* F_4.

46. *prunes*] Pope. *Prewyns* Ff. *pruns* Rowe (ed. 1). *pruins* Id. (ed. 2).

raisins] Pope. *reysons* F_1F_2. *reasons* F_3F_4. *rasins* Rowe.

47. [Grovelling...] Rowe.

Clo. I' the name of me—

Aut. O, help me, help me! pluck but off these rags; and then, death, death!

Clo. Alack, poor soul! thou hast need of more rags to lay on thee, rather than have these off.

Aut. O sir, the loathsomeness of them offends me more than the stripes I have received, which are mighty ones and millions.

Clo. Alas, poor man! a million of beating may come to a great matter.

Aut. I am robbed, sir, and beaten; my money and apparel ta'en from me, and these detestable things put upon me.

Clo. What, by a horseman, or a footman?

Aut. A footman, sweet sir, a footman.

Clo. Indeed, he should be a footman by the garments he has left with thee: if this be a horseman's coat, it hath seen very hot service. Lend me thy hand, I'll help thee: come, lend me thy hand.

Aut. O, good sir, tenderly, O!

Clo. Alas, poor soul!

Aut. O, good sir, softly, good sir! I fear, sir, my shoulder-blade is out.

Clo. How now! canst stand?

Aut. Softly, dear sir [*picks his pocket*]; good sir, softly. You ha' done me a charitable office.

Clo. Dost lack any money? I have a little money for thee.

Aut. No, good sweet sir; no, I beseech you, sir: I have a kinsman not past three quarters of a mile hence, unto whom I was going; I shall there have money, or any thing I want: offer me no money, I pray you; that kills my heart.

Clo. What manner of fellow was he that robbed you?

Aut. A fellow, sir, that I have known to go about with troll-my-dames: I knew him once a servant of the prince:

48. *me—*] Rowe. *me.* Ff. *the—* Theobald conj. om. Johnson conj. See note (XIII).

53. *offends*] $F_2F_3F_4$. *offend* F_1.

59. *detestable*] *derestable* F_1.

65. [Helping... Rowe. om. Ff.

71. [picks......] Capell. om. Ff. Cuts his purse. Collier (Collier MS.).

72. *ha'*] *ha* Ff.

81. *troll-my-dames*] *troll-madams* Hanmer.

him] *him him* F_2.

I cannot tell, good sir, for which of his virtues it was, but he was certainly whipped out of the court.

Clo. His vices, you would say; there's no virtue whipped out of the court: they cherish it to make it stay there; and yet it will no more but abide.

Aut. Vices I would say, sir. I know this man well: he hath been since an ape-bearer; then a process-server, a bailiff; then he compassed a motion of the Prodigal Son, and married a tinker's wife within a mile where my land and living lies; and, having flown over many knavish professions, he settled only in rogue: some call him Autolycus.

Clo. Out upon him! prig, for my life, prig: he haunts wakes, fairs and bear-baitings.

Aut. Very true, sir; he, sir, he; that's the rogue that put me into this apparel.

Clo. Not a more cowardly rogue in all Bohemia: if you had but looked big and spit at him, he'ld have run.

Aut. I must confess to you, sir, I am no fighter: I am false of heart that way; and that he knew, I warrant him.

Clo. How do you now?

Aut. Sweet sir, much better than I was; I can stand and walk: I will even take my leave of you, and pace softly towards my kinsman's.

Clo. Shall I bring thee on the way?

Aut. No, good-faced sir; no, sweet sir.

Clo. Then fare thee well: I must go buy spices for our sheep-shearing.

Aut. Prosper you, sweet sir! [*Exit Clown.*] Your purse is not hot enough to purchase your spice. I'll be with you at your sheep-shearing too: if I make not this cheat bring out another and the shearers prove sheep, let me be unrolled and my name put in the book of virtue!

89. *a bailiff*] *to a bailiff* Edd. conj.

compassed] *compos'd* Long MS.

90. *where*] *of where* Keightley conj.

92. *rogue*] *a rogue* Warburton.

101. *do you*] *do you do* F_4.

105. *the way*] *thy way* F_4.

107. *fare thee well*] *fartheewell* F_1. *farewell* F_2. *farewel* F_3F_4.

buy] F_1. *to buy* $F_2F_3F_4$.

109. [Exit Clown.] Capell. Exit. Ff (after line 108).

112, 113. *unrolled*] *unrold* Ff. *enrolled* Collier (Collier MS.). *unrogued* W. N. L. (N. and Q.). conj.

Song. Jog on, jog on, the foot-path way,
And merrily hent the stile-a:
A merry heart goes all the day,
Your sad tires in a mile-a. [*Exit.*

SCENE IV. *The* Shepherd's *cottage.*

Enter FLORIZEL *and* PERDITA.

Flo. These your unusual weeds to each part of you
Do give a life: no shepherdess, but Flora
Peering in April's front. This your sheep-shearing
Is as a meeting of the petty gods,
And you the queen on't.
Per. Sir, my gracious lord,
To chide at your extremes it not becomes me:
O, pardon, that I name them! Your high self,
The gracious mark o' the land, you have obscured
With a swain's wearing, and me, poor lowly maid,
Most goddess-like prank'd up: but that our feasts
In every mess have folly and the feeders
Digest it with a custom, I should blush
To see you so attired, sworn, I think,

115. *hent*] *hend* Hanmer.

115—117. *stile-a...mile-a*] *stile, o... mile, o* The Dancing Master (1650). *stil-e...mil-e* Lewis conj.

SCENE IV.] SCENE III. Capell.

The Shepherd's cottage.] The prospect of a Shepherd's Cotte. Theobald. A Room in the Shepherd's House. Capell.

Enter F. and P.] Rowe. Enter F., P., Shepherd, Clowne, Polixenes, Camillo, Mopsa, Dorcas, Servants, Autolicus. Ff.

2. *Do*] Theobald. *Do's* Ff. *Does* Rowe.

4. *Is as*] *Is* Rowe.

a meeting] F_1. *a merry meeting* $F_2F_3F_4$.

5. *Sir*] *Sure* Collier (Collier MS.).

12. *Digest it*] $F_2F_3F_4$. *Digest* F_1.

12, 13. *custom, I should blush... think,*] *custom* (*sworn I think*) *To see you so attired, I should blush* Steevens conj.

13. *sworn*] F_3F_4. *sworne* F_1F_2. *swoon* Hanmer (Theobald conj.). *scorn* Mitford conj. *so worn* Collier (Jackson conj.).

13, 14. *sworn, I think...glass*] *swoon, I think, To see myself i' the glass* Theobald conj. *and more I think... a glass* Ingleby conj. *frown, I think, ...a glass* or *sorely shrink...i' th' glass* or *more, I think...a glass* or *more, I think...i' th' glass* Bailey conj.

To show myself a glass.
Flo. I bless the time
When my good falcon made her flight across
Thy father's ground.
Per. Now Jove afford you cause!
To me the difference forges dread; your greatness
Hath not been used to fear. Even now I tremble
To think your father, by some accident,
Should pass this way as you did: O, the Fates!
How would he look, to see his work, so noble,
Vilely bound up? What would he say? Or how
Should I, in these my borrow'd flaunts, behold
The sternness of his presence?
Flo. Apprehend
Nothing but jollity. The gods themselves,
Humbling their deities to love, have taken
The shapes of beasts upon them: Jupiter
Became a bull, and bellow'd; the green Neptune
A ram, and bleated; and the fire-robed god,
Golden Apollo, a poor humble swain,
As I seem now. Their transformations
Were never for a piece of beauty rarer,
Nor in a way so chaste, since my desires
Run not before mine honour, nor my lusts
Burn hotter than my faith.
Per. O, but, sir,
Your resolution cannot hold, when 'tis
Opposed, as it must be, by the power of the king:
One of these two must be necessities,
Which then will speak, that you must change this purpose,
Or I my life.
Flo. Thou dearest Perdita,

22. *Vilely*] Hanmer. *Vildly* Ff.
28. *the green*] *sea green* Anon. conj.
31, 32. *now. Their...beauty rarer,*] Rowe. *now. Their...beauty, rarer,* Ff. *now:—Their ... beauty rarer,—* Dyce.
33. *in a way*] *any way* Collier (Ritson conj.).
35. *faith*] *faith does* Keightley conj.
sir] F_1. *deere sir* F_2. *dear sir* F_3F_4.
38. *must be necessities*] *necessities must be* Hanmer.
40. *dearest*] F_3F_4. *deer'st* F_1. *deerest* F_2.

With these forced thoughts, I prithee, darken not
The mirth o' the feast. Or I'll be thine, my fair,
Or not my father's. For I cannot be
Mine own, nor any thing to any, if
I be not thine. To this I am most constant,
Though destiny say no. Be merry, gentle;
Strangle such thoughts as these with any thing
That you behold the while. Your guests are coming:
Lift up your countenance, as it were the day
Of celebration of that nuptial which
We two have sworn shall come.

Per. O lady Fortune,
Stand you auspicious!

Flo. See, your guests approach:
Address yourself to entertain them sprightly,
And let's be red with mirth.

Enter Shepherd, Clown, MOPSA, DORCAS, *and others, with* POLIXENES *and* CAMILLO *disguised.*

Shep. Fie, daughter! when my old wife lived, upon
This day she was both pantler, butler, cook,
Both dame and servant; welcomed all, served all;
Would sing her song and dance her turn; now here,
At upper end o' the table, now i' the middle;
On his shoulder, and his; her face o' fire
With labour and the thing she took to quench it,
She would to each one sip. You are retired,
As if you were a feasted one and not
The hostess of the meeting: pray you, bid
These unknown friends to's welcome; for it is
A way to make us better friends, more known.
Come, quench your blushes and present yourself
That which you are, mistress o' the feast: come on,

46. *gentle*] *gentlest* Hanmer. *girl* Collier (Collier MS.).
49. *your*] *you* F_4.
it were] *'twere* Pope.
54. Enter...] Enter All. $F_2F_3F_4$ (after *auspicious!* line 52). om. F_1.
55. SCENE V. Pope.
60. *and*] *and on* Keightley conj.
61. *thing*] *things* F_4.
68. *come on*] Pol. *Come on* Theobald conj.

And bid us welcome to your sheep-shearing,
As your good flock shall prosper.
Per. [*To Pol.*] Sir, welcome:
It is my father's will I should take on me
The hostess-ship o' the day. [*To Cam.*] You're welcome, sir.
Give me those flowers there, Dorcas. Reverend sirs,
For you there's rosemary and rue; these keep
Seeming and savour all the winter long:
Grace and remembrance be to you both,
And welcome to our shearing!
Pol. Shepherdess,
A fair one are you, well you fit our ages
With flowers of winter.
Per. Sir, the year growing ancient,
Not yet on summer's death, nor on the birth
Of trembling winter, the fairest flowers o' the season
Are our carnations and streak'd gillyvors,
Which some call nature's bastards: of that kind
Our rustic garden's barren; and I care not
To get slips of them.
Pol. Wherefore, gentle maiden,
Do you neglect them?
Per. For I have heard it said
There is an art which in their piedness shares
With great creating nature.
Pol. Say there be;
Yet nature is made better by no mean,
But nature makes that mean: so, over that art
Which you say adds to nature, is an art
That nature makes. You see, sweet maid, we marry

70. [To Pol.] *Sir, welcome*] Malone. *Sir, welcome*, Ff. *Sirs, welcome* [To Polix. and Cam. Rowe. *Sirs, you're welcome* [To Pol. and Cam. Hanmer. *Welcome, sir* Capell.

72. [To Cam.] Malone.

sir] *sirs* Rowe.

76. *to you*] *unto you* Pope.

78, 79. *well...winter.*] *will...winter?* Staunton conj.

81. *fairest*] *fair'st* S. Walker conj.

82. *gillyvors*] *Gilly-vors* Ff. *gilly-flowers* Rowe. See note (XIV).

83. *call*] *cail* F_2.

84. *garden's*] F_2 F_3 F_4. *gardens* F_1.

90. *over*] *o'er* Capell. *ever* or *e'er* Anon. conj. *even* Craik conj.

A gentler scion to the wildest stock,
And make conceive a bark of baser kind
By bud of nobler race: this is an art
Which does mend nature, change it rather, but
The art itself is nature.

Per. So it is.

Pol. Then make your garden rich in gillyvors,
And do not call them bastards.

Per. I'll not put
The dibble in earth to set one slip of them;
No more than were I painted I would wish
This youth should say 'twere well, and only therefore
Desire to breed by me. Here's flowers for you;
Hot lavender, mints, savory, marjoram;
The marigold, that goes to bed wi' the sun
And with him rises weeping: these are flowers
Of middle summer, and I think they are given
To men of middle age. You're very welcome.

Cam. I should leave grazing, were I of your flock,
And only live by gazing.

Per. Out, alas!
You'ld be so lean, that blasts of January
Would blow you through and through. Now, my fair'st friend,
I would I had some flowers o' the spring that might
Become your time of day; and yours, and yours,
That wear upon your virgin branches yet
Your maidenheads growing: O Proserpina,
For the flowers now, that frighted thou let'st fall
From Dis's waggon! daffodils,
That come before the swallow dares, and take

93. *scion*] Steevens (1793). *sien* Ff. *scyon* Pope. *scyen* Capell. *cyon* Steevens (1778).
wildest] *wilder* Anon. conj.
98. *your*] *you* F_1.
gillyvors] *Gilly 'vors* Ff. *gillyflowers* Rowe.
104. *mints*] *mint* S. Walker conj. (withdrawn).
105. *wi' the*] Capell. *with'* Ff. *with th'* Rowe.
108. *You're*] *Y'are* Ff.
very welcome] *welcome* F_4.
112. *my fair'st friend*] Ff. *my fairest friends* Rowe (ed. 2). *fairest friend* Hanmer.
118. *Dis's*] *Dysses* F_1. *Disses* $F_2F_3F_4$.
daffodils] *early daffadils* Hanmer. *golden daffodils* Coleridge conj. *yellow daffodils* Keightley conj.

The winds of March with beauty; violets dim
But sweeter than the lids of Juno's eyes
Or Cytherea's breath; pale primroses,
That die unmarried, ere they can behold
Bright Phœbus in his strength, a malady
Most incident to maids; bold oxlips and
The crown imperial; lilies of all kinds,
The flower-de-luce being one! O, these I lack,
To make you garlands of; and my sweet friend,
To strew him o'er and o'er!

Flo. What, like a corse?

Per. No, like a bank for love to lie and play on;
Not like a corse; or if, not to be buried,
But quick and in mine arms. Come, take your flowers:
Methinks I play as I have seen them do
In Whitsun pastorals: sure this robe of mine
Does change my disposition.

Flo. What you do
Still betters what is done. When you speak, sweet,
I'ld have you do it ever: when you sing,
I'ld have you buy and sell so, so give alms,
Pray so; and, for the ordering your affairs,
To sing them too: when you do dance, I wish you
A wave o' the sea, that you might ever do
Nothing but that; move still, still so,
And own no other function: each your doing,
So singular in each particular,
Crowns what you are doing in the present deeds,
That all your acts are queens.

Per. O Doricles,
Your praises are too large: but that your youth,
And the true blood which peeps fairly through 't,

125. *bold*] *gold* Hanmer.

127. *flower-de-luce*] *flower-de-lis* Rowe.

134. *Whitsun*] Johnson. *Whitson* Ff. *Whitsund'* Hanmer.

137, 138. *I'ld*] $F_1F_2F_3$. *I'le* F_4. *I'll* Rowe.

142. *move*] *but so move* Keightley conj.

still so] *still so, my fair* Capell.

142, 143. *still so, And own no*] *still so, and own No* Malone.

145. *you are*] *you're* Pope.

deeds] *deed* Spedding conj.

146. *queens*] *queen's* Singer.

148. *peeps......through 't*] F_3 F_4.

Do plainly give you out an unstain'd shepherd,
With wisdom I might fear, my Doricles,
You woo'd me the false way.
Flo. I think you have
As little skill to fear as I have purpose
To put you to't. But come; our dance, I pray:
Your hand, my Perdita: so turtles pair,
That never mean to part.
Per. I'll swear for 'em.
Pol. This is the prettiest low-born lass that ever
Ran on the green-sward: nothing she does or seems
But smacks of something greater than herself,
Too noble for this place.
Cam. He tells her something
That makes her blood look out: good sooth, she is
The queen of curds and cream.
Clo. Come on, strike up!
Dor. Mopsa must be your mistress: marry, garlic,
To mend her kissing with!
Mop. Now, in good time!
Clo. Not a word, a word; we stand upon our manners.
Come, strike up!
[*Music. Here a dance of Shepherds and Shepherdesses.*
Pol. Pray, good shepherd, what fair swain is this
Which dances with your daughter?

peepes...through't F_1F_2. *peeps forth.... through it* Rowe. *peeps so...through t'* Capell. *fairly peeps through it* Steevens (1793). *peeps...through it* Collier. *through it...peeps* Staunton conj. *peepeth...through 't* Anon. conj.

152. *to fear*] *in fear* Hanmer.

155, 156. Per. *I'll...'em.* Pol. *This*] Pol. [Aside] *I'll...This* Johnson conj.

155. *I'll swear*] *Elsewhere* Jackson conj.

for 'em] *for them* [Music. Dance forming. Capell. *for one* Rann (Theobald and Ritson conj.).

157. *green-sward*] Steevens. *green-sord* Ff.

seems] *says* Collier (Collier MS.). *deems* Anon. conj.

160. *makes...out*] *wakes her blood: look on't* Collier (Collier MS.).

look out] Theobald. *look on't* Ff.

162, 163. Arranged as in Capell. As prose in Ff.

marry, garlic, To......with!] *marry Garlick to...with.* Ff. *marry, garlick to...with—* Johnson.

165. *strike up*] *strike up, pipers* Capell, ending lines 166, 167 at *what ...daughter?*

165. [Music.] Malone. om. Ff.

166. *Pray*] *I pray* Hanmer. *Pray you* S. Walker conj.

167. *Which*] *Who* Pope.

Shep. They call him Doricles; and boasts himself
To have a worthy feeding: but I have it
Upon his own report and I believe it;
He looks like sooth. He says he loves my daughter:
I think so too; for never gazed the moon
Upon the water, as he'll stand and read
As 'twere my daughter's eyes: and, to be plain,
I think there is not half a kiss to choose
Who loves another best.

Pol. She dances featly.

Shep. So she does any thing; though I report it,
That should be silent: if young Doricles
Do light upon her, she shall bring him that
Which he not dreams of.

Enter Servant.

Serv. O master, if you did but hear the pedlar at the door, you would never dance again after a tabor and pipe; no, the bagpipe could not move you: he sings several tunes faster than you'll tell money; he utters them as he had eaten ballads and all men's ears grew to his tunes.

Clo. He could never come better; he shall come in. I love a ballad but even too well, if it be doleful matter merrily set down, or a very pleasant thing indeed and sung lamentably.

Serv. He hath songs for man or woman, of all sizes; no milliner can so fit his customers with gloves: he has the prettiest love-songs for maids; so without bawdry, which is strange; with such delicate burthens of dildos and fadings, 'jump her and thump her;' and where some stretch-mouthed rascal would, as it were, mean mischief and break a foul gap into the matter, he makes the maid to answer 'Whoop,

168. *and boasts*] *and he boasts* Rowe. *he boasts* Capell. *'a boasts* Steevens conj.

169. *feeding*] *breeding* Hanmer.
but I have it] *I have it but* Hunter conj.

176. *Who loves another*] *Which loves the other* Hanmer. *Who loves the other* Mason conj.

177. *So she*] *She* Warburton.

181. SCENE VI. Pope.

185. *grew*] *grow* Rowe (ed. 2).

193. *fadings*] *fapings* Rowe (ed. 2). *fa-dings* Theobald.

196. *gap*] *jape* Singer (Collier MS.).

do me no harm, good man;' puts him off, slights him, with 'Whoop, do me no harm, good man.'

Pol. This is a brave fellow.

Clo. Believe me, thou talkest of an admirable conceited fellow. Has he any unbraided wares?

Serv. He hath ribbons of all the colours i' the rainbow; points more than all the lawyers in Bohemia can learnedly handle, though they come to him by the gross: inkles, caddisses, cambrics, lawns: why, he sings 'em over as they were gods or goddesses; you would think a smock were a she-angel, he so chants to the sleeve-hand and the work about the square on't.

Clo. Prithee bring him in; and let him approach singing.

Per. Forewarn him that he use no scurrilous words in's tunes. [*Exit Servant.*

Clo. You have of these pedlars, that have more in them than you'ld think, sister.

Per. Ay, good brother, or go about to think.

Enter AUTOLYCUS, *singing.*

Lawn as white as driven snow;
Cypress black as e'er was crow;
Gloves as sweet as damask roses;
Masks for faces and for noses;
Bugle bracelet, necklace amber,
Perfume for a lady's chamber;
Golden quoifs and stomachers,
For my lads to give their dears;
Pins and poking-sticks of steel,
What maids lack from head to heel:
Come buy of me, come; come buy, come buy;
Buy, lads, or else your lasses cry:
Come buy.

200. *admirable conceited*] Ff. *admirable-conceited* Theobald.

201. *unbraided*] *braided* Johnson conj. *embroided* Collier (Collier MS.).

wares] *warres* F_2.

206. *or*] *and* Pope.

207. *sleeve-hand*] *sleeve-band* Hanmer. *Silesia* or *sleasie holland* Peck conj.

211. Exit...] Capell.

212. *them*] *'em* Warburton.

216. *Cypress*] *Cyprus* Rowe (ed. 2).

219. *Bugle bracelet*] *Bugle-bracelets* F_4.

225. *come;*] *come buy;* Keightley conj.

226, 227. *Buy...Come buy.*] *Buy...Come buy, &c.* Theobald. As one line in Ff.

Clo. If I were not in love with Mopsa, thou shouldst take no money of me; but being enthralled as I am, it will also be the bondage of certain ribbons and gloves.

Mop. I was promised them against the feast; but they come not too late now.

Dor. He hath promised you more than that, or there be liars.

Mop. He hath paid you all he promised you: may be, he has paid you more, which will shame you to give him again.

Clo. Is there no manners left among maids? will they wear their plackets where they should bear their faces? Is there not milking-time, when you are going to bed, or kiln-hole, to whistle off these secrets, but you must be tittle-tattling before all our guests? 'tis well they are whispering: clamour your tongues, and not a word more.

Mop. I have done. Come, you promised me a tawdry-lace and a pair of sweet gloves.

Clo. Have I not told thee how I was cozened by the way and lost all my money?

Aut. And indeed, sir, there are cozeners abroad; therefore it behoves men to be wary.

Clo. Fear not thou, man, thou shalt lose nothing here.

Aut. I hope so, sir; for I have about me many parcels of charge.

Clo. What hast here? ballads?

Mop. Pray now, buy some: I love a ballad in print o' life, for then we are sure they are true.

Aut. Here's one to a very doleful tune, how a usurer's wife was brought to bed of twenty money-bags at a burthen and how she longed to eat adders' heads and toads carbonadoed.

Mop. Is it true, think you?

238. *bear*] *wear* Warburton.

239, 240. *kiln-hole*] Malone. *kill-hole* Ff.

240. *whistle off*] Hanmer. *whistle of* Ff. *whisper off* Collier MS.

242. *clamour*] *charm* Hanmer. *chamber* Jackson conj. *chommer* Cornish conj. *clammer* Keightley conj. *chawmer* Singer conj.

253. *ballad*] F_3F_4. *ballet* F_1F_2.

253, 254. *o' life*] *o'-life* Collier. *a life* Ff. *or a life* Rowe (ed. 2). *a'-life* Malone.

256. *of*] F_1F_2. *with* F_3F_4.
burthen] *birth* Anon. conj.

Aut. Very true, and but a month old.

Dor. Bless me from marrying a usurer!

Aut. Here's the midwife's name to't, one Mistress Tale-porter, and five or six honest wives that were present. Why should I carry lies abroad?

Mop. Pray you now, buy it.

Clo. Come on, lay it by: and let's first see moe ballads; we'll buy the other things anon.

Aut. Here's another ballad of a fish, that appeared upon, the coast on Wednesday the fourscore of April, forty thousand fathom above water, and sung this ballad against the hard hearts of maids: it was thought she was a woman, and was turned into a cold fish for she would not exchange flesh with one that loved her: the ballad is very pitiful and as true.

Dor. Is it true too, think you?

Aut. Five justices' hands at it, and witnesses more than my pack will hold.

Clo. Lay it by too: another.

Aut. This is a merry ballad, but a very pretty one.

Mop. Let's have some merry ones.

Aut. Why, this is a passing merry one and goes to the tune of 'Two maids wooing a man:' there's scarce a maid westward but she sings it; 'tis in request, I can tell you.

Mop. We can both sing it: if thou'lt bear a part, thou shalt hear; 'tis in three parts.

Dor. We had the tune on't a month ago.

Aut. I can bear my part; you must know 'tis my occupation: have at it with you.

SONG.

A. Get you hence, for I must go
Where it fits not you to know.
D. Whither? *M.* O, whither? *D.* Whither?

262. *midwife's*] Rowe. *midwives* Ff.
263. *wives*] *wives'* Steevens. See note (XV).
266. *moe*] *more* Rowe (ed. 2).
268. *ballad of*] Ff. *ballad, Of* Capell.
269. *Wednesday*] *Wensday* F_1F_2.
270. *fathom*] Johnson. *fadom* Ff.
272. *cold*] *cod* Anon conj.
288. SONG] See note (XVI).
289. *Where it*] *Whither* Collier (Collier MS.).
290, 299. *whither*] F_4. *whether* $F_1F_2F_3$.

M. It becomes thy oath full well,
Thou to me thy secrets tell:
D. Me too, let me go thither.

M. Or thou goest to the grange or mill:
D. If to either, thou dost ill.
A. Neither. *D.* What, neither? *A.* Neither.
D. Thou hast sworn my love to be;
M. Thou hast sworn it more to me:
Then whither goest? say, whither?

Clo. We'll have this song out anon by ourselves: my father and the gentlemen are in sad talk, and we'll not trouble them. Come, bring away thy pack after me. Wenches, I'll buy for you both. Pedlar, let's have the first choice. Follow me, girls. [*Exit with Dorcas and Mopsa.*

Aut. And you shall pay well for 'em. [*Follows singing.*

Will you buy any tape,
Or lace for your cape,
My dainty duck, my dear-a?
Any silk, any thread,
Any toys for your head,
Of the new'st, and finest, finest wear-a?
Come to the pedlar;
Money 's a medler,
That doth utter all men's ware-a. [*Exit.*

Re-enter Servant.

Serv. Master, there is three carters, three shepherds, three neat-herds, three swine-herds, that have made themselves all men of hair, they call themselves Saltiers, and they have a dance which the wenches say is a gallimaufry of gambols, because they are not in't; but they themselves

293. *thither*] F_3F_4. *thether* F_1F_2.
301. *gentlemen*] Rowe. *Gent.* Ff.
304. Exit...] Dyce om. Ff. Exeunt Cl., A., D., and M. Rowe (after line 314).
305. [Follows singing.] Edd. Song. Ff.
306—314. As six lines in Ff.
306. *buy*] *by* Pope (ed. 1).
307. *cape*] *cype* F_1.
309. *Any...any*] *And...and* Theobald.
311. *wear-a*] *ware-a* Rowe.
315. SCENE VII. Pope.
Re-enter...] Enter a Servant. Rowe.
Master] *Mayster* F_1.
there is] *there are* Rowe.
carters] *goatherds* Theobald.
316. *three swine-herds*] *and three swine-herds* Rowe.

are o' the mind, if it be not too rough for some that know little but bowling, it will please plentifully.

Shep. Away! we'll none on't: here has been too much homely foolery already. I know, sir, we weary you.

Pol. You weary those that refresh us: pray, let's see these four threes of herdsmen.

Serv. One three of them, by their own report, sir, hath danced before the king; and not the worst of the three but jumps twelve foot and a half by the squier.

Shep. Leave your prating: since these good men are pleased, let them come in; but quickly now.

Serv. Why, they stay at door, sir. [*Exit.*

Here a dance of twelve Satyrs.

Pol. O, father, you'll know more of that hereafter.
[*To Cam.*] Is it not too far gone? 'Tis time to part them.
He's simple and tells much. How now, fair shepherd!
Your heart is full of something that does take
Your mind from feasting. Sooth, when I was young
And handed love as you do, I was wont
To load my she with knacks: I would have ransack'd
The pedlar's silken treasury and have pour'd it
To her acceptance; you have let him go
And nothing marted with him. If your lass
Interpretation should abuse and call this
Your lack of love or bounty, you were straited
For a reply, at least if you make a care
Of happy holding her.

328. *squier*] *squire* Ff. *square* Rowe. See note (XVII).

331. Serv. *Why...sir*] Ff. Omitted by Rowe and all Edd. before Capell.

[Exit.] Capell.

Here...] Ff. Enter twelve Rusticks, presenting Satyrs. Company seat themselves. Dance, and Exeunt Rusticks. Capell.

332, 333. Pol. *O, father......Is it*] Flo. *O, father......hereafter* (Here a dance of twelve Satyrs). Pol. *Is it* Hanmer.

332. [Aside. Johnson. [Rising from beside the Shepherd. Capell.

333. [To Cam.] Edd. [Aside. Capell.

337. *handed*] *handled* Collier (Collier MS.).

344. *reply, at least*] *reply, at least,* Theobald. *reply at least,* Ff.

a care] *care* Theobald.

Flo. Old sir, I know
She prizes not such trifles as these are:
The gifts she looks from me are pack'd and lock'd
Up in my heart; which I have given already,
But not deliver'd. O, hear me breathe my life
Before this ancient sir, who, it should seem,
Hath sometime loved! I take thy hand, this hand,
As soft as dove's down and as white as it,
Or Ethiopian's tooth, or the fann'd snow that's bolted
By the northern blasts twice o'er.

Pol. What follows this?
How prettily the young swain seems to wash
The hand was fair before! I have put you out:
But to your protestation; let me hear
What you profess.

Flo. Do, and be witness to't.

Pol. And this my neighbour too?

Flo. And he, and more
Than he, and men, the earth, the heavens, and all:
That, were I crown'd the most imperial monarch,
Thereof most worthy, were I the fairest youth
That ever made eye swerve, had force and knowledge
More than was ever man's, I would not prize them
Without her love; for her employ them all;
Commend them and condemn them to her service
Or to their own perdition.

Pol. Fairly offer'd.

Cam. This shows a sound affection.

Shep. But, my daughter,
Say you the like to him?

Per. I cannot speak
So well, nothing so well; no, nor mean better:
By the pattern of mine own thoughts I cut out

349. *life*] *love* Theobald.

350. *who*] *whom* F_1.

353, 354. *Or...o'er*] Arranged as in F_1. In $F_2F_3F_4$ line 353 ends at *snow*.

353. *Ethiopian's*] *Ethiop's* Dyce conj. *Ethiop* Lettsom conj.

354. *blasts*] F_1. *blast* $F_2F_3F_4$.

356. *I have*] *I've* Pope.

360. *the heavens*] *and heavens* F_4.

363. *force*] *sense* Collier MS.

369. *him?*] Rowe. *him.* Ff.

The purity of his.
Shep. Take hands, a bargain!
And, friends unknown, you shall bear witness to't:
I give my daughter to him, and will make
Her portion equal his.
Flo. O, that must be
I' the virtue of your daughter: one being dead,
I shall have more than you can dream of yet;
Enough then for your wonder. But, come on,
Contract us 'fore these witnesses.
Shep. Come, your hand;
And, daughter, yours.
Pol. Soft, swain, awhile, beseech you;
Have you a father?
Flo. I have: but what of him?
Pol. Knows he of this?
Flo. He neither does nor shall.
Pol. Methinks a father
Is at the nuptial of his son a guest
That best becomes the table. Pray you once more,
Is not your father grown incapable
Of reasonable affairs? is he not stupid
With age and altering rheums? can he speak? hear?
Know man from man? dispute his own estate?
Lies he not bed-rid? and again does nothing
But what he did being childish?
Flo. No, good sir;
He has his health and ampler strength indeed
Than most have of his age.
Pol. By my white beard,
You offer him, if this be so, a wrong
Something unfilial: reason my son
Should choose himself a wife, but as good reason
The father, all whose joy is nothing else
But fair posterity, should hold some counsel

378. *your*] *you* F_4.

380. *awhile, beseech you;*] Capell. *a-while, beseech you,* F_1. *a-while; 'beseech you,* $F_2F_3F_4$.

389. *dispute*] *compute* Johnson conj. *dispose* Collier MS. *dispense* Anon. conj.

395. *my*] *the* Anon. conj.

In such a business.

Flo. I yield all this;
But for some other reasons, my grave sir,
Which 'tis not fit you know, I not acquaint
My father of this business.

Pol. Let him know't.

Flo. He shall not.

Pol. Prithee, let him.

Flo. No, he must not.

Shep. Let him, my son: he shall not need to grieve
At knowing of thy choice.

Flo. Come, come, he must not.
Mark our contract.

Pol. Mark your divorce, young sir,
[*Discovering himself.*
Whom son I dare not call; thou art too base
To be acknowledged: thou a sceptre's heir,
That thus affects a sheep-hook! Thou old traitor,
I am sorry that by hanging thee I can
But shorten thy life one week. And thou, fresh piece
Of excellent witchcraft, who of force must know
The royal fool thou copest with,—

Shep. O, my heart!

Pol. I'll have thy beauty scratch'd with briers, and made
More homely than thy state. For thee, fond boy,
If I may ever know thou dost but sigh
That thou no more shalt see this knack, as never
I mean thou shalt, we'll bar thee from succession;
Not hold thee of our blood, no, not our kin,
Far than Deucalion off: mark thou my words:

406. [Discovering...] Rowe.
408. *acknowledged*] *acknowledge* F_1.
409. *affects*] Ff. *affect'st* Pope.
410. *I am*] *I'm* Pope.
410, 411. *can But shorten*] *can but Shorten* Warburton.
412. *who*] *whom* F_1.
413. *copest with,—*] *coap'st with—* Pope. *coap'st with.* Ff.
Shep.] Per. Theobald conj.
415. *fond*] *found* F_4.
417. *shalt*] Rowe. *shalt never* Ff. See note (XVIII).
420. *Far than*] F_4. *Farre then* F_1. *Farre than* F_2 F_3. *Less than* Hanmer. *Far' than* Warburton. *Far as* Capell (Johnson conj.). *Farther than* Heath conj. *Far'r than* Grant White.

Follow us to the court. Thou churl, for this time,
Though full of our displeasure, yet we free thee
From the dead blow of it. And you, enchantment,—
Worthy enough a herdsman; yea, him too,
That makes himself, but for our honour therein,
Unworthy thee,—if ever henceforth thou
These rural latches to his entrance open,
Or hoop his body more with thy embraces,
I will devise a death as cruel for thee
As thou art tender to't. [*Exit.*

Per. Even here undone!
I was not much afeard; for once or twice
I was about to speak and tell him plainly,
The selfsame sun that shines upon his court
Hides not his visage from our cottage, but
Looks on alike. Will't please you, sir, be gone?
I told you what would come of this: beseech you,
Of your own state take care: this dream of mine,—
Being now awake, I'll queen it no inch farther,
But milk my ewes and weep.

Cam. Why, how now, father!
Speak ere thou diest.

Shep. I cannot speak, nor think,
Nor dare to know that which I know. O sir!
You have undone a man of fourscore three,
That thought to fill his grave in quiet; yea,
To die upon the bed my father died,
To lie close by his honest bones: but now
Some hangman must put on my shroud and lay me
Where no priest shovels in dust. O cursed wretch,
That knew'st this was the prince, and wouldst adventure

423. *dead*] *dread* Anon. conj. *you*] *your* F_3F_4. *thou* Anon. conj.

426. *thee,—if*] *thee. If* Ff.

428. *hoop*] *hoope* Pope. *hope* Ff.

430. *to 't*] *to it* Rowe. [Exit.] Rowe. SCENE VIII. Pope.

431. *afeard*] *afraid* Rowe.

435. *on*] *on both* Malone conj. *on all* Singer (Hunter conj.). *on's* Anon. conj. *Will't*] Hanmer. *Wilt* Ff. [To Flo. Rowe.

437. *this dream of mine,—*] Johnson. *this dream of mine,* Ff. *from this my dream* Hanmer. *as for this dream of mine,—* Capell conj.

441. [To Flo. Rowe.

444. *died*] *died on* Keightley conj.

447. [To Perdita. Rowe.

To mingle faith with him! Undone! undone!
If I might die within this hour, I have lived
To die when I desire. [*Exit.*

Flo. Why look you so upon me?
I am but sorry, not afeard, delay'd,
But nothing alter'd: what I was, I am;
More straining on for plucking back, not following
My leash unwillingly.

Cam. Gracious my lord,
You know your father's temper: at this time
He will allow no speech, which I do guess
You do not purpose to him; and as hardly
Will he endure your sight as yet, I fear:
Then, till the fury of his highness settle,
Come not before him.

Flo. I not purpose it.
I think, Camillo?

Cam. Even he, my lord.

Per. How often have I told you 'twould be thus!
How often said, my dignity would last
But till 'twere known!

Flo. It cannot fail but by
The violation of my faith; and then
Let nature crush the sides o' the earth together
And mar the seeds within! Lift up thy looks:
From my succession wipe me, father, I
Am heir to my affection.

Cam. Be advised.

Flo. I am, and by my fancy: if my reason
Will thereto be obedient, I have reason;
If not, my senses, better pleased with madness,
Do bid it welcome.

Cam. This is desperate, sir.

451. SCENE IX. Pope. *upon me*] om. Steevens conj.
452. *afeard*] *afraid* Rowe.
456. *your*] *my* F_1.
459. *sight as yet*] Hanmer. *sight, as yet* Ff.
462. *Camillo?*] *Camillo?*—Johnson. *Camillo.* Ff. *Camillo*— Theobald.
465. *fail*] *fall* Anon. conj.
469. *my*] *thy* Capell.
473. *better pleased with madness,*] F_1. *better* (*pleas'd with madness*) F_2 F_3 F_4.

Flo. So call it: but it does fulfil my vow;
I needs must think it honesty. Camillo,
Not for Bohemia, nor the pomp that may
Be thereat glean'd; for all the sun sees, or
The close earth wombs, or the profound sea hides
In unknown fathoms, will I break my oath
To this my fair beloved: therefore, I pray you,
As you have ever been my father's honour'd friend,
When he shall miss me,—as, in faith, I mean not
To see him any more,—cast your good counsels
Upon his passion: let myself and fortune
Tug for the time to come. This you may know
And so deliver, I am put to sea
With her whom here I cannot hold on shore;
And most opportune to our need I have
A vessel rides fast by, but not prepared
For this design. What course I mean to hold
Shall nothing benefit your knowledge, nor
Concern me the reporting.

Cam. O my lord!
I would your spirit were easier for advice,
Or stronger for your need.

Flo. Hark, Perdita. [*Drawing her aside.*
I'll hear you by and by.

Cam. He's irremoveable,
Resolved for flight. Now were I happy, if
His going I could frame to serve my turn,
Save him from danger, do him love and honour,
Purchase the sight again of dear Sicilia
And that unhappy king, my master, whom
I so much thirst to see.

478. *thereat*] *thereout* Hanmer.
all] F_1. *all that* $F_2F_3F_4$.
or] om. Long MS.

479. *sea hides*] Capell. *seas hides* F_1. *seas hide* $F_2F_3F_4$.

480. *fathoms*] Johnson. *fadomes* Ff.

482. *As you have ever*] Ff. *As you have e'er* Malone. *As y' have e'er* S. Walker conj.
honour'd] F_1. om. $F_2F_3F_4$.

488. *whom*] $F_2F_3F_4$. *who* F_1.

489. *our*] Theobald. *her* Ff. *the* Capell.

495. [Drawing...] Capell.

496. [To Camillo. Theobald.
irremoveable] *immoveable* Anon. conj.

497. *Resolved*] *Rosolv'd* F_2.

Flo. Now, good Camillo;
I am so fraught with curious business that
I leave out ceremony.
Cam. Sir, I think
You have heard of my poor services, i' the love
That I have borne your father?
Flo. Very nobly
Have you deserved: it is my father's music
To speak your deeds, not little of his care
To have them recompensed as thought on.
Cam. Well, my lord,
If you may please to think I love the king,
And through him what is nearest to him, which is
Your gracious self, embrace but my direction,
If your more ponderous and settled project
May suffer alteration, on mine honour
I'll point you where you shall have such receiving
As shall become your highness; where you may
Enjoy your mistress, from the whom, I see,
There's no disjunction to be made, but by
As heavens forefend! your ruin; marry her,
And, with my best endeavours in your absence,
Your discontenting father strive to qualify
And bring him up to liking.
Flo. How, Camillo,
May this, almost a miracle, be done?
That I may call thee something more than man
And after that trust to thee.
Cam. Have you thought on
A place whereto you'll go?
Flo. Not any yet:
But as the unthought-on accident is guilty

503. *curious*] *serious* Collier MS.
504. [Going. Malone. See note (XIX).
511. *through him what is*] Hanmer. *through him, what's* Ff. *thorough him, what's* Theobald.
nearest] *near'st* S. Walker conj.
514. *alteration, on*] *alteration. On* F_1. *alteration: On* $F_2F_3F_4$.
520. *And*] *I'll* Long MS.
521. *discontenting*] *discontented* Rowe.
strive to qualify] *I'll strive to qualifie* Rowe (ed. 2). *I will strive To qualifie* Hanmer.
522. *him up*] om. Rowe.

To what we wildly do, so we profess
Ourselves to be the slaves of chance, and flies
Of every wind that blows.
Cam. Then list to me:
This follows, if you will not change your purpose
But undergo this flight, make for Sicilia,
And there present yourself and your fair princess,
For so I see she must be, 'fore Leontes:
She shall be habited as it becomes
The partner of your bed. Methinks I see
Leontes opening his free arms and weeping
His welcomes forth; asks thee the son forgiveness,
As 'twere i' the father's person; kisses the hands
Of your fresh princess; o'er and o'er divides him
'Twixt his unkindness and his kindness; the one
He chides to hell and bids the other grow
Faster than thought or time.
Flo. Worthy Camillo,
What colour for my visitation shall I
Hold up before him?
Cam. Sent by the king your father
To greet him and to give him comforts. Sir,
The manner of your bearing towards him, with
What you as from your father shall deliver,
Things known betwixt us three, I'll write you down:
The which shall point you forth at every sitting
What you must say; that he shall not perceive
But that you have your father's bosom there
And speak his very heart.
Flo. I am bound to you:
There is some sap in this.
Cam. A course more promising
Than a wild dedication of yourselves
To unpath'd waters, undream'd shores, most certain
To miseries enough: no hope to help you,

528. *To*] *Of* Rowe. *Towards* Hanmer.
538. *asks*] *ask* Long MS.
thee the son] F_3F_4. *thee there Sonne* F_1F_2. *there the son* Ritson conj.
539. *kisses*] *kiss* Long MS.
540. *divides*] *divide* Long MS.
546. *comforts*] *comfort* Anon conj.
550. *sitting*] *fitting* Theobald. *sifting* Thirlby conj.

But as you shake off one to take another:
Nothing so certain as your anchors, who
Do their best office, if they can but stay you
Where you'll be loath to be: besides you know
Prosperity's the very bond of love,
Whose fresh complexion and whose heart together
Affliction alters.

Per. One of these is true:
I think affliction may subdue the cheek,
But not take in the mind.

Cam. Yea, say you so?
There shall not at your father's house these seven years
Be born another such.

Flo. My good Camillo,
She is as forward of her breeding as
She is i' the rear o' our birth.

Cam. I cannot say 'tis pity
She lacks instructions, for she seems a mistress
To most that teach.

Per. Your pardon, sir; for this
I'll blush you thanks.

Flo. My prettiest Perdita!
But O, the thorns we stand upon! Camillo,
Preserver of my father, now of me,
The medicine of our house, how shall we do?
We are not furnish'd like Bohemia's son,
Nor shall appear in Sicilia.

Cam. My lord,

558, 559. *another: Nothing*] *another Nothing* Hanmer.

559. *who*] *which* Hanmer.

569. *She is*] Pope. *She's* Ff.

570. *She is i' the rear o' our birth*] Rowe (ed. 2). *She is i' th' reare 'our birth* $F_1F_2F_3$. *She is i' th' rear 'our birth* F_4. *She is i' th' rear o' her birth* Rowe (ed. 1). *I' th' rear of birth* Hanmer. *She is i' th' rear of birth* Johnson. *She is i' the rear our birth* Boswell. *She is i' th' rear 'f our birth* Grant White.

572. *sir; for this*] Hanmer. *sir, for this,* F_1. *sir, for this.* $F_2F_3F_4$.

576. *medicine*] *medecin* Theobald conj.

578. *appear in Sicilia.*] *appeare in Sicilia.* F_1. *appeare in Sicily.* F_2. *appear in Sicily.* F_3F_4. *appear in Sicily—* Rowe. *appear in Sicilia—* Boswell. *appear 't in Sicilia.* Collier (Collier MS.). *appear so in Sicilia.* Staunton conj.

Fear none of this: I think you know my fortunes
Do all lie there: it shall be so my care
To have you royally appointed as if
The scene you play were mine. For instance, sir,
That you may know you shall not want, one word.
[*They talk aside.*

Re-enter AUTOLYCUS.

Aut. Ha, ha! what a fool Honesty is! and Trust, his sworn brother, a very simple gentleman! I have sold all my trumpery; not a counterfeit stone, not a ribbon, glass, pomander, brooch, table-book, ballad, knife, tape, glove, shoe-tie, bracelet, horn-ring, to keep my pack from fasting: they throng who should buy first, as if my trinkets had been hallowed and brought a benediction to the buyer: by which means I saw whose purse was best in picture; and what I saw, to my good use I remembered. My clown, who wants but something to be a reasonable man, grew so in love with the wenches' song, that he would not stir his pettitoes till he had both tune and words; which so drew the rest of the herd to me, that all their other senses stuck in ears: you might have pinched a placket, it was senseless; 'twas nothing to geld a codpiece of a purse; I would have filed keys off that hung in chains: no hearing, no feeling, but my sir's song, and admiring the nothing of it. So that in this time of lethargy I picked and cut most of their festival purses; and had not the old man come in with a whoo-bub against his daughter and the king's son and scared my choughs from the chaff, I had not left a purse alive in the whole army.
[*Camillo, Florizel, and Perdita come forward.*

582. *mine*] *true* Collier MS.
583. [They talk aside.] Rowe.
587. *brooch*] Steevens. *browch* Ff. *broch* Capell.
588. *fasting*] F_1. *fastning* F_2F_3 F_4.
589. *throng*] *thronged* Collier (Collier MS.).
591. *picture*] *pasture* Anon. conj.
592. *My clown*] *My good clown* Rowe.
594. *wenches'*] Johnson. *wenches* Ff.
596. *ears*] *their ears* Rann (Mason conj.).
598. *would*] *could* Long MS.
filed keys off] F_3F_4. *fill'd keyes of* F_1F_2.
600. *nothing*] *noting* Anon. conj.
604. [Camillo...] Theobald.

Cam. Nay, but my letters, by this means being there
So soon as you arrive, shall clear that doubt.

Flo. And those that you'll procure from King Leontes—

Cam. Shall satisfy your father.

Per. Happy be you!
All that you speak shows fair.

Cam. Who have we here?
[*Seeing Autolycus.*
We'll make an instrument of this; omit
Nothing may give us aid.

Aut. If they have overheard me now, why, hanging.

Cam. How now, good fellow! why shakest thou so?
Fear not, man; here's no harm intended to thee.

Aut. I am a poor fellow, sir.

Cam. Why, be so still; here's nobody will steal that from thee: yet for the outside of thy poverty we must make an exchange; therefore discase thee instantly,—thou must think there's a necessity in't,—and change garments with this gentleman: though the pennyworth on his side be the worst, yet hold thee, there's some boot.

Aut. I am a poor fellow, sir. [*Aside*] I know ye well enough.

Cam. Nay, prithee, dispatch: the gentleman is half flayed already.

Aut. Are you in earnest, sir? [*Aside*] I smell the trick on't.

Flo. Dispatch, I prithee.

Aut. Indeed, I have had earnest; but I cannot with conscience take it.

607. *Leontes—*] Rowe. *Leontes?* Ff.

609. *Who*] *Whom* Collier.
[Seeing A.] Theobald.

612. [Aside. Theobald.

613, 614. As three lines in Ff, ending *fellow...man...thee*; as prose first in Malone.

613. *why*] *come, why* Hanmer. *wherefore* Capell, reading 613, 614 as two lines of verse.

619. *a necessity*] *necessity* Steevens.

621. [Giving money. Dyce.

622, 626. [Aside]. Indicated by brackets in Ff.

624. *dispatch...gentleman is*] *now dispatch...gentleman 'S* Capell, reading as verse.

625. *flayed*] *fled* Ff. *flead* Rowe.

Cam. Unbuckle, unbuckle.

[*Florizel and Autolycus exchange garments.*

Fortunate mistress,—let my prophecy
Come home to ye!—you must retire yourself
Into some covert: take your sweetheart's hat
And pluck it o'er your brows, muffle your face,
Dismantle you, and, as you can, disliken
The truth of your own seeming; that you may—
For I do fear eyes over—to shipboard
Get undescried.

Per. I see the play so lies
That I must bear a part.

Cam. No remedy.
Have you done there?

Flo. Should I now meet my father,
He would not call me son.

Cam. Nay, you shall have no hat.

[*Giving it to Perdita.*

Come, lady, come. Farewell, my friend.

Aut. Adieu, sir.

Flo. O Perdita, what have we twain forgot!
Pray you, a word.

Cam. [*Aside*] What I do next, shall be to tell the king
Of this escape and whither they are bound;
Wherein my hope is I shall so prevail
To force him after: in whose company
I shall review Sicilia, for whose sight
I have a woman's longing.

Flo. Fortune speed us!
Thus we set on, Camillo, to the sea-side.

Cam. The swifter speed the better.

[*Exeunt Florizel, Perdita, and Camillo.*

631. [Florizel...] Capell.

635. *your*] *thy* Boswell.

638. *over*] *over you* Rowe. *ever* Collier (Egerton and Collier MS.). *overt* Jervis conj.

642, 643. *no hat...friend*] As one line in Hanmer.

642. [Giving...] Capell.

643. *Adieu, sir.*] *Adieu, sir.* [retiring. Capell.

645. [Talking with her aside. Capell.

646. [Aside] Rowe.

649. *whose*] *his* Anon. conj.

653. [Exeunt......] Capell. Exit. Ff. Exit Flo. and Per. (after line 652). Exit (after line 653) Rowe.

Aut. I understand the business, I hear it: to have an open ear, a quick eye, and a nimble hand, is necessary for a cut-purse; a good nose is requisite also, to smell out work for the other senses. I see this is the time that the unjust man doth thrive. What an exchange had this been without boot! What a boot is here with this exchange! Sure the gods do this year connive at us, and we may do any thing extempore. The prince himself is about a piece of iniquity, stealing away from his father with his clog at his heels: if I thought it were a piece of honesty to acquaint the king withal, I would not do't: I hold it the more knavery to conceal it; and therein am I constant to my profession.

Re-enter Clown *and* Shepherd.

Aside, aside; here is more matter for a hot brain: every lane's end, every shop, church, session, hanging, yields a careful man work.

Clo. See, see; what a man you are now! There is no other way but to tell the king she's a changeling and none of your flesh and blood.

Shep. Nay, but hear me.

Clo. Nay, but hear me.

Shep. Go to, then.

Clo. She being none of your flesh and blood, your flesh and blood has not offended the king; and so your flesh and blood is not to be punished by him. Show those things you found about her, those secret things, all but what she has with her: this being done, let the law go whistle: I warrant you.

Shep. I will tell the king all, every word, yea, and his son's pranks too; who, I may say, is no honest man, neither to his father nor to me, to go about to make me the king's brother-in-law.

Clo. Indeed, brother-in-law was the farthest off you

654. SCENE XI. Pope.
hear] *heard* Hanmer.

663, 664. *thought it were...would not do 't*] *thought it were not...would do 't* Hanmer. *thought not it were... would do 't* Capell.

665. Re-enter...] Dyce. Enter... Ff.

666. *here is*] F_1F_2. *here's* F_3F_4.

677. *those*] *these* Theobald.

could have been to him and then your blood had been the dearer by I know how much an ounce.

Aut. [*Aside*] Very wisely, puppies!

Shep. Well, let us to the king: there is that in this fardel will make him scratch his beard.

Aut. [*Aside*] I know not what impediment this complaint may be to the flight of my master.

Clo. Pray heartily he be at palace.

Aut. [*Aside*] Though I am not naturally honest, I am so sometimes by chance: let me pocket up my pedlar's excrement. [*Takes off his false beard.*] How now, rustics! whither are you bound?

Shep. To the palace, an it like your worship.

Aut. Your affairs there, what, with whom, the condition of that fardel, the place of your dwelling, your names, your ages, of what having, breeding, and any thing that is fitting to be known, discover.

Clo. We are but plain fellows, sir.

Aut. A lie; you are rough and hairy. Let me have no lying: it becomes none but tradesmen, and they often give us soldiers the lie: but we pay them for it with stamped coin, not stabbing steel; therefore they do not give us the lie.

Clo. Your worship had like to have given us one, if you had not taken yourself with the manner.

Shep. Are you a courtier, an't like you, sir?

Aut. Whether it like me or no, I am a courtier. Seest thou not the air of the court in these enfoldings? hath not my gait in it the measure of the court? receives not thy nose court-odour from me? reflect I not on thy baseness court-contempt? Thinkest thou, for that I insinuate, or

687. *know*] *know not* Hanmer.

688. [Aside] Rowe.

690, 700. *fardel*] Steevens. *Farthell* $F_1F_2F_3$. *Farthel* F_4. And passim.

691, 694. [Aside] So marked by Capell.

693. *at palace*] *at 'Pallace* F_1. *at Pallace* $F_2F_3F_4$. *at the palace* Rowe. See note (XX).

696. [Takes off...] Steevens (1793).

698. *an*] Hanmer. *and* Ff.

701. *ages*] *age* Rowe (ed. 2).

702. *to be*] *for to be* Rowe (ed. 2).

707. *not stabbing*] *note-stabbing* Theobald conj.

not give] *give* Hanmer.

709. *manner*] *manour* Hanmer.

710. *an't*] Hanmer. *and 't* $F_1F_2F_3$. *and'* F_4. *and* Rowe.

715. *or*] $F_2F_3F_4$. *at* F_1. *to* Capell. *and* Malone. See note (XXI).

toaze from thee thy business, I am therefore no courtier? I am courtier cap-a-pe; and one that will either push on or pluck back thy business there: whereupon I command thee to open thy affair.

Shep. My business, sir, is to the king.

Aut. What advocate hast thou to him?

Shep. I know not, an't like you.

Clo. Advocate's the court-word for a pheasant: say you have none.

Shep. None, sir; I have no pheasant, cock nor hen.

Aut. How blessed are we that are not simple men!
Yet nature might have made me as these are,
Therefore I will not disdain.

Clo. This cannot be but a great courtier.

Shep. His garments are rich, but he wears them not handsomely.

Clo. He seems to be the more noble in being fantastical: a great man, I'll warrant; I know by the picking on's teeth.

Aut. The fardel there? what's i' the fardel? Wherefore that box?

Shep. Sir, there lies such secrets in this fardel and box, which none must know but the king; and which he shall know within this hour, if I may come to the speech of him.

Aut. Age, thou hast lost thy labour.

Shep. Why, sir?

Aut. The king is not at the palace; he is gone aboard a new ship to purge melancholy and air himself: for, if thou beest capable of things serious, thou must know the king is full of grief.

Shep. So 'tis said, sir; about his son, that should have married a shepherd's daughter.

Aut. If that shepherd be not in hand-fast, let him fly:

718. *pluck*] *push* Rowe (ed. 2).

722, 759, 781. *an't*] Hanmer. *and 't* Ff.

723. *pheasant*] *present* Kenrick conj.

725. *pheasant, cock*] Capell. *pheazant cock,* Ff (*pheasant* F_4).

726. *blessed*] Ff. *bless'd* Pope.

729. *be but*] *but be* Hanmer.

732. *to be*] *to me* S. Walker conj.

733. *on's*] *of's* Capell conj.

734. *fardel*] Steevens. *Farthell* F_1F_2. *Farthel* F_3F_4.

747. *hand-fast*] *band, fast* Grant White conj.

the curses he shall have, the tortures he shall feel, will break the back of man, the heart of monster.

Clo. Think you so, sir?

Aut. Not he alone shall suffer what wit can make heavy and vengeance bitter; but those that are germane to him, though removed fifty times, shall all come under the hangman: which though it be great pity, yet it is necessary. An old sheep-whistling rogue, a ram-tender, to offer to have his daughter come into grace! Some say he shall be stoned; but that death is too soft for him, say I: draw our throne into a sheep-cote! all deaths are too few, the sharpest too easy.

Clo. Has the old man e'er a son, sir, do you hear, an't like you, sir?

Aut. He has a son, who shall be flayed alive; then 'nointed over with honey, set on the head of a wasp's nest; then stand till he be three quarters and a dram dead; then recovered again with aqua-vitæ or some other hot infusion; then, raw as he is, and in the hottest day prognostication proclaims, shall he be set against a brick-wall, the sun looking with a southward eye upon him, where he is to behold him with flies blown to death. But what talk we of these traitorly rascals, whose miseries are to be smiled at, their offences being so capital? Tell me, for you seem to be honest plain men, what you have to the king: being something gently considered, I'll bring you where he is aboard, tender your persons to his presence, whisper him in your behalfs; and if it be in man besides the king to effect your suits, here is man shall do it.

Clo. He seems to be of great authority: close with him, give him gold; and though authority be a stubborn bear, yet he is oft led by the nose with gold: show the inside of your purse to the outside of his hand, and no more ado. Remember 'stoned,' and 'flayed alive.'

Shep. An't please you, sir, to undertake the business for us, here is that gold I have: I'll make it as much more and leave this young man in pawn till I bring it you.

752. *germane*] *Iermaine* F_1 F_2. *Jermain* F_3F_4.

763. *then stand*] *there stand* Capell.

774. *behalfs*] *behalf* F_4.

775. *man*] F_1F_2. *a man* F_3F_4. *the man* Long MS.

Aut. After I have done what I promised?

Shep. Ay, sir.

Aut. Well, give me the moiety. Are you a party in this business?

Clo. In some sort, sir: but though my case be a pitiful one, I hope I shall not be flayed out of it.

Aut. O, that's the case of the shepherd's son: hang him, he'll be made an example.

Clo. Comfort, good comfort! We must to the king and show our strange sights: he must know 'tis none of your daughter nor my sister; we are gone else. Sir, I will give you as much as this old man does when the business is performed, and remain, as he says, your pawn till it be brought you.

Aut. I will trust you. Walk before toward the sea-side; go on the right hand: I will but look upon the hedge and follow you.

Clo. We are blest in this man, as I may say, even blest.

Shep. Let's before as he bids us: he was provided to do us good. [*Exeunt Shepherd and Clown.*

Aut. If I had a mind to be honest, I see Fortune would not suffer me: she drops booties in my mouth. I am courted now with a double occasion, gold and a means to do the prince my master good; which who knows how that may turn back to my advancement? I will bring these two moles, these blind ones, aboard him: if he think it fit to shore them again and that the complaint they have to the king concerns him nothing, let him call me rogue for being so far officious; for I am proof against that title and what shame else belongs to't. To him will I present them: there may be matter in it. [*Exit.*

799. *look*] F_3F_4. *looke* F_1F_2. *leake* Theobald conj.

801, 802. *blest*] *bless'd* Ff.

804. Exeunt S. and C.] Rowe. Exeunt. $F_2F_3F_4$. om. F_1.

809. *back*] *luck* Collier (Collier MS.).

815. [Exit.] Rowe. [Exeunt. Ff.

ACT V.

SCENE I. *A room in* LEONTES' *palace.*

Enter LEONTES, CLEOMENES, DION, PAULINA, *and Servants.*

Cleo. Sir, you have done enough, and have perform'd
A saint-like sorrow: no fault could you make,
Which you have not redeem'd; indeed, paid down
More penitence than done trespass: at the last,
Do as the heavens have done, forget your evil;
With them forgive yourself.

Leon. Whilst I remember
Her and her virtues, I cannot forget
My blemishes in them, and so still think of
The wrong I did myself: which was so much,
That heirless it hath made my kingdom; and
Destroy'd the sweet'st companion that e'er man
Bred his hopes out of.

Paul. True, too true, my lord:
If, one by one, you wedded all the world,
Or from the all that are took something good,
To make a perfect woman, she you kill'd
Would be unparallel'd.

Leon. I think so. Kill'd!
She I kill'd! I did so: but thou strikest me
Sorely, to say I did; it is as bitter
Upon my tongue as in my thought: now, good now,
Say so but seldom.

Cleo. Not at all, good lady:
You might have spoken a thousand things that would
Have done the time more benefit and graced

SCENE I. A room...] Capell.

Enter...] Rowe. Enter L., C., D., P., Servants: Florizel, Perdita. Ff.

12. Paul. *True, too true*] Theobald. *true.* Paul. *Too true.* Ff. Paul. *'Tis true, too true* Long MS.

17. *She I kill'd!*] *kill'd?—She I kill'd?* Theobald.

21. *spoken*] *spoke* Pope.

Your kindness better.
Paul. You are one of those
Would have him wed again.
Dion. If you would not so,
You pity not the state, nor the remembrance
Of his most sovereign name; consider little
What dangers, by his highness' fail of issue,
May drop upon his kingdom and devour
Incertain lookers on. What were more holy
Than to rejoice the former queen is well?
What holier than, for royalty's repair,
For present comfort and for future good,
To bless the bed of majesty again
With a sweet fellow to't?
Paul. There is none worthy,
Respecting her that's gone. Besides, the gods
Will have fulfill'd their secret purposes;
For has not the divine Apollo said,
Is't not the tenor of his oracle,
That King Leontes shall not have an heir
Till his lost child be found? which that it shall,
Is all as monstrous to our human reason
As my Antigonus to break his grave
And come again to me; who, on my life,
Did perish with the infant. 'Tis your counsel
My lord should to the heavens be contrary,
Oppose against their wills. [*To Leontes.*] Care not for issue;
The crown will find an heir: great Alexander
Left his to the worthiest; so his successor
Was like to be the best.
Leon. Good Paulina,
Who hast the memory of Hermione,
I know, in honour, O, that ever I

24. *so*] om. Hanmer.
26. *name*] *dame* Reed (1803). *little*] *a little* Heath conj.
30. *queen is well?*] *queen? This will.* Hanmer (Warburton).
36. *fulfill'd*] *fulfill'n* F_2.
37. *said,*] F_4. *said?* $F_1F_2F_3$.
42. *Antigonus*] *Antigomus* F_2.
45. *contrary*] *contray* F_2.
46. [To L.] To the King. Theobald.
49. *Good*] *Ah! good* Hanmer. *Thou good* Capell. *My good* Keightley conj.

Had squared me to thy counsel!—then, even now,
I might have look'd upon my queen's full eyes;
Have taken treasure from her lips,—

Paul. And left them
More rich for what they yielded.

Leon. Thou speak'st truth.
No more such wives; therefore, no wife: one worse,
And better used, would make her sainted spirit
Again possess her corpse, and on this stage,
Where we offenders now, appear soul-vex'd,
And begin, 'Why to me?'

Paul. Had she such power,
She had just cause.

Leon. She had; and would incense me
To murder her I married.

Paul. I should so.
Were I the ghost that walk'd, I'ld bid you mark
Her eye, and tell me for what dull part in't
You chose her; then I'ld shriek, that even your ears
Should rift to hear me; and the words that follow'd
Should be 'Remember mine.'

Leon. Stars, stars,
And all eyes else dead coals! Fear thou no wife;
I'll have no wife, Paulina.

Paul. Will you swear
Never to marry but by my free leave?

Leon. Never, Paulina; so be blest my spirit!

54. *lips,—*] Capell. *lips.* Ff. *lips!* Pope.

58, 59. *stage...appear*] *stage, (Where we offenders now) appear,* Knight. *stage (Where we offendors now appeare)* Ff (*appear* F_3F_4). *stage, (Where...now) appear* Theobald. *stage, (Where we offended anew) appear* Hanmer. *stage, Were we offenders now—appear* Heath conj. *stage (Where we offenders now appear, soul-vex'd)* Steevens conj. *stage (Where we offended,) now appear* Jackson conj. *stage (Where we offend her) new appear* Spedding conj. *stage, (Where we offenders move) appear* Delius conj. *stage, Where we're offenders now, appear* Anon conj.

60. *And begin, 'Why to me?'*] *And begin, why to me?* F_1. *And begin, why to me;* F_2F_3. *And begin, why to me.* F_4. *Begin, 'And why to me?'* Capell. *And begin, Why? to me.* Rann (Mason conj.). See note (XXII).

61. *cause*] F_3F_4. *such cause* F_1F_2.

63. *walk'd*] *wak'd* Rowe (ed. 2). Servant post. Collier MS.

67. *Stars, stars*] *Stars, very stars* Hanmer.

71. *blest*] *bless'd* Ff.

Paul. Then, good my lords, bear witness to his oath.
Cleo. You tempt him over-much.
Paul. Unless another,
As like Hermione as is her picture,
Affront his eye.
Cleo. Good madam,—
Paul. I have done.
Yet, if my lord will marry,—if you will, sir,
No remedy, but you will,—give me the office
To choose you a queen: she shall not be so young
As was your former; but she shall be such
As, walk'd your first queen's ghost, it should take joy
To see her in your arms.
Leon. My true Paulina,
We shall not marry till thou bid'st us.
Paul. That
Shall be when your first queen's again in breath;
Never till then.

Enter a Gentleman.

Gent. One that gives out himself Prince Florizel,
Son of Polixenes, with his princess, she
The fairest I have yet beheld, desires access
To your high presence.
Leon. What with him? he comes not
Like to his father's greatness: his approach,
So out of circumstance and sudden, tells us
'Tis not a visitation framed, but forced
By need and accident. What train?
Gent. But few,
And those but mean.
Leon. His princess, say you, with him?
Gent. Ay, the most peerless piece of earth, I think,

75. Cleo. *Good madam,*— Paul. *I have done*] Capell. Cleo. *Good madam, I have done* Ff. Cleo. *Good madam, pray have done* Rowe.

78. *you a*] *your* Anon. conj.

84. Enter a Gentleman.] Theobald. Enter a Servant. Ff. Enter a Servant-post. Collier MS.

85. SCENE II. Pope.

Gent.] Ser. Ff (and throughout the scene).

out himself] *himself out* Pope.

87. *fairest I have*] Ff. *fair'st I've* S. Walker conj.

94. *Ay,*] *I:* Ff. *Yes;* Rowe.

That e'er the sun shone bright on.
Paul. O Hermione,
As every present time doth boast itself
Above a better gone, so must thy grave
Give way to what's seen now! Sir, you yourself
Have said and writ so, but your writing now
Is colder than that theme, 'She had not been,
Nor was not to be equall'd;'—thus your verse
Flow'd with her beauty once: 'tis shrewdly ebb'd,
To say you have seen a better.
Gent. Pardon, madam:
The one I have almost forgot,—your pardon,—
The other, when she has obtain'd your eye,
Will have your tongue too. This is a creature,
Would she begin a sect, might quench the zeal
Of all professors else; make proselytes
Of who she but bid follow.
Paul. How! not women?
Gent. Women will love her, that she is a woman
More worth than any man; men, that she is
The rarest of all women.
Leon. Go, Cleomenes;
Yourself, assisted with your honour'd friends,
Bring them to our embracement. Still, 'tis strange
[*Exeunt Cleomenes and others.*
He thus should steal upon us.
Paul. Had our prince,
Jewel of children, seen this hour, he had pair'd
Well with this lord: there was not full a month
Between their births.
Leon. Prithee, no more; cease; thou know'st
He dies to me again when talk'd of: sure,

97. *grave*] *grace* Collier (Egerton MS.).
100. *than*] *on* Hanmer.
103. *you have*] *you've* Pope.
106. *This is*] *This is such* Hanmer. *This'* S. Walker conj.
creature] *creature, who* Keightley conj.
109. *who*] *whom* Hanmer.
bid] *did* Collier (ed. 1).
114. Exeunt C.......] Exeunt C., Lords, and Gentlemen. Capell. Exit. Ff.
117. *full a*] F_1F_2. *a full* F_3F_4.
119. *Prithee*] *Pray* S. Walker conj.
cease] om. Hanmer.

When I shall see this gentleman, thy speeches
Will bring me to consider that which may
Unfurnish me of reason. They are come.

Re-enter CLEOMENES *and others, with* FLORIZEL *and* PERDITA.

Your mother was most true to wedlock, prince;
For she did print your royal father off,
Conceiving you: were I but twenty one,
Your father's image is so hit in you,
His very air, that I should call you brother,
As I did him, and speak of something wildly
By us perform'd before. Most dearly welcome!
And your fair princess,—goddess!—O, alas!
I lost a couple, that 'twixt heaven and earth
Might thus have stood begetting wonder, as
You, gracious couple, do: and then I lost,
All mine own folly, the society,
Amity too, of your brave father, whom,
Though bearing misery, I desire my life
Once more to look on him.

Flo. By his command
Have I here touch'd Sicilia, and from him
Give you all greetings, that a king, at friend,
Can send his brother: and, but infirmity
Which waits upon worn times hath something seized
His wish'd ability, he had himself
The lands and waters 'twixt your throne and his
Measured to look upon you; whom he loves,
He bade me say so, more than all the sceptres
And those that bear them living.

Leon. O my brother,

123. Re-enter C.......] Re-enter Cleomenes, &c. with Florizel and Perdita. Capell. Enter Florizell, Perdita, Cleomines, and others. Ff.

124. SCENE III. Pope.

131. *your*] *you* Boswell.

princess,—goddess] *princesse (goddese)* F_1F_2. *princess (goddess)* F_3 F_4. *princess-goddess* S. Walker conj.

136. *whom,*] *whom,*— Malone.

138. *on him*] *on* Theobald. *upon* Steevens.

By] *Sir, by* Theobald.

140. *at friend*] F_1. *as friend* F_2 F_3F_4. *a friend* Steevens conj. *and friend* Harness (Malone conj.). *at friends* Seymour conj.

Good gentleman! the wrongs I have done thee stir
Afresh within me; and these thy offices,
So rarely kind, are as interpreters
Of my behind-hand slackness! Welcome hither,
As is the spring to the earth. And hath he too
Exposed this paragon to the fearful usage,
At least ungentle, of the dreadful Neptune,
To greet a man not worth her pains, much less
The adventure of her person?

Flo. Good my Lord,
She came from Libya.

Leon. Where the warlike Smalus,
That noble honour'd lord, is fear'd and loved?

Flo. Most royal sir, from thence; from him, whose daughter
His tears proclaim'd his, parting with her: thence,
A prosperous south-wind friendly, we have cross'd,
To execute the charge my father gave me,
For visiting your highness: my best train
I have from your Sicilian shores dismiss'd;
Who for Bohemia bend, to signify
Not only my success in Libya, sir,
But my arrival, and my wife's, in safety
Here where we are.

Leon. The blessed gods
Purge all infection from our air whilst you
Do climate here! You have a holy father,
A graceful gentleman; against whose person,
So sacred as it is, I have done sin:
For which the heavens, taking angry note,
Have left me issueless; and your father's blest,
As he from heaven merits it, with you

157, 166. *Libya*] *Libia* F_1F_2. *Lybia* F_3F_4. *Lydia* or *Lycia* Douce conj.

159. *Most...daughter*] Hanmer. As two lines in Ff, ending *Sir...daughter*.

160. *his, parting*] Hanmer. *his parting* Ff. *her parting* Thirlby conj. *at parting* Heath conj.

168. *we are*] *we happily are* Hanmer.

The blessed] *Oh! may the blessed* or *And may the blessed* Mitford conj. *The ever-blessed* Anon. apud Halliwell conj.

170. *holy*] *noble* Collier MS.

174. *blest*] *bless'd* Ff.

Worthy his goodness. What might I have been,
Might I a son and daughter now have look'd on,
Such goodly things as you!

Enter a Lord.

Lord. Most noble sir,
That which I shall report will bear no credit,
Were not the proof so nigh. Please you, great sir,
Bohemia greets you from himself by me;
Desires you to attach his son, who has—
His dignity and duty both cast off—
Fled from his father, from his hopes, and with
A shepherd's daughter.

Leon. Where's Bohemia? speak.

Lord. Here in your city; I now came from him:
I speak amazedly; and it becomes
My marvel and my message. To your court
Whiles he was hastening, in the chase, it seems,
Of this fair couple, meets he on the way
The father of this seeming lady and
Her brother, having both their country quitted
With this young prince.

Flo. Camillo has betray'd me;
Whose honour and whose honesty till now
Endured all weathers.

Lord. Lay't so to his charge:
He's with the king your father.

Leon. Who? Camillo?

Lord. Camillo, sir; I spake with him; who now
Has these poor men in question. Never saw I
Wretches so quake: they kneel, they kiss the earth;
Forswear themselves as often as they speak:
Bohemia stops his ears, and threatens them
With divers deaths in death.

Per. O my poor father!
The heaven sets spies upon us, will not have

178. SCENE IV. Pope.
186. *your*] *the* Reed (1803).
189. *Whiles*] *Whilst* Rowe.
203. *sets spies upon*] *which sets spies on* Hanmer.

Our contract celebrated.

Leon. You are married?

Flo. We are not, sir, nor are we like to be;
The stars, I see, will kiss the valleys first:
The odds for high and low's alike.

Leon. My lord,
Is this the daughter of a king?

Flo. She is,
When once she is my wife.

Leon. That 'once,' I see by your good father's speed,
Will come on very slowly. I am sorry,
Most sorry, you have broken from his liking
Where you were tied in duty, and as sorry
Your choice is not so rich in worth as beauty,
That you might well enjoy her.

Flo. Dear, look up:
Though Fortune, visible an enemy,
Should chase us with my father, power no jot
Hath she to change our loves. Beseech you, sir,
Remember since you owed no more to time
Than I do now: with thought of such affections,
Step forth mine advocate; at your request
My father will grant precious things as trifles.

Leon. Would he do so, I'ld beg your precious mistress,
Which he counts but a trifle.

Paul. Sir, my liege,
Your eye hath too much youth in't: not a month
'Fore your queen died, she was more worth such gazes
Than what you look on now.

Leon. I thought of her,
Even in these looks I made. [*To Florizel.*] But your petition
Is yet unanswer'd. I will to your father:
Your honour not o'erthrown by your desires,

214. *worth*] *birth* Hanmer (Warburton).

216. *Fortune, visible*] *Fortune visible,* Hanmer.

220. *affections,*] Ff. *affections.* Warburton.

228. [To Florizel.] Theobald.

I am friend to them and you: upon which errand
I now go toward him; therefore follow me
And mark what way I make: come, good my lord. [*Exeunt.*

SCENE II. *Before Leontes' palace.*

Enter AUTOLYCUS *and a* Gentleman.

Aut. Beseech you, sir, were you present at this relation?

First Gent. I was by at the opening of the fardel, heard the old shepherd deliver the manner how he found it: whereupon, after a little amazedness, we were all commanded out of the chamber; only this methought I heard the shepherd say, he found the child.

Aut. I would most gladly know the issue of it.

First Gent. I make a broken delivery of the business; but the changes I perceived in the king and Camillo were very notes of admiration: they seemed almost, with staring on one another, to tear the cases of their eyes; there was speech in their dumbness, language in their very gesture; they looked as they had heard of a world ransomed, or one destroyed: a notable passion of wonder appeared in them; but the wisest beholder, that knew no more but seeing, could not say if the importance were joy or sorrow; but in the extremity of the one, it must needs be.

Enter another Gentleman.

Here comes a gentleman that haply knows more. The news, Rogero?

Sec. Gent. Nothing but bonfires: the oracle is fulfilled; the king's daughter is found: such a deal of wonder is

231. *I am*] *I'm* Pope.
friend] *a friend* Reed (1803).
SCENE II.] SCENE V. Pope.
Before...] The same. Before the Palace. Capell. Near the court in Sicily. Theobald.

2. First Gent.] Gent. 1. Ff.
12. *very*] *every* Anon. conj.
13. *as they*] *as if they* Rowe.
18. *haply*] Collier. *happily* Ff.
20. Sec. Gent.] Gent. 2. Ff (and throughout).

broken out within this hour, that ballad-makers cannot be able to express it.

Enter a third Gentleman.

Here comes the Lady Paulina's steward: he can deliver you more. How goes it now, sir? this news which is called true is so like an old tale, that the verity of it is in strong suspicion: has the king found his heir?

Third Gent. Most true, if ever truth were pregnant by circumstance: that which you hear you'll swear you see, there is such unity in the proofs. The mantle of Queen Hermione's, her jewel about the neck of it, the letters of Antigonus found with it which they know to be his character, the majesty of the creature in resemblance of the mother, the affection of nobleness which nature shows above her breeding, and many other evidences proclaim her with all certainty to be the king's daughter. Did you see the meeting of the two kings?

Sec. Gent. No.

Third Gent. Then have you lost a sight, which was to be seen, cannot be spoken of. There might you have beheld one joy crown another, so and in such manner, that it seemed sorrow wept to take leave of them, for their joy waded in tears. There was casting up of eyes, holding up of hands, with countenance of such distraction, that they were to be known by garment, not by favour. Our king, being ready to leap out of himself for joy of his found daughter, as if that joy were now become a loss, cries 'O, thy mother, thy mother!' then asks Bohemia forgiveness; then embraces his son-in-law; then again worries he his daughter with clipping her; now he thanks the old shepherd, which stands by like a weather-bitten conduit of many kings' reigns. I never heard of such another encounter, which lames report to follow it and undoes description to do it.

28. Third Gent.] Gent. 3. Ff (and throughout).

31. *Hermione's*] *Hermiones* Ff. *Hermione* Rowe.

50. *which*] *who* Rowe.

51. *weather-bitten*] F_1F_2. *weather-beaten* F_3F_4.

53. *to do it*] *to draw it* Hanmer. *to do it justice* Singer conj. *to show it* Collier (Collier MS.).

Sec. Gent. What, pray you, became of Antigonus, that carried hence the child?

Third Gent. Like an old tale still, which will have matter to rehearse, though credit be asleep and not an ear open. He was torn to pieces with a bear: this avouches the shepherd's son; who has not only his innocence, which seems much, to justify him, but a handkerchief and rings of his that Paulina knows.

First Gent. What became of his bark and his followers?

Third Gent. Wrecked the same instant of their master's death and in the view of the shepherd: so that all the instruments which aided to expose the child were even then lost when it was found. But O, the noble combat that 'twixt joy and sorrow was fought in Paulina! She had one eye declined for the loss of her husband, another elevated that the oracle was fulfilled: she lifted the princess from the earth, and so locks her in embracing, as if she would pin her to her heart that she might no more be in danger of losing.

First Gent. The dignity of this act was worth the audience of kings and princes; for by such was it acted.

Third Gent. One of the prettiest touches of all and that which angled for mine eyes, caught the water though not the fish, was when, at the relation of the queen's death, with the manner how she came to 't bravely confessed and lamented by the king, how attentiveness wounded his daughter; till, from one sign of dolour to another, she did, with an 'Alas,' I would fain say, bleed tears, for I am sure my heart wept blood. Who was most marble there changed colour; some swooned, all sorrowed: if all the world could have seen 't, the woe had been universal.

First Gent. Are they returned to the court?

Third Gent. No: the princess hearing of her mother's

57. *matter*] *matters* F_4.
58. *with*] *of* Capell conj.
63. *Wrecked*] *Wrackt* Ff.
70. *locks*] *lock'd* Hanmer.
71. *losing*] *losing her* Collier (Collier MS.).
75. *caught*] *and caught* Keightley conj.
75, 76. *caught...fish*] omitted by Hanmer (Warburton).
77. *bravely*] *heavily* Collier (Collier MS.).
81. *marble there*] F_3. *marble, there* F_1F_2. *marble there,* F_4.
82. *swooned*] Pope. *swownded* F_1 F_2. *swounded* F_3F_4.

statue, which is in the keeping of Paulina,—a piece many years in doing and now newly performed by that rare Italian master, Julio Romano, who, had he himself eternity and could put breath into his work, would beguile Nature of her custom, so perfectly he is her ape: he so near to Hermione hath done Hermione, that they say one would speak to her and stand in hope of answer:—thither with all greediness of affection are they gone, and there they intend to sup.

Sec. Gent. I thought she had some great matter there in hand; for she hath privately twice or thrice a day, ever since the death of Hermione, visited that removed house. Shall we thither and with our company piece the rejoicing?

First Gent. Who would be thence that has the benefit of access? every wink of an eye, some new grace will be born: our absence makes us unthrifty to our knowledge. Let's along. [*Exeunt Gentlemen.*

Aut. Now, had I not the dash of my former life in me, would preferment drop on my head. I brought the old man and his son aboard the prince; told him I heard them talk of a fardel and I know not what: but he at that time, overfond of the shepherd's daughter, so he then took her to be, who began to be much sea-sick, and himself little better, extremity of weather continuing, this mystery remained undiscovered. But 'tis all one to me; for had I been the finder out of this secret, it would not have relished among my other discredits.

Enter Shepherd *and* Clown.

Here come those I have done good to against my will, and already appearing in the blossoms of their fortune.

Shep. Come, boy; I am past moe children, but thy sons and daughters will be all gentlemen born.

Clo. You are well met, sir. You denied to fight with

99. *wink*] *winking* S. Walker conj., reading lines 98—101 as four lines of verse, ending *benefit...eye...makes us... along.*

101. Exeunt Gentlemen.] Capell. Exit. Ff. Exeunt. Rowe.

102. *had I not*] *had not I* Rowe (ed. 2).

108. *extremity*] *and extremity* Keightley conj.

112. SCENE VI. Pope.

114. *moe*] F_1. *more* $F_2F_3F_4$.

me this other day, because I was no gentleman born. See you these clothes? say you see them not and think me still no gentleman born: you were best say these robes are not gentlemen born: give me the lie, do, and try whether I am not now a gentleman born.

Aut. I know you are now, sir, a gentleman born.

Clo. Ay, and have been so any time these four hours.

Shep. And so have I, boy.

Clo. So you have: but I was a gentleman born before my father; for the king's son took me by the hand, and called me brother; and then the two kings called my father brother; and then the prince my brother and the princess my sister called my father father; and so we wept, and there was the first gentleman-like tears that ever we shed.

Shep. We may live, son, to shed many more.

Clo. Ay; or else 'twere hard luck, being in so preposterous estate as we are.

Aut. I humbly beseech you, sir, to pardon me all the faults I have committed to your worship and to give me your good report to the prince my master.

Shep. Prithee, son, do; for we must be gentle, now we are gentlemen.

Clo. Thou wilt amend thy life?

Aut. Ay, an it like your good worship.

Clo. Give me thy hand: I will swear to the prince thou art as honest a true fellow as any is in Bohemia.

Shep. You may say it, but not swear it.

Clo. Not swear it, now I am a gentleman? Let boors and franklins say it, I'll swear it.

Shep. How if it be false, son?

Clo. If it be ne'er so false, a true gentleman may swear it in the behalf of his friend: and I'll swear to the prince thou art a tall fellow of thy hands and that thou wilt not be drunk; but I know thou art no tall fellow of thy hands and that thou wilt be drunk: but I'll swear it, and I would thou wouldst be a tall fellow of thy hands.

117. *this other*] *the other* Hanmer. 140. *an*] Hanmer. *and* Ff.

Aut. I will prove so, sir, to my power.

Clo. Ay, by any means prove a tall fellow: if I do not wonder how thou darest venture to be drunk, not being a tall fellow, trust me not. Hark! the kings and the princes, our kindred, are going to see the queen's picture. Come, follow us: we'll be thy good masters. [*Exeunt.*

SCENE III. *A chapel in* PAULINA'S *house.*

Enter LEONTES, POLIXENES, FLORIZEL, PERDITA, CAMILLO, PAULINA, Lords, *and* Attendants.

Leon. O grave and good Paulina, the great comfort
That I have had of thee!
Paul. What, sovereign sir,
I did not well, I meant well. All my services
You have paid home: but that you have vouchsafed
With your crown'd brother and these your contracted
Heirs of your kingdoms, my poor house to visit,
It is a surplus of your grace, which never
My life may last to answer.
Leon. O Paulina,
We honour you with trouble: but we came
To see the statue of our queen: your gallery
Have we pass'd through, not without much content
In many singularities; but we saw not
That which my daughter came to look upon,
The statue of her mother.
Paul. As she lived peerless,
So her dead likeness, I do well believe,
Excels whatever yet you look'd upon
Or hand of man hath done; therefore I keep it

158. *masters*] F_1. *master* $F_2F_3F_4$.
SCENE III.] SCENE VII. Pope.
A chapel...] A Chapel in Paulina's House: at upper End a Nich; a Curtain before it. Capell.
Lords and Attendants.] Rowe. Hermione (like a Statue:) Lords, &c. Ff.
16. *you*] *you've* Anon. conj.

Lonely, apart. But here it is: prepare
To see the life as lively mock'd as ever
Still sleep mock'd death: behold, and say 'tis well.

[Paulina draws a curtain, and discovers Hermione standing like a statue.

I like your silence, it the more shows off
Your wonder: but yet speak; first, you, my liege.
Comes it not something near?

Leon. Her natural posture!
Chide me, dear stone, that I may say indeed
Thou art Hermione; or rather, thou art she
In thy not chiding, for she was as tender
As infancy and grace. But yet, Paulina,
Hermione was not so much wrinkled, nothing
So aged as this seems.

Pol. O, not by much.

Paul. So much the more our carver's excellence;
Which lets go by some sixteen years and makes her
As she lived now.

Leon. As now she might have done,
So much to my good comfort, as it is
Now piercing to my soul. O, thus she stood,
Even with such life of majesty, warm life,
As now it coldly stands, when first I woo'd her!
I am ashamed: does not the stone rebuke me
For being more stone than it? O royal piece
There's magic in thy majesty, which has
My evils conjured to remembrance, and
From thy admiring daughter took the spirits,
Standing like stone with thee.

Per. And give me leave,
And do not say 'tis superstition, that
I kneel and then implore her blessing. Lady,
Dear queen, that ended when I but began,
Give me that hand of yours to kiss.

18. *Lonely*] Hanmer. *Louely* F_1. *Lovely* $F_2F_3F_4$. See note (XXIII).
20. [Paulina...] Rowe.
28. *much*] om. Seymour conj.
41. *thy*] *my* Theobald.
44. *then*] *thus* Collier (Collier MS.).

Paul. O, patience!
The statue is but newly fix'd, the colour's
Not dry.
Cam. My lord, your sorrow was too sore laid on,
Which sixteen winters cannot blow away,
So many summers dry: scarce any joy
Did ever so long live; no sorrow
But kill'd itself much sooner.
Pol. Dear my brother,
Let him that was the cause of this have power
To take off so much grief from you as he
Will piece up in himself.
Paul. Indeed, my lord,
If I had thought the sight of my poor image
Would thus have wrought you, for the stone is mine,
I'ld not have show'd it.
Leon. Do not draw the curtain.
Paul. No longer shall you gaze on't, lest your fancy
May think anon it moves.
Leon. Let be, let be.
Would I were dead, but that, methinks, already—
What was he that did make it? See, my lord,
Would you not deem it breathed? and that those veins
Did verily bear blood?
Pol. Masterly done:
The very life seems warm upon her lip.
Leon. The fixure of her eye has motion in't,
As we are mock'd with art.
Paul. I'll draw the curtain:
My lord's almost so far transported that
He'll think anon it lives.

47. *colour's*] *colours* S. Walker conj.

48. [Staying Perdita. Capell.

52, 53. *sorrow But*] *sorrow but It* S. Walker conj.

58. *is mine,*] *i' th' mine* Tyrwhitt conj.

61. *moves*] *move* Pope.

62. *already—*] Rowe. *alreadie.* F_1. *already.* $F_2F_3F_4$. *already I am but dead stone, looking upon stone* Collier (Collier MS.). *already I'm in heaven, and looking on an angel.* Anon. apud Singer conj.

67. *fixure*] *fixture* F_4. *fissure* Warburton conj.

68. *As*] *And* Capell. *So* Mason conj.

are] *were* Rowe (ed. 2).

Leon. O sweet Paulina,
Make me to think so twenty years together!
No settled senses of the world can match
The pleasure of that madness. Let't alone.

Paul. I am sorry, sir, I have thus far stirr'd you: but
I could afflict you farther.

Leon. Do, Paulina;
For this affliction has a taste as sweet
As any cordial comfort. Still, methinks,
There is an air comes from her: what fine chisel
Could ever yet cut breath? Let no man mock me,
For I will kiss her.

Paul. Good my lord, forbear:
The ruddiness upon her lip is wet;
You'll mar it if you kiss it, stain your own
With oily painting. Shall I draw the curtain?

Leon. No, not these twenty years.

Per. So long could I
Stand by, a looker on.

Paul. Either forbear,
Quit presently the chapel, or resolve you
For more amazement. If you can behold it,
I'll make the statue move indeed, descend
And take you by the hand: but then you'll think,
Which I protest against I am assisted
By wicked powers.

Leon. What you can make her do,
I am content to look on: what to speak,
I am content to hear; for 'tis as easy
To make her speak as move.

Paul. It is required
You do awake your faith. Then all stand still;
On: those that think it is unlawful business
I am about, let them depart.

Leon. Proceed:

73. *Let 't*] *Let* Johnson.
74. *I am*] *I'm* Pope.
75. *farther*] F_1F_2. *further* F_3F_4.
80. *my*] *me* F_2.
96. *On: those*] Ff. *And those* Pope. *Or those* Hanmer.

No foot shall stir.
Paul. Music, awake her; strike! [*Music.*
'Tis time; descend; be stone no more; approach;
Strike all that look upon with marvel. Come,
I'll fill your grave up: stir, nay, come away,
Bequeath to death your numbness, for from him
Dear life redeems you. You perceive she stirs:
[*Hermione comes down.*
Start not; her actions shall be holy as
You hear my spell is lawful: do not shun her
Until you see her die again; for then
You kill her double. Nay, present your hand:
When she was young you woo'd her; now in age
Is she become the suitor?
Leon. O, she's warm!
If this be magic, let it be an art
Lawful as eating.
Pol. She embraces him.
Cam. She hangs about his neck:
If she pertain to life let her speak too.
Pol. Ay, and make't manifest where she has lived,
Or how stolen from the dead.
Paul. That she is living,
Were it but told you, should be hooted at
Like an old tale: but it appears she lives,
Though yet she speak not. Mark a little while.
Please you to interpose, fair madam: kneel
And pray your mother's blessing. Turn, good lady;
Our Perdita is found.
Her. You gods, look down
And from your sacred vials pour your graces

98. [Music.] Rowe.

100. *upon*] *on you* Hanmer. *upon you* Keightley conj. *upon't* Anon. conj.

103. [Hermione...] Rowe.

109. *suitor?*] Ff. *suitor.* Rowe (ed. 2).

[Embracing her. Rowe.

112, 113. *She hangs...too*] Arranged by S. Walker as two lines, ending *pertain...too.*

114. *make't*] Capell. *make it* Ff. *make* Hanmer.

121. [Presenting Perdita, who kneels to Her. Rowe.

122. *vials*] Pope. *viols* Ff.

Upon my daughter's head! Tell me, mine own,
Where hast thou been preserved? where lived? how found
Thy father's court? for thou shalt hear that I,
Knowing by Paulina that the oracle
Gave hope thou wast in being, have preserved
Myself to see the issue.

Paul. There's time enough for that;
Lest they desire upon this push to trouble
Your joys with like relation. Go together,
You precious winners all; your exultation
Partake to every one. I, an old turtle,
Will wing me to some wither'd bough and there
My mate, that's never to be found again,
Lament till I am lost.

Leon. O, peace, Paulina!
Thou shouldst a husband take by my consent,
As I by thine a wife: this is a match,
And made between's by vows. Thou hast found mine;
But how, is to be question'd; for I saw her,
As I thought, dead; and have in vain said many
A prayer upon her grave. I'll not seek far,—
For him, I partly know his mind,—to find thee
An honourable husband. Come, Camillo,
And take her by the hand, whose worth and honesty
Is richly noted and here justified
By us, a pair of kings. Let's from this place.
What! look upon my brother: both your pardons,
That e'er I put between your holy looks
My ill suspicion. This your son-in-law,
And son unto the king, whom heavens directing,
Is troth-plight to your daughter. Good Paulina,

129. *Lest*] F_3F_4. *Least* F_1F_2.

144. *by the*] om. Collier (Collier MS.).

147. [To Her. Hanmer.

149. *This*] *This'* S. Walker conj.

150. *whom heavens directing,*] *from heav'n's directing,* Hanmer. *who, heavens directing,* Capell. (*whom heavens directing,*) Malone.

Lead us from hence, where we may leisurely
Each one demand, and answer to his part
Perform'd in this wide gap of time, since first
We were dissever'd: hastily lead away. [*Exeunt.*

155. *We were*] F_1F_2. *Were* F_3F_4.

NOTES.

Note I.

I. 2. 42. Warburton, who reads 'good heed' with the later Folios, says that Mr Theobald, not understanding the phrase, altered it to 'good deed.' In reality Theobald recalled the reading of the first Folio, which Warburton had not taken the trouble to collate.

Note II.

I. 2. 154. 'Methoughts' is of course a form grammatically inaccurate, suggested by the more familiar 'methinks.' It occurs, however, sufficiently often in the old editions to warrant us in supposing that it came from the author's pen. We therefore retain it.

Note III.

I. 2. 272. Mr Collier tells us that some copies of the second Folio read 'think it.' Ours has 'think.'

Note IV.

I. 2. 459. Johnson says: 'Dr Warburton's conjecture is, I think, just; but what shall be done with the following words of which I can make nothing? Perhaps the line, which connected them to the rest, is lost.' In fact we should have expected Polixenes to say that his flight without Hermione would be the best means not only of securing his own safety but of dispelling the suspicions Leontes entertained of his queen.

NOTE V.

II. I. 136. The Folios spell 'than' and 'then' indifferently 'then.' In this passage Malone was inclined to restore 'then.'

NOTE VI.

II. I. 143. If 'land-damn' be the right reading it has not yet received a satisfactory explanation. The word 'lamback' which in his first edition Mr Collier offered as a conjecture, he afterwards found in the corrected copy of the second Folio. But with the sense which he assigns to it 'to beat,' it seems an anticlimax after the threat contained in the line preceding. We omitted to record in our note that Dr Nicholson proposes to read 'Lent-damn.'

NOTE VII.

II. 3. 177. 'It,' as a possessive pronoun, is found again in this play (III. 2. 99). In the latter place Rowe was the first to make the correction 'its.' In *The Tempest* (II. I. 157), as here, the change is made by the third Folio. See our note on that passage. It is remarkable that the only comedies in which this ancient usage occurs, viz. *The Tempest* and *The Winter's Tale*, are among the latest of our author's works. Perhaps the printer is responsible for the singularity.

Mr Staunton has mentioned the following instances in the Histories and Tragedies: *King John*, II. 1, *Timon of Athens*, V. 2, *King Lear*, I. 4, *Hamlet*, I. 2 and V. 1. 'It' occurs besides in *Henry V.* V. 2, *Cymbeline*, III. 4, *Romeo and Juliet*, I. 3, and *Antony and Cleopatra*, II. 7.

In *Hamlet*, I. 2, the first Quarto has *his*, the first Folio, published twenty years later, has *it*. In the same play, V. 1, one of the Quartos has *it's*. Professor Craik quotes also from the Quarto, *ith* or *it* in *King Lear*, IV. 2. But the two Quartos of 1608 in Capell's collection both read *it*. 'Its' is found in *The Tempest*, I. 2. 95, 393, *Measure for Measure*, I. 2. 4, *Winter's Tale*, I. 2. 151, 152, 157, 266, III. 3. 46, 2 *Henry VI.* III. 2, *Henry VIII.* I. 1. On the whole we think it most probable that Shakespeare would not deliberately have written *it* for *its*, or *his*, except when imitating the language of rustics or children. It is only fair, however, to mention that Mr Staunton and Professor Craik are of a different opinion. After all it is not of very great consequence which form we preserve in the text, as we carefully record all the minutest variations at the foot of the page.

NOTE VIII.

III. 2. 10. The first Folio prints 'silence' in italics, like a stage-direction. The subsequent Folios have 'Silence. Enter,' also in italics. Rowe printed it, as we have done, as part of the officer's speech. Capell assigned it to a crier, and Mr Dyce, in support of this, quotes the commencement of Queen Catharine's trial, in *Henry the Eighth*, II. 4. But there is no reason why in this play the officer who has already spoken should not also command silence.

NOTE IX.

III. 2. 41. "It is surprising," says Mr Staunton, "that this passage should have passed without question, for grief must surely be an error. Hermione means that life to her is of as little estimation as the most trivial thing which she would part with; and she expresses the same sentiment shortly after in similar terms,—'no life,—I prize it not a straw.' Could she speak of grief as a trifle, of no moment or importance?"

Is not the meaning this, that Hermione now holds life and grief to be inseparable and would willingly be rid of both? Johnson's note is to this effect.

NOTE X.

III. 3. 59. If written in Arabic numerals 16 would be more likely to be mistaken for 10 than 13, which Capell suggested. Besides 'sixteen' seems to suit the context better than 'thirteen.' Another mistake of one number for another occurs IV. 2. 3, but this may have been an error on the author's part.

NOTE XI.

III. 3. 122. Capell's copy of the first Folio has distinctly 'fight.' A copy in the possession of the Rev. N. M. Ferrers, Fellow of Gonville and Caius College, has as distinctly 'sight.'

NOTE XII.

IV. 1. 1. Johnson followed Theobald and Warburton in printing Time's speech at the end of the third act, but said in his note: 'I believe this speech of Time rather begins the fourth act than concludes the third.' He had not referred, apparently, to the Folios or to Rowe and Pope. Theobald did not mean to include the speech in either act, but drew a line above it to mark that it was an interlude between the third and fourth. Warburton, and Johnson after him, omitted the line.

NOTE XIII.

IV. 3. 48. A writer in *The Gentleman's Magazine*, 1st series, Vol. LX. p. 306, suggests that by 'me—' in this place is meant 'mercy,' and that the clown's exclamation is interrupted by Autolycus.

NOTE XIV.

IV. 4. 82. We have retained here the spelling 'gillyvors' in preference to the more familiar form 'gillyflowers,' because the latter is due to an etymological error. The original word is 'caryophyllus,' which becomes 'girofle' in French, and thence by metathesis 'gilofre,' 'gillyvor.'

NOTE XV.

IV. 4. 263. We have retained *wives* in this passage because Steevens' reading *wives'* is too strictly grammatical to accord with the reckless volubility of the charlatan. To be consistent, Steevens ought to have printed *witnesses'* for *witnesses* in line 275.

NOTE XVI.

IV. 4. 288. The first three Folios read thus:

Song. *Get you hence for I must goe*
Aut. *Where it fits not you to know.*

The fourth thus:

SONG.

Get you hence for I must go,
Aut. *Where fits not you to know.*

Rowe first set it right.

NOTE XVII.

IV. 4. 328. We have adopted the spelling 'squier' here, as in *Love's Labour's Lost*, V. 2. 474, because the word in this sense is now obsolete, and because this spelling comes nearest to 'esquierre,' from which it is derived.

NOTE XVIII.

IV. 4. 417. We have followed Rowe in ejecting the first 'never' from the line, for these reasons. 1. The misprint is of a very common sort. The printer's eye caught the word at the end of the line. 2. The metre is improved by the change. The line was made doubly inharmonious by the repetition of 'never.' 3. The sense is improved. Polixenes would rather make light of his son's sighs than dwell so emphatically upon their cause.

NOTE XIX.

IV. 4. 504. We think Malone's stage direction 'going' was inserted under a mistaken view of Florizel's meaning. He apologises to Camillo for talking apart with Perdita in his presence. At the commencement of this whispered conversation he said to Camillo, 'I'll hear you by and by,' and at the close of it he turns again to him with 'Now, good Camillo;' &c.

NOTE XX.

IV. 4. 693. In the first Folio the reading is 'at 'Pallace,' the apostrophe, if it be not a misprint, pointing either to the omission of the article or its absorption in rapid pronunciation, as in IV. 4. 105, 'with' Sun.' Perhaps the Clown speaks of the King being 'at palace' as he would have spoken of an ordinary man being 'at home.'

NOTE XXI.

IV. 4. 715. The first Folio has 'at toaze,' which is apparently a corruption. The subsequent Folios read 'or toaze,' which in default of a more certain correction we have adopted. It is not improbable, however, that Autolycus may have coined a word to puzzle the clowns, which afterwards puzzled the printers.

NOTE XXII.

V. 1. 60. Steevens distinctly claims as his own the emendation which is due to Capell, and credit has been given him for it by Malone and subsequent editors. In a similar manner he appropriates Capell's division of the speeches in line 75 as a conjecture of his own. Malone proposes to retain the reading of the Folios in lines 58—60, with a different punctuation, thus:

"Again possess her corpse, (and on the stage
Where we offenders now appear soul-vex'd)
And begin, 'why to me?'"

In the last words there is probably a corruption which cannot be removed by simple transposition.

NOTE XXIII.

V. 3. 18. Mr Halliwell says that 'Lonely' is the reading of the first Folio. Capell's copy has 'Lowely,' and the same is found in Mr Ferrers' copy.

CPSIA information can be obtained
at www.ICGtesting.com
Printed in the USA
LVHW110932160522
718424LV00013B/95

9 783375 004453